# SENTINEL
## A PROTECTOR'S PURPOSE
### JESSIE KREIDLER

# Acknowledgements

To my family, who believed in me more than I believed in myself.
Hey, Dad, I wrote the book!

# HIDE
## CHAPTER 1

HOLY MYTHOS, IT'S BEEN a long night. Bathory Boarding Institute may be the death of me after all. I'm not meant to thrive in academics—that's why Rodney's *my* Vampire. He could do all the hard thinking stuff and I'd do all the ass-kicking.

Clutching my books to my chest, a swell of energy awakened the blood in my veins at the set of broad shoulders slumping ahead of me. All the staff and students wrapping up their day, headed to dinner, then bed.

"Rainy days are the worst," I declared, skipping to catch up to my mentor.

Kade didn't even startle, knowing my voice well. "Yes, they are. They seem to bring out the worst in everyone." He slipped his fingers into the front pockets of his black jeans.

"No kidding. Ms. Way gave us an eternity of homework. I think I'll be writing essays long after I graduate."

His tired eyes crinkled as his lips stretched into a crooked grin. "You'd never stay on task that long."

"You're my mentor!" I gasped. "You're supposed to have faith in me."

"As your mentor—" he slowed at the door to the gym "—I know all too well your capabilities and passions. Unless it's physical training, you don't have the attention span."

"Fair enough." I lifted one shoulder.

The education process was important, understandably. But my job as a Protector is to keep my Vampire safe. My chronically ill and especially weak Vampire. One of us had to be strong, and he wasn't.

"Speaking of training, do you wanna spar?"

He tilted his head back, looking down his sharp nose. "I won't get rid of you until I fight you, will I?"

I giggled. "You'll get plenty of rest once I'm graduated."

Then I'd have to find someone else to occupy his position. If I didn't practice daily, I'd lose my edge. Rodney relied on me, and I refused to let him down. Being petite, I had to prove myself as a Protector, especially when my charge is such a special case.

Kade backpedaled into the gym, stretching his arms and staring at the ceiling. He'd dimmed the lights to keep other students from entering—though we both knew that wouldn't happen. Not a soul here took their career as seriously as me. They all did the bare minimum, more interested in dating and parties.

Rodney's frail body had strayed me from that path long ago. He couldn't keep up with the others, couldn't risk hangovers like the others, either. We'd found out the hard way—He'd gone to a party after our first school dance without me. Disinterested in fraternizing with boys privately, I went to bed, trusting Zoon's—the third member of our trio—promise to monitor him. Little did we know he'd end up vomiting blood and falling down the stairs trying to get to his dorm room. His disease wouldn't allow him to tolerate alcohol the same way everyone else could—like most things.

I thought we'd lose Rodney that day and swore to him nothing like that would happen again. I'd always be there to protect him, even from a treacherous fall or every bully he'd endured over the years.

"Ready to get your ass kicked?" I gloated, unable to control the giddy grin on my face.

Kade rolled his eyes and dropped his arms at his sides. "I relish the day you'll be able to, smartass."

I folded my arms. "Do you have this little faith in all your students?"

He crooked a smirk. "Only the cocky ones."

I had good reason to be. I'm undefeated on the mat. No one else wants this like I do. Of course, a challenge may present itself if a single one of my peers had a change of focus. None of them wanted to fight, falling into the social opinion that Protectors were becoming obsolete. They called me "eccentric".

"Follow me." Kade gestured vaguely.

We crossed the gym to a heavy wooden door leading outside to the institute's ornamental garden. Rain still fell from the sky, keeping it dark despite the sun's approach. A labyrinth of hedge bordered the perimeter, shielding the fountain and stone benches at the center. The rain drops echoed off the water and rattled the foliage.

I cradled myself and ducked my head to follow into the garden, rounding the opening between the pair of shrubs sculpted to look like cones.

"Kade?"

*He disappeared.*

I shivered, craning my neck to see where he went. Maybe he ran ahead to get out of the rain? There's a shed on the other side of the garden for the fountain pumps. Unfolding my arms, I jogged to get out of the rain.

"Ow! Shit,"

He barreled out of the hedge, clashing into my compact frame like a train. My boots slipped on the stone pathway, and I crashed into the hedgerow on the other side. Grappling with my arms, he impaired my ability to gather my footing.

I pinched my eyes shut to keep the hedge branches from scratching them and pitched forward. Driving my knee into his thigh, my cheek smashed against his sternum.

Kade folded, but tightened his grasp on my arms, whirling to use me as a cushion for his landing.

*This sucks!*

I put my boot in his abdomen and thrust him away, drawing my institute issued dagger from my boot. He already had his out and jumped to his feet.

"Are you crazy?" I panted.

"This is training you for real life," he replied, rolling his dagger side to side with his thumb. "You're never going to be in a controlled environment when you protect your Vampire. It can be during nights like this. Say you're walking him home from work or a friend's house."

He's right, but it still sucks! It's cold and wet!

Tightening my hold on my dagger, I charged. *Big mistake.* He buckled down to return my momentum, delivering me into his waiting shoulder. He seized my wrist, twisting it until I dropped my weapon.

*Rookie mistake.* Why am I sucking so badly?

I pushed with my shoulder to get some space between us, sweeping a boot through the air. He caught my ankle, dropping his dagger, too. At least now the playing fields matched.

"You need to think ahead. You're flailing, kid."

*Ugh.* I hated when he called me that. He wasn't much older than me and I wasn't a kid anymore. *I'm a grown ass woman!*

"You didn't give me time to think!" I complained.

He twisted my leg until it made me grimace. "Do you think someone trying to hurt Rodney will give you time to think?"

*Ugh.* I hated it even more when he's right! I jerked my ankle from his hold and switched legs. My boot punted into his jaw, knocking his head to the side.

*Ha! One point.*

"Keep going, Jo." I muttered to myself. With all my momentum, I tackled him to the ground, splashing into a muddy puddle consuming the stone path.

Slipping on the soupy ground, my elbow drove into his gut—fortunately—as I scrambled to straddle him. He tangled a fist in my soaked hair, ripping me off with one sharp pull.

"Ouch!" My spine vibrated as the stone beneath me stole my breath. That's a new bruise.

Kade rolled on top of me, struggling in the mud to get his arms beneath him and flipping the bangs out of his face.

*Fuck, he's heavy!*

I wound my arm around his neck, using it as a pivot point to roll us once again. My hair whipped against my lips, pelting mud into my mouth. *Gross.* Rodney better not make any enemies willing to fight in this sort of weather.

Dragging his head tight against my chest, I crawled out from under Kade. I tucked his chin into the crook of my elbow and squeezed. *Got him.*

*Shit. Shit. Shit.*

He stood up, and I lost my hold. He swiveled and kicked me in the chest. My back slapped into the mud pit and my breath caught in my throat, pinned by the sole of his boot. I clutched his ankle, realizing I'd have to submit.

Recognizing that in my bulging eyes, Kade gave yield. "You're getting better." He held out a hand to help me up.

"You're crazy," I panted, massaging my throat where the tread of his sole left an imprint.

He swept a hand over his hair, mud dripping down his face. "Anyone who attacks Rodney will be crazy."

*Fair point.*

Chests heaving, we entered the gym.

"Make sure you stretch." Kade fetched some towels from the wall shelf.

My chest quaked with stifled laughter. Rarely did I leave a mark on Kade. A purple bruise colored the spans of his jaw where I'd kicked. "You, too."

He rolled his eyes. "One day, someone will not go so easy on you."

Easy on me? "I didn't ask you to go easy on me!"

"I do it for the sake of your ego,"

I scrubbed my hair with the towel before turning my glare onto him. "You're kidding, right? I want to be the best—"

"And you will be." He sighed, suddenly decades older. "It all comes with experience on the job. I can't prepare you for everything."

"Next time, don't hold back."

"And what would you learn, then?"

"What it's like to actually fight!" I snapped. "Like you said, the people who try to hurt Rodney won't hold back."

"But they also won't be trained Protectors—"

"How do you know?" I struggled to keep my voice level. "Anyone could hate him! Plus, it's not like we're even remotely close to being the strongest race—"

"I know." He held up a hand, white-blue eyes taken by a serious sheen. "You do not have to lecture me about the dangers of the world. I am your mentor and I decide how I teach. If you're unsatisfied with that, ask to transfer to a different one and see how they tolerate your schedule."

*He's right.* No one else would meet with me as frequently as he did. In fact, I don't even know why *he* agrees to meet with me regularly.

"I'm sorry,"

"Don't be sorry." His words were clipped, making it difficult to believe him. "Think before you speak. Just like I tell you to think before you strike, kid."

"Don't call me kid."

"I'll call you kid until you act otherwise."

I pitched my towel in the hamper. I should have kicked him harder.

A smile threatened to cross his lips. "Go eat with your peers."

"I'll eat," I grumbled. "I just want to be sure I'm ready to graduate."

"Has it ever occurred to you *I* would like to eat?"

I grinned and fixed my ponytail. "Three more months and you'll be rid of me."

He scoffed. "Sounds too good to be true." He may claim to be ready for me to leave, but I knew he'd miss me.

If I did my job well, he wouldn't worry about me bothering him again. Protectors rarely had recreational time once they entered the field. My Vampire required plenty of attention, especially if he couldn't afford more than one. Some families had multiple Protectors, but those were usually Vampires of high caliber.

Kade gathered my textbooks from the bleachers and dropped them into my arms. "Go eat," he instructed, "and go to sleep."

I gave a mock salute as I backed toward the exit to head to the cafeteria. It should be cleared out now. *I could eat and catch up on some homework—*

"Oof,"

Startled forward, I pivoted to see what frail creature I'd bumped into.

Ms. Way, the astronomy teacher, stepped around me. Her celestial, Space Pixie eyes flickered like a vortex of rage. My stomach dropped and I clutched my books to my chest, prepared for a lecture.

"Josephine," she snapped, scowl tracking over Kade.

I avoided my mentor's eye contact, embarrassed he found himself involved in this.

"I struggle to believe you *forgot* about the detention you were required to serve." Her vicious glare staked through my perfectionist image.

I surveyed my books in hopes she would stop there.

"She was held back on my account," Kade lied, which inclined me to raise my head.

"As if that would matter to you Protectors. My time is as valuable as yours," she sneered, nose turned up.

He folded his arms, straining to remain stoic. "I didn't know she had prior responsibilities,"

Ms. Way's upper lip curled under her thin nose. "Typical Protector,"

I tightened my hands on my books. His help was appreciated, but it wasn't his duty to quarrel with this tortuous woman. I'd forgotten to attend my detention, solely I deserved to suffer for it.

She flipped her cropped red hair over her shoulder and whirled toward the hallway. "Come along, Josephine, your little friends are waiting," she called. "Time starts when we step into my classroom."

I clenched my jaw hard enough it hurt and trailed after her. One solid kick to her spine would send her in a clatter to the floor. *And create another round of detention.*

Kade caught my upper arm to stop me in the doorway. "Try to keep your temper in check," he whispered near my ear.

I acknowledged his recommendation, but would never promise. Ms. Way got under my skin. She believed her students were the reason bad things happened in the world and her attitude ensured we solidified that claim.

I surveyed her small boots, stricken by how much noise each heeled step invoked against the stone floor. Her pressed slacks stopped beneath her tiny rib cage, pooched paisley button up tucked into her pant line.

"Once you graduate, you'll learn," she preached, "Protectors are swiftly becoming antiquated. They're a dying luxury."

I focused my breath to prevent an outburst. While other races didn't need our expertise, the Vampires preferred us. My instructors worked hard to educate a generation of Protectors who would persuade future

Vampires to keep us employed. No security system in the world was as efficient as one of us at their side.

Regardless, her beliefs breeched mine. Why else would Bathory waste precious time and finances to lock us away in this institute? We'd graduate with useless skills and no purpose. My throat tightened; would I still have a place in Rodney's life?

"Especially that one." She tossed her hand towards the gym we'd left. "A talented Protector wouldn't waste his time here."

I expelled a breath. If only her classroom stood closer to the training hall. Then I wouldn't be tempted to defend Kade's qualifications—the certifications he'd worked hard to earn. The many recommendations he'd been awarded by his instructors and employers.

"He's respected because he entices hormones. He has no impressive lineage."

My hands trembled. Kade could be defined as easy on the eyes, but it had nothing to do with his popularity. He was a good person—unlike the scuttling wretch before me who felt inferior to him. She would say anything to tempt me to earn additional detention.

To my relief, we rounded the hallway to her classroom. The smell of antiques hung in the air.

Both Vampires perched on the surfaces of opposite faced desks. They were thin and tall, their chosen seats dwarfed.

Rodney's narrow shoulders hunched as he read a book, his black hair with chunky white highlights shielding his expression from view. Zoon gawked without interest at the projection ceiling, not actually studying the artificial stars glimmering there.

I could imagine the tongue lashing they received while waiting. Zoon presumably earned himself extra time, unable to control himself.

"Since you three find it necessary to disrupt my classroom with your commentary," she shuffled paperwork behind her cluttered desk, "I find it suitable for you to clean it."

The amount of disorganized papers and hidden discarded pens suggested she never bothered to do so herself.

Zoon threw back his feathery haired head to groan, and his shoulders sagged.

"You won't receive any sympathy here, Vampire." She stopped to glare. "After as much time as you've spent in detention, you should know better than to act out."

The toe of Rodney's boot met Zoon's shin and a snarky retort formed on his lips. Grabbing his knee, he poked a fang into his lip to stifle it.

Enveloped in her search within the messy desk, Ms. Way somehow missed the encounter. She produced a feather duster and scraper from the bottom drawer, then traipsed around the desk akin to an enchantress marching into battle against dust mites.

Across the room, she handed the duster to Rodney. No further explanation needed for him; he set to work dusting the hand crafted shelves and trinkets lining the walls.

Typical behavior for him. He didn't deserve to be in detention; Zoon and I belonged here. Zoon started the commentary and Ms. Way's incapability to handle the situation without retaliating inspired me to join the party.

She held out the scraper for the remaining Vampire. "You get to remove gum from the desks and chairs."

He pinched his thin lips. "Sounds great,"

"Josephine," she trilled.

Begrudgingly, I followed to the extensive bookshelf at the rear of the classroom. Often during her endless lectures, I'd examine this disaster. Collections of senseless objects clung to the edge of each shelf and buried the contents behind. Zoon shouldn't have commented about her monotone voice. *Then we wouldn't be stuck here.*

"You'll organize these constellation charts. Be careful, they're very old and some of them are original copies."

My shoulders dropped at the abundance of aged scrolls. They'd occupied space here as long as Ms. Way's perpetual lifespan and would require later than dinner hour to sort.

Zoon's shriek redirected everyone's focus. He nursed his sore head beneath a desk, scraper held next to his grimace. "There's a tooth in this one!"

I rolled my eyes and returned to the scrolls—*definitely past dinner hour*.

Drained from the pointless chores, we dragged our feet out of Ms. Way's classroom. She gloated at the door and watched us slump away while we cradled our backaches and paper cuts.

"Of course, she'd make us miss dinner." I clutched my textbooks.

The castle bore little sound, the bulk of students already in their rooms. We weren't the only stragglers, however. The castle almost always stirred with life, considering the wide age range of its occupants.

"I'm starving," Rodney agreed. Ms. Way didn't care if she'd suffer repercussions for endangering an immunocompromised student. He couldn't skip meals.

Zoon swooped close behind me, leaned to place his head near my shoulder. A chill shot down my spine, goosebumps in its wake. I hated to be touched unless in a fight. My instincts demanded I deflect the creep who encroached on my personal space.

"We could eat JoJo,"

"That would be hard to do with no teeth in your head,"

I swatted him in the face, then rushed to the Protector's wing, opposite the stairwell to the Vampire story. No one fed from the source anymore, unless in an emergency or for pleasure. I couldn't fathom participation in such an act. How could Vampires tell when to stop? The concept terrified me, afraid to be drained. I existed to protect them, not feed them.

"Goodnight, you two," I called, not bothering to listen for a reply.

Kade leaned against the door to his room and my depleted energy recharged some.

"You shouldn't let the older mentors bully you into babysitting," I teased.

He rolled his bloodshot eyes and pushed from the heavy wooden door to face me. "I wouldn't have to stay up so late if you could stay out of detention on a regular basis."

I stopped to gape. "This is the first time for me this year!"

"Forgive me." He smirked. "It all blurs together."

"I graduate this year, I have to do better,"

He raised his brows in disbelief. "How did it go, then? Did she force you to write sentences on how useless Protectors are?"

"We're an excellent use as a janitorial service,"

"Much better time spent than eating—"

An ear-splitting scream erupted from the institute's depths. The hair at the nape of my neck stood up. I'd never heard such genuine fear in my life. Books forgotten, I threw myself into motion while they clattered to the floor.

The sound of boots against the stone floor doubled, Kade in stride beside me. His brief focus cast on me as we rounded the end of the hall to the commons, noting I didn't hesitate to follow suit. He'd already whipped the knife from his belt, trained gaze darting about the open room.

A handful of students and faculty pushed past us in a frenzy. But the bulk of the screams were further in the castle.

While I'd collected many hours of instruction, we'd never prepared for this. Never once had it occur to me a threat would find its way into our school. We should have practiced drills for this!

He signaled for me to continue while he stilled near the commons entryway. I refused to let him face the intruders on his own. Or maybe I was afraid.

"Let me help. You don't know what we're up against," I argued.

"It's pointless for us both to defend the same room!" He jabbed a finger at the cafeteria. "Go to the cafeteria and search for your Vampire!"

His order cut me to the bone, a reminder of my sole purpose to protect Rodney. While all the other lives within the school mattered, his should matter to *me*.

Providing one last stern glare, Kade proceeded without me. Into the commons, where the sounds of attack increased. I had to lock away the urge to follow and focus on finding Rodney.

I darted past the commons, as Kade instructed, only slowing once I reached the cafeteria. An ice-cold hand clapped over my mouth and wrenched me from the entrance.

Rodney's crystalline eyes met mine, wide with fear. "We need to hide. Mages are killing everyone."

I reached to pull his hand from my face to scan the area. "Where's Zoon?"

He swiped at the ash on his face. "I lost track,"

My lungs felt too big for my chest as the castle became a foreign labyrinth.

"Let's go. We have to find him..." And Kade. *He'd know what to do.*

My heart sank deep within my rib cage as I peered into the commons. Heaps of dead bodies were scattered about the room, students and faculty marred beyond recognition; their bones splintered from their skin and a metallic smell choked the air.

They'd collected into groups to defend one another, some cowered behind the inflamed furniture. Their charred and bloody corpses displayed their futile efforts.

Mages were unstoppable, unbeatable fountains of power. The face of every war in history. *Pure evil.*

"We have to find Kade." I lunged toward the bodies.

Rodney looped an arm around my waist. "You don't know he's in there."

"I just left him!" I sobbed.

"If he was in there, he's gone—"

"You don't know that!"

"It isn't safe to stay here and find out!" he snapped.

I had to channel Protector mode, shut off the feelings, as practiced.

*How had we not heard a single sound during detention?*

A blot of crimson liquid dripped onto my forearm, inclining me to lift my head to the ceiling. From the great wrought iron chandelier swung Kade, pierced like a kebab. Blood dripped from every puncture point in his chest, thick black char marks obscured his face.

"No," I gasped, weak with horror. *It couldn't be him. He was unstoppable.*

Rodney tugged on my arm. "Jo."

He couldn't be dead. This couldn't happen.

"Jo!"

The explosions and horrific screams shifted deeper within the castle. I knew better than to stand here and grieve, but still had to bite my tongue to tear my eyes from *him.*

I gathered Rodney's hand into mine, then pushed into a sprint. A resonant boom sounded as a bright light erupted ahead. Stone fell from the shaken walls.

Once my sight adjusted, adrenaline filled my senses.

*Run.*

A faded tapestry of Bathory's crest hung loose from its fixture, touching the floor at an unflattering angle. Years snooping around the castle served me well. Behind the tapestry, a slender hidden door led to an old sentry tower in a part of the institute no one used anymore.

A scream ripped through my lungs as a body whizzed past us to crash against the stone wall. A cloaked figure stood in the doorway ahead, engulfed in a cloud of dust.

Pressure built in my throat, our footsteps echoing in the eerie silence. The Mage's head tipped to listen.

*Shit, he heard us!*

I thrust Rodney against the wall and dragged him along. As soon as the dust settled, we'd be sitting targets.

*It's right there!*

The cloaked figure turned to study the hall, balled fists at his sides. I drove my shoulder into Rodney's back to push the pace faster.

Flipping aside the heavy handstitched fabric, he pulled open the stiff old door.

150 years ago, Mages waged war on the Mythos, one of the lengthiest, brutal battles the mythical world ever saw—the Blood Crusade. Or, as the Vampires called it, the Blood Persecution. As a result, most schools no longer allowed visitation by families. Children were accepted at infancy and resided at the school until they graduated. As far as we understood, the races were at peace—still well hidden from the humans.

*Something's changed.*

We stumbled up the narrow, crumbled stairs to the sentry tower attic; storage occupying the dust blanketed room. The grime layer suggested no one touched anything here in decades. A cobweb clung to every nook and a stagnant, musty smell tainted the air.

Rodney dropped to the ground in front of the window, careful to avoid the sunlight spilling in, the rain gone. He wrapped his thin arms around his trembling legs and gasped for air. His sharp fangs caught on his bottom lip as he did his best to hold it in.

*I'd saved us for what?* We'd be traumatized for life.

Adrenaline still pumping through my veins, I positioned a dresser in front of the door. I couldn't risk our discovery, even by a fellow student. I had to keep Rodney alive; it's my duty, as his friend and Protector.

*I have to do this.*

The hunk of wood proved difficult to relocate, chest level to my short frame. My limbs quaked and with a hefty screech, it gave way. Slumping against it, I sucked in several deep breaths.

"Jo,"

I spun at Rodney's whimper to listen for any sound beyond the door. He motioned for me to join him. His black and white hair obscured his eyes, fixed on the courtyard below. Careful to stand out of direct sight of the third-story window, I crouched beside him.

Several hooded figures worked together to throw bodies haphazardly into a pile outside. The orange glow of sunlight which crept over the trees around the institute ensured the Vampire's deaths. They'd turn to stone after a few hours in direct light.

I hoped other student Protectors saved their Vampires, although I'd often chastised them for their uselessness. In the end, I wanted them to succeed, too.

"No!" He pivoted to sit, hiding from the sight of our best friend as he was added to the pile.

"We were just with him," I whispered. It's my fault he'd gotten separated from us.

I pressed a hand to my lips as tears spilled, refracting in the sunlight to blur the image of Zoon's lifeless body. I, too, adjusted to sit flat on the floor to escape the misery sunlight brought.

*Where did these terrors come from? How did they get inside?*

The institute held a staff of well-trained Protectors from around the world; it should have proven difficult for intruders to enter the castle without notice. The wards set in place by the professors alone should have prevented a breach of the gates.

Without these precautions, I wasn't sure how they expected us to fight off a foe quite like this. We were outnumbered and underqualified against magic. Our professors rendered it clear we stood no chance against it without purchasable aid. Therefore, they'd taught us to either submit, negotiate or run when encountered by a Sorcerer.

Rodney's voice broke the awful silence, "We came to see if the lunch ladies would pity us and let us have a snack."

I gathered his fingers and he squeezed mine, the gesture minuscule in comparison.

"We heard an explosion," he continued, voice shaken.

Able to fill in the rest, I buried my face against his boney chest. Feeling him quiver with restrained sobs, I pinched my eyes closed to do the same.

The recall of Kade as he dangled from the chandelier assaulted the peace I hoped to achieve and Zoon's limp corpse intensified the horror. I begged my brain to stop.

I'd kept Rodney alive. The purpose of my existence was to protect my Vampire; I couldn't save everyone.

# RUN
## CHAPTER 2

As if it were any regular day, the lack of light through the dusty window told me nighttime arrived. Usually the rest of the institute would get up, too, preparing for the school day. Not this day.

I stretched away from Rodney, snuggled close against my side, to peer out the thin, aged glass. The body piles were gray and still, like hundreds of statues discarded in the courtyard. A pit developed in my chest, the loss too great to bear.

We had to get out of here.

Were the Sorcerers still on the premises? The cocky assholes probably stuck around to bask in their victory.

Even so, we couldn't stay or we'd find ourselves amongst the pile and the only way out was down.

The wooden frame warped along the seam where the window and its track came together. I slid my nails between the wood and it shifted—*it could open!* My pulse raced faster; *we could get out.*

We had to cross the sculpted courtyard decorated with natural stone, marble benches, and floral shrubbery. If we were careful, the landscape could conceal us from any lookouts who might exist.

But we had to hurry.

I bent to shake Rodney awake. "We need to leave,"

His rose-colored eyes opened abruptly, and he sat up. I waited patiently while he adjusted to the darkness; the urgency of our situation clarifying with each serene blink. He slept harder than most, due to his disease.

"Are they still out there?" he asked, voice groggy.

"I don't see anyone," I confessed, at the window again. "Not that it means much."

He stood to loosen his limbs and rub his tired eyes. "Do you think they're looking for something?"

"I'm not sure. Not sure why anyone would—" I couldn't finish, the words crumbling in my throat.

With one giant pull, I opened the window to let in a blast of cool air. Fortunately, it yielded only a *slight* hollow scrape. To be sure no one heard, I stuck my head out to search the darkness.

"The gates aren't a far trek from here." While quite the fall, we could descend the stone wall to the ground.

"Are you crazy?" he blurted.

"We need to get out of here while the courtyard is clear." The shrubbery at the tower's base twisted as my nerves disagreed with my confidence.

"Where would we go? We're in the middle of nowhere!" he objected.

"If we try, we could make it to a city. We can't be that far away from the rest of the Mythos."

"What if the entire world is screwed up, too?"

"What if it isn't?"

His anxious stare suffocated my fleeting confidence. "There's no way—"

We couldn't sit here and hash out all the possibilities waiting for us at the gates. Because one thing's for certain. If we stay here, we're dead.

"We can't just let them find us," I stated. Gripping the window frame tight, I searched, with both feet, for the lip of a stone.

"You can't be serious!" Rodney rushed to the opening.

My entire body shook as I continued to forge a path down the tower. Doing my best not to think about the possibility a Sorcerer may wait at the bottom.

"Dammit." My boot slipped, and I lost my vantage, a scream plugging my throat. Digging my nails into the stone, I clung to the wall. *It hurts.*

"Shit. Jo!" Rodney hissed, swinging his leg out the opening, which brought attention to the fact I hadn't gotten as far as my aching muscles insisted. "I swear to the Mythos, you're the most insane person I've ever met. What would you do if I stayed in that tower? Huh?"

"We have to go or they'll kill us,"

"What if you fell?" He grunted through bared teeth as he extended his arms, same as I had.

Afraid he would step on my fingers, I analyzed where my next footfall would lie. To avoid another scare, each action must be gauged. I swung my short leg to reach a protruding stone with my toe and my heart stuttered.

Was I more afraid to miss the brick or that Rodney's boney ass would crush me?

Taking the chance, I fused to the wall with all my might, despite the quake of my worn out body.

"Are you alright?" he asked and craned his neck to see.

The momentum assisted as I slid against the raucous tower for my next step.

"I'm alright," I whimpered and my legs convulsed. While in shape due to rigorous training, flexibility wasn't my strong suit. The splits in particular weren't my favorite way to stretch, but I pressed on. "Are you alright?"

His wide, graphite colored eyes beamed past me at the ground, so far away, and he trembled worse than me.

My muscles tensed in anticipation. If I fell, I'd be seriously injured or dead. Would his weakened bones stand the fall any better than mine? "Rodney?"

My nails caught on a collection of debris between a set of stones. A gust startled me and, once again, I teetered.

*The debris was actually a nest.*

I ducked around the chattering bird as it dive bombed my head, its wings fluttering like thunderclaps.

"Shoo!" I hissed, shaking hard enough my fingers began to slip.

*If it doesn't shut up, we're toast!*

Shoulders hunched against the territorial nightmare, I pressed on before one of us fell. If there were any Sorcerer's left, I hoped they weren't outside to witness this.

The tower seemed twice as tall as I remembered, and the bird's fury proved endless. Mere feet from the ground, Rodney collapsed, and we crumpled into a pile, my body cushioning his fall.

"Fucking asshole!" I grumbled. The incessant bird circled one last time to declare its displeasure at anyone who would listen. No magic blasted through the air, so perhaps its racket had gone undetected after all.

My pulse never slowed as I searched Rodney for any breaks or abrasions, drawing his arms into my lap to twist at awkward angles. Despite the moon's plentiful light, it helped I possessed special sight. Generations ago, our exclusively bred race hired witches to enhance our vision. Throughout time, the trait genetically transferred from those chosen Protectors, from parent to child. Not all of us retained these special abilities.

"I'm fine," he whispered.

"Are you sure?"

"Yes. You broke my fall." He smirked.

"Right." I exhaled a heavy sigh.

*We made it.*

I feared we'd fallen hard enough to break him. With his condition, any break could be fatal. His body already attacked itself on a regular basis; no one could predict how it would handle even the most basic trauma.

The castle door's distinct, ear-splitting creak thrust us into a nearby shrub. A shrouded silhouette exited the large wooden doors and froze.

*Dammit, they saw us!*

Systematic shouts ensued as the figure raced back inside to gather his comrades.

"Go!" I ordered, propelling Rodney into a run.

I stayed on his heels to block any attack that may come our way, a hand in the small of his back to push him to the limit. His speed was slow and clumsy. If our lives weren't in danger, I may have chastised him for it. At present, I'm sure the Sorcerers behind us were enough.

A ball of orange flame soared past to strike a nearby bush. A scorched mass left behind.

"Why did it have to be Spellcasters?"

Protectors were hardly a threat against such a powerful race. They were versed in battle tactics *and* they had *fire* magic.

We took refuge behind the stone wall, through the wide-open gates. Another blast of fire followed, consuming the beautiful cherry blossom tree mere feet from the entrance. The acrid smell of burnt wood filled the air and a quick plume of heat swept over us.

"That could've been us," Rodney murmured, dragging his feet in awestruck horror.

My adrenaline spiked out of control and I dragged him to the nearest path, in hopes the dark of the night would blanket us from sight.

Panting, he cradled himself and stumbled along the path. Still charged with adrenaline, I stabilized him while he caught his breath and dabbed at his cold sweat. Many times I carried him to the nurse's office from gym class. He struggled to keep up and would grow so fatigued he required a blood pouch to rejuvenate.

"They're not far behind." His feet caught on each other and sent him to the ground.

I stopped to help him up from his scuffed knees, and he clung to me. I hated when he got to this point. Unfortunately, it never got easier, and he grew impatient.

"It's okay, as long as we keep moving, they can't catch us," I reassured him as well as myself.

Together, we gathered his balance and trudged on.

"Why did you pick me?" He coughed breathlessly. He was the weakest link in our class, while I was the strongest. It made sense for us to be paired.

"What do you mean?"

"Out of everyone you could have protected last night, you chose me?"

"You're my best friend—"

He sighed. "I'm a pathetic excuse for a Vampire. You should have picked someone who deserves life."

The only other Vampire I could have chosen would be Zoon. We'd grown together, learned together, and formed a unique bond.

I raked my teeth. "You're my best friend. I couldn't let you die."

"Any other Vampire would have made this easier for you—"

"I wasn't worried about easiest. I worried for your safety." No time for choices, I did as any friend would do when he came to me.

He dragged a fang along his lower lip and surveyed the ground, unsatisfied with my answer. It wasn't me who frustrated him; he was once more disappointed in his ill body. Time after time, his rapid blood absorption proved to be a hindrance. It didn't matter to me, though. His illness was a part of him and I swore to protect *him*, regardless the cost. I'd done this as a best friend, not yet given the opportunity to do so as a professional—and may never be able to, if no one remained to certify me as such.

When my legs shook, same as Rodney's, we stopped to rest. The landscape grew denser with greenery and the ground rose in slight hills. In our twenty-one years, we'd roamed the institute's perimeter yet never ventured this far out. We never traveled from campus, not even for a field trip. This realization empowered me. Without extensive survival skills and no idea where we headed, we were still alive.

No thanks to the institute. We should be able to navigate off the land, survive without commodities! How did they expect us to live on the outside? Some of us wouldn't step into a life filled with riches and caretakers. We'd have to work for our own possessions.

"We should find some place to rest," I decided. Birds chirped in proclamation of dawn, the warning carried away in the autumn wind.

"There," Rodney panted. He pointed to trees fused together in a concave shape big enough we could fit inside.

Too exhausted to care if another animal may duel us for disturbing its home, I motioned for him to squeeze inside. "I'll stay out here just in case. You get some rest."

"You need sleep, too."

"I'll sleep! You're the one allergic to the sun."

His jaw shifted side to side. He wanted to argue, and it surprised me he had the patience to hold his tongue. Reluctantly, he complied with my instructions.

I put my back to him and leaned against the small cavity. Instantly, my lids grew heavy with delusions of my dorm bed—the comfort of the pillow top mattress as it resisted my tired muscles, and the soft sheet's caress.

A stick jabbed my hipbone as I shifted to find a suitable position—*on the forest floor, without a blanket or pillow.*

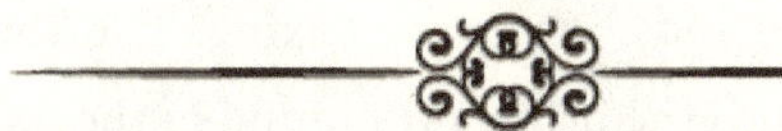

The unmistakable crunch of footsteps on rocks shocked my senses to life. The sun peeked over the horizon and brought light to the shadows, where a cloaked figure slouched. His malicious chuckle rendered my spine straight as a board.

*Protect Rodney.*

"Josie," Rodney squeaked, his voice nearly inaudible over my heart.

"Where's your Vampire, little girl?" the Sorcerer rasped.

*I'm a grown woman, asshole.* I slipped my fingertips into the top of my boot for my dagger.

"Shy, are we?" He chuckled.

Fear intertwined with my resentment as I rose gradually, gaze locked on his approach. This would be my first proper hand-to-hand combat. I'd have to fight for my life. Unlike with Kade, there wouldn't be any delays to allow for my reactions, only continuous attempts at my life.

I realized my hesitation and charged, grip tight on my knife. The sudden advance caught the Sorcerer by surprise, and he held his arms up to catch me as I dove.

Luckily, his vantage wasn't strong, and he fell to the ground. Locked in a power play, my dagger inches from his chest.

"All of this for a Leech?" he rasped.

*He's my best friend.* I'd do anything for him.

He twisted to slam me hard against the ground, and my head crashed into a relentless rock. Everything spiked white and blurred.

"Wanna give up now? He's not worth it," the Sorcerer taunted. He moved so fast, his knuckles contacting my face in a burst of pain.

"Agh!" I roared. My lip stung and blood flooded my mouth. *I'll never give up.*

A primitive groan erupted, seemingly all around me, as I pushed the dagger with both hands, my arms quaking. The Sorcerer's grip faltered, and he fell onto the blade, eyes round in shock.

Relief washed over me—*I did it*. Granted, the experience proved morally fruitless. I pinched my swollen lips, tepid blood cascading down my arms and onto my chest.

This much blood sickened me, more so because it largely wasn't mine. I could taste it, smell it, and—*Holy Mythos*—it soaked most of my skin and clothes.

"So gross," I complained.

I struggled to maintain a sturdy grasp while heaving the body off me. *The body*. I'd killed a man. I'd expected to divert burglars, not *this*.

Rodney hurried to assist with the lifeless husk. Once free, I retracted my knife and wiped it clean on the dead man's clothes.

Hardly allowing me time to do so, Rodney set to work dragging the deceased Sorcerer into the shade provided by the trees. His brows cinched low over his obsidian eyes.

"It's okay. He's dead. He can't hurt us," I assured.

"I know." He caught his bottom lip with his fangs. "I'm hungry."

He couldn't care less if the man was dead or alive. I rose and stepped back, hands up. "Don't let me stop you."

Unable to look away, I watched him crouch to tear into the Sorcerer's throat. My stomach churned at the sight of more blood as he gulped the discharged liquid.

In all my time on campus, I never saw a Vampire feed. They sipped from bottles of blood the school distilled prior to mealtime. The fact he fed from others to survive didn't bother me anywhere near as much as the gush of fluid into his mouth.

*Yuck.*

I returned to my prior station outside our woodsy motel. No matter how natural it was supposed to be, I preferred not to watch him feed. My roiling stomach stilled once my feet were no longer beneath me.

I directed my vision upwards to avoid further assessment of my gross condition. Yet I couldn't ignore the soaked sweater clinging to my crunchy skin as it cooled.

A man's life source stained my flesh. I'd taken his life. Avenging my schoolmates should've felt empowering—Why did it leave a dark place in my chest?

Rodney crawled into the tree, passing me a sealed baggie of trail mix, warm from the Sorcerer's pocket.

"Thanks," I murmured, only able to muster a halfhearted smile as I tore open the package. A deep breath threatened to capsize my lungs, and I dropped my hands into my lap. "Have you...ever..."

"Have I ever fed from a human?" he provided the words I couldn't.

My eyes fell closed, and I nodded, inhaling slowly as I unpacked the contents from inside the baggie. Gradually, my stomach settled to digest the scant food source.

"No," he whispered. "It's instinct, I guess..."

It somewhat surprised me the institute hadn't prioritized the Vampire's education on the hunt for food if the occasion ever arose. Then again, they failed to teach us how to survive in conditions such as these.

Failed to prepare us for the unpredictable.

The silence between us lasted long enough I suspected he'd gone to sleep. Then his chilled fingers touched my arm. "I was so hungry. I didn't mean to frighten you."

I twisted away. "I'm fine. Get some sleep."

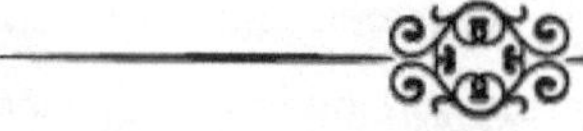

The last one alive, Rodney stalked me, eyes fluorescent green. His nearly nonexistent pupils stood out in the eerie darkness of the crumpled institute. Blood dripped from his rabid lips and the lifeless corpse of our classmate fell from his arms.

He'd drained everyone on campus; now he sought me.

He wanted my blood, my soul.

I thrust the image from my mind, sitting upright to rub the sleep out of my eyes. He'd never do that.

*Unless hungry enough*—No.

There was no reason for my dreams to invent these nightmares. Not when they were usually something tame, like failing a class or flirting.

"Wake up." I shook his leg.

With slow, disjointed movements, he stirred. Vampires slept like the dead; Whereas, any ordinary noise woke me—for example, birds fluttering from their nests at all hours. Which I desperately needed to get used to if I hoped to get any rest, instead of assuming they were a Sorcerer, strapped with weapons of war.

"Remind me to leave a bad review," he grated, crawling out onto the cool, damp dirt then stretched to his feet. "The bed really could've used some fluffing."

I winced, the dried blood along my swollen lip cracking with my smile. The world twirled faster with every pound of my head and I swayed to my feet.

"You look like shit," he stated. His gray eyes and brow line creased with worry.

"I'm fine, let's go." I smoothed my long-sleeved shirt and pulled my tights up. Regardless if he was right, I refused to inform him of my suffering.

I led us along the path, pushing my miserable body forward, Rodney close behind, head hung, and hands tucked into the pockets of his skinny jeans. Kade hadn't prepared me for how taxing it would be to protect Rodney while defending myself. *It hurt to exist.* Every step withered my spirit.

As we passed the pale and pungent corpse from yesterday, my thoughts trailed to our kill. It was a little easier to stomach now. One less Sorcerer meant fewer chances they'd take my best friend from me. Like they'd taken Zoon and Kade.

Tears surfaced and along with them, the memory of Kade's body swinging from the chandelier. My chest cracked all over again, as if finding him for the first time. He's gone. The closest person I had to family taken from me in the most horrific way possible.

An ember of rage revived the hollow chasm within my ribcage. I wasn't entirely sure how, but the Sorcerers would pay for what they'd done to our school. It may not be me who makes them, but it would happen. They couldn't just do this.

Rodney's voice jolted me from my sorrows. I'd been so focused, I nearly didn't hear him.

"Jo, look."

As I wiped my eyes clean, I could see the campus gates stretched high towards the night sky, its stone walls around us.

"How did I not notice?" My entire being quaked with rage and defeat. The sky seemed to swirl, cranking faster with my increasing frustration. *I should've noticed!*

Rodney pulled me from the path into the pine trees. My initial reaction was to resist, muscles constricted enough they cramped.

"What do we do now?" my voice shook. I couldn't believe this happened. That we hadn't noticed we'd made a loop!

He tucked me tight against his side, cradling my head, and I fell limp in his arms.

"We'll figure it out. Okay? The schools existed long enough some paths have outlived their purpose. So we just gotta figure out which ones lead somewhere. There's nothing out here anymore," he explained.

After the Blood Persecution and progressive modern living, there was no need to have direct access to resources. Frequent deliveries provided the school with necessities. Designed to be hard to get to, so the students' families wouldn't be tempted to visit and to assist in solidarity.

"Where do we even start? We can't keep going in circles." A sob threatened to break my voice.

"Just pick one. It's the only way," he whispered.

I shook my head, embarrassed by my obliviousness. Not only had I led us on the wrong path, but I'd loitered in the open, making us easy targets. Attentiveness was a key attribute for a Protector. Kade often said I was too hotheaded, throwing myself into action without a thought. Failing to think forward.

We must be proactive.

I pulled from Rodney's hold to survey the ground ahead. This time, an educated guess would prove profitable. The best choice appeared to be the larger path, less overgrown with grooves in the exposed dirt, suggesting recent travel.

His arm cinched in mine, we set off in search of civilization.

"No way," he hissed. A cluster of Mages emerged from the castle, as casually as if at a nightclub.

*Assholes.*

"Why are they still here?" I muttered.

Rodney's tense frame replicated my fear as we weaved between the wilted foliage along the trail. If they indeed hunted us, the rustle of the leaves would give us up.

The Spellcaster's voices silenced, and my heart raced in terror. Afraid to dare a glance over our shoulders, we kept our heads ducked and ran as best we could.

Certain of their discovery, the Spellcasters shouted to organize a search for the source of the leaves' crunch.

"Faster!"

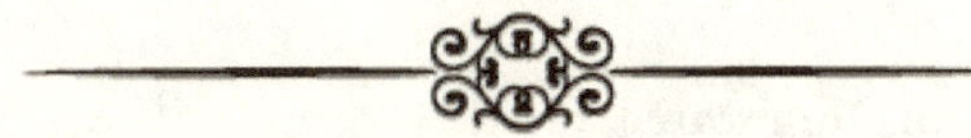

I pushed our limit for hours until my lungs burned, and my legs felt like gelatin. "Do you think we've gotten far enough ahead?"

He slowed to lean against a tree, gasping for air, an arm wrapped around his stomach. "They're Sorcerers, Jo. They can use tracking spells. There's no such thing as far enough ahead."

"Instead of learning about useless star formations, they should have taught us about our allies and enemies!" I lashed out at a low branch. These people possessed capabilities unimaginable.

I lifted my arms above my head and kept my sights on the sky. We required rest and nourishment—despite the risk of a tracking incantation.

"I'm starved," he uttered.

My already pained stomach cramped. The impossible likeliness we'd run into another being meant *I* was on the menu. I bowed my head and set pace. Maybe I would get lucky, and we'd find civilization in time for him to feed.

"Jo,"

"Any chance you could drink squirrel blood?"

"That only works in the movies, and you know that."

Sure, I knew it; didn't mean I preferred the answer to be different. It was common knowledge Vampires required human blood to survive. It made no sense to dispense animal blood into a different species.

I folded my arms across my chest and trudged on.

*He wants my blood.*

My stomach churned, and my breath fell short. He wanted to drink from me.

*Would it hurt?*

"Jo,"

I spun on him. "I'm scared, okay!"

His mouth snapped shut, and he bowed his head. His irises flickered pink, suggesting he felt guilty. With each emotion, they changed color, like a kaleidoscope. The more common ones were easy to distinguish, while his complex or torn sentiments could overlap with the limited color options.

Many creatures had unique eye qualities, however, I had yet to see another Vampire with eyes like Rodney's. We'd always assumed it to be a unique familial trait—something we hoped to confirm upon graduation.

He lagged as we traveled further into the forest where the trees grew thicker, and the path long since faded away. I'd picked every possibility apart about him feeding from me. For one, it would be painful, scary, and an all-around horrid experience. Two, my dehydrated and malnourished body left little sustenance to offer.

He collapsed to the ground with a thud and a muffled grunt. Too weak to continue, there wasn't time for me to come to terms with my fears. *I had to do this.*

"Are you alright?" I swallowed the lump in my throat.

His lips trembled as he shifted his weight onto one hip, averting his hazy glare. His metal band hoodie was ratted and dirty. Sticks and rocks had found their way into his holey jeans, scratching his knees.

"Rodney,"

"I need to eat,"

I'd committed myself to the Vampire and if that meant feeding him, it would be done. Somehow, I had to trust he would know when to stop, so my heart rate would slow down.

I crouched to thrust both trembling wrists in his face. His irises danced painfully, lips parted to reveal needle-sharp fangs. My gag reflex demanded to react, and I sucked in a deep breath to redirect the flow.

"I can't—"

"You have to. I refuse to let you die over something so stupid."

"I don't want to scare you,"

"Too late. Eat." I pinched my eyes closed and turned my face away.

His icy hands clasped the wrist closest to him. I'd never considered this. Never thought he'd ask me to.

Gossip had circulated about Protectors feeding their Vampires for as long as I could remember. It was shameful. Scandalous even. Although that wasn't what happened between us now, it didn't feel...okay. No one would see, so no one could spread rumors.

But it didn't make it any easier.

He pulled my wrist towards his face, and I clenched my teeth tight, rocking forward to rest my weight on my knees.

"Relax," he murmured.

No comfort surfaced as his lips brushed my skin.

*This is it.*

I whimpered and twisted my free fist in my blood-soaked shirt as he bit into my flesh. In a flash, the pain disappeared and time slowed. I floated—at least it felt like it—and my breath became lighter.

*Endorphins.*

Now I understood the whispers about blood lounges where workers allowed Vampires to feed directly from the source for money. All fears and pain drifted away same as if I'd taken a drug to numb my entire body. This feeling I could appreciate.

*I enjoyed it.*

My heartbeat echoed in my ears, and a great weight crushed my leg. Through the numbness, I considered it to be a side effect. Maybe since I was dehydrated, my muscles suffered—*Ow!*

I cracked open my eyes to find he clutched my leg with his free hand. A greedy moan echoed against my skin as he gulped.

"Rodney, stop!" I jerked my wrist away, terrified by the animalistic gleam in his black eyes. The creature who returned my stare was not my best friend. His instincts ruled him, just like my nightmare.

I scrambled in reverse and broke free, bloody arm clutched to my chest. He slumped on the ground, head tilted toward the dirt.

*Run.*

A deer would run from a hunter. A mouse would run from a cat. *But not me.*

Heartbeat in my ears, I waited for my friend.

"Why did you do that?" he snapped. His blood glossed lips sickening.

I put pressure on my chewed skin, unable to believe my own ears. *He dared to blame me?*

"I had complete control!" He rose to loom over me, throwing his hands in the air. "You shouldn't have done that."

"You're lying!" I declared, staggering to my feet. The world spiraled out of control as I did my best to storm through the trees in a straight line.

If he said one more thing to me, I would rip his head off—all three of them!

*Excuse me for panicking when my leg teetered on the verge of shattering!*

We gave one another the cold shoulder for the next several hours, left to our own reflections. I freed my hair from its ponytail so it could flow down my shoulders, the light brown waves matted with blood and filth. Aside from that, my head felt free, the pressure on my skull lessened some.

The sun lightened the sky and with each step, our exhausted bodies seemed to be drawn to the thick tree enclosure with enough space to sleep in. The foliage here was bigger and spaced further apart, the ground littered with decayed leaves that tumbled in the chilly, whipping wind.

Rodney climbed inside and I leaned against the nearest tree to relax. Sleep pledged to fill the drunken void left behind by the endorphins.

"Jo,"

"What?" I bit out.

There was a long pause.

"Earlier... I didn't mean to lose control. I waited too long to eat, and I didn't know how else to stop myself. If I had gone much longer..."

I wouldn't have enough blood to survive—*as suspected*. Since he's irresponsible, it's my obligation to ensure he never got hungry enough to let such worries occur. I'd signed up to be his Protector, not a babysitter—*or a living, breathing bottle*.

Arms across my chest, I settled on the leaf cushioned ground.

He deserved the guilt.

# HUNTED
## CHAPTER 3

AN EERIE HOWL SENT me onto my feet faster than my vision cleared. Silvery light shined on the trees and shrubbery we'd traveled past the previous night. The radiance appeared to pulse in the cool mist as it drifted closer.

"Get up," I hissed, kicking Rodney awake.

I retrieved my knife, sight trained on the light. The Sorcerers sent their hounds to track us, but why? Why bother hunting down two students who'd likely end up dying of exposure anyway? What did they want?

Rodney crawled to his feet. "What is it?"

"A silver wolf,"

In school, we learned about the silver wolves bred and trained by the Vampire's foes. One bite from the creature was fatal for Vampires. They were designed in pure silver and blessed water ran through their veins.

The hair at the nape of my neck stood up as the enormous wolf stepped from the foliage mere feet away. Twice the size of an average wolf. Saliva dripped from its snarl, the sound making my heart pound faster.

"I need you to climb that tree,"

"Jo—"

The wolf's white eyes gleamed onto the leaves as they scattered. The foliage didn't interest the creature, its focus centralized on Rodney.

"It isn't a suggestion. Climb the tree and don't come down until I say."

"But—"

"NOW!"

The tree limbs' shuffle confirmed he'd done as asked, and I finally sucked a deep breath into my lungs. Bracing myself only seconds before the wolf pounced, it knocked me to the ground. My appendages screamed as we writhed beneath its massive weight.

Its surreal white-blue glow illuminated my skin as it snarled and saliva spattered my face. The way its hollow chest spanned over my body was enough to send me into a terror, afraid the chasm would suck me up.

Knife forgotten, I scrambled to shove the wolf away. Its body was jagged, constructed of less than cared for silver that splintered into my palms. Tarnish painted my skin, accentuating the scratches already there. I gritted my teeth against the pain.

*Its teeth are worse.*

Silver wolves were built stronger than Vampires and I was weaker than both, so I'd be lucky to get the animal off. All my conditioning didn't hold a candle to the weight this creature carried.

*Can I stop this thing?*

My legs were my strongest offense; unfortunately, they weren't able to bend at the angle needed to put power behind them. Any false move and the wolf's jaws would seize my limbs. Hands slipping, the animal's jagged chest sliced my forearm open like butter. Hot blood dripped onto my sweater and white spikes limited my vision.

I twisted the wolf's neck, and a scream ripped from my lungs. Metal teeth sank into my arm and shook me until my shoulder burned. Trapped by a machine that couldn't eat I was a plaything. It should be focused on getting to Rodney, discarding me as swiftly as possible.

As if it could hear my thoughts, the wolf released, lifting its snout to survey me. Why would it let go now?

One arm to my chest, I reached to pick up my knife. Prepared, it sprang at me. Slower than I would have preferred, I slashed wildly. The blade grazed the wolf's skin, nowhere near enough power behind it to do any damage—Though it proved to be enough to tick it off further.

*Fantastic.*

The wolf snapped and caught my mutilated shoulder. I screamed through closed lips as the canine's teeth carved my flesh away from the bones like a thousand little knives. Tears burned my vision as I fought to keep control.

"Are you alright?" Rodney's voice rang out from the tree canopy above.

"Stay back!" I ordered as fiercely. He'd shifted to a lower set of branches.

The wolf's ears pricked up, and it licked the scarlet liquid from its snout, standing at the tree's base.

I crawled in slow pursuit, repositioning my knife. Every inch of ground covered took an eternity.

*Too slow.*

The wolf scratched impatiently, searching for the Vampire among the leaves. Its neck stretched at the perfect angle, I slammed my knife straight into its shoulder, buckling its front legs and it yelped.

Snapping jaws sent me back, scrambling away as fast as I could despite my injuries.

*Not fast enough.*

I fell flat on my face, the wolf's teeth latched onto my leg and yanking me backward. Mouth full of rubble from the forest floor, I grappled for my dropped knife.

"No!" I screamed, clawing the dirt.

The wolf dragged me, teeth hooked deep into my skin. My knife grew farther and farther away—too far to reach. I was weaponless and useless to my Vampire.

*I failed him.*

A hollow *tink* echoed like a ball against a bat. Then, a yelp came from my canine adversary as the pressure on my leg released. Thankful for the miracle, I crawled away, peering over my shoulder.

"Rodney!" I screeched.

He hovered behind me, stuck in limbo between helping and retreat. He'd acquired a branch as big around as my leg and used it as a weapon to distract the wolf.

My idiot Vampire protected me and endangered himself! Alt*hough I needed it, he's still an idiot.* I was almost finished, even he could sense it.

Rodney pulled the limb over his shoulder and swung at the wolf's head. The impact rattled its brain and loose bark roughed its skin.

"Dammit! Run!" I screamed.

He stood frozen in the face of danger. The wolf wouldn't nurse its wounds! He needed to run.

I crawled faster to retrieve my knife. Hands raw from all they'd endured, it was painful to wield the weapon. I favored my freshly injured leg, counter balanced by nursing my bleeding arm as I limped between the wolf and Rodney.

The wolf circled, waiting for a sign of his next move. It still toyed with us. Ears laid back, it crouched into a hunter's stance, snarling.

I cursed my slow advances. I had to persevere. Even if this fight felt undefeatable.

I squared my posture as a wave of pain in my wounded leg overcame me. My weak breath evolved into a whimper as I launched myself onto the wolf. Landing on its spine, I delivered my momentum into its shoulder with my elbow. Unable to support our combined weight, it collapsed.

*I had it.*

Drawing my knife over my shoulder, I brought the blade down hard into its metal flesh.

*Would it get back up?*

I stabbed again. We couldn't take much more. Again and again I buried the blade between the animal's vertebrae, its spine severing into segments.

*It can't attack if it's in pieces.*

"Jo! It's dead."

Someone tugged my arms, yet my motions didn't cease. Locked in a trance.

The wolf deserved death.

"Josie!" Rodney ripped me off the wolf's limp body. "It's dead! We're going to be alright!"

I dropped my knife and turned into his arms. *We're safe.*

"Ah!" He tensed and held his left hand in the air.

My heart stopped—*The wolf?*

A red rash spread across his palm, ignited by the silver flecks tainting my clothes. Resentment swelled in my chest as I twisted to view the deconstructed creature. Once the spine separated, it came apart like a piece of magical machinery.

"Are you alright?" I asked, my voice a croak. The wolf had been subdued. We could make it. We *had* to make it.

"I'm fine. Don't worry about me," Rodney insisted. "Let's get out of here."

He scooped me into his tremulant arms. My Protector morals insisted I walk, while the paralyzing pain allowed him to carry me. The blood, muscles, and exposed bone convinced me I shouldn't fathom walking.

"I'm so sorry," I breathed. Frailly, I swiped the silver flecks accosting him. Even in death, the wolf hurt him. "I should've done better."

"You did fine. We're still alive," he whispered harshly, pointedly focused on our path ahead.

All the agony inflicted upon me swelled with each unsteady footfall. The weight of it crushed my shoulders and blackness encroached.

*Maybe we couldn't do this.*

The sensation of falling irked me awake, heart in my throat. With a quick assessment, I discovered we were in a clearing a few yards from the forest. Wildflowers sprouted here and there amongst the brown, brittle grass growing sparse at the towering pine tree's edge.

I'd slept. Was falling unconscious the same as sleeping?

Rodney supported himself against the same tin shed supporting my crumpled figure. It wasn't a well-maintained building by any means—leaning to one side; the door rusted on the ground. Various sized holes adorned the walls, providing a dappled portrait of the saplings on the outside.

A wave of nausea reminded me of what we'd overcome. How much longer could we continue with him as my crutch? It didn't matter if we couldn't slow my bleeding.

"Are you okay?" he gasped, sliding to the ground beside me. His brows wavered, and he bared his fangs in the struggle to get down.

"We barely escaped that wolf," I confessed. "If the Sorcerer's send another one, we're as good as dead."

*It's the truth.* I had once believed myself to be the best Protector at the institute. Now, I questioned my capabilities. None of us were cut out for this.

He shook like a leaf, so I thrust my pain away. "What's the matter?"

He hung his head, weak. "I'm fine,"

Without further consideration, I held my wrist out for him.

"You've lost too much blood and you're dehydrated,"

"You need to eat."

"You haven't eaten either!"

"I'm *your* Protector," I insisted. "Let me do my job."

"I can't do that." He leaned away from me.

I sat up to hold my bloody arm beneath his nose, whimpering in agony. The smell should tempt him, since my insistence didn't seem to help. He lifted his grateful gaze to mine as he slipped his fangs into fresh skin.

At this point, what was a little more blood? At least he would gain the strength to assist me. Because if we didn't find civilization soon, another silver wolf would kill us, if starvation didn't get us first.

*I should have done better.*

The high was different this time, probably due to my condition. My limbs grew heavy first, then my thoughts. Soon after, my lids fluttered closed.

At some point, Rodney dragged me inside the rickety shed amongst the rotted barrels and burlap bags. Every inch of muscle in my body ached, and I felt so weak. Even opening my eyelids hurt.

The silhouette of a large man blocked the doorway, silent and unmoving.

I scrambled backwards until I collapsed against Rodney's stomach. He seized my arm, startled awake by the collision.

"Ow," I whimpered.

"It's alright." The man held his hands up.

Fingers in my boot, I prepared to fight. Even if it killed me.

His sharp, stubbled chin shifted, noting the gesture. *Good;* Nothing would stop me from defending my Vampire.

"There's lots of blood out here. Is everyone okay?"

*Lots of blood?* How much had I lost to leave behind easy evidence?

"We had a minor issue with a wolf," Rodney deepened his voice for effect. "Thank you for your concern. We've got it covered."

The man stepped inside, dwarfing the rickety structure. His jacket snagged on the tin wall, only slowing his approach mildly.

I gripped my knife until my arm screamed in pain, watching his gauged actions warily. His boots scraped against the litter on the floor, the scattering items loud enough to alert a silver wolf miles away.

"That much blood on the ground tells me one of you is severely injured. Let me take you to the hospital."

I threw a glance at Rodney. "That isn't necessary."

Besides, we couldn't afford a hospital stay—if they even knew how to treat Mythos beings.

"Please, let me help you. I can dress your wounds," the man's voice was resonant, yet tranquil, "and food never hurts." He dipped his head considerately at the dried blood.

*Food.*

My stomach growled. Had I the strength to care, my face may have reddened. Conversely, the man's persistent regard kept me distracted. We shouldn't trust this guy. We had no reason to.

*Did we?*

Although I hadn't seen the blood, I could feel it. The fatigue and cloudiness in my mind. I'd lost so much if we stayed here, our survival chances were far less than if we accompanied the stranger. Assuming he didn't lie about his supposed medical knowledge.

"No questions asked," the stranger promised. Genuine concern displayed in his tight brow line and pleading eyes.

While I refused to admit defeat, what other options did we have? If we declined his offer, we'd perish in this shed. Neither of us had another day on our own left. If he revealed himself as a serial killer, at least we'd be put out of our misery.

"Alright. Food and bandages, then we're gone." I decided.

His shoulders relaxed, and he appeared a little less gigantic. Not that it slowed the pounding drum inside my head.

With Rodney's help, I still couldn't keep my legs under me. Flashes of the wolf's razor-sharp teeth reminded me how much I'd endured. How mutilated my limbs were.

"Careful!"

"It's fine,"

"No, you're stubborn!"

My leg gave way, and I crumbled to the floor, sparks of darkness pelting my vision.

"Oh Mythos," I breathed. My heart scattered—*Had the stranger heard me?*

He rushed to sweep me up like a stack of timber. Not a bone in my body could muster the strength to fight him off. He didn't stumble or shake under my weight the way Rodney did. He had toned muscles, or so I imagined, from the excellent cushion they provided.

*Perfect for overpowering and killing us.*

"How long has she been like this?"

Rodney hesitated to answer, "Not long."

Despite my conscience, I observed the man—and my upturned head invited him to look at me, too. A bewitching simper split across his face, and he winked, stealing all the breath from my lungs.

*Damn.*

Recovering what little sanity remained, I directed my attention across the clearing to the city lights overshadowing the stars in the sky. They stretched far across the horizon, painfully abundant.

*How had we missed them?*

The apartment wasn't far. Under the complex lights, it was easier to inspect the stranger. Without a production this time, I noted his features—*in case of emergency*. An olive green V-neck smoothed over his defined chest and a silver necklace plummeted into his shirt collar. His now torn, thin black jacket protected his arms from the chilled fall air.

In my lightheaded state, I still found myself paranoid others would see us. Was this city accustomed to the Mythos? If they were, were they trustworthy? Humans wouldn't venture what to think of a bloodied and marred woman. Would they alert the authorities if they were awake to witness?

I *must* assume this human didn't know of our world in order to protect it.

With one arm, he unlocked the front door and pushed it open. Crossing the threshold, he set me on the living room couch. A small television hung on the wall to the right, parallel to the couch. To the left of the door was an armchair and floor lamp, clustered together.

Hastily, he disappeared into an adjacent hallway, and Rodney crouched between the coffee table and couch.

"I shouldn't have fed from you." He gathered my hands into his. "This is all my fault. I should be stronger, so I could've helped you. You shouldn't have to do everything."

I stared at the popcorn ceiling while he lowered himself into a sitting position. Too weak to tell him otherwise, I allowed him to wallow in guilt.

"I'm so sorry, Jo."

Our host returned with two bowls and water, herding Rodney to occupy the armchair. He thrust one bowl into the Vampire's hands before crouching to offer me a forkful of macaroni and cheese.

"Here, Love," his voice soft and subtly accented. The affectionate nickname differed from any I'd ever been given. My peers called me names out of spite, besides Jo, of course. *Love* awakened bats inside my chest.

I met his warm butterscotch eyes and opened my mouth expectantly for the bite. Not that I would've ever considered it—it felt nice to be taken care of. Regardless, if it meant the food got to my belly slower than preferable.

His expression contorted in studious fixation, giving my heart a thrill. A faint scar caressed the edge of his pinched lips. Chewing idly, I found myself immersed in his mouth's movement while he concentrated. How adorable he was—*For a potential murderer.*

After a few more administered bites, I apprehended the bowl with my operable arm to scarf the remnants. Cheesy noodles never tasted so good. Especially when they were a great distraction from the inappropriate thoughts in my head about a man we knew nothing about.

Rodney sat awkwardly with the still full bowl and glass of water. He had no use for either—I, however, would've consumed them for him.

Gingerly, the stranger lifted my battered leg from the couch, and sympathy wrinkled his brow. Avoiding eye contact with my wounds, I gauged their severity by the tightness in his jaw. They must be pretty bad, because he rose to disappear once more in the hallway, muttering under his breath about bandages.

While he was gone, I gestured for Rodney to trade his full containers for my empty ones.

"This isn't a good idea," he declared, sights on the hall. "What human allows strangers into their home?"

"It's no worse than risking it out there," I stated.

"He could be as dangerous as a silver wolf. I know you're in pain, but we can't stay here. We can find help elsewhere." The remainder of his speech stilled on his lips as I devoured my meal in time for the man to reappear and discard my dishes.

"You need to bathe so I can tend to these," he expressed, brushing away the mud and blood caked to my wound.

"Ow!" I growled. "Are you sure you know what you're doing?"

"Sorry, Love." He released my leg and sat back. His concentration melted into empathy. Without knowing me, he chose compassion. Something I never believed existed without strings attached.

Rodney's hesitations echoed through my skull. Had he lied about letting us go? *Did he want me to bathe so he could eat me?*

His mouth opened briefly, and his hand lifted as if he might comfort me. My chest fluttered and nearly stopped under Rodney's icy stare. Less windswept with the stranger, his irises blurred gray and purple; fingers curled tightly into his palms.

Ultimately, my wounds needed cleaned, or they'd become infected. "Okay," I amended.

"Let me help you," he insisted.

Carefully, I shifted and allowed him to assist me through the hall and into the bathroom. The tight room filled with the smell of warm water as he twisted on the faucet. While he set out a bath towel and washcloth, I surveyed the cream tile floors and uniform textured walls.

He had the bare necessities, suggesting he lived alone and guests didn't visit often, decreasing the need for decorative flair. A bachelor? Divorced? Arguably, there wasn't much to decorate in the modest apartment.

"I'll find you some clean clothes." He backed out of the room and pulled the door closed behind him.

A bubble of excitement floated into my chest as I bunched my shirt around my neck. It's been days since my last bath. Working my protesting arms carefully, I drew my shirt over my head just as the door swung open again.

"By the way," he gave a wicked smile, "my name's Preston."

Scrambling as best I could to conceal my chest, I provided an awkward smile, cheeks warm as the water awaiting me. "Thanks...Preston,"

The smile curled tighter, indenting his cheek as he finally left. Leaving me to wade through the emotions crowding the room as swiftly as the steam.

*He's a stranger. A potential murderer.* Who'd given me a name to provide in the event things took a turn for the worst.

Vision rendered useless by tears and steam, I turned away from the dirty, crimson hued water swirling into the shower drain. I didn't recall the scratches on my face, some broken open by my vigorous scrubbing. As if pressure could wash away what happened to us.

Clutching the edge of the vanity, I attempted to steady my labored breath. To cast aside the agony plaguing my swollen muscles. There was little doubt in my mind the leg I couldn't put weight on was broken. While the fracture may be small, it was miserable to endure and saturated with stubborn silver fragments.

I picked out what I could and washed them down the drain. Hopefully Preston wouldn't put too much thought into what remained. The last thing we needed was a human asking questions.

"Holy Mythos, I look like a Gargoyle." I murmured, prodding the abundance of bruises throbbing as my skin tightened from the cool air. "He has to be a madman to offer to help us. I'm terrifying."

I traced the puncture marks on my wrist and winced.

Over time, I had my fair share of injuries, but none like *this*.

My earliest profound injury happened when Kade first agreed to oppose me in hand-to-hand combat. He took it easy on me, simply blocking and resisting my efforts. I got frustrated and attempted to punch him in the face. Of course, he'd easily avoided the hit and my fist connected with the brick wall behind his head. The wall I should have used to my benefit, having him cornered and all.

Kade helped me to the nurse's office to have my broken hand mended. He stayed at my side the entire time. Formerly, I believed he remained out of mentorly compassion, since I was his favorite student. He'd never said it out loud, but it was obvious by his efforts to cultivate my talents.

While he escorted me to my room, he lectured about the importance of awareness of one's surroundings. Crushing my delusion he stayed to be sure I was alright. Using my pain as yet another educational experience.

*"Unfortunately,"* he said, *tipping his head toward my bandaged hand, "some have to learn lessons the hard way."*

At the angsty age of sixteen, this wasn't what I wanted to hear. Not that I wanted to be coddled, but I definitely didn't want someone to tell me I had executed my reaction in a fight improperly.

With no parents to look forward to, I had little need for someone to educate me about emotions. I wanted to be strong and feared by opponents.

So, I went to my bedroom to sulk, sure to slam the door in his face.

A wavering sigh exhausted my lungs, drawing more tears. I yearned for his wisdom, for him to tell me all the different ways I'd screwed up the wolf fight. How I could have done better and used the environment to my advantage.

Instead, his life ended on chandelier hooks. All the knowledge and wisdom he had to share taken from me and future students.

"Pull yourself together, Josie." I breathed. Time to get dressed and slip into Protector mode again.

My clothes were gone, a shirt and hot pink shorts on the vanity. Allegedly, he lived alone, then he presented me with these? *Did he have a girlfriend?*

More importantly, *when* had he brought them in?

I pinched my eyes shut—*Should've paid better attention!* He could've killed me—and he definitely saw me naked!

After struggling to dress, I dragged my ragged body into the living room. Preston waited with a first aid kit, perched on the coffee table's edge. He put his back to Rodney, an apathetic twist to his lips.

Hopefully, the Vampire hadn't said something to compromise our situation. The way he dashed to claim the vacated shower didn't instill confidence. Nor did it set a great vibe in his absence.

I deposited my boots and knife beside the couch, tucking them near the wall to hide the weapon.

*Shit.*

Preston could've seen it while swapping the clothes. Would he call the police? Forcing me to subdue him until we could safely escape?

"Feel better?" he asked, situating me on the couch so my legs were in front of him.

The filth washed away, the wounds were more gruesome to view. Peeled open with jagged edges of torn tissue, the tendons did their best to cover the exposed white flecks of bone.

"Uh-m," I stammered as my stomach crept into my throat.

"Here, drink this." He offered a small vial of an amber solution.

"What is it?" Poison came to mind.

"It's an old family recipe for pain relief,"

*Here's to hoping he isn't a liar.*

A ghastly smell assaulted my senses as I choked down the bitter liquid. Once it entered my system, my misery decreased—So did my fear.

*It isn't poison.*

Humans undoubtedly practiced alchemy themselves—*thank the Mythos.*

His tender fingers roamed my limbs to apply ointments and bandages. Occasionally, he'd stop to remove debris caught in the grooves of my battered skin.

*Would he notice the fang marks differed from the wolf's bite?*

I twirled a hand in my hair. Humans don't know Vampires exist.

*There's nothing to worry about.*

Maybe he wouldn't see the silver flakes, or would assume it's debris from something else.

*Of course he would; humans don't know about silver wolves, either.*

He studied my leg the longest, gingerly turning it for better observation. I dug my nails into the couch, defying the urge to cry. Feeling my muscles squeeze, his brows raised, and he let go. While the pain dulled from the medicine, it couldn't combat it all.

His face paled, and he glanced at me. "This may need stitches,"

"No hospitals." I sat up to view the garbled wound. The wayward skin chunks and exposed bone caused my stomach to lurch, and I lay down.

*No wonder it hurt so badly.*

Preston rocked on his heels, palms on his knees. "I'll wrap it then."

I nodded, willing the wooziness to go away by absorbing his soft smile.

He shifted to filter through the first aid kit, producing a gauze roll. Pacing my breath, I closed my eyes tight and tried not to think about what he did. Like when I had my wrist tended to at the institute.

Numbness washed over the wound as he carefully worked the wrap. Had my body decided to no longer engage pain receptors or did the medicine finally kick in?

"Must've been some wolf," he observed. An errant grin revealed his perfect teeth and light dimples.

I vehemently studied the room, anything to distract from his curiosity. "Yeah, it was."

"Why were you out in the woods?"

Bitter annoyance bubbled in my chest. He didn't stick to his promise. "We were on a walk. Why else would anyone go into the forest at night?"

"It's just...Wolf attacks aren't common so close to the city."

His attention stayed on my arm as he smoothed the last bandage. His steady hands were warm and soft, which I could have enjoyed if their pressure wasn't so unwelcome. Not to mention, he made it difficult to relax when he asked questions.

I cleared my throat and shifted away. "Any chance I could have another water?" Before I stabbed him and escaped after all.

With a nod, Preston left to do as asked. His questions made me worry he was on to us. Or, as suspected, his hospitality would prove too good to be true.

He returned with a fresh water glass and more questions. "Do you guys live around here?"

His gaze was impossible to meet as I scrambled for a valid lie. I didn't know any human cities—didn't even know the name of the city we're in!

Sooner than one came to mind, he crooked another grin. "I suppose I said no questions asked, didn't I?"

Casting a dark visage upon him, I said, "If I'm not mistaken, that's yet another question."

"You're right." The grin on his face didn't waver, and his eyes glinted with interest. Which awakened the bats in my chest, fluttering erratically the longer he held my gaze.

I let out an anxious giggle.

*How soon was too soon to leave?*

He's playful, despite all my paranoia. So perhaps I shouldn't fret too much, at least not until I had the strength to.

"You need to rest, Love." His bemusement faded as he rose. "I'll get you a blanket."

I relaxed into the cushions, into the belief he simply wanted to help. Temporarily shunning the fact I couldn't trust anyone other than Rodney. Many Mythos races presented themselves as simple humans to the naked eye.

The smell of shower gel wafted through the air, a welcome scent compared to old blood. Rodney returned dressed in a loose gray shirt and too big, black athletic pants cinched tight around the waist, the material bunched together. He sank into the nearby recliner, more untroubled than I'd seen him in days. It hurt to know the feeling was temporary. We'd swiftly be thrust into the wild once more in search of a place to go. Someone to inform of the tragedy we'd survived.

"Sorry, I don't have better sleeping accommodations. I rarely have guests." Preston brought an armload of pillows and heavy blankets, handing Rodney his share first. He placed the pillow on the couch, then spread the blanket over me.

Settled in, I absorbed his pause to appreciate his work tucking me in. I twisted my fists in the fabric and pulled the blanket close against me, creating the illusion of security.

"I'll leave you two to rest." He gave a curt nod as he backed into the hall.

*Kinda weird he tucked me in.* Sure, I was pretty injured, but a blanket wasn't hard to handle. Regardless, I snuggled into the couch and his sweet, musky cologne. Allowing myself to enjoy the security within the ruse.

Rodney's soft voice shattered my peace. "I'm sorry I wasn't more help."

Over my shoulder, he perched on the coffee table's edge, leaned forward so I could hear him.

"You did plenty. If you hadn't helped, I'd be dead." Although apparent by my wounds, it hit harder to hear it said out loud.

The overconfidence I'd possessed plummeted the second we stepped outside Bathory Boarding Institute. We were alone in a world foreign to us. No money or safe haven. We didn't even know how to get to Carthage, the Vampire capital.

I pulled the blanket to my chin.

One measly silver wolf nearly took me out.

*Why had Kade bothered with me?*

Rodney lifted his head to observe the hallway. Busy noises suggested Preston was still active within the apartment.

"It's fortunate someone found us who wants to help, not kill us." I yawned.

His knees bounced with anxiety. "I disagree. There's something about this guy."

"You say that about everyone new," I grumbled and faced the couch cushions. My lids fell closed, heavy with sleep. He hated Kade for the longest time, then his focus shifted to our new algebra professor and any person who expressed interest in our friend group.

"This is different," he insisted. "Just...Try not to end up alone with him, okay?"

"I can take care of myself, Rodney."

If he said anything further, I didn't hear it. The weighted arms of rest swept me up, hauling me into blissful numbness. Where reality couldn't reach me.

# COMPELLING
## CHAPTER 4

My spine still ached from enduring the forest floor. The sticks and stones leaving a permanent impression in my bones. Making me regret anything I ever said about Bathory's dorm rooms and their comfortability. Rolling over, I tucked an arm beneath my head.

Cool air whipped through the room as Preston slipped through the front door. Where did he have to go that's so important he'd leave *strangers* in his home?

Breathing through the pain, I pushed myself to follow, using the furniture along the way as a crutch. Cigarette smoke blasted away the fresh air and sent me back a step.

"Gross," I grumbled, clutching the doorjamb to steady myself. *Damn, my legs hurt.*

Preston twisted to view me, his hips against the lattice wrapped porch railing. Smoke drifted over his shoulder, cigarette held in front of his chest between his thumb and index finger. "You shouldn't be up so soon," he stated, taking a drag from the cigarette.

Drawing the door shut, I slumped against it, squinting into the crude early morning sunlight. My eyes stung, unused to the brightness having lived in low light conditions my entire life. "I wanted to thank you for your help."

His polite simper exhausted another toxic cloud, creating an understanding of why the institute banned any such paraphernalia from entering its perimeter. It smelled awful.

I cleared my throat, looking past him at the teenagers loading into a vehicle. They were loud and jolly. I envied them. Being a Protector appeared to be such an exciting lifestyle until recently. My delusion of our future crushed within a few days.

Preston shifted to follow my gaze. "Friends of yours?"

Supporting my quaking frame with the door handle, I suppressed a snort. "I'm not a teenager."

*I'm twenty-one!*

We were about to be released into the real world as promising young adults. I'd earned my title and refused to be proclaimed a child. Although we hadn't formally graduated, the work was done.

Ready to stand at Rodney's side and conquer his plan to forge a fulfilling career.

"My apologies. I know better than to ask a woman her age." He rested his palms on the railing and the cigarette clung to his lips as he spoke, drooping dangerously as they stretched into a subtle grin.

One I promptly ignored.

"We're not from around...here." I winced, a little too close to putting my foot in my mouth. "What about you?"

"I've lived here a short time." He elevated his chin in my direction and removed the cigarette from his lips to flick away ash. "Where are you two headed?"

"We're just, uh...drifting." I limped to join him along the railing. The bone deep ache had set in again, creeping through the wall erected by the medicine.

Would it be inappropriate to ask for more so soon?

He held up a hand. "I broke the agreement. I forgot."

An amused breath escaped against my will; he forgot quite a lot for someone who said they wouldn't ask questions.

"If you're trying to get out of town, I could spot you some cash." He slouched to rest an elbow on the rail.

His generous offer astounded me. Why would a complete stranger offer such a thing?

I provided a polite, tight-lipped smile. "That won't be necessary." My legs trembled, warning me they were about to give out. I should go inside.

"If you change your mind, don't hesitate to ask."

To my relief, he pushed away to enter the apartment. Further displaying his thoughtfulness, he held the door open and assisted me to the couch.

Buried beneath a blanket, Rodney remained asleep in the recliner. Thankfully. I couldn't tolerate anymore fretting over my condition.

"Taking the bus would be helpful," Preston insisted, an ornery gleam in his shadowed eyes, "if you want to get where you're going this century."

"You're so thoughtful!" I grumbled, dropping into the couch's depths. We'd figure it out. It's what we do.

He sank onto the coffee table, retrieving my bandaged leg so I could lie down. Elevating the limb for better inspection, he scowled at the brown tinted dressing.

"Is that bad?" I asked, even though I didn't want to hear the answer. There had to be some way to get the wound to clot. I couldn't protect anyone in this state.

"I'll re-wrap it." He fetched the first aid kit from the end table.

"Great." I hoped to avoid viewing my wounds again until they were much less jarring.

"If the bleeding doesn't slow, you *will* have to go to the hospital," he said sternly, regarding me from beneath his lashes as he unraveled the bandage.

I grimaced, both at him and the pain. We couldn't go to the hospital. We *had* to make it work.

Mirroring my expression, he bowed his head to clean the wound. Why did he care about my welfare, anyway? He didn't know me.

"Are you a doctor?" I dug my nails into the couch as he tended to a specifically miserable spot.

One side of his mouth tightened, and he cast a smoldering glimpse my way. He was breathtaking; a wind gust should have tousled his hair. Or time should have slowed. "I've been called many things."

Swallowing hard, I redirected my sight to the bundle of Vampire in the corner. "I'm sure you have," I murmured.

"He sleeps hard." Preston's firm hands set to re-wrapping my leg in medical tape.

I stiffened. "Our...trip has been taxing for him."

"Both of you," he amended.

We'd endured a lot. But this stranger wouldn't understand our situation—*couldn't* understand.

"Since you seem to forget," he chastised, pressing the tape to seal the wrap, "you need to rest and keep off that leg as much as possible." He returned the first aid kit to the end table.

"Yes, doctor." I scrunched my nose and twisted to lie on the couch.

Again, his cheek wrinkled under the threat of a smile as he stepped into the hall.

*Damn, he was...something.*

Pushy—and compelling. Without knowing his motives, I could pretend he cared. He probably did, in a way I didn't comprehend. A way that would swiftly change if he found out what we were. Creatures from the horror movies he likely watched on this very couch.

Chewing my bottom lip, I forced myself to study Rodney once more, envious of his ability to sleep so soundly. To enter a stasis of comfort that would allow this blanket to feel like an embrace warm enough to stave off the sadness creeping in. Slowly consuming me.

My vision burned, wishing I could've said goodbye. Wishing I would've helped Kade and saved Zoon. Deep down, I knew they'd be proud I'd kept Rodney from harm, but wished I could hear them say it.

The distant murmur of a television echoed through the apartment, dragging me from the dark place my thoughts traveled. The voices mulled together as Preston flicked through the channels and I strained to hear the news anchor's practiced tone.

"...many lives lost. At this time, we are uncertain if there were any survivors."

I pushed into a sitting position. Had a similar attack happened in this city? Was Bathory's decimation part of a series of raids?

Gritting through the pain, I got up. Maybe if I stood in the hallway, I could hear better and not disturb Preston. He'd done enough for us, he deserved to rest.

Careful not to make a sound, I leaned against the wall outside his bedroom door. It stood halfway open, the flickering light from the TV illuminating the hallway.

"...more on this tragedy as soon as authorities release further information."

An obnoxious tune played as the focus shifted.

"You can come in if you want," Preston's voice startled me.

*Damn.* We'd spent an entire semester practicing the art of stealth! Kade would be ashamed. Inhaling a breath to fight off the blush warming my cheeks, I pushed through the door into the room.

He sat at the head of the bed beside an open chip bag, ankles crossed at the comforter's center. My lip caught between my teeth, and I twirled a finger tight in my hair. His thin pajama pants left his chest available for my visual pleasure.

If he had a girlfriend, what would she think about strangers being in his apartment? Me ogling him like this?

Ignoring the amusement painted on his face, I shuffled to watch the screen perched on top of a dresser. A small woman reviewed the weather for the week and none of the headlines referred to the previous topic.

Adjusting my weight from my injured leg, I glanced at him. He folded his arms behind his head, blatantly observing me out of his peripheral. As if I wasn't doing the same—admiring the way his bronze skin stretched over his rib cage and into his flexed biceps.

"Was there an accident?" I remained vague in case my assumptions were wrong.

He jeered, dropping his arms to his sides. "We're in the city, Love. Accidents are equal to oxygen."

I pinched my lips. If the news reported an attack similar to the institute, he would have known my allusion. "Shit!" I caught myself as my knee buckled.

"Sit down," he instructed, leaning towards me.

"I'm fine." I waved a hand in the air. To prove me wrong, my leg shook. I held through the pain as long as I could, afraid to let him be right. Only to end up surrendering. I lowered onto the edge of the bed. "I'll leave in a second."

He smiled, nostrils flared. "I would say, don't rush on my account. But, you can't."

My cheeks warm, I fidgeted with my shirt's edge. "Your bedside manner is awful," I stated, throwing him a glower.

His ridiculous smirk crinkled the stubble on his golden cheek. "Believe it or not, I'm not a doctor."

"Hm," I twisted to adequately scrutinize him, "you could have fooled me with your wound care expertise."

"Those are excellent wrappings." His eyes glittered with light from the TV.

I raised my brows. "The best embalmer would be impressed."

A low rumble resonated in his chest, the sound stirring an unfamiliar feeling within my own.

*What is wrong with me?*

The news proved to be a waste, unrelated to the attack on Bathory. Knowing better than to bother acting tough, I groaned as I left the room.

"Goodnight,"

"Sleep tight, Love."

*Love.* My chest contracted, squeezing the breath out of me. What was it about this man? *I had a Vampire to protect.*

Supported by the wall, I limped to the couch. Sleep would be easy this time, the trek outside as well as across the apartment had done me in.

I'd never dreamed of being so injured I'd be able to admit defeat. Usually, Rodney hindered our travel. Would I recover and be able to return to my accomplished strength and agility? Or would this damage forever ail me?

Tears surfaced, and I forced myself to forget about it, my face buried in the blanket. I'd address the future obstacles as they arrived. Nothing would stand in my way of delivering Rodney to Carthage.

Driven by my vicious stomach, I ventured after the fragrant smell of bacon. Taking every step carefully, I avoided direct eye contact with the blood-stained bandage around my leg. He's right, stitches were needed. Something had to be done, but I refused to believe we couldn't figure it out on our own. A hospital would complicate things.

The unmistakable sizzle of bacon led me to the end of the hall and into the kitchen. The sinking sun peaked through the open curtains, glinting off a spatula. A spatula manning a skillet of scrambled eggs to ensure they don't burn. As if my brain couldn't compute it, I rubbed my eyes and waited for them to focus.

The utensils were making breakfast.

*A Mage!*

My quaking legs pushed me backwards into the entryway. I'd allowed us to stay the night in the enemy's apartment! *Delivering my Vampire like takeout.*

I whirled to face the broad chest, brushing against my head as he attempted to bypass me. Heart in my throat, I braced for an altercation. We hadn't come all this way to die in a stranger's apartment.

"Sleep well, Love?" Preston's greeting faltered and the corners of his mouth wavered.

"Who are you?" I demanded. "And don't lie, *Spellcaster*!"

He didn't react to the insult. Allegedly, Sorcerers despised being referred to as Spellcasters, claiming it diminished their capabilities, essentially calling them stupid.

His gaze flicked to the scrambled eggs behind me, then rebounded to my squared stance. Uncertainty shook his voice as he begged me to understand, "I am a friend; a rogue Archmage."

"No Spellcasters are a friend to us!" I argued. According to my limited Sorcerer education, if he *is* an Archmage, he's older than he appeared and incredibly powerful. We were in enormous danger, unable to compete with such high-level magic. There wasn't enough time for me to retrieve my knife for protection!

A mistake a Protector should never make.

Settling on the nearest object, I fumbled to wield a ceramic coffee mug from the kitchen counter.

"I don't intend to hurt either of you." He shouldered past to pull the skillet from the stovetop and set the spatula aside. I tracked him with the mug poised to strike. Amusement traced his scarred lips. "Although you've given me plenty of reasons to be skeptical. 'No questions'."

Speechless, I tightened my hold on the mug. How could I be sure this Archmage wasn't a member of the militia who raided our school? "My name is Josephine,"

A light glinted in his eyes. "Are you a survivor of the massacre?"

I narrowed my gaze; *the report he'd brushed off on the news.* "How do you know about...that?"

"Everyone in the mythical world knows what happened. Hundreds of Vampires and their Protectors slain. Allegedly, no one survived."

Whoever discovered the carnage undoubtedly received a great shock. Had they arrived sooner, maybe someone could have stopped it. Maybe more of our classmates could've survived—maybe Kade and Zoon would be here.

I lifted my chin and squared my shoulders, depositing my makeshift weapon onto the counter. "We escaped."

Each ashen face marred beyond recognition blurred my vision. Somehow, we'd survived, and it didn't seem fair in the grand scheme. What about the families who would never get to meet their adult children? How will they cope?

My pride flickered when my legs shuddered. I rushed to collapse into a chair at the nearby table. Fresh blood seeped through the already saturated bandage and trickled down my leg to my bare foot.

"This is humiliating," I complained. *What threat am I in this condition?*

He flashed to my side, concern creasing his forehead. "Please, let me heal you."

I leaned away, further discomforted by his proximity. Not that he needed to be close to kill me—*he's a Spellcaster.*

"You've bandaged me and you aren't a doctor. What more can be done?" My voice shook same as my hands, terrified to bleed out.

"With magic, I can heal your wounds," he explained, impatience in his constricted neck muscles.

I didn't want his help if it involved magic. Magic took Bathory—and strung my mentor up like decor.

I shook my head. "How do I know you won't kill me?" There was no one to stop him or prevent Rodney from suffering a similar fate.

Preston hefted an exasperated sigh. "If I intended to kill you, I would've done it already."

He had a point. The Mages stormed our school in a matter of hours. This one wasted time if his intentions were the same as theirs.

Spreading my palms across my abdomen, I inhaled a slow breath. "How is it done?"

My mind raced in anticipation—*Would it be painful? Were there side effects, like a Vampire bite?*

A breath hitched in my throat at the notion of the endorphins from feeding a Vampire. The numbness they provided would soothe my pain—*While also inhibiting me to protect anyone.*

He cradled my leg. "Let me show you."

I had no weapon to defend myself, couldn't run. The most I could do was call for help, but wouldn't dare subject Rodney to that. There was no choice. Either I bled out from my leg or I took the chance, letting him heal me—and dammit, the soft honey color of his eyes and pinched brows persuaded me to.

He placed an open palm over my shin and his warm eyes bore deep into mine. My breath hitched as a flash colored my vision and a falling sensation swept me into—a daydream?

My skin warmed—*wait, my theoretical skin felt warm?* This wasn't real life, yet I could feel the sun on my skin—and my eyes didn't burn!

A beautiful hilled landscape with lush green grass surrounded me. Weeping willow trees cast great shadows under clear blue skies. Stepping from their reach, the warmth intensified.

Face tilted upwards to experience the sunlight on my cheeks, I spread my arms and spun in a circle. My pain melted away under the sensation the sun dispensed. No ache left in its wake.

At the end of the spin, I threw myself into the lush grass below.

The impact never came; my vision cleared into Preston's kitchen. Hands trembling, I looked upon my arms. Bruises blemished my skin now, the gruesome bite marks all gone. The discarded dressings piled on the table, no longer necessary.

He stood to watch me marvel at my nearly flawless skin.

"That's amazing. Thank you." I gushed.

"No need to thank me." He smiled curtly as he retrieved a plate of eggs and bacon.

My stomach rumbled at the delicious food placed in front of me beside the steaming mug I'd used as a weapon. He sat with me under the darkened windows, the streetlights outside projecting strange shapes on his face.

Between bites, I cast wary glances, unnerved by the way he watched me from across the small round table. *Should I trust him?* Now healed, we no longer needed to stay here. We could return on our journey before he turned on us.

Every time our gazes met, he lowered his interest to the coffee between us. Once my focus returned to the fork scraping my plate, he would train his eyes on me. As if I was the one who'd just used magic to do something extraordinary.

"Now the secret's out, I suppose I can stop trying to force feed your Vampire food and you can stop hiding you've eaten it all." he teased, lips dancing with laughter.

I paused mid bite to discard my fork, embarrassed he knew I ate every mac and cheese serving provided. While chewing idly, I gripped the coffee mug in my hand as a distraction.

"I, uh, noticed the bite marks on your arm—"

"They were from the wolf attack," I blurted. Just because he'd revealed his secrets, didn't mean we had to share ours.

The chair beneath me screeched as I rose to abandon my meal. He'd promised not to ask questions, yet here he pried about our feeding situation. It's none of his business how I cared for my Vampire. Let alone, I hadn't much choice in the matter. He either fed or died.

Which reminded me Rodney was likely starving. A whole day without food wasn't ideal for his condition. Monitoring Preston out of my peripheral, I left to wake the Vampire. He'd gone out of his way to keep his race from us, which didn't instill confidence in his claim to not want to harm us.

Especially since he was so specific about his classification. An Archmage. *Arrogant much?* Confessing to be a Sorcerer would've been plenty. Specifying he's the highest rank in power was more than arrogant—it was intimidating.

"Where is he?" I condemned the mysterious Mage with a glance as I rushed from room to room, even Preston's bedroom.

*Nothing.*

"Where is he?" I tugged on my boots and unsheathed my dagger.

His brows rose high, and he threw his hands up dejectedly. "He was here when I came into the kitchen. I swear."

I swept outside, scanning the balcony for a shock of black and white hair. He'd warned me not to trust a stranger. *This is my fault.*

"Where are you going, Love?" Preston dashed after me.

"Where did they take him?" I whipped around to level my blade on him.

He lifted his hands, and I tightened my grip on the hilt. "There's a ward over my apartment. No one could have come in."

*Who did he need protection from?*

"If you're lying, I'll slit your throat." I warned, turning to resume my search.

I raced into the parking lot, and cold air blasted my exposed legs once outside the protection of the shrubbery encompassing the complex.

The nightlife was still, as were the vehicles in their stalls. In the distance, faint horns and sirens echoed. *He could be anywhere.*

A waft of cigarette smoke choked a cough out of me. Preston paced at my side, cigarette between his lips, and loose wavy hair in his eyes. "Mythos, you're disgusting."

"Ouch." He placed a hand over his heart, as if I'd stabbed him.

"What did you do to him?" His lack of concern erected so many red flags. Some *friend*.

"Me?" He sounded taken aback, blinking exaggeratedly. "Are you sure he didn't leave to feed, Love?"

My stomach hardened; I hadn't considered he might try to hunt. Something he should never do on his own without his Protector in an unfamiliar city. If there's a Spellcaster in the area, then there were unlimited threats to consider.

"Dammit, Rodney, where are you?" I whispered.

A narrow alleyway merged the apartment complex and a neighboring building on the other side of the parking lot. He would've stuck to the shadows, weak enough to need the brick building's support to walk.

I jogged across the asphalt pad to search the trash littered alley.

The frantic flutter of my heart reminded me of another time I searched for him like this. The heavy weight of his disappearance driving my footfalls faster.

Zoon came to me as the sun crested the horizon. The two idiot Vampires thought it would be fun to sneak out to swim in the Vivika river not far outside the campus walls.

*"The dean is gonna kill me!" Zoon howled.*

*"Everything's going to be fine." I insisted, pushing aside overgrown bushes to clear our way to the river.*

*"JoJo, what if he drowned?" He put his hands on either side of his head, clutching onto his feathery hair. "I killed my best friend! I'm a murderer!"*

*"Zoon," I jerked one arm from his head, "calm down and show me where you started."*

*"Okay." He cleared his throat and straightened to lead the way.*

*It wasn't far until we came to the river's edge. Rodney frantically swam in circles, diving into the water for extended periods of time.*

*"Dude!" Zoon threw his arms in the air, relief washing over him. "What are you doing?"*

*Rodney froze, swiping hair out of his eyes. The panic in his expression relaxed and his irises became a rose color. "I thought…I thought you—Why is Jo here?"*

They both believed one another drowned. Of course, I never let them live it down and they often wished the river had swept them away. Anything to avoid the taunts I distributed in honor of my lost sleep.

*I missed that blundering idiot.*

For now, I brushed away the memory. It wouldn't do any good to be emotional. I had to find Rodney.

Squinting, I craned my neck to see around a heaped dumpster and hopped over a fallen stack of boxes. Mere feet past the garbage pile, a bundle of tarps mingled. "Oof!"

I stumbled over something solid. In these low light conditions, the glint of his studded belt nearly went unnoticed.

"Rodney?"

I threw myself onto the sidewalk over his crumpled frame. Red foam soaked his graphic shirt front, and he reeked of bile.

"What happened to you?" I squeaked, uncertain how to search for internal injury. It wasn't unordinary for him to get hurt, however he'd always gone to the nurse and she cared for him. *Why weren't we taught first aid?*

"Is he alright?"

Having forgotten Preston, I jumped. "I don't know!"

I turned Rodney's face and his geode eyes fluttered to alert the arrival of vomit. I flew back, fumbling to pull my shirt over my nose, and breathed through my mouth. The smell alone would cause a chain reaction.

Yet, the Mage didn't hesitate to heft the frail Vampire over his shoulder to dangle limply.

"Be careful!" I snapped. "Something's wrong with him."

"I can see that," Preston fired back, then tipped his head at the complex. "Let's get him to the apartment."

He retrieved a small trash can from the bathroom for Rodney to cuddle while hurling his guts up. Although the sound upset my stomach, it didn't stop my desire to help. I ached to console my best friend and fought the entourage of questions begging to escape my mind.

What happened?

How long had he been gone?

How bad was he hurt?

I sat across from him on the floor and twirled the hilt of my dagger between my palms. The polished metal blurred like a vortex, a visual representation of my mind. I shouldn't watch him suffer; there had to be something I could do. If someone poisoned him, then we were definitely being watched. Or Preston had done it while I was asleep or in the kitchen.

We'd made a mistake staying here this long. Either the Spellcasters caught up or Preston led them straight to us.

Now, Rodney couldn't travel, trapping us here until he's better. Meanwhile, I could gather supplies from Preston's apartment.

Top of the list—a bag to transport a steady food and water supply. Blankets, two since cold weather approached. Which brought the benefit of shorter daytime, so we could travel longer.

I stopped spinning my blade; travel would be difficult once snow arrived.

"Where were you two headed when I found you?"

My gaze locked onto Preston's. The questions never stopped. "Away from campus."

It wasn't a lie. We knew little about navigation. Our primary concern to escape the Spellcasters, not our destination.

"Then where will you go now?" His gaze went to Rodney.

"The lone creatures we can trust are Vampires..." I didn't see the need to elaborate further. Rodney, obviously poisoned, was explanation enough to the danger of our situation.

Preston stroked his chin, lifted toward the ceiling as he wracked his brain. Did he intend to help us or report to whoever led the massacre?

"Carthage," he guessed. "Do you have a map?"

It hadn't occurred to me to possess a map, nor had there been time to acquire one.

"I'll take that as a no." He pushed away from the wall where he leaned. "The Vampire will be fine. Come with me."

"Unless you have something to tell me, you can't possibly know he's alright!" I proclaimed.

He stopped in the doorway and hefted a sigh. "He's drunk,"

"Excuse me?"

"The Vampire fed from a drunk person and now he is hurling up the poisoned blood. Amateur mistake." He came from a more daring standpoint than informative.

Relief swept over me—*It's not poison.*

I scowled at Rodney. "Is this true?"

Were he well enough, he'd demand to understand why Preston acted so casually about all this. Preoccupied by shame, he nodded his head into the trash can in time to vomit.

"Guess you won't go wandering off on your own again, now will you?" I grumbled, rising to follow Preston. I kept my blade ready. While he may be right about the vomiting, I didn't trust the circumstances weren't part of a malicious, organized plan. "Where are we going?"

Contiguous to the apartment, Preston rapped on the Management Office door prior to swinging it open.

"Should we be here?" I hissed, trailing behind. Uninterested in getting arrested for breaking and entering. A flare of fear ignited in my chest. Had he taken me to be ambushed?

A metal desk sat to one side, a graciously muscled blond man behind it. He raised his head, square framed glasses perched on his nose as he wrote on a document.

"Good evening, Beau," Preston greeted.

"Mister Crosstone, always a pleasure." The man's gaze shifted to me, and he set down his pen. *Crosstone.* I knew that name. "Who's this?"

Preston gestured loosely to me. "This is Josie. She needs a map."

Another torrent of red flags erected. Another stranger knew my name. While it could be irrelevant, it could also create problems if they worked for whatever force destroyed our school.

Beau settled in his chair and put his hands in his lap. "Of what kind?"

After first surveying the room like someone—or something—should pop out of the shadows, Preston replied, "Carthage."

Again, I wondered who—or what—he needed protection from. Or was this typical with humans in the community?

Beau did not budge, and I squirmed under his piercing stare. Why would a human apartment manager have a map of the Mythos?

*This Spellcaster's off his rocker.*

"Coincidentally, I have a map to Carthage." Beau laced his fingers on the desk. "What do you need it for?"

Obligated to explain, I consulted the man who brought me here. If he trusted this human, he must know more. Taking his persistent stare at Beau as permission, I proceeded with caution. "I'm transporting a Vampire there,"

"Hm." He adjusted his glasses and leaned forward in his chair, a tired squeal escaping the hardware. "Also, coincidentally, another Mage has asked for it."

A darkness cast over Preston's face, developing into a sneer. Another Mage seeking a map to the Vampire city couldn't be good after what happened to Bathory.

"However," Beau lifted a finger, "I am going to give it to you because I trust you to understand this is a loan and it will need to be returned. I suspect you two are more than informed of the tragedy bestowed upon the mythical world."

Preston nodded, his demeanor abruptly tense.

Should we accept this map unaware if we could return it? What were the repercussions should anything happen to it under our care?

His desk drawer shrieked as he retrieved a tightly rolled document from its confines. "In my position, I have to remind you to keep this map confidential due to the secrecy it protects. Especially if it falls into the wrong hands against a world as fragile as us humans'."

The secrecy Beau referred to was the Vampire city itself. Exclusively Vampires could find it and only Vampires lived there, their Protectors the exception.

"Of course." Preston procured the map.

Holding the door open for me, he paused in the doorway to listen.

"Good luck to you both," Beau said, a crease forming between his brows.

The darkness that overcast them both settled in my chest. The Bathory massacre was clearly just the beginning of a scheme larger than I could ever imagine.

# FLEE
## CHAPTER 5

"Who was that guy?" I asked, struggling to keep up with Preston's strides.

He flipped on the living room light—or rather, his magic did—and a groan erupted from the tangled blankets on the floor. "He's a human employed to protect the treaty between the humans and the Mythos." The agreement to coexist in cities protected by our wards. There were humans on the other side who knew about us, but they were bound by secrecy to keep our existence safe.

As we settled around the coffee table, Rodney unraveled from his cocoon to join us. He appeared recovered from his dinner binge, his pale skin its natural hue. Upright, he clutched a throw blanket beneath his chin, fabric draped over his head like a hood. The trashcan stayed between his knees in case the hiatus didn't last long.

"Feeling better?" I asked.

He grunted again.

Preston unrolled the parchment paper, and it crinkled against the coffee table. Stained and worn with age, there was nothing more on the inside.

I slumped. "It's fake."

Preston flipped it over. "I have a hard time believing Beau would trick us—"

"You guys can't read it?" Rodney quirked a brow.

"There's nothing on the paper!" Frustration spilled from my lips.

He seized the empty parchment, amethyst eyes flicking as if studying a detailed ledger. Often, he could be found settled in with a stack of books. Due to his lack of physical attributes, he excelled in literature. Hopefully, map reading fell into that category.

"I should've known." Preston swiped a hand through his hair as he stood. "Strictly Vampires can read the ink. Of course."

I gestured hopelessly. "That's inconvenient."

"Not really, Love," he chastised. Like he was so superior in intelligence.

*'Not really, Love.' Whatever, Smartass!*

The map creator was smart to use invisible ink to a Non-Vampire, regardless I was bitter about relying on someone else to navigate. While my routing skills weren't the best, I had little faith Rodney's were much better—he'd lost Zoon in a river, for goodness' sake.

"Does it make sense to you?" Preston asked.

"Yeah." Rodney's face brimmed with amazement. "I knew Carthage was hidden from the world. But we weren't allowed to see maps or illustrations either."

We were taught about the different cities throughout the Mythos. Yet, the institute ensured we were ignorant of their precise locations to prevent students from running away. If we didn't know where to go, what was the point?

I rose, too, eager to reach our destination and, more importantly, get away from the know-it-all. "We'll head out tomorrow."

Rodney's shoulders fell. "It'll take days to get there."

*Days.*

It's been four days. It felt like an eternity since our journey started. How much longer did we have to go?

"It would go a lot faster if you didn't have to travel during the shortest part of the day," Preston pointed out, crudely.

"We have no choice in our travel hours," I sneered. No matter how long, we wouldn't get there any faster if we stayed here. "We have to keep moving."

"I could go with you?" Preston offered, fulfillment in his snarky tone.

"What good would that do?" Rodney growled, rolling up the map. I couldn't agree more. His attitude's less than helpful.

Preston's golden eyes narrowed. "No offense, the state I found you two in is enough to convince me you don't have a clue how to protect yourselves."

I clenched my fists. "I am a *trained* Protector. We were fine."

The Archmage scoffed. "One more night and you would have died. There is an entire army after you two—"

"How do you know so much?" Rodney swayed as he got to his feet.

"You want to help us so your little Mage friends can find us easier!" I spat, shifting to Rodney's side to better glower. Why else would he want to go with us? Complete strangers!

"A *Mage*?" Rodney's voice boomed throughout the room and into my bones. His mouth hung open to display his fangs.

*Crap.* There hadn't been time to tell him.

"Once again," Preston overshadowed any explanation I could've mustered, "I am a rogue Archmage. That doesn't mean I don't have connections to the Mythos. There's the news. Other people. Beau is a prime example."

"Beau?" Rodney's shoulders tensed higher, and his obsidian eyes flashed in my direction.

Preston sighed. "Beau is a human who knows about the Mythos. The government employed him as a go between. He helps keep us hidden from the humans, while providing amenities we require from our world."

"He's also the apartment manager," I provided. It wasn't my fault he went on a bender. Had he remained here, he'd be caught up.

"If this information was so widely known, why weren't our administrators aware? Did you know it was going to happen? Why didn't you tell someone?" His pointed face grew stone cold.

Preston floundered and hesitated to answer, a solemn shadow sweeping over him. "There's no way to predict such a timeline."

"What do you mean?" my voice shook. "How can you not be one of them and know they were going to slaughter a school?"

His expression remained patient, head tilted with burden. "It's complicated, Love."

"Don't call me *Love*!" I shouted, nails biting into my palms. "I should kill you."

"I want to help you. Again, these Mages—"

"Are they the reason you have wards? Or are you worse than they are?" I shook, narrowly containing the will to harm him.

"I cannot stress enough, I am your ally!"

"I need to think!" I stormed outside, slamming the door behind me. Silencing their shouts, which all seemed to be a direct hit on me. Highlighting the fact every decision made the second we stepped outside Bathory was mine, along with every consequence when it's not the right one.

Somehow, intuitively, I had to know if Preston was trustworthy. If he told the truth and wasn't hoping we'd be stupid enough to parade a Mage into Carthage so he could slaughter the rest of our people.

I stomped about the complex sidewalks to clear my head. I'd never felt so helpless, without a clue what we were supposed to do. Preston's jab at my survival skills destroyed my self-esteem. While in the comfort of Bathory, I'd proclaimed myself well qualified for most instances. Kade trained me to be the best Protector of my generation. Yet, I couldn't navigate the forest or detect a Mage under my nose. We could've died—We had been dying. Until Preston found us.

Running a hand through my hair, I stopped to lean on the balcony railing outside the apartment. Cars passed by, my attention on the wheels and their strange driving patterns. How did it feel to live without sole responsibility for another's safety? Having the freedom to choose where to go to school? And not to be stalked by individuals who could end your entire livelihood with a simple whisper?

I sighed. Would I still have a family if we lived in the human world? While it would've proven easy to begrudge my family for dying, it was a more solemn curiosity. Everyone at Bathory grew up without their parents' influence. Not so unlike them, I wasn't sure I had any living relatives to search for, since I didn't have a surname to start.

The pedestrian traffic distracted me, car doors slamming and children screeching. Beau's office acted as the grand central station of the complex. Someone ventured in and out almost constantly.

I cradled my head in my hands. If Preston knew to find us in the forest, then he's more involved with the Mage army than he'd let on. He couldn't have known we'd survive—and even if he did, he couldn't predict we'd end up in that shed.

Could we afford to travel without him? Even with a map, we weren't qualified to navigate the Mythos alone. Rogue Sorcerer or secret agent to the Mage army, he was useful. If we were careful, maybe once in Carthage we could dispose of him before he caused any harm.

Getting to the Vampire city was our priority and risks would have to be taken to do so.

I watched the sun come up, basking in the magical orange glow. For a second, I closed my eyes and pretended the world wasn't falling around me. That we were back at Bathory, studying hard for graduation. Our biggest threat a pop quiz from Ms. Way.

The apartment door opening startled me. An ironic metaphor of my new life.

"Sorry to interrupt." The Mage in question closed the door, much quieter than he'd burst through it. He settled beside me, within reach of the shrub engulfing the rail.

He didn't appear to be sorry. So absorbed in himself he didn't seem to notice the waves of irritation radiating off me should disintegrate him.

A smooth snap of his fingers flicked a tiny flame to life above the joining place of his pointer finger and thumb. The cigarette ignited and smoke billowed from his mouth.

"So awful." I waved a hand in front of my face and paced away.

"Speaking of awful. The bites on your wrists..."

I folded my arms across my chest. *Here comes some more know-it-all bullshit.*

"I assume you understand the risks of feeding a Vampire?"

"Of course, I understand." They pounded the risks into us every day. Coupled with being Rodney's Protector and his special condition. In his poor health, the probability of him losing control and killing me was higher. Then there's the limited resource of my blood compared to how often he needed to feed.

Preston stroked his chin, head tilted toward his boots. "This was your last year in school, wasn't it?"

I swallowed the lump in my throat and nodded stiffly. We'd gotten so close to living our lives just to have it ripped away. We'd miss our final semester. When they taught us real world politics and helped find our careers.

"Had they presented your files yet?"

I shook my head.

"Do you know your family name?"

I quirked my lips to the side. "All I know is they are dead."

"I'm... sorry to hear that." He didn't lift his head.

Rodney's poor health kept him in the administrative office more often than the typical child. One day, he found my file open on the dean's desk.

Luckily, my lifestyle made it relatively easy to cope. Instead of worrying about a relationship with a family I didn't have, I focused on becoming a successful Protector.

"What is the Vampire's surname?"

"Harper,"

Preston nodded and set off for the management office, smoke idly in the air behind him. Flicking the cigarette out, he entered Beau's office. What information would they scrounge up this time?

A pit of worry grew within the depths of my chest. How would I know if we could trust him? Even with the knowledge of Carthage's location?

Returning to the apartment, I lowered myself onto the coffee table, gripping the edge. Rodney sat on the couch and held a towel to his head, steadying his labored breaths. He'd thrown up all he could.

"Why didn't you wait for me to feed you?" I tried not to scold, which proved difficult in this situation.

"You'd done enough for me. It didn't feel right to ask you again." He lowered the towel to cast his bloodshot gaze on me. "I also thought we should be careful so Preston wouldn't catch us."

"So, you *leave* the safe place to go find someone? You can't hunt!"

"Seriously?" he snapped. "I wasn't aware we were staying with a *Spellcaster*!"

I pretended to study the blank walls. So often I scolded his poor decisions, as well as Zoon's. I didn't like, nor was I accustomed to his tone—a tone I typically received from our educators.

"How long have you known?" he accused.

"I found out right before I went searching for you." I met his glare with equal ferocity.

"And you trusted him to heal you?" His accusatory glare swept from my head to my feet, making my skin scrawl.

"As opposed to what? Bleeding out? My leg wouldn't heal on its own."

He folded his arms and looked away. "I'm sorry. I don't want anything else to happen to you because of me."

I rolled my eyes. "Don't worry about me. It's not your job."

He scoffed. "One of us has to worry. You left me with him on my own, in a vulnerable position."

"I was right outside." Chewing my bottom lip, I turned my remorse on the lamp in the corner. The prospect had crossed my mind; I hadn't abandoned him—not completely.

He ran a hand through his hair and squared his shoulders. "Yeah. That makes me feel safe—"

"He's a Sorcerer. What do you expect me to do? If he wanted us dead, we'd be dead!"

Silence stretched between us. Both of us adequately scolded. For now, Preston had to be tabled as something akin to an enemy and an ally. He obviously meant to help us, we just had to be cautious and wait to find out why.

"Did the person you drank from suspect you were a Vampire?" I asked, worried I needed to track the human. What would they do with the information?

He shifted his weight, focus on the door behind me. "She had bites all over her skin. She knew what I was and approached me. I didn't know I would get sick from her being drunk."

"Drunk?" I rebuked. "You were wasted!"

The Vampire's face turned green, and he rushed to retrieve the trash can. After several heaves, he lay on the couch and wiped the drool from his lips.

"If she had prior bites, and she came to you...do you think...someone sent her?"

"She's probably an addict, looking for her next fix. It's not out of the norm in cities like this."

A shudder rolled through me; if I weren't careful, I'd suffer the same fate. "What do you mean by cities like this?"

"Little Hope has the highest population of humans because it's the closest to the edge of the wards," he explained, burping into the towel.

Little Hope. Bathory was this close to a city all along?

"I'm worried," I confessed. "There's another Mage after the map to Carthage—"

"Do you think it's the ones who attacked Bathory?"

"Why else would a Mage want a map to the Vampire city?"

"To extinguish us..."

A wave of doom swept over me as I lowered myself to the floor between the couch and coffee table. Just when I thought things were at their worst, they were about to get worse.

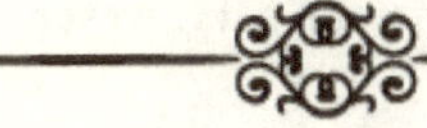

My lids flashed open, and I didn't recognize my surroundings for a split second. A sliver of sunlight shone through a space in the curtains. Another hour or two until night time.

I slept in Preston's bed, snuggled beneath the thick black comforter. Vaguely, I recalled falling asleep on the floor in the living room. A flicker of panic swept over me. He must've transported me here—he could've killed us.

But he didn't and, like he said, if he planned to, he would've done it already.

Rolling onto my side, I buried my face in the silky soft pillow, laced in his warm, spiced scent. No residual smell from his late-night snacks. A slow smile etched my lips, imagining him watching TV in his pajamas.

*Such a compelling know-it-all.*

Being in this room made it difficult to watch over Rodney. Yet, the desire to care failed to rise. He'd insisted repeatedly he's our ally and perhaps I'd begun to believe him.

Because the idea of Preston carrying me to this glorious bed gave me a thrill. I'd never considered someone could care for *me*.

I chewed my bottom lip and imagined if this room was mine.

At Bathory, I had a tiny dorm with minimal furniture, the nicest part a black fur rug. A metal frame twin bed sat under the small, stained-glass window, facing the wooden dresser with an aged mirror on top. I'd taped posters to every inch of the stone walls to make the room more *mine*. It was nothing akin to this spaciousness.

The underlying draw was the concept of sharing a room. How it felt to come to bed each night to someone so—*I shouldn't finish that thought*.

I sat up; *I should find my Vampire*. However, a small chest on the bedside table distracted me.

Paranoid, I glanced at the door while reaching for the chest. Heavier than expected, I had to use two hands to lug it into my lap. The lid opened with a soft click of the hinges and rested on my knees. Envelopes filled the coffer, pressed together so tight it was a wonder they didn't compromise the integrity of the wooden structure.

Peripheral vision trained on the door; I filtered through the many envelopes. Each one addressed to Preston from a woman named Desma Crosstone. The last name's the same as his. I selected one to open and skim.

Whoever the woman was, she's angry he ignored her many letters and missed him dearly. Did she own the clothes I borrowed? Perhaps an abandoned wife?

Distantly, dishes clattered, and I hurried to return the envelope and chest to the table. Putting distance between it and myself to devoid any suspicion I may have snooped. My frequent visits to the dean's office were due to sneaking about. We'd learned the hard way I wasn't a reliable stealth source.

*Zoon and I exchanged notes in Ms. Ways' classroom that would've gotten us detention for life. Somehow, the idiot left the notes tucked in his desk cubby. If she found them, we were doomed.*

*Which didn't seem to bother him. If I spent all my spare time in punishment for silly mistakes, I wouldn't have time to train extra.*

*Fortunately, her classroom was unlocked. The lights were shut off and not a soul lingered in the hallway. All students were supposed to be in their rooms right now.*

*I'd be in unequivocal trouble if busted.*

*Checking the hall on either side one last time, I pushed the door open. The luminescent galaxy mural projected on the ceiling provided some guiding light. Just in case, I kept a sweaty hand outstretched as I shuffled to our desk row.*

*The note was still folded and tucked away in Zoon's. I retrieved it and froze, heel clicks approaching. Dropping to my hands and knees, I crawled under the desk. The classroom lights came on and Ms. Way entered from the hall. She appeared to be in a foul mood, accentuated by her swinging arms.*

*Craning my neck, I watched her shuffle through her desk drawers for a few folders and a paper stack.*

*"Ungrateful Leeches...think they run the Mythos..." she muttered.*

*I bit my tongue. Why did she work here if she disliked them?*

*She slammed the drawers closed with her hip and left the room, flipping the lights off. I waited until I could no longer hear footsteps before leaving.*

*Zoon would get an earful when I saw him. Considering Ms. Way's mood, I would have found myself buried beneath the school.*

*As I rounded the corner in the hall, I stopped dead in my tracks.*

*"Josephine!" The Space Pixie jumped. A sheet of paper escaped the clutches of a folder and fluttered to the ground. "Why are you up at this hour?"*

*Her galaxy eyes narrowed, focusing the faint light emitted from their depths, while struggling to balance her paperwork.*

*Shaking hands behind my back, I sought courage. "I, uh, forgot a book in one of my classes. I suppose I can get it tomorrow. I'll be more responsible."*

*She righted her papers and tossed the hair from her guarded expression. "Seems we both are forgetful today. Go on to your room and I'll not report you."*

*I gave a curt nod prior to rushing off to my room. It wasn't typical of Ms. Way to dismiss a chance to reprimand a student.*

Even today, I recognized the encounter as strange. If only I had gotten a chance to look at the loose papers.

Had my stomach not insisted, I would've stayed in bed forever. Whether because of impending doom or because this mattress was *so* inviting.

My clothes sat at the foot of the bed, clean and mended. Another magic trick, I assumed. Stretching the fabric, I cursed the school for not teaching us more about the other races in the Mythos.

As a Protector, I should understand what we faced. Even coexisting alongside a magically inclined janitor would've provided some insight. At present, the definition of Sorcerer in a dictionary surpassed what I knew.

Dressed in clean clothes, I joined Preston at the kitchen table, glasses on and a coffee in hand. Across from him sat a full plate aside another cup of coffee for me.

The glasses aged him and suggested he may be nearly as smart as he perceived himself. Catching my bottom lip between my teeth, I admired the wisdom it gave him. Were the glasses for show? If he could heal my wounds, couldn't he heal his poor vision?

*Damn the institute and their lack of valuable curriculum!*

"What is that?" I trailed my index finger across the table to the collection of papers he studied.

His fatigued gaze fell on mine, and guilt pelted my chest from sleeping in his bed. While I'd enjoyed myself—albeit more than I should have—he deserved rest as well. "Beau located the Vampire's family,"

An enormous weight lifted from my shoulders so rapidly I fell short of breath.

Preston toyed with the chain around his neck. "When you said the school hadn't given your files yet, I wanted to be sure Carthage was where you needed to go. If his family's here close by, it would save you some trouble."

Once more, he rendered admirable efforts to assist us beyond my expectations. At this rate, he'd complicate my plan to use and dispose of him.

"Will they be able to help us?"

He sipped from his coffee and flipped through the paperwork. His brows rose with interest as he read a certain bit of information. "Conveniently, they'll be able to help you more than any other family. He's the son of the Mayor of Carthage."

The entire apartment shuddered as an explosion shook the complex. I braced myself on the table and sprang to my feet, knocking the chair to the ground. Preston beat me to the living room to peer through the blinds. Behind him, Rodney rubbed his bleary eyes, craning his neck to see around the Sorcerer.

"What's going on?" I demanded, tempted to throw open the door. I stood behind two men whose height limited my view. Faintly, I could make out a swirl of glittering smoke in the parking lot, illuminated by the streetlights.

"We need to go," Preston said, voice low as if a threat could hear despite the wards he insisted protected the apartment.

I reached for my knife instinctively, recognizing the glittery smoke. *Spellcasters.*

Rodney retrieved the map from the table beside the couch, falling into step behind me as we darted outside.

The complex parking lot was alive with bodies and magic. Sorcerers and Sorceresses stood guard throughout the lot, shouting and firing magic. Residents who found themselves caught in the chaos cowered, heeding their command.

Three Sorcerers with hoods pulled over their heads approached the management building. The center man of the trio, in a maroon cloak, stood out amongst the others under the fluorescent glow of the streetlights. He walked a few paces ahead, head held high—like a leader.

*The other Mage come to collect the map?*

"We've gotta hurry, Love." Preston jerked me by the arm to lead us around the side of the apartment complex. I clutched Rodney's wrist, dragging him with me into the sudden blast of autumn wind.

A black sedan was parked along the curb, outside the compass of the lively lot. Where the darkness felt serene, so close to the production to scare Beau into giving them the map.

We clamored into the back seat while Preston settled behind the wheel. No sooner than we'd closed the door, the engine fired to life, and we pulled away from the curb.

"I didn't know you had a car," I observed, trying to distract from the seriousness of what was happening.

"I don't," Preston confessed.

My eyes bulged. "We can't be arrested for—"

"It's Beau's. Trust me, he won't mind."

"Considering what we left behind, he might." Rodney countered, black eyes wide.

"He has plans set in place for such occurrences,"

Somehow, I doubted he'd prepared to ward off an army prepared to exterminate the Vampire race.

"They must really want that map,"

Preston sighed, weaving between traffic. "How else would they infiltrate Carthage?"

"Is it the Sorcerer Beau mentioned?"

"What other Sorcerer would storm an apartment complex in Little Hope?"

Rodney gripped my hand, focus out the window as we passed car after car. Clasping his icy hand, a pit developed in my stomach. Bathory was just the start.

"Now would be a good time for you to tell me which way to go."

Rodney scrambled to open the map, shaking from the adrenaline rush. His eyes flicked side to side as he deciphered coordinates. "We're in Little Hope?"

"Yeah." Preston glanced in the rearview mirror.

An unanticipated crater in the road jostled the car like dead weight. My stomach twisted, and I heaved for a calming breath. This wasn't as magical as I'd often dreamt it would be.

"As soon as possible, we need to exit the city on the south side."

I clutched onto the seat as Preston flipped the car around. It took all my strength to stifle a scream as I squished against the door nearest me from the momentum. The engine growled as we weaved between traffic in the opposite lane.

"They're following us!" I declared.

Hooded figures filtered into the sidewalks, their heads whipping to track our car.

"They know we have the map!"

We flew into the ditch at the dead end of a dusty dirt road, brakes locked tight. The map showed this would conclude our travel via vehicle, the city miles behind. From here we would voyage by foot through a wooded area, once *again*.

Preston left the car in the deep ditch where it wouldn't be seen from the road, hidden by the tall dry grass. I was relieved to leave the dreaded monstrosity behind.

We trudged through the brittle, autumn colored foliage, headed south. Rodney led the way, map held up, with Preston hot on his heels; a cigarette perched between his lips. Maintaining a close eye on him, I scanned for other suspicious Mages.

The further from the car we got, more bushes sprouted, intertwined with ivy. Full sized, healthy trees covered the ground with early autumn leaves. The cool air would prove more difficult to endure as time continued. Hopefully, we'd reach Carthage before winter.

Deep in the woods, the silver moonlight dimmed behind the thicket of trees. Preston shifted his gate to peer over his shoulder. His pace slowed, ear tilted one way to listen better.

*What did he hear?*

Rodney's pale hand clasped mine, pulling me close against his side. A chill zipped down my spine, triggering my Protector's instinct. His enhanced hearing picked up on a sound inaudible to mine. I followed Preston's gaze across the knoll's crest to the faint glow between the brier's leaves.

*A silver wolf.*

Fear buckled my legs out from beneath me. The last time I'd faced one, I'd nearly died. I had to remind myself we had help this time before the fear consumed me.

Mist illuminated the shadows, awakening the many rodents in the trees. Preston stood in a braced stance, hands held palm outward at his sides to follow the vapor's motion. It rippled the longer it permeated the air and, with the same frequency, a vibration tickled my skin. The sensation beckoned me to a revealed silhouette.

*They'd caught up to us.*

"Fuck. All this for a map." A Sorcerer stumbled from behind a nearby tree, compelled by the spell. He threw out an arm, muttering inaudibly, and a gust knocked me and Rodney flat on our backs.

Preston remained faced away from us and our attacker. Another silhouette approaching from the north.

*How many are there?*

"Run!" He twisted his head to bark the order, eyes a wild and piercing yellow.

I'd never realized they changed when he used magic, given my pain preoccupied my mind most of the time he'd used it in my presence. The haunting neon orbs imprinted my memory, rattling me to the core. His power's both terrifying and mesmerizing when not used for harm.

Perhaps his cockiness *was* called for. He moved like Kade, with sureness and a level of force only someone with experience could accomplish.

"Go!" He cast a spell at the approaching foe.

An agonized scream carried on an unnatural wind gust. The foliage between Preston and his victim blasted through the air at tornadic speed, spearing tiny, thin sticks through his forearms and dry grass splintered his eyes.

Hauling us onto our feet, I pushed Rodney away from the chaos. "Don't let them catch you!"

He twisted the map closed, watching me over his shoulder. I couldn't blame him for being hesitant to leave my side, but he had to stay safe. "Lookout!"

I met the Sorcerer's chest with my boot, knocking him to the ground. He fell hard on his shoulder, the wind knocked out of him; giving me plenty of time to dart ahead.

The silver wolf slipped from the bushes to fall into step behind us.

*Rodney's not fast enough to get away.*

"Just give us the map, kid!" The Sorcerer panted, cradling his ribs as he hurried to catch up.

"Rodney, get in a tree!"

He sized up the next biggest tree and threw himself against the trunk, pulling onto the nearest branch. His arms trembled as he climbed, but nothing like they usually did. Not even at school, in a safe environment, had he climbed so swiftly.

"You can't run forever!"

I screamed; my legs swept out from under me and leaves skittered across the dry dirt, blurring the wolf jumping at the tree, clawing the bark.

Not a soul stood near me—no wolf, no person.

*Magic.* My ass had been handed to me by an invisible force. *Great.*

"Where did you get the pet Mage?" the Sorcerer asked as I rolled onto my back.

Past him, Preston battled another Sorcerer and his silver wolf. The wolf paced, impatient to fulfill its duty. Preston wouldn't let it pass. He danced from side to side, trails of magic emitted from his hands.

The impending Sorcerer swiveled to witness a burst of magic explode between the trio like a firework. Sparks stretched into the air, lighting the forest broad as daylight and leaving behind a sulfur scent. Smoke drifted into the air, the dry grass on fire.

I scrambled to my hands and knees to hide in a thicket. The hair on the nape of my neck rose as the silver wolf preying on Rodney let out an impatient, eerie whine and I gripped my knife tight.

The Sorcerer's pace slowed, head lowered to search for me.

I took a deep breath, then swiped my knife across his Achilles tendon. "Agh! Bitch."

The wolf whipped in our direction.

*Was it his?*

I dove from the bushes, driving the blade into the Sorcerer's back. He crumpled to the forest floor, and the wolf whined as its light flickered out. Piece by piece, its body tumbled apart, making sharp, metallic *tinks* as they became a pile.

I froze in awe; too hysterical before to witness the previous silver wolf dismantle. We'd studied little about their design in school. Our training focused instead on the wolf's intent so we'd know how to kill them.

I toed the dismantled parts. If my suspicions were right, then the previous silver wolf hadn't been alone. Had its Sorcerer been hiding and watched their creation die?

A simmer of empathy filled my chest. No one's safe from the Sorcerers.

Pushing aside my feelings, I waited at the tree base for Rodney to climb down. My Vampire's safe. That's all that matters.

"Everyone okay?" Preston lumbered to us, his brows pinched and sweat on his forehead collected curled hair strands. His eyes flickered as he healed his bloody forearm, which appeared to bother him little.

"We're fine," I replied, dusting myself off.

Rodney tapped his waist line. "The map is safe."

"What about you? Are you alright?"

"Physically? I'm fine." He crooked a grin. "Mentally? I don't think we have enough time to go over that."

He'd selflessly defended us and had the strength to joke. "Thank—"

A distant growl stopped the words on my lips.

There's more. There will always be more.

"Time to go!" Preston ushered us on.

Running's a frivolous and unachievable ambition. Silver wolves matched Vampires' enhanced speed.

We had to find the wolf's Sorcerer. They'd be easier to take down—*in theory.*

Operating like a well-oiled machine, Rodney screeched to a halt to climb a tree. Simultaneously, Preston and I whirled to confront the wolf. I crouched with my knife, squared into a fighter's stance. This was my opportunity to show him I could defend us. We weren't completely hopeless on our own.

Preston held his hands up, yellow eyes casting a harrowing sheen on his face as he concentrated all his energy on the creature. Sheer gray light emitted from his fingertips, paling his skin in an imitation of the many dead faces I'd witnessed all too frequently.

A dark cloud materialized above the animal.

*Once again, Mister Arrogant must prove himself.*

The veil flashed with silver flecks, increasing in intensity as unabridged lightning loosened from its depths. The wolf's fur stood on end in response to the electricity. Head whipping from side to side in panic, it fled.

"That's not very heartless predator of you," Preston chastised. Several bolts struck the canine, eliciting an ear-splitting crackle as the wolf dismantled in a heap.

Nerves already on edge, I jumped at the following thunder boom. Similar to nature, magic was a force to be reckoned.

"Let's go." Preston spun on his heel to run. "The Sorcerer that thing belongs to won't be far behind!"

I'd always assumed they were created in mass quantities and released into the world as a species project. Until now, I hadn't considered they belonged to each Sorcerer individually. A pet death machine to do their bidding.

If they got their hands on the map to Carthage, there wouldn't be a city left for us to find.

# GIFTS
## CHAPTER 6

Rodney slowed, using the trees to keep up until his toes dragged, and he stumbled. Excitement staked my chest, recognizing his signs of fatigue. I shouldn't, but I wanted to feed him. To feel the apathy.

"You need to feed," I said, dragging him to a stop.

"Already?" Preston complained, upper lip curled. "We shouldn't stop now—"

"Just because you zapped a wolf, Mister Badass, does not crown you leader. He has to feed more frequently, not that it is *any* of your business." If he couldn't handle Vampires needing blood to survive, then he was no ally to us. Rodney had no choice. I put my back to Preston and muttered, "Go choke on a cigarette."

Towing Rodney with me, we hid behind a hedge far enough away to get some privacy; close enough to monitor the pissy Archmage while he smoked.

"Did he mention his echelon or sect?" Rodney asked in a whisper.

"What's their sect again? He said he's an Archmage." I folded my arms and grumbled, "An arrogant one."

Rodney's lips and brow quirked. A telltale sign he's about to educate me. "They each have certain magics they're better at. Like fire and water." He gestured dramatically for emphasis. "He's able to do it all and, from my research, he does it well. I'm no expert, but I think he's an Anteomancer."

I glanced in the smoker's direction, miffed he knew it all, and could do it all. "So?"

"So, he's powerful," he spoke matter-of-factly.

"Why would someone so powerful hide like a coward?" I challenged.

"Even powerful people have enemies."

Well, hopefully his skills would prove to be our advantage. The last thing we need is a super powerful Sorcerer as *our* enemy. Which further complicated my plan to ditch him. Could we afford to?

"Great," I sighed. "Let's get this over with. I prefer not to leave him out of my sight. Believe it or not, I don't completely trust him."

The obsidian shade of his eyes suggested he didn't believe me. As if his safety wasn't at the forefront of my mind every second. We'd both witnessed the damage Sorcerers could cause. I'd be a fool to throw all caution to the wind just because this one fed and healed me.

"If you don't trust him, then why are we letting him stick around?"

"Because he's useful," I stated, holding my arm out to him.

Rodney grasped my wrist. "We were doing fine without him."

"Were we?" I didn't like to admit it, but we needed him. "I would've died from my wounds. I don't like the situation any better than you do, but we have no other choice right now."

Setting his jaw, he bent to bring my forearm to his lips. As his fangs pierced my skin, a slight pinch made me gasp. I twisted to rest my chin on my shoulder to avoid watching. Just feeling his tongue skate over the puncture points soured my stomach.

The endorphins gushed over me, washing away my concerns—the residual rush from the fight, worry for our wellbeing, distrust for Preston and the never fading pang of loss. *Gone.*

It made the bite worth the initial fear. Worth risking my reputation as Rodney's Protector. The moment he'd been assigned to me, I'd never relaxed, not truly. We'd hang out with one another, sure, but I still had to watch out for him. Bullies, falling risks, and reminding him not to miss a feeding.

The endorphins took all that away.

He drew me against him, raking his tongue over my flesh one last time, before cinching me in an embrace. He tucked his chin against my neck, eliciting a sweep of awareness I hated to acknowledge—the craving for *more* endorphins.

"You okay?" I murmured. Usually, I initiated the hugs. *Maybe he was scared?*

"Mhm,"

His icy body temperature leached into mine, driving me to slip from his hold.

*Maybe not.*

His cheeks reddened, and he fidgeted with his hair. *No, no, no.* This was *not* happening.

We're best friends. He knew that. *Right?*

I tucked my arm against my chest and trudged in the direction of Carthage. For now, I had to compartmentalize my problems the best I could, considering my brain's scrambled. Rodney was just being weird because we nearly died a few days ago and Preston wasn't a shifty Sorcerer waiting to enact our demise. Whatever that may be.

"You two coming?" I hollered, keeping my momentum. If I stopped, my legs would crumple.

"Gladly," Preston grumbled, striding to catch up.

"Asshole," I muttered, tossing a glance at Rodney behind me. He'd have to get over his inhibitions about our feeding arrangement if he planned to stick with us. Rodney had to feed.

"This is ridiculous," Preston complained, gesturing to me as I stumbled and staggered. "No wonder you were in terrible shape when I found you."

"I'm doing fine. We're still moving!" I insisted. Even if it wasn't at the rate he'd like to travel, we were putting distance between us and the Sorcerers chasing us.

"You're definitely doing a lot of moving," he chastised, flicking away his cigarette.

"You didn't have to come with us, you know." I reminded him, gathering my steps into rhythm. I could do this, my head would clear soon.

"I disagree." He reached for me. "You're going to hurt yourself."

"I don't need your help!" I jerked away from him and lost my balance. A tree stopped me, knocking the wind out of me as I slammed into it.

"You're being childish and slowing us down!" he snapped.

"Don't touch me!" I swatted his hand out of the air.

He took the weak smacks in stride, scooping me into his steely arms. Hardened gaze on the forest ahead, he grated, "Rest. We'll travel faster this way and you'll be better off."

"Better off?" I kicked and pried at his fingers cinched tight on my arm. "You're not the boss of me! Put me down!"

"You're making a fool of yourself, Love."

"Let her go!" Rodney hissed, inching to our side. "She'll be fine—"

"Keep walking, Vampire." Preston ordered, his golden eyes turning dark.

I recognized that tone. It's the one Kade used when he was done arguing and expected us to obey. Something, as a twenty-one-year-old, I knew better than to fight. Rodney knew better. Pinning our lips closed, we let him have this one. Relaxing against his shoulder, as if controlled by him, my lids lulled, and sleep took me.

The jostle as he walked eventually woke me, and the ache in my spine that radiated into my feet. Although I fought him, maybe it wasn't so bad being carried by someone so sturdy and warm.

Without a show, I peered through sleepy lashes at Preston's determined features. If I must guess, he appeared to be in his late twenties, early thirties. Likely far older since Mage's physical aging slowed significantly after eighteen. Truly, the utmost confirmed information I possessed about Sorcerers from Bathory.

His light brown hair curled around his eyes and chin, stuck to his stubble. Something I hadn't quite grown accustomed to yet—Vampires rarely had facial hair.

"She'll be fine after the endorphins wear off," Rodney grumbled. "You don't need to carry her all the time."

Preston's arms tensed. "The endorphins aren't the problem. She's lost blood. It takes time to recover and at the rate you feed from her—and her lack of adequate rest and nourishment—she needs the break."

"We could stop and rest then, instead of giving you a reason to put your hands all over her!"

"I'll not stoop to your level of immaturity. You know as well as I, we can't stop. She won't withstand another attack so soon."

"You underestimate Jo—"

"I do not doubt her capabilities. I wish to keep her from collapsing due to your selfish needs."

Silence followed. Preston struck a chord, sending Rodney into a cold shoulder sulk. He couldn't help he must feed from someone, and I'm the one available to do so. I hated to see him frustrated with himself, but

Preston had a point. I had little self-control with Rodney and would give him my last drop of life in exchange of a break.

"We need to stop for shelter anyway," Rodney muttered. The sky grew lighter by the minute as dawn neared.

"You get your wish, Vampire. She's awake." Preston set me on my feet, and I had to pretend not to grieve the loss of his comfortable embrace.

A small hill sat between a cluster of trees; a burrow carved into its depths. Large enough, a bear could occupy it, or gnomes—who preferred to keep to themselves and thus were rarely sighted.

Rodney settled in once we ensured it was indeed unoccupied. Then Preston and I assembled a haul of weeds and leaves over the opening to shield him from the sun.

He still wasn't talking, and it made my chest hurt. He didn't deserve to pout, but there's nothing I could say to drag him out of the dark place his mind ventured. In time, he'd move on.

A smoke plume swept from Preston's side of the burrow, cigarette burning in his hand. I rocked my head back against the tree behind me and sighed. It's a wonder he had any lung capacity left. *Could he heal the damage cigarettes caused?*

"If you're going to continue to feed him, we need supplies," he stated, lifting the cigarette to his lips.

I pinned him with a glare. "We have no choice. How else would he eat?"

"It's not that he has to eat." His copper gaze pierced through me, daring me to argue. "It's that you seem to be okay with the toll it takes on you. Forgetting how dangerous it is to your health when you don't have the proper supplies to recover. I'd even venture to say you like it."

A metaphorical stake pierced my chest, envisioning myself covered in marks identical to the woman from the alley. Lost to the addiction of the endorphins.

I lowered my head to my lap, fidgeting with a lock of hair. "I'll do anything to keep him alive."

"Seems rather illogical to pick an ill Vampire to escape a school massacre,"

"He's my *best* friend," I reminded him in a steely tone. "There's no one else in the Mythos who matters more to me. I'd never leave him behind just because he's more challenging to look after. Only a coward would do that to someone with a disease like his."

I hoped Rodney wasn't awake to hear what Preston said. He already hated himself because of the illness he couldn't control. As if he wasn't a unique case, no one had yet to study.

"What's his disease?"

"There isn't a name for it. The closest we could get is leukemia. But even that isn't a proper diagnosis. He has to eat more frequently because his energy depletes so quickly. Which makes it hard for him to heal, or run—especially at human speed."

Preston pulled the cigarette from his lips, and smoke illustrated his slow exhale. "He has good reason to love you,"

His positive observation rendered me momentarily speechless. Had he seen the way Rodney embraced me? Unfortunately, it appeared to mean more to him than a friendly exchange. In school, he hadn't touched me much. He'd always respected my boundaries, knowing how much it irritated me that Zoon didn't.

Clearing my throat, I insisted, "We've been friends a long time. We're like family."

Preston sat straighter, forehead wrinkled in sour amusement. "So you've friend zoned him?"

"It would be inappropriate otherwise." Social standards considered it poor taste. In the Protector class, a relationship between a Protector and their charge was the same as sleeping with your boss. Rumors spread like wildfire and the Protector's abilities were questioned.

"Do you share his feelings?"

"Of course not!" My stomach tightened as I got the absurd notion Preston might be *interested*. "Why do you care?"

"Hm." He took a drag of his cigarette and looked into the crimson sky. His pinched brows withholding any indicator of his actual deliberations.

Why else would he care if I shared feelings for Rodney? *Mythos.* I couldn't even entertain the idea. He's like my brother. A few times I'd considered other Protectors but never pursued any of them. They were either too arrogant or weak for me.

The sunlight cast a beautiful filter over Preston's skin, bringing a natural blush to his cheeks. A breath hitched in my chest, and I quickly cleared my throat. Forcing my attention elsewhere.

A glint of silver along his collarbone did the trick.

His fingers closed around the charm, and he tossed away his cigarette. "I've had this a long time." He removed the necklace and held it out to me. "Since I was your age."

Hesitantly, I took it into my outstretched palm and traced the thorny silver vines and worn edges of the dagger. "It's beautiful."

"You can have it,"

"Oh no, I couldn't!"

"I have no use for it anymore." He held my gaze a long minute. "Try it on."

What did he mean by no use for it?

I slid it over my head. As if radiant energy nested within the charm itself, a capsizing weight caused me to hunch my shoulders.

"It suits you,"

*Well, if he insists.*

"Thanks," I murmured, tucking the necklace into my shirt collar. I pressed it against my chest. If the metal didn't emit energy, perhaps it was my swelling heart.

If he had this necklace most of his long life, wouldn't he want to gift it to someone more significant than me? A quick blip in his existence once we made it to Carthage and separated from him forever.

He cleared his throat and got up to escape my stare—*Oh, Mythos, how embarrassing.*

"Since you've caught up on some rest, we can go get what we need while the Vampire sleeps." He offered me a hand, only reinforcing the lump wedged in my throat.

"From where?" I fidgeted with the necklace, keeping my hands busy so I didn't have to take his.

"Luxor's outskirts. They sell wares there at a bazaar." Luxor, the Sorcerer city. Likely fraught with soldiers prepared to dispose of us and take our map.

"So, is that your plan?" I asked, lifting my condemning glare to his annoyed one. "To give me to the Mages? What'll you do with Rodney and the map?"

"Of course not!" he growled. "It's the best place to get what we need quickly. How many times do I have to tell you I'm not your enemy? I've just given you a very expensive piece of jewelry. Why would I do that if I planned to get rid of you?"

"I don't know! Why would you give it to me in the first place? You barely know me."

"Consider it a pledge of peace."

No matter how hard we fought to carve a confession from him, he surprised me. Maybe he wasn't our enemy.

I slid my hand into his warm and calloused palm. He swept his thumb along my knuckles before pulling me to my feet. My heart scattered—*Floosy.*

"We can't just leave Rodney," I stated, turning out of his reach to check the camouflage hiding the burrow.

"A concealment ward will keep him safe." Preston crouched, then held his hands above the foliage and it glittered with white light.

"Wards didn't keep them out of Bathory." I stated, anxiety clenching my nerves. "I'll stay here while you go get supplies."

"The wards protecting your school weren't being maintained. A Sorcerer has to reinforce them regularly for the magic to work efficiently." Creases stretched from the edges of his eyes and he combed his fingers through his hair. "I swear on my life, no harm will come to your Vampire while we are gone. My magic is strong. No one can get through it."

"How do I know you're not just arrogant?"

"I am." He grinned, offering his hand again. "But, trust me, Love, I have reason to be."

I'd never teleported, and I did not fancy doing so a second time. My stomach twisted, my skin vibrated, and for an instant, I feared my conscience tore from my skull.

We materialized in an oak tree row on the outskirts of a bustling clearing. Vendor tents littered the market, people filtering between them in a quantity I hadn't anticipated. Not that I had much to compare it to, considering I'd never seen anything like this.

"Wow," I breathed. Luxor lit up the not so distant horizon, glamorous in comparison. The architecture even put Little Hope to shame, being much older and bearing character.

My admiration was cut short, Preston suddenly blocking my view. He pressed me into his chest and squeezed my forearm with the bite. It tingled as he rapidly mended it, the experience nothing like when he'd healed me in his kitchen.

"I'm sorry, Love." I stiffened as his stubble raked against my cheek and his hot breath tickled my ear. "To cover our bases, no one can know you're a Vampire Protector. Not even smell you've been around one. You're here with me, which means they'll think you're my Protector and here, that title won't get you much respect. At least, not like what you're used to."

I recalled Ms. Way's discount of my career. Was there some truth to her words?

"What are you doing?" I gasped as warmth spread across my skin like a summer breeze and a swell of awareness inflated in my chest. It was magic—*right*?

"Cleansing your scent." He pulled me along by my fingers. "Keep close."

Perhaps I should've questioned him more about where he was taking me. Weren't we in enough danger without adding more to the load?

Merchants called out to us, tempting me with what they offered. Preston ignored them all, his arm snaked around my hips to pin me to his side. As much as I wanted to fight it, my instincts ushered me to follow his lead. If he told the truth, this wasn't a place to test boundaries.

Twirling a finger in my hair, I chanced a glance at his hand on my waist.

"Sorry, Love," a smile danced along his lips, "formalities."

Twisting into him, I said, "Are you sure this isn't just another excuse to touch me?"

A pleasant laugh rumbled in his chest, weakening the support in my knees, and he squeezed my hip. "Forgive me."

The tingle of awareness from earlier swept through me. I expected him to counter me, not confirm my suspicions. All logic evaporated from my mind, which rapidly turned to mush. *This was not who I am.* I'm a Protector, not a flirt!

Righting myself, I returned to my surroundings. I'd never shopped, let alone in a place like this. Where I had to whip my head around to ensure

I didn't miss a thing, making me dizzy. Had Preston let go, I would've gotten lost in the crowd.

"This is amazing," I said, baffled by the lively atmosphere.

The soft smile on his lips tugged higher on one side, indenting his cheek. "I told you it would be the best place for supplies."

Canopies protected the endless city of display booths. Some were homemade foods and spices, others were crystals, flowers and handmade jewelry, then there were the weapons, clothes and hiking supplies.

The mixture of floral scents and food wafted through the air, awakening my stomach. Which led me into the clutches of a bread cart. A petite Sorceress moved like a dancer, swinging her hips as she passed a handful of samples to Preston.

"Here, Love." One cube pinched between his index finger and thumb, he waited for me to accept the offering. His golden eyes mimicked the Sorceress's movements as he tracked my lips. Without consulting me first, they parted expectantly for him to carefully deposit the fluffy piece of bread on my tongue.

"Mmm." It was somehow the best sample of food I'd ever had.

*Holy Mythos.*

His stare consumed me, every inch of my face and especially the red tint to my cheeks. I sounded like an idiot.

"Would you like some more?" He held out his palm, full of more bread.

Abashedly, I grazed from his hand while we migrated into the crowd once more. The clamor of voices occupying the bazaar reminded me of the institute lunchroom. After a while, it became a roar that washed out most things—like my embarrassment.

As we rounded a bend, bread long gone, Preston's arm slipped from me and a solid shoulder collided against mine. I stumbled backwards to catch my balance, all the while losing Preston in the crowd.

A scream plugged the base of my throat, caught by my escaping heart as a set of large, unfamiliar hands grappled my shoulders.

The notion to pivot and give the stranger a piece of my mind withered as a man loomed over me, his face buried within a bushy beard. Two barely visible green orbs peeked out from within the depths of curls. He wore a heavy cloak, blanketing his figure. His rough hand cupped my chin to twist my head side to side. His intrusive ogle emulated how one would examine a juicy piece of meat.

I yelped, his other hand squeezing my butt.

"You're not a Sorceress," he observed, a pink tongue darting out to lick his lips.

*What gave me away?*

"You're a Protector then, aye?" his voice boomed and shook me to the core. Plucking my clothes away with his mind.

"I—"

He abruptly tumbled away, thrust by Preston's persistent shoulder.

"Hands off," he snarled. "She belongs to me."

I rushed to Preston's open arms, deciding his touch was preferable to anyone else's here. At least with him, I knew I was safe.

The man curled his lips. "You should keep a better hold on her then,"

Preston squeezed me tighter, reminding me of his warning that Protector meant something very different here. Something I wasn't sure I wanted to understand.

The man's beady eyes narrowed. "Do I know you?"

Wheeling me along beside him, we rode the current of the crowd, leaving the brute behind. Lips close to my ear, he whispered, "Try to keep close, Love, this is not the most reputable place to be."

"No shit!" It wasn't like I wandered off! I needed him to return to Rodney.

I gripped Preston's hand tighter and stayed directly in front of him. He pulled my wrist in the direction we needed to go. Crowding me from behind any time we viewed an exhibition.

I clenched the necklace charm to still a shiver as his breath tickled the base of my neck. His body heat melted away the glaze of fear lingering now that I knew how Sorcerer's Protectors were treated. Convincing myself it was the faint chill in the air, I didn't shy away. Basking in the comfort of his proximity.

Or maybe it was the way he'd rushed to my aid that made it so easy to forget he was the reason we were in this frightful bazaar. Letting my thoughts drift to places it shouldn't, imagining his arms sliding around me and pulling me closer. Stealing me away from my responsibilities.

*What am I thinking?*

We came upon a weaponry display when the sun hid behind the trees, near the last of the bizarre. I'd never seen so many diverse knife styles and handguns. Behind us were swords and large firearms.

This tent was popular, packed with shoppers who lacked the decency to keep their distance. Preston tactically positioned himself around me, hands resting near my hips. I leaned to better view the weapons, and every time I rocked to examine another, he brushed against my backside.

The more it happened, the less I feared it.

"Pick something you like," he instructed, trailing his fingers along my arm.

"Are you sure?" I didn't have any money, and it didn't feel right letting him pay for them.

"They're necessary," he insisted, gesturing to the table of daggers. His stony gaze darted to track everyone slipping past. Not missing a thing.

My thudding heart slowed a beat, knowing he strived to keep us safe. A position I wasn't used to sharing.

A set of matching daggers called to me; the sapphire inscriptions intricately carved into the knives the drawing feature. I held them in my palms, judging their light weight and size. The sturdy black material binding the hilts was comfortable. The blades were flawless and unbelievably sharp, much better than my knife. I'd always dreamed of a similar set, but the institute's salary could never afford such luxuries.

"Are those the ones, Love?" Preston murmured in my ear and squeezed my hips.

A jolt scaled through me and I brought the knives close to my chest. He'd already given me his necklace, I couldn't ask for more.

He deemed my silence as an answer and straightened beside me. Had I the courage, I would have told him he didn't have to.

"We'll take the pair and a small handgun, doesn't matter which." He spoke to the gristly Sorcerer behind the table, motioning towards the items he wanted.

The man narrowed his bloodshot eyes. "Payment?"

A heavy weight came over Preston as he rolled his sleeve to display a chevron pattern in bold black. Upon further inspection, I realized it was a multitude of V's tattooed on his skin. Three solid bars encircling his forearm just below the V's.

The merchant's brow creased, and he nodded, passing a .22 to Preston and an ammunition box.

"Thanks," Preston said, although he didn't sound genuine. Shame laced his tone and overshadowed his features.

We sauntered into the traffic of bodies.

"What are the V's for?" I asked as he smoothed the sleeve over his arm.

He avoided my gaze, his face strangely devoid of emotion. "The V stands for Veiled and the bars state my rank as general. Each V represents five men killed."

A chill split down my spine. Preston stole *hundreds* of lives. "How does that pay for the weapons?"

"It doesn't." The merchant gifted them to preserve his own life.

Any forward steps he made in my wavering trust for him disintegrated.

*Who is he?*

"A lot of these items are sold illegally," Preston explained. "Luxor allows this bizarre operation with the understanding its habitants will keep crime out of the main city. They're under close supervision and will avoid any dispute if possible."

So, they operated out of self-preservation? What an odd way to earn a living selling illegal goods—*Does that make me a fugitive for procuring some?*

The crowd came to a standstill and voices raised. I couldn't see what had everyone so stirred up. Hopefully Preston's right and everyone did their best to avoid conflict. That little fact didn't quite sit right with me. How could criminals be allowed to thrive like this?

How was I able to stick by a criminal's side as we traipsed along on a shopping spree?

*A general?*

He must've fought in the Persecution against Vampires that ended just a little over twenty-one years ago. My stomach sank—No wonder he didn't like stopping for Rodney to feed. The Persecution existed purely because a Sorcerer decided he didn't like how Vampires lived and wanted to wash them out of the Mythos.

He had some explaining to do.

While we waited for those ahead to move, I tucked one of my new daggers into my waistband and the other into my weaponless boot. Preston wrapped my hands around the gun, his steady gaze boring into mine as many words passed through. Kade taught me how to wield a gun. I'd just never expected to own one.

"Are you sure?" I asked. "The daggers are more than enough—"

"I'm sure."

I appreciated the sentiment, but I was running out of places to hide weapons.

Hooded figures milled about the bazaar. Here, their presence was considered normal and unmenacing—no more so than anyone else who shopped here. Even so, I inched closer to Preston. The sooner we left, the better. If anything happened, Rodney would wake up alone, with no idea what happened to me.

Preston drew me to his side, and I relaxed a fragment. Without Rodney at my side, they shouldn't recognize me. We're just a Sorcerer and their Protector shopping. *There's nothing to fear.*

"It's alright, Love," he insisted, hauling us into the crowd as it shifted.

We slid ahead, leaving behind the weaponry section of the bazaar and entering a corral of food trucks and vendors. Various spices wafting in the wind called to my stomach.

Preston stopped us at a sandwich truck, not even consulting me as he placed an order. He kept me cinched against his side like an unruly child, while retrieving a wallet from his pocket to pay for the food. Why hadn't he paid for the weapons if he had money?

"I don't know what century you were born. In this one, women order their own food." I sassed.

A crooked grin and crow's feet creased one side of his face. "Didn't figure you cared, so long as it's food."

"Fair," I grunted, hungry enough to eat just about anything.

While waiting for our sandwiches to be prepared, we migrated to a small enclosure to purchase a backpack crammed full of nonperishables. Evidently, criminals spent a lot more time traveling than I realized. I'd always imagined them wealthy, dining in fine restaurants while strategizing their big plans.

As we returned for our sandwiches, I warily inspected his arm of V's. He'd lived an entire life before we'd met, one that should incline me to ditch him the first second we could.

"I am not proud of my tattoos." He saw the apprehension in my expression and squeezed my hand.

"How did you earn so many?" my murmur was nearly inaudible over the market.

He reached to extract the prepared food from the truck window, then guided us away from the crowd. He kept his voice low, "I am…older than you think and lived through some dark times."

The Persecution—*how old is he*?

He'd fought for the Veiled Army, killing many Vampires and their Protectors—nearly entire bloodlines. So why was he helping us?

The lines between his brows suggested he carried a lot of weight from that time of his life. A lot of regret for the things he'd done. Perhaps he helped us out of guilt.

We traveled across the clearing and ducked into the oak tree row, where he stopped to hand me a sandwich. Amid the market, I hadn't realized how much time we'd spent in the different shops. The sun sank in the sky.

"Shouldn't we get back?" I narrowly refrained from stating we could eat while in Rodney's company.

"Five more minutes won't hurt," he assured.

It was plenty of time to allow anything to happen. For Rodney to wake and assume something terrible happened. For Sorcerers to capture him.

My shoulders ached, burdened by everything we'd done while Rodney slept. The walking, shopping, nearly getting kidnapped, and the close call with the hooded Mages.

I needed sleep. Not a nap while being carted through the forest.

I adjusted the weapons in my waistband to comfortably succumb to the deli sub, hoping for rejuvenation.

Preston ate his, then paced away, giving space for his smoke to waft without disturbing me. Close enough, his steadfast regard unnerved me.

"Why are you helping us?" I blurted, squirming in place.

"It's not every day the survivors of a school massacre stumble into your life…I suppose it was right to do." He exhaled, the cigarette at his side so his lips could curl and his mischievous eyes twinkled. "Then there's the bonus of good company along the way."

My stupid heart fluttered, resembling a panicked bird, and my lips dried eternally. Licking them, I gathered the trash from my sandwich, making an obvious display of preparation to leave this place. No amount of flattery should overshadow the fact he'd blatantly dodged my question.

But I let it.

# An Alliance
## Chapter 7

Food in my system this time, the teleportation didn't affect me as strongly. Preston wrapped his arm around my shoulders then engaged the magical pulls. The atmosphere became dense, squeezing our bodies like the air would vacate between us. My vision blurred, and a tremor crept along my skin as it had previously, yet I didn't become nauseous. In a flash, the world dispersed, the smell of smoke in the wind.

We materialized mere feet from the burrow where we'd left Rodney hours ago. Preston's fingers bit into my arm, anchoring me in place. I tracked his wide stare, lifting a leg to retrieve a knife from my boot.

Rodney sat next to a fire beside a formidable man who ate what I assumed to be a rabbit, cooked over the fire. They spoke comfortably—laughing!

An odd thing for him to do considering he didn't know this man.

Together, Preston and I emerged to let our presence be known. Neither one appeared surprised by our arrival, suspiciously. Granted, the stranger's glance did cast towards the knife clutched in my hand.

"Mercy," he rasped. "I do not intend to harm anyone."

"Who are you?" I demanded. Gathering Rodney's arm into my hand, I gave him a quick inspection. He didn't appear to have any injuries.

My ferocity dwindled as the man's sky-blue eyes watered and his freckled nose crinkled. The distinct sneeze indicators drove me back as he fell into a sneezing fit, loud enough to startle birds from their nests. He pawed his face and the fire dimmed from his rhythmic puffs.

Minutes passed until his reaction reduced to a sniffle. "It's your necklace. I'm allergic to silver."

"My necklace?" My hand went to the jewelry under my sweater. *It hadn't touched him. Why would silver cause him to sneeze?*

"What necklace?" Rodney rose to his feet and the color drained from his expression as he recognized the charm.

"Preston gave it to me," I mumbled, incoherently. It meant a lot to me, in a way I couldn't explain—especially not to Rodney.

Besides, we should be focused on the stranger! Not locked in a standoff between him and the necklace.

*This is humiliating.*

The man cleared his throat. "I'm Reginald Rayham." He delivered a theatrical bow from his seat on the forest floor. "You may call me Reggie."

Judging by his height and build, he wasn't human. His skin was kissed by the sun, brown and golden from exposure. His wild hair fell from its ponytail, caressing his jawline and lightly pointed ears. He lifted his beard laden chin to assess Preston and me.

I squeezed my knife. "Why are you here?"

"I live in a nearby village when I'm not on a stroll in the woods to exercise my creature," he explained. "Might I ask why *you* are here?"

'Exercising his creature'—a Werewolf. At least, that's the first creature I could recall. Where did their loyalty lie in all this?

"We're passing through," Preston replied, shifting the supply bag onto his shoulder.

Reggie's frame tightened, and he spoke to me awkwardly out the side of his mouth, as if to prevent others from hearing, "Are you safe, girl?"

"I'm fine." I glanced at Preston. So far, he hadn't indicated I was in indefinite danger. Buying me new weapons and feeding me artisan bread didn't exactly fall into the villain category.

Reggie's gaze flicked toward the burrow. "I saw you leave him earlier and decided I better stay with him until you got—"

"Were you following us?" Preston snapped, squaring his shoulders.

"You aren't stealthy travelers. Anyone could follow the battle trail in your wake." Reggie pulled his hair into a more secure ponytail. "Initially, I expected to find a Spellcaster troop. From what I've gathered, you are the Protector and Vampire the Mythos is talking about. The Bathory survivors."

"You seem to know a lot for a Werewolf innocently passing by." Preston lifted his chin and his shoulders seemed to grow wider. Had he picked up on something I missed?

Reggie rose to his full height—close on to seven feet, and I ogled like a child. Fighting with the nostalgic reminder of Zoon's tall and lanky build. *Damn, I missed him.*

"Be careful where you cast your suspicions, Spellcaster. It is far more concerning that you are with them than it is for me to know about them. Were they to suggest you are part of the army that destroyed their school, your entrails would be swinging from my snout."

Preston's elevated chin lowered as the implication sank in. We were right to be hesitant to trust him and Reggie had every right to do the same. Combing a hand through his hair, he paced away to soothe his afflicted ego with a cigarette.

"With that said, it would be my honor to help in any way I can," Reggie turned towards me as he spoke, never pulling his visage away from the Sorcerer.

I twirled a finger in my hair, the natural highlights shimmering different shades in the moon and fire light. "I'm not sure that's necessary. We're traveling straight through and I'm not sure what our journey looks like..."

"I know this forest well." He gestured his large arms broadly. "Ever since I was a pup, I've been exploring every inch. Befriended many creatures who call it home."

His unbuttoned autumn colored flannel exposed his chest, laden with sun-bleached chest hair. The flannel stood no chance against his broad frame. Had he buttoned it, the fabric would've split. A hard cut abdominal V guided the eye to the black jeans hugging his muscular legs. I averted to his well-worn boots to hide the blush on my cheeks. He was a massive and attractive man—it wasn't often I'd seen a developed shirtless man-chest. The most I'd ever experienced were lean, young Vampires.

"Why would you want to help us? You don't even know us." I said, studying his boots that appeared to have many hard miles on them. The weathered material pulled away from the sole.

"Because it is the right thing to do. After what you've been through, the Mythos owes you kindness." His lips disappeared into his beard, pressed into a fine line.

More of us meant a higher risk of being found. It also meant we stood a better chance at winning battles—Although silver wolves may prove a problem for him.

"Alright. If you're sure it is what you want to do." I decided. Perhaps this would even the field if Preston turned out to be a spy after all. After the revelation of his war tattoos, I struggled to believe he'd completely abandoned his distaste for Vampires. Anyone who fought in the Persecution couldn't just throw away whatever drove them to join the Veiled Army.

"As I said before, it would be my honor." Reggie insisted.

"I think it's a good idea," Rodney added, standing so he could squeeze my hands. His character judgment couldn't be trusted—the only person he tolerated aside from me, had been Zoon. Which is why we hadn't welcomed anyone else into our friend group.

Only time would tell if allowing either man into our current company was a mistake.

"We need to go." Preston gestured impatiently, snuffing out his second cigarette since our arrival. "Better get out your map, Vampire."

Rodney grumbled under his breath as he unrolled the map, and led the way. Preston kept on his heels, as if we were cattle needing direction, not the reason for this expedition in the first place.

Reggie lifted a worn leather backpack from where he'd sat to sling it over one shoulder. Extinguished fire smoke behind him, he caught up to our group in one quick stride.

I sucked in a deep breath, and lowered my head to where I twisted my dagger between my hands. I'd fidgeted with the weapon so often over the years, it was muscle memory and often didn't notice it even happened. The faint scars littering my forearms were a testament to that.

I scurried to Rodney's side. "I have something to give you."

His brows arched like two mountain peaks over the map's edge.

Sucking on my bottom lip, I held out my campus issued dagger. "I want you to have this, just in case."

His brows didn't lower as he rolled up the map and accepted the blade. "Are you sure?"

I nodded. It brought me peace he had a way to defend himself if I were unable. Two daggers were all I could use at a time, anyway.

"I guess I don't understand." He turned the dagger over, as if checking its authenticity, and his brows came together. "Don't you need this?"

Excitement built within my chest as I retrieved the dagger from my waistline. I held it out for him to view, cradled in both hands. "Preston got it for me—well; he got me two, actually."

Darkness crept across his face, turning his eyes obsidian as his head snapped in Preston's direction. The Mage weaved between the trees several feet away, tainting his lungs and studying the night sky. "Why would he buy you knives or give you a *necklace*?"

My cheeks burned so hot my hair felt heavy on my shoulders. "He—"

"He's trying to bribe you into something, Jo. Did you really not notice that?" Rodney scolded, pointing the tip of the blade at the Mage. "He's either one of *them* or he's... A fuckin' creep."

Which was worse? A creep or a Veiled Army soldier? It's almost like he'd been trying to tell me by showing me his tattoos. I slid the new knife into the old one's place in my boot, and bowed my head. What kind of Protector was I?

Preston twisted in our direction, noticing my sudden change in stature. "What's the matter, Love?"

"She's not interested in whatever game you're trying to play, " Rodney sneered, the sharpness in his tone jerking my chin up.

"*What*?" Preston's mouth hung slightly open with distaste.

"I'm fine. Just stay out of it," I begged. Until we had proof of his intentions, I didn't want to spoil his generous gift. My stomach clenched, reminding me his feelings shouldn't matter. My Vampire's safety was more important.

Rodney clenched his fists and stopped abruptly. "Why buy her new weapons? What do you want?"

Reggie snorted, a wicked grin on his face. He kept a hearty distance away from me and my necklace.

*At least one of us found this situation amusing.*

Preston took a long drag off his cigarette, narrowing his exceedingly bored stare on Rodney. "It gives me peace of mind knowing she has more options to protect you *and* herself." He acknowledged the dagger in Rodney's hand. "It appears now you have a way to defend yourself in the event she cannot."

Rodney's fang stabbed into his lower lip and he bowed his head.

"Jealousy is an ugly characteristic, Vampire."

I couldn't agree more. While I agreed Preston's behavior had layers, I didn't appreciate Rodney's either. Gifts weren't exactly a reason to accuse the Mage of treachery.

I hefted a sigh. The tension radiating from the pair as we continued walking was stifling. If we were to travel to Carthage together, they'd have to figure something out.

Rodney slid the campus issued knife into his belt to hug me tight against his side. "I'm sorry. I didn't mean to discount your gift."

"Don't be." I squeezed him too. We shouldn't have to worry about trusting strangers, at least not to this magnitude. We were supposed to be preparing to graduate in three months, safely tucked away on campus.

I slipped out of his hold, not liking the weight of his hand on my waist. He accused Preston of making inappropriate advances when he did exactly that, damaging the bond we'd forged since the third grade.

"How do you fit into this expedition, Spellcaster?" Reggie asked, his tone wavering on accusatory.

Preston heaved an irritated sigh and lifted his sights towards the sky. "Same as you."

Both were strangers to us who we permitted the chance to assist us as we made the trek to Carthage. Possibly a dangerous misjudgment on my part.

"What proof have you given them that you can be trusted? That you're not leading them into a trap?" he asked the very question that haunted me.

"I had nothing to do with what happened at Bathory," Preston stopped to square his shoulders and face Reggie, "and I owe you no explanation."

Except some justification would be nice. I intended to extract one from him prior to our arrival in Carthage.

Reggie mirrored his stance without a glint of distress. Standing over a foot taller than the Mage and spanning just as wide, he didn't appear to need to fear him.

Bats fluttered in my chest and my fingers squeezed for the comfort of my blade. Were they to engage in a flurry of fists, should I bother to stop them? Or would it be the perfect opportunity to continue on our own?

Preston's chin tipped up, his cheek sinking in a moment before he decided the fight wasn't worth it and moved on. His strength to do so impressed me. I wouldn't have had the sense to walk away.

Reggie appreciated the reaction differently. A smirk teasing his lips as he followed Preston's lead.

A chill rolled across my shoulders, and I strode faster to spread out from the others. How messed up that we had to question one another like this.

Preston fell into step beside me. His hunched shoulders bearing the weight of our constant judgment. It must be tiring to continually advocate his intentions. He helped considerably thus far. Without his aid, we would have died in the forest the day he found us.

"Thank you," I murmured, timidly touching his arm, "for everything."

Preston unfurled from the dark place he'd receded to. Untwisting his lips to smile softly. "No need to thank me, Love."

"Love?" Reggie scoffed from behind us, nose wrinkled.

"Right? Creep's a try-hard." Rodney grumbled, shoulders squared huffily.

A smirk played on my lips, and I did my best to hide it behind my hair. I, too, was still getting accustomed to the new nickname.

Reggie stopped to burst into a sneezing fit, several intricate swear words sewn between each gasp. I gauged the space between us, afraid I'd gotten too close.

When Preston stiffened, I drew my knives from my boots and caught Rodney's wrist, jerking him behind me. He stumbled, previously enveloped in the map.

The nearby foliage came alive and a silver wolf emerged. Moments later, a coven of Spellcasters materialized around us and the silver wolf.

"Stay," Preston directed, his voice low so only I could hear.

Reggie swore under his breath, darting from our group, barreling past the Mages with little hesitation. *Was he retreating? He had offered to help us!*

"Coward!" Rodney snapped, inching closer behind me. His eyes trained on the silver wolf, and the wolf reflected the libation.

"Give up!" the Mages persuaded. "You kids don't know who you're up against."

They wouldn't stop until they had the map, no matter how many Spellcasters they had to send.

Preston spread his feet apart in a supportive stance and outstretched his hands. Thrusting down in a push motion, the ground rumbled and rippled forward in a half moon, knocking our opponents off balance.

"Neither do you," he countered.

His arrogance baffled me. We're outnumbered, now wasn't the time to taunt them.

As the Mages regained their balance, a large mousy brown wolf barreled from the forest to ambush the silver wolf head on.

"Reggie." I grinned.

He was double the size of the silver wolf and much more vicious, using his massive claws instead of his sharp teeth. Likely due to his allergy. Something that didn't go unnoticed by me. He not only risked his life by fighting to protect us, but by facing his silver allergy head on.

Preston launched forward to apprehend a Sorceress working to get to her feet. He seized her by the face and thrust an arm into her chest, pinning her to a tree. Keeping pressure on her for a second, he leapt to watch as his spell took effect.

She screamed and fell to her knees, steam rising from her boiling skin as it fell away from her bones. The *smell*. It thrust me into the same fear that nearly crippled me in Bathory as I saw Kade's swinging corpse.

I pinched my eyes shut, imagining his screams as the magic seared into his skin, taking his life same as the Sorceress crumpled on the forest floor.

A battle cry forced my eyes open, as a Sorcerer darted for me. I had to stop him before he charred my bones, too. I put my weight behind my knives, plunging them both into his shoulders. He groaned and jerked away, dodging my swinging blades.

Preston caught the Sorcerer by his cloak hood, grasping his face long enough to cast another skin boiling spell, then discarding him.

*Two left.*

Reggie had the silver wolf between his powerful jaws, shaking the animal's life from its body. As it disassembled, he dropped it to the ground then stood on his hind legs, stretching towards the lower tree branches where a Sorcerer posed to attack. In one leap, his large fangs ripped the man's throat with a vile crunch.

Preston trained his focus on the last Sorcerer, whose pace slowed. "You can't run forever!"

With a whip of his arm, a burst of flame shot through the air to engulf the man. A vibrant flash turned his body to ash.

"Let's go!" Preston ordered.

"They're after the map!" Rodney declared. Our duty surpassed delivering him to his family. We were now responsible for protecting the confidentiality of Carthage.

"If they sent this many, there are more close behind!"

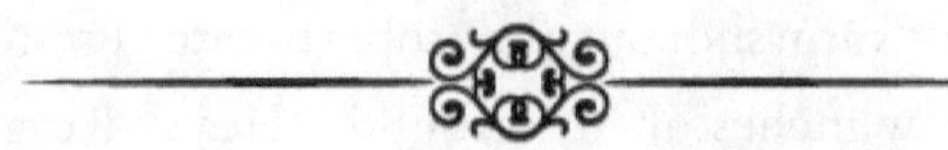

High in the night sky, the moon illuminated the darkness and our footsteps broke the silence of the sleepy woodland. The threat of more soldiers remained heavy on our minds.

A horrible wheeze stopped us in our tracks. Reggie bent to rest his hands on his knees, heaving for air. His lips were swollen to twice their size, and his face flushed with splotchy red.

"Are you alright?" I asked, and he held out a hand to stop me from approaching. The silver wolf had been in his mouth, no wonder he's suffering.

Preston placed a hand to his chest, boiling over with amusement. "You sound ridiculous," he gasped between bouts of laughter.

Reggie's irritated and watering eyes narrowed.

"He fought the silver—"

"You're whistling!" Preston laughed harder. Completely insensitive to Reggie's sacrifice.

I punched the Archmage. "Quit being an asshole and help him!"

"Fine." He rubbed his arm while gathering his composure. "Damn,"

"I shouldn't have to tell you to help him. He didn't have to fight the silver wolf for us, knowing his allergy could easily kill him faster than the wolf." I stated.

"I didn't ask him to," Preston pointed out, inching closer to the Werewolf.

Reggie straightened, his whistle now a wheeze. We couldn't let him die this way, not when we owed him for his protection.

Yet Preston's eyes watered from his internal war to keep his laughter at bay.

*Asshole.*

The Werewolf's arm shot out like a cobra to catch Preston's throat, lifting him a few inches off the ground. "Heal," Reggie uttered, fighting for every syllable, "me."

Instantly sobered, Preston's nostrils flared and his jaw tightened, the muscles pronounced against his skin. He allowed the wolf to suffer one more minute before grasping Reggie's arm. I recognized the dreamy state that overcame Reggie, slower than it felt, and his grip on Preston slackened, lowering the Archmage to the ground, then releasing him.

Rodney and I rushed to help him into a sitting position before he collapsed as the magic took full effect. Sweeping through his body to heal his inflamed sinuses.

When Reggie's lips returned to their natural state, Preston removed his hands. The reddish hue no longer tainted his face, and the whistle ceased. Airways now clear, he heaved a whole breath.

"Thank you,"

Preston ignored Reggie, too busy lighting a cigarette placed between his lips with a snap.

He motioned for me to come near; the cigarette clinging for life to the edge of his tightened mouth.

I hesitated to heed his beckon. *What did he want with me?* I had no injuries—that I was aware of. Arms crossed, I timidly stood in front of him.

Preston reached to lift the necklace from my chest by the chain, careful to be a gentleman. His fingertips brushed my sweater as he pinched the necklace and pulled it away.

"What are you doing?" I demanded. Although he'd tried to execute the gesture without awkwardness, it was.

He cupped his hand around the charm, and the metal vibrated against my icy skin. Once the vibration ceased, his gaze met mine. "I placed a sealing charm on the necklace so Reggie can get some sinus relief."

"You mean so he won't inconvenience you again?" I sassed, disbelieving it was for the Werewolf's comfort.

"That's exactly why," Preston amended.

Reggie harrumphed and rifled through his backpack for water.

Preston released the jewelry and proceeded to finish his cigarette. Initiating travel once more. Something I noticed he did when our company's at odds with him. Which could easily be solved by an attitude adjustment. It's like we'd never left Bathory.

As we resumed, the battle replayed itself for me. Specifically, the way Preston responded so effortlessly to their attacks. A display of his time serving for the Veiled Army. Something I hadn't been sure I could look past, but he hadn't hesitated to end those soldiers and didn't appear phased by their passing.

What changed his beliefs? Specifically, what led him to fight for us?

But he wasn't the only one selflessly throwing himself into battle for complete strangers.

"I noticed you ran away to change into your wolf form. Why?" I paced Reggie, my voice light. I didn't intend to embarrass him, I was genuinely curious.

He smiled, first at me, then his feet. Voice still hoarse, he said, "Thirty years of being a wolf, you would assume I'd be more comfortable transforming in front of folks. To tell you the truth, I've never come around to the idea of strangers seeing me naked."

My cheeks warmed, and I suppressed the urge to laugh. Meanwhile, Preston didn't. I punched him in the arm, aiming for the same place as before.

He flinched and cradled his arm. "Ow,"

Reggie laughed.

"It isn't a crime to be modest. Reggie is a gentleman," I scolded, holding in the remark that playing mediator was getting old.

Preston grunted, flicking the ash off his cigarette.

Reggie patted me on the head. "Also, it gets old carrying a bag of clothes. If I have time, I find a place to stash my stuff before transforming. It's a lot of work to find decent apparel when traveling; most often people don't throw away satisfactory pieces."

That explained his bedraggled flannel, likely found in someone's dumpster.

"Does it deplete your energy to change?" Rodney asked. He hoped he wasn't the only one wiped out. He'd been the only one at Bathory.

Reggie shrugged. "It does leave me tired once the adrenaline runs out. It's why I carry a pack with rations, but it's nothing I can't quickly recover from."

Rodney dipped his head in the shadow of disappointment, and I looped my arm in his, squeezing. He pulled away to weave between the row of trees at our side, where he could sink into the pit of self-loathing established in his chest.

A flame of fight ignited within me. I'd engaged in many disputes with classmates about the way they affected him, sometimes on purpose. Unfortunately, there weren't any words I could offer him to stop the embarrassment he felt.

"Won't your pack have something to say about you disappearing in the woods?" Preston's inquiry wasn't one of curiosity, more a jab at our newest addition's presence.

Reggie shrugged one shoulder. "It isn't uncommon for me to do so. I'm gone often to fulfill my responsibility in my pack to patrol the forest surrounding our village. Since it bothers you so much, I can drop by to gather some supplies and update my family. It's not far from here."

*A Werewolf village.*

In school, others joked the Werewolves were centuries behind in structural development. Allegedly, they were neglected in education and their livelihood suffered from it. Planting them securely in an outdated lifestyle and endangering their population's future.

Was Reggie's village folkish or did the Vampire community have a harsh sense of humor?

"What is your village like?"

A fond smile glanced across Reggie's features. "Compared to the big city, it's a breath of fresh air. We're a small community. Basically, one extensive family, we take care of one another."

I imagined it quaint, like the villages in story books, where princesses found their fairy tale endings.

Rodney and Reggie lumbered ahead, their voices more prominent than their silhouettes, shrouded by the tree canopy, blocking the moonlight.

"More of the Mythos should be like your village," Rodney decided.

"Unfortunately, it would never work." Reggie said, explaining how there are too many people with ugly personalities in the world. "My village has lived in the same area for many generations, we've learned to appreciate the land and our families with the same grace. Much different than the way the rest of the Mythos operates."

"That's what we should be teaching the future generations."

Preston held his cigarette tilted inward between his index finger and thumb, so he could study the burning end, turning it side to side to change his view of the shadow it cast on his palm. "If the way your village operates is so great then why do you spend so much of your time outside it?"

Reggie growled over his shoulder. "Because not all of the enjoyable parts are within the city limits. The surrounding wildlife and nature have much to offer as well."

"Sounds like a roundabout way of saying you prefer getting away from home,"

"All of it is my home."

"Delusional…" Preston muttered.

Snapping off a twig from a nearby shrub, I placed the piece of wood between my lips. It was sweet with sap, growing damp with my saliva. Arms across my chest, I stomped to walk equal to Preston.

Nose upturned, I grumbled in imitation of the Sorcerer.

His head whipped in my direction.

"Are you making fun of me?" he demanded, putting out his cigarette.

"Maybe." I tossed the twig.

It bounced off his chest and tumbled to the ground. He watched it as well, then turned on me. Surveying me from head to toe thoroughly, a slow dimple surfaced in his cheek.

My pulse quickened—I'd stoked the fire. He'd enact revenge if I didn't escape now. Throwing myself into a run, I gained a few paces. The avid smoker proved more capable than I gave him credit for. He grappled my arm, failing to capture me. I spun, dodging his hands precisely.

Laughter danced on his lips each time he missed, echoing in my chest. He finally lunged, arms swooping over my head as I ducked under his attack. Pivoting, he thrust me against the tree trunk nearest us.

The wind knocked out of me, he easily lifted me off the ground by my arms. The bark bit into my shoulder blades, affecting the smile on my face.

Preston's victorious grin gleamed. "That'll teach you—"

Bending my knees, I thrust him off his feet. Landing haphazardly in a crouched position, I used his stomach to keep from face planting. The stupid grin on his face never wavered, even as he lay in the dirt.

"I'm sure there's a logical explanation as to why you two are fighting?" Reggie quirked an eyebrow.

Rodney fumed at his side, appearing to quiver with venom. His accusations from earlier drifted into my shoulders and filled my chest with regret. No matter how much Preston fought to prove his loyalty to us, Rodney wouldn't want me to befriend him.

Rising to my feet, I offered Preston a hand to stand. I'd behaved childishly and the realization inflamed my skin.

"The fight isn't important," Preston resolved, smoothing his dusty jacket. "What matters is *I* won."

Reggie snorted, the concern slipping from his brows. "Won a dirt bath?"

"You're probably the most nosey Werewolf I've encountered," Preston wagered, stalking past the pair of interrogators.

I synced with him, afraid to linger behind in case Rodney exploded. "We are known for our keen senses,"

A giggle swelled in my chest, but I didn't dare let it out, knowing Rodney's temper all too well. Nor did I wish to encourage the seemingly endless banter between the three.

# FORTUNATE
## CHAPTER 8

REGGIE DRIFTED AHEAD, MORE accustomed to the terrain, and Preston straggled behind, chain smoking. The quiet allowed my mind to reel, dissecting the fight, searching for any wrong move I may have made. Anything I could've done better, because it's what Kade would've told me to do.

"Ah," Rodney's sharp gasp ripped me from my analysis. He held the map in one hand, the other cradled to his chest.

"Are you okay? What happened?" I swooped in front of him.

I should've been alert! Rookie mistake!

He averted his eyes, tears in their depths, as I carefully pulled the limb from his chest and slid his sleeve past his elbow. The wrist lay limp, tweaked at an unnatural angle, and turned an ugly shade of red and blue.

"When did this happen?" Reggie loomed over us, his voice stern.

*I'm such an awful friend. This shouldn't have happened.*

Rodney wouldn't meet my gaze, his eyes flicking toward Reggie, diffidently. Preston, however, stood idly nearby, watching his smoke pollute the air.

"While you were fighting. I fell when Preston cast the first spell that shook the ground. It hurt, but I didn't want to bother anyone."

Preston's eyebrows rose, and he decided to come inspect the damage done.

"You should have told me," I scolded. "I am your *Protector*. Do you need to feed?"

His lips twinged eagerly.

"Feed?" Preston scoffed. "Let me heal him. He hasn't lost any blood and it'll prevent you from slowing us."

Once again, he held all the answers. Our way would work fine, if the Archmage wasn't right. We didn't have time to waste, the sun daring to rise soon.

"Fine. I'll feed him later." I released Rodney and folded my arms across my chest. We had to stretch his feedings as best we could anyway, for my safety. Were it not obvious before, I'd waved a bright flag disclosing my addiction to the endorphins. Twirling a finger in my hair, I hoped to shrink away from the spotlight. That everyone would forget how quickly I'd jumped to the offer.

"Give me your wrist." Preston placed his cigarette in the corner of his lips, hands held out.

Rodney scowled sufficiently, placing his broken wrist in Preston's upturned palms, and Reggie secured his shoulders. The Vampire soon fell into the dreamy state, a repulsive crack emanating from the wound as it healed.

Fidgeting with the necklace charm, I recalled the first time I'd accompanied Rodney to the nurse's office. He'd tripped over his own feet during a game of dodgeball and fallen on the same wrist he'd broken today.

*The nurse was an older Vampire. Her gray hair tied into a perfect bun, paired well alongside her pressed scrubs. She laid him onto the small cot in her office, so she had plenty of space to assess the damage.*

*"Poor wee Vampire," she crooned. "If you didn't have the equivalent of human leukemia, this fall wouldn't have hurt you."*

*She thrust a straw into the top of a blood pouch, similar to a juice box. He accepted it gratefully, sucking down its contents. I curled my lips as the thick liquid disappeared and stained his lips.*

*The nurse winced with him as she bound the wrist into a splint. He would heal faster due to the provided plasma, as Vampires always did.*

Except it still took days, maybe a little over a week, for his wrist to heal. His other abrasions took days—far more time than it seemed to take him when he drank my blood. Something I hadn't noticed until now, because I'd been far too preoccupied with my own injuries. Maybe since he drank directly from a living source, it worked quicker?

Satisfied with the repair, Rodney retracted his arm and rolled his shoulders to shake off the dream world and Reggie. "That was...weird," he decided, shuffling away to unfurl the map from his zipped jacket.

It was weird how Preston could take you out of this world into another. One that felt so warm and safe. Much unlike the one we're in.

"I assume you mean the magic and not the Spellcaster?" Reggie said unnecessarily as we fell into sync, trudging through the forest.

"Both,"

The pair giggled like old friends, a sound I missed hearing shared between Rodney and Zoon. Heat washed over my skin, a burning reminder I'd never truly hear that sound again. Our best friend was gone.

I ran a hand through my hair to tie it into a ponytail. Maybe it wasn't the memory, and it was my adrenaline finally burning out from the fight. Or just *burning*. It's been hours. No one else seemed to be sweating—at least, not now that their injuries were taken care of.

I fanned myself, considering the removal of my sweater. The humiliation would be well worth the cool down.

Again, I studied the male counterparts.

A playful smirk curled Preston's lips.

"You!" I whipped around.

He averted his gaze, fumbling with an unlit cigarette.

I hit him once in the chest, twice in the arm in succession to leveling a finger with his nose. "Do it again," I warned, "and I'll cut your hands off."

One less distraction from keeping my Vampire safe. His absence would lighten the mood considerably.

"You looked chilly," he lied, unable to hide the mischievous gleam in his eyes.

I kicked him in the shin. Perhaps he'd placed wards on his apartment to hide from other women who vowed to remove his hands. Stalking off, I joined Rodney while Preston chuckled to himself, finally lighting his cigarette.

Reggie shook his head. "We would all benefit from him losing a hand."

"Who would heal you then?" Preston countered, exhaling a smoke cloud. Apparently fine with being chastised by me, not anyone else.

Rodney's fangs bit into his lower lip, and he focused intently on the map. Had his shoulders hunched anymore, his neck would have disappeared.

"We'd manage," Reggie grated.

I hefted a sigh and folded my arms. *What game did the Mage play this time?* As the oldest member of the group, I expected him to behave more maturely. Instead, he acted as a fine replacement for Zoon.

*The stupid grin on his face...* I threw a glance over my shoulder, fingers curling into fists.

*He winked!*

My teeth clicked together as I faced forward. By journey's end, I would stab him.

The grassland turned rocky, stubborn trees pushing between the gravel surface. We walked uphill for some time and I found myself at the back of the group, wishing I had slept some before we left our last camp. To our luck, a cave came into view—a perfect shelter from the sun. Preston and Reggie offered to stand guard outside while Rodney and I slept inside. Judging by the silence between the two, they were both too tired to squabble anymore.

I glanced over my shoulder at the others outside. "Can I ask you a question?"

Rodney's eyes widened eagerly. "Of course,"

I rubbed my arm, hoping no one else could hear us. "When Preston healed you...did you see anything?"

His eyes narrowed, turning a slate gray. "Yeah. I was in a field, for some reason."

"Is it the magic?"

Lifting one shoulder, he brought my speculations to an end. He didn't want to talk about Preston, or anything associated with him.

"It just felt so real. Like I crossed into another world."

"I'm not an expert on Sorcerers, Jo. I'd say you could ask him, but I really don't feel like anything he says is the truth."

"Care to share why?"

"No. Not really."

Because he didn't have a reason, not a real one, anyway. We're best friends, we should be able to talk about anything. Including the person who got on his nerves—For whatever reason.

I led us further into the cave for the privacy needed to feed. While he sank his teeth into my arm, I surveyed the space we'd occupy for the night. It was tall enough I could stand comfortably. Rodney, however, hunched his shoulders to prevent scraping his head along the stone ceiling.

It was the depth that made the tiny hairs on my head stand up. The further it went, the darker it got, just out of reach of the encroaching sunlight. Nighttime didn't bother me—complete and utter darkness did. When you couldn't see even a few inches from your face. Couldn't predict if a threat approached. Couldn't focus on anything but the rasping sound of your breath.

I bit back a gasp of relief as the endorphins flowed through my veins, relaxing the tightness in my shoulders and pushing aside the lingering fear Spellcasters might lurk nearby. Making room for the bubbly, giggly place I shouldn't enjoy. Because it made Rodney an easy target.

Even after he pulled away, I fought with the desire to enjoy what the endorphins offered. Grappling with the bit of honed instincts Kade had worked so hard to perfect—I had worked so hard to perfect.

We lowered to the cave floor. I stretched my legs out in front of me with my ankles crossed and he settled with his head in my lap.

"After drinking from you, I couldn't stomach the crap the school gave us from a bag." He laughed lightly.

My stomach twisted, and I massaged my temples, as if what I'd just heard had been a misunderstanding. That he hadn't just told me I was his favorite meal.

*Is this what food feels like when we say it tastes good?*

He sighed heavily. "Most of my life I wished something terrible would happen to Bathory, because I hated it there...Now I wish we could go back."

"Yeah." Cool relief washed over me that the subject changed. "Classes and trivial drama seem like a cakewalk compared to this."

"I miss Zoon," his voice wavered.

Tears surfaced, and I promptly wiped them away. I never expected to miss Zoon. He was the insufferable addition to our trio, always getting us into trouble and begging me to get us out of it. Never once had he thanked me. Unless his constant attempts at my affection counted.

He didn't deserve the death he received.

As annoying as he could be, he was lovable. Freshman year, he gave me a teddy bear with a heart-shaped pillow stitched to its paws. I'd thrown it at him, only to find it in my bed later.

*How had he done that?*

Sophomore year, he asked me on a date. I threatened him with physical harm every time he brought it up. Which didn't deter him any.

Junior year, he stole me a rose bouquet from the campus garden. I'd tucked a petal away for safekeeping, but never told him.

Senior year, he'd finally given up, and his sights were set on another Protector.

My chest convulsed, wishing he was here to help me get Rodney to Carthage. He'd make it far less insufferable and maybe the world would seem a little less daunting.

Noticing Rodney's breath evened out, I carefully shifted him to the ground so I may lie down, well aware my mind wouldn't allow sleep despite how exhausted I was. I scooted closer to the cave entrance to put distance between the Vampire's chilled body and mine. Not that it made much difference. It was drastically colder since we'd left Bathory, nearly a *week* ago, and we weren't dressed for it.

To distract myself from the cold seeping through my clothes and into my bones, I focused on the two outside.

"I know you don't owe me an explanation, but I don't owe you anything either. Which makes it hard to trust a *Spellcaster* who's conveniently helping the Bathory survivors. Especially since compassion doesn't seem to be in your nature."

"I'm plenty compassionate." Preston snapped. "I cannot help that you and the Vampire make every effort to test my patience. Nor can I change what is done. I *can* assure you, I wish to help them."

I hadn't forgotten about the wards on his apartment. No honorable person needed to seal themselves from the world that drastically. Which should erect a vibrant red flag because that meant he endangered my Vampire.

Not open up another opportunity for me to fawn over him. He's mysterious and smells nice...and—*A know-it-all.*

"The Vampire lad..." Reggie paused. "He didn't jump to fight?"

"He's..." Preston sighed. "Different."

"I understand fear, but the lass threw herself into combat—"

"She is trained to. The Vampire is a special case. He is to be protected."

I appreciated Preston's attempt to keep Rodney's illness private. It embarrassed him for anyone to know. Once his weakness was discovered, he often became the target of cruel humor. If he could let others live in the lie he's a perfect, healthy Vampire, I would allow him.

Their voices grew softer, and I gave in to the exhaustion contributing weight to my lids.

Thunder rumbled, and a flash woke me up. Preston and Reggie clamored into the small cave, drenched to the bone. Heavy rain spouted from the sky outside, forming puddles near the cave entrance.

Once my quick breaths evened out, after convincing myself there was no actual threat, I enjoyed the view of the drenched duo. Their hair matted to their faces, lips drawn into frowns.

"Now it's going to smell like wet dog," Preston grumbled, peeling off his jacket.

"It'll mask the stench following you at least." Reggie glowered.

Preston twisted his jacket so water dripped to the stone floor. "Stench?"

Though I'd never admit it aloud, I thought he smelled nice.

"Roughing it doesn't mean you have to smell," Reggie explained. Scooting so his back was against the stone wall, he stretched his legs into the puddle created by Preston's jacket. The water splashed into the Sorcerer's lap.

"I don't smell," Preston grumbled, organizing his bag and jacket. Perhaps the Werewolf's enhanced sense of smell was picking up on something we couldn't. Or maybe it was yet another subject for them to argue over. Something they'd likely do until night time.

I folded my arms, noting there wasn't much light outside due to the rainstorm that turned the cool air icy. Which meant the darkness within the cave crept closer. The shadows stretching, reaching for us like tentacles.

"Did we wake you, Love?" Preston asked, throwing Reggie a condemning glare.

I opened my mouth to respond, but Reggie interrupted. "Told you. Your stench woke her."

"Wolf—"

"When did it start raining?" I scooted closer, doing my best to distract them from their senseless bickering.

"Not long ago,"

"Came in like a flock of Harpies," Reggie said, pivoting on his hip to gather nearby rubble.

Preston folded his arms and leaned into the stone wall behind him. Wet as he was, he couldn't appear more...ridiculous. Nothing like a know-it-all Archmage.

I chewed my bottom lip, a bubble of laughter crowding in my chest.

"Looks like it'll rain most of the day," he claimed, gaze on the cave entrance.

"Hopefully it lets up by nightfall," I said. We should've gotten coats at the bazaar.

Dramatically dropping sticks on the ground between us, Reggie assembled a small fire, briefly filling the cave with smoke.

"I could've done that," Preston stated, an arrogant smirk tugging at one side of his lips, "much faster and with less mess."

Reggie narrowed his eyes. "We're fortunate to have this cave." He ignored the Archmage's statement as the storm's intensity picked up.

"And why's that, oh-wise-one?"

A wave of irony brought a grin to my face. Now he got a taste of what it's like to be on the receiving end of his attitude.

"With these temperatures, we could catch a cold." Reggie stoked the fire, glare intensified by the flame's light on his face. Despite Preston's remark, the Werewolf's ability to light a fire so effortlessly impressed me. I'd freeze before I ever got one to take off.

Preston wiggled his fingers. "How scary."

I rolled my eyes. "It is getting pretty cold out there."

"Thank goodness Reggie has built a fire—"

"It's not for me, Spellcaster—"

"Don't call me that, *Dog*." Preston combed his hair back, and the light brightened his golden eyes until they were an ominous shade of yellow.

"The fire is for her," Reggie finished, maintaining his stare.

"Thank you," I mumbled, scooting closer and tucking my arms beneath my head.

He dipped his head and sat against the cave's wall, preparing to sleep upright. "I intend to get you and the Vampire to your destination safely. Even if it isn't the way *he* prefers."

My spine hurt, my hips ached, and it felt like I hadn't slept a wink all night. My stomach rumbled to let me know I forgot to count it in my list of miseries. The sooner we got to Carthage, the better.

I rubbed my face, begging my brain to wake up to process what Reggie and Rodney discussed. Something about the cave and its natural formation—maybe even its uses. All in all, it sounded like cluttered facts, clashing against my ears like flies trying to escape a window.

"Come on, Jo." I whispered, shaking my head for emphasis.

Perhaps geography wasn't the best thing to wake up to.

Staggering away from the pair, I found Preston on a collection of rocks, studying the sky like he so often did. The moonlight blanched his skin and reflected in his eyes, making them a pale yellow.

He withdrew the cigarette from his lips to smile. "The mutt fetched breakfast," he said, producing a wad of foil.

"Thanks."

The contents were a combination of fruits and some white meat. I refused to speculate what it might be and scarfed it all down as we walked. I hadn't slept well since Bathory and couldn't help but fear I never would sleep like that again. Because even when I could stay asleep, the horrors we'd endured tormented me.

I winced, startled by Reggie's sudden dramatic gesture as he elaborated on the intimate information he knew about the forest. He'd spent many hours here and learned a lot from its inhabitants—the hierarchy of the animals and the tree's cycles.

Things I never would've valued in school. I'd skipped science class as much as possible, more interested in defense against danger rather than its design.

"Are you alright, Love?" Preston tossed his cigarette and turned his worried expression onto me.

His concern caused the others to pause—All three stares on me.

I attempted a false smile, rubbing one eye. "I'm fine, just a little tired."

Calling my bluff, Reggie came to my aid. He removed his backpack and held it out for Rodney to take, resentfully. Rushing to crouch in front of me, he tapped a heavy paw on his shoulder blade. "Climb aboard. You could use the rest."

The glare Rodney pinned on us sent me stammering. "I'm alright. Really."

"I insist," Reggie pressed.

My muscles twinged, as if giving me the permission Rodney withheld. "You don't have to do this. Thank you."

It was quite a feat to wrap my arms around his meaty neck while also trying to hook my legs over his massive hips. He's large, but I hadn't realized how *thick* he was.

As he stood, my stomach did a flip and a sheepish grin stretched across my face.

*This is how it feels to be seven feet tall!*

I could see the tops of Rodney's and Preston's heads.

He tucked an arm beneath me to hold my small body in place while I clung to his expansive back.

My head barely missed low branches, something I wasn't used to. All the times in my life height could have benefited me came to mind. I never would've had to ask for help to get things from shelves. No one could have intimidated me, and everyone would've feared me in school.

"Is this how it is for you guys?" I teased, pushing through the fog infringing on my mind.

Preston laughed. "Yes, it's empowering to look down on you."

I ripped a small branch from a passing tree to lob. "You're a troll!"

He flinched as the brittle timber contacted his skull. "That's insulting," he feigned.

Rodney pointed and laughed, eliciting a quick, rude gesture from Preston.

"He smells much worse than a troll," Reggie declared, chuckling to himself. He proceeded to explain how they weren't native to the area, living higher in the Yorik Mountains to the west.

No one appeared to be as interested as before in what Reggie had to say and I tried not to think about why.

When we entered a narrower trail, following the bluff's edge, Reggie returned me to the ground. I lingered, catching myself on the jagged outcrop in the hillside as I stumbled.

*Thanks, nature, for the careful placement of sturdy objects.*

The others took no notice due to their constant bickering.

"There is so much evidence of the existence of sasquatch," Rodney insisted.

"I've scouted these lands for decades and never ran into one. It's all just children's stories." Reggie's tone cut sharply.

"Are you sure you aren't a distant relative of the sasquatch?" Preston had little investment in the debate. He simply wanted to stoke the fire.

Whatever retort followed, I couldn't hear. My hearing grew cloudy, then whistled as if my ears depressurized.

*Maybe the berries from breakfast were poisonous.*

Darkness closed in, weighing on my shoulders and pressing me into the earth. Was that?

*No.* Vines couldn't crawl out of the ground like that. *Could they?*

The toe of my boot caught on one, pitching me off a steep bluff into rocks and fallen limbs. Somehow, I missed the established timber that would easily stop my fall—and life.

I screamed, cognitive words too far to grasp.

*Could they hear me?* I couldn't hear them.

I tumbled faster and my vision blurred until my stomach heaved to dump the food from my belly.

My ribs collided with a set-in-spot boulder to end my infinite fall. All the air left my lungs, driving me to heave for more.

Nature had officially given me the worst ass beating of my life.

I pinched my eyes shut and cradled myself against the hearty stone. No way could I die this way.

*How embarrassing.*

I pulled my legs towards my sickened stomach. The spinning slowed with each heart beat, my stomach churning with every pulse. I wasn't sure how far I'd fallen.

Could they hear me from here?

My voice box couldn't muster a sound anyway. If they hadn't heard my scream, they'd never find me.

Undoing my trembling arms, I attempted to sit up. With less pressure on my ribs, I could get a good breath in and the pain would stop.

My arms buckled under the heavy weight dropped onto my back, thrusting me into the moist dirt; adding to the filth already coating my body. White spikes flashed in my vision, my breath gone.

I dug my fingers into the silt, icy hands holding me hard in place. Frigid breath lingered near my ear, forming a language I did not understand.

Strange as the accent was, I recognized one word—*"aeternum"*.

*Eternal.*

Dagger sharp teeth broke the skin at my neck and a scream erupted from somewhere deep in my lungs. In my current state, I didn't know I could emit such a noise and it raked against my ribs, pushing them to their breaking point.

A sensation I imagined solely the dead experienced swept over me as my blood turned ice cold, freezing in my veins; My pulse lethargic.

The teeth retracted from my body, and I heard retreating footsteps in the fallen leaves. I never saw my attacker's face, merely the strange blue-hued hands keeping me in place.

I pinched my eyes closed as a dull pound filled my ears, growing with strength in time. My blood pumped in my veins once more. It thawed and broke away into painful, jagged pieces.

Ice Pixie's had blue skin.

*Why would an Ice Pixie attack me?*

When I feared I'd die here alone, next to a shallow creek bed, muscular arms lifted me from my crumpled state. My breath hitched, transitioning to a weak whimper, as I lay eyes on my savior—a stranger. A maroon cloak hid his features, face shielded by the hood.

*A Sorcerer?*

# GRATITUDE
## CHAPTER 9

I DIDN'T DREAM AND sleep seemed to stretch on forever. Forcing my eyes open, I swallowed my heart, climbing up my throat.

My tender muscles were a painful reminder of every stick and stone that crossed my path down the hill. Forfeiting my attempt to sit up, I crumbled into the velvety soft sheets of the twin bed. The muted lamplight from the nightstand stretched to the dresser at the foot of the bed and the chair at the center of the room—mere feet away.

*Where's the hooded stranger?*

Had he been watching me sleep?

Pressure built behind my eyes as my pulse pounded faster. None of them had noticed me fall, so could I trust them to care for Rodney as I would? Would they take him to Carthage no matter what happened to me?

The bedroom door opened, and I braced myself as bright light poured in ahead of the man in the maroon cloak. He stood less than six feet tall and his shoulders filled the doorway.

I cowered under the blankets, wrenching them tight in my fists. Had I lost my weapons in the fall?

"You're awake," his voice was soft as he lowered into the rickety wooden chair. His dark eyes twinkled in the low light, like when a predator stalks its prey. "I was beginning to wonder if you hit your head hard enough to cause permanent damage."

He leaned toward me, his subtle upturn to his lips more apparent in the lamplight. Drawing my focus from his lawless black hair, his brilliant white teeth complimented the glossy black hoop pierced through his nostril.

I stiffened, as if moving would entice him to pounce.

"Thank you—um—for your help," the words felt foreign to my mouth.

"Of course. It's my pleasure." He held out a sandwich wrapped in a napkin and placed water on the nightstand. "You need to eat."

I accepted the sandwich, despite the pain it caused me to do so. Grateful, I ate, never taking my sight off the man in case he indicated somehow the food was poisoned.

"You're lucky I fished nearby," he stated, removing the cloak from his shoulders. He folded the fabric and draped it over his arm. No one wore cloaks anymore except the Sorcerers who swarmed Bathory and tracked us. What was the significance of the maroon? It seemed I should know, like I'd seen it before.

"Fishing?" I stammered, trying to process where he'd been fishing. I didn't recall any water, just mud.

My lids lulled, and my head rolled—for a second, I feared it would fall off my neck.

*So tired.*

"There's a stream there with the best shade," he explained. The glimmering in his eyes almost seemed to emit from their depths.

I blinked slowly and slumped into the pillows. The subtle recline was enough to turn him into a blurred figure and pushed my crumbling disposition to its breaking point.

Had he drugged me—or worse, *cursed* me?

It wasn't safe to sleep here. We'd already cashed in our miracle, stumbling across two strangers who hadn't tried to kill us upon sight. It's unlikely to happen again so soon.

"No one would've found you in that ravine," he explained. He grew further away, and the room narrowed, haziness enveloping the shadows. "You were covered in mud. Even I nearly missed you."

His suggestion struck like a threat. As if he wanted me to know how vulnerable I was and could do anything about it.

"Why were you near the ravine, anyway?"

"I...fell,"

"Were you injured formerly?"

My lips twitched, and my speech slurred an unintelligible response.

"Your wounds could get infected..."

His words blurred together as my lids snapped closed, willing the pain to sink deep into my muscle tissue, stowed away for later. No matter how desperately I reached, his voice grew too muffled to hear, and the darkness wrapped itself around me like a blanket. Lulling me to sleep.

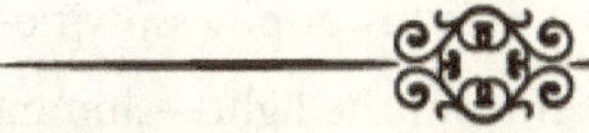

"Good afternoon." He was still there. Waiting while I slept for any amount of time. As if he expected something to happen. Whatever his reasoning, it couldn't be good.

A ripple of agony flashed through me as my muscles tensed. He's closer—within arm's reach.

I pushed into a sitting position and winced as a spike of pain shot up my spine. The blankets settled around my hips, giving me a glimpse of the assorted bruises coloring my flesh. Very little went unscathed.

He scooted to the edge of his seat. "I wanted to wait until you'd eaten before I healed you. Good thing, too. You needed the energy, judging by the nap you took. Your body would've gone into shock." He held out a hand. "May I?"

Not just a hooded stranger, but a cloaked Sorcerer. Same as the ones who decimated Bathory and tracked us. The same fear that rendered me paralyzed at the bazaar struck me. Even if I had a weapon, could I wield it? It hurt to make a fist.

"I have some hesitations with magic," I said. Shifting subtly, I craned my neck for something to use in defense. I'd rather die fighting than let him keep me from finding my Vampire.

"You're gravely wounded," he insisted. "If you plan to survive, you need to decide quickly."

His hand lowered and the dull ache deep in my muscles radiated like wild fire. I pitched forward, clapping a hand over my mouth. Although the blankets hid them from sight, I felt every gash, bruise, and internal inflammation.

He hadn't drugged my food, he'd used magic to dull my pain.

With a subtle tip of his head, the magic numbed me once more.

"You're very convincing," I choked out between sharp gasps. A shudder swept through me as I met his pupilless, wine-colored eyes. White flecks—not the reflection from the light—shimmered on their surface, unnatural for a Sorcerer. At least as far as I knew, their eyes weren't typically multicolored.

"Pain has a way of doing that. You whimpered in your sleep, so I thought you'd appreciate the relief." He gathered my arms into his hands, and I noted the disgusted countenance on his face.

*The bite marks.*

No matter this Sorcerer's plan, I would escape to find my Vampire. I wouldn't allow my fear to overcome my sense of duty. I'd endure whatever he put me through until I had the strength and weapons to do otherwise.

For no longer than a breath, it felt like I was tumbling off the ravine again. Instead of landing in the mud, it was his healing world. Preston's shimmered with sunshine, while this one snowed. Flakes swirled in the night sky, the moon reflecting on the glittering powder beneath me like a sea of ice. The trees surrounding a quaint little cabin resembled cotton candy, covered in icicles and heavy snow.

I hurried inside, eager to escape the cold.

"Thank the Mythos!" I muttered. A fire roared in the fireplace, a gray fur rug on the floor in front of it. Like a moth to flame, the warmth drew me in and I sprawled out on the rug.

Often at Bathory, we studied in front of the fire until bedtime. The three of us spent more time talking than getting anything done. I wished more than ever before we'd be able to do that again. School work felt so unimportant now.

My eyelids fluttered closed, and I inhaled the smoky scent from the burnt wood. This dream world lasted longer than usual, and I questioned exactly how serious my wounds had been since I never got a good look at them.

Heat radiated from my toes, through my legs, and across my torso. Once the sensation reached my face, the illusion dissipated.

The Sorcerer straightened in his seat, waiting as I settled into the present world.

"I heard you scream," he said, abruptly.

I dropped my chin, fidgeting with the blanket's seam. He didn't need to know why I'd fallen, although he'd likely dredged up his own theories after seeing the bite marks. The swell of defense in my chest crowded out the bitter taste of fear from recalling my plummet into the unknown.

"I saw the Ice Pixie first. He left you there, unconscious." His lips twitched strangely, almost fighting a smile.

"You saw him?" I croaked. "He attacked me."

"He cursed you," he corrected, gesturing towards his neck.

My hand flew to my neck, where the bite had been. Faint imprints remained in the shape of a halfmoon. "Why? Who hides in the forest, waiting to prey on people falling to their deaths?"

"Did he say anything when he attacked you?"

"I couldn't understand him." The memory was fuzzy, eventually putting itself together one piece at a time. "He did say 'aeternum'."

"*Eternal*. I've heard of this ritual." He stroked his chin. "It's forbidden in the Pixie community. He froze your biological clock."

"I'm immortal?"

*Immortal like a Vampire?*

Eternal life seemed so long and...lonely. Even though I had no family to watch grow old, it would be just as hard to watch the world age when I didn't.

He shrugged. "I wouldn't say *completely* immortal. After all, you nearly died from your injuries."

*I'd nearly died?*

The ravine must've been much deeper than I realized.

Had the Pixie been following us? How else would he appear so swiftly after my fall?

"How does something like that even work? Why would he leave me to die?" A wave of emotion rolled over me, tears threatening to slip free. On the verge of death, a Pixie *attacked* me. Either this Mage lied or the Pixie stalked me, waiting for the opportune moment.

His expression flickered, and his tone was off. "I suppose we'll never know, will we?"

He claimed to know the spell. Now he appeared to be hiding *something*.

Panic threatened to rear its ugly head.

He swept to his feet. "Let's get the memory of those wounds washed off you."

*A bath sounded excellent.* I discarded the blankets, swinging my legs from the bed. The muscles tingled to life, stiff from all they'd suffered.

"By the way," he held his hand out to assist me off the bed, "my name is Ramone."

I hesitated to accept his hand, searching the swirling orbs in his eyes, begging them to give me a sign. Could I trust him, or was this all a trap?

I stood, tilting my head to hold eye contact. "Josie,"

The crooked smile returned to his face, and a chill crept across my spine.

*Definitely not a stranger to trust.*

He led me by the hand through the hall to a large, gray-scale bathroom with an elaborate granite sink vanity. However, this proved to be the least impressive feature.

Beautiful stones covered in moss surrounded a thermal spring. Steam rolled from the bubbling surface, a natural fragrance emitted into the air. I became weak in the knees, eager to delve in.

Ramone gestured toward the water. "I'll return with fresh clothes,"

*Déjà vu.*

The amount of times I'd recently needed men to fetch me clothes was a little alarming.

I cradled myself. Where had they gotten off to? Had they even noticed I was missing?

Anger broiled in my chest. *They'd abandoned me.*

The three typically were invested in everything I did; how could they overlook my fatal fall? I'd never let them live it down, if I ever saw them again. Immortality would give me the opportunity to ensure the reminder would be painful for them.

I peeled off my filthy clothes and lowered into the bubbles. My skin tingled from the heat, my sore muscles now relaxed. A satisfied moan escaped me as I ran my wet fingers through my hair. I'm never leaving this place, even if I shriveled into an unrecognizable raisin.

A throaty chuckle from behind startled me. Ramone returned, as promised, with clean clothes. He set them on the vanity, alongside a rolled towel, lotions, and perfumes.

I narrowed my gaze. *Did a woman reside here?*

He folded his arms and leaned against the counter's edge. I felt extra naked and vulnerable.

Scrubbing shampoo into my hair helped to distract from the fact a strange man spectated while I bathed. At least my body was hidden in the bubbling water, shielding me from his prying stare.

"The Pixie's bite wasn't the only one ailing you," he expressed, challenge in his tone.

His words echoed off the walls and through my soul. I could imagine what he thought of Rodney's bite—that I craved it.

Embarrassment ignited my cheeks an instant before the rush of anxiety. He knew I had a Vampire. What would he do with the information?

I splashed water onto my face to conceal my reaction. Maybe if I didn't respond, he'd let it go. The dirt and grime turned to mud on my skin, dripping into the murky water.

*Yuck.*

"Were you willing?"

*About as willing as I am to have an audience while bathing.*

I glanced in Ramone's direction, not intending to provide him with an actual answer. It was none of his business how I associated with Vampires. Especially if it meant protecting mine.

"It isn't fair they need our life source to survive,"

Using a folded cloth from a stone along the water's edge, I scrubbed my face clean. "They explicitly consume what they need and most don't feed from the source anymore." I grumbled.

The steaming water rippled, my words reverberating along with the motion, back to me, and I flinched, realizing most weren't breathing anymore either. The entire next generation of Vampires faced genocide.

*Genocide led by Sorcerers!*

Impatience stole the satisfaction of the spring. Rodney needed to make it to Carthage—I had to make sure of it. Which meant I had to get out of here.

"Excuse me; I'd like to dry off, please."

I side eyed Ramone as he departed without a word, left to my devices.

*Was this guy with the enemy?*

Surely, if he was, he wouldn't allow a prisoner to bathe in such a beautiful space.

I dragged myself from the spring's embrace. Maybe there's a chance he shared similar beliefs as Preston and he'd help me.

Toweling off, I sidled up to the vanity. The clothes supplied were an oversized sweatshirt and leggings.

"Well, he has good taste for a weird dude."

I wandered from the bathing room, the cold floor a shock to my bare feet and an immediate reminder my boots were missing, too.

Ramone relocated to a living room, where he sat in an armchair, staring silently at the hardwood floor. His chair and another faced a vintage television adjacent to a beautiful bay window beholding a well-manicured, sunbathed lawn. A broadleaf forest trimmed the yard's edge, the trees much different than the ones I'd slept under since Bathory.

How far away had he taken me?

I lowered into the chair beside him, twisting a finger in my hair. Had he kidnapped me or rescued me? Rather swiftly, he'd gone from convincing me I needed his help to interrogating me about Vampires and not withholding his biased opinion of them.

"You seem hesitant to trust me." Ramone steepled his fingers, pointing their tips at me. His pierced brow quirked, as if the challenge pleased him.

I crossed my legs. "Spellcasters attacked my school, forcing me to navigate a world I know little about with a map I can't read, and now you, yet another Spellcaster, has me."

"I'll pretend to not fret over such basic terminology of my craft and focus on the interesting part of your sad spectacle of a life," he grumbled. "A map you cannot read?"

His confusion reflected my own upon discovering the map's qualities. Yet, his offense over being called a Spellcaster somewhat entertained me.

"Specifically, only Vampires can read the map," I spoke tentatively.

His already dark eyes deepened as he gripped the arms of the chair he occupied. The change in his demeanor inclined me to regret mentioning any information to him. I didn't know this man well enough to spout off important knowledge such as I had.

*Dammit.*

"How intelligent," his voice dripped with distaste.

My heart thrummed against my chest, and my breath shortened. *What?*

"I thought so." Not at the time, but it wasn't his business.

He rose to his feet, a sneer on his lips. "I shouldn't be surprised the method is brilliant. They employed accomplished Mages to conceal their city."

"How ironic," I mumbled, finding it difficult to believe with the world's current state.

His shoulders squared, and he lifted his chin to cast a vicious glare down the bridge of his nose. "Mages they promptly drained of their life source to ensure they couldn't be doublecrossed."

The way he spoke of Vampires left me uneasy. Never had I experienced this level of prejudice. Although, I'd never viewed anything the Vampires had done from his perspective. It wasn't hard to see why he believed they were cruel if they killed their helpers.

My stomach flipped. If his sentiments reflected the other Mage's hunting us, Rodney was in more danger than I'd realized. This was so much bigger than the school.

If anything happened to him while we were apart, I would never forgive myself.

"Do you know where my Vampire is?" Tears burned my throat, driving me to my feet. "Will you please take me to him?"

Ramone gave a simple nod. "In time, I will. I've got further questions for you."

He'd asked about the map, made it painfully obvious how he feels about Vampires—he had to work for the army chasing us.

I wouldn't answer anymore of his questions. Rodney needed me.

"You don't understand," I snapped. Without feeding, he's basically a sitting target while carrying the map. Especially now that I'd told yet another Sorcerer about it. "He's special. He needs me."

That's if he's even still alive. Many more than a few days without feeding...I didn't want to think about the condition Rodney could be in.

"How long have I been away?"

"You've been here two days." He loomed over me, citrus cologne assaulting my senses. "Does the Vampire need you, or are you addicted to his bite?"

"He needs me," I vomited information, because hearing someone call me addicted was worse than wondering myself. It didn't scare me anymore. Which could easily be written off as either I fed Rodney or he died.

*Simple.*

"You must be special to him,"

I folded my arms across my chest. "I'm his Protector."

"Your behavior suggests more,"

"What?"

"Have you kissed?"

"Excuse me?" I was taken aback.

*How was it his business?*

He waved a hand in the air. "Never mind,"

We'd never engaged in any inappropriate behavior! Our relationship was professional. How dare he—a stranger—accuse me of *anything!*

This is exactly what I'd been afraid of. People assumed if a Protector fed their Vampire, then there were complicated feelings that jeopardize their ability to perform the job.

Maybe he was right. I'd let a Sorcerer into our circle, one we knew nothing about. Now I couldn't even protect him if something happened. Or worse, Preston funneled information to this Sorcerer.

*Rookie.*

"I apologize for wasting your time." Ramone gathered my hands, gaze boring into mine. "If you'll allow me, I can track your Vampire with a spell."

"What do you mean?" I almost pulled my fingers from his grasp but refrained with the hope if I cooperated, he'd help me.

It frustrated me we never studied the types of magic used by Mages. I searched his eyes for *something*. Any subtle sign.

"It's simple and quick. We'll find him much faster this way."

*Faster.* He wants the map, and I'd given him the heads-up that he'd need a Vampire to read it. *My* Vampire.

"I will warn you, the spell is...invasive,"

This was magic we talked about. Couldn't he do it with a snap of his fingers? Rodney was my best friend, and I'd do *anything* for him. Nevertheless, there had to be some boundary.

What sort of conditions was he implying?

"What's your interest in my Vampire?"

"To help reunite you with your friend," he said, his whirling eyes a little too invested in mine. "I'm sure he's worried about you."

He's *one* Sorcerer. How much of a threat could he be against me and the others? Assuming Preston wasn't his minion.

I dropped my wrist at my side. "If I agree, will you take me to him tonight?"

Ramone pinched his lips, twisting them theatrically as he considered my inquiry. "I suppose time is of the essence,"

I sucked in a slow breath as he grasped my arms, muttering in a foreign language. He placed my palms together, then pulled them apart and inched closer. His mouth still ambled, and I found myself focused on the movement.

He was entrancing, or maybe it was the effects of the magic shaking my mind. Nothing else came into focus except him. The curvature of his lips accentuated the stubble against his tan skin and sharp chin. His hair curled around his ears, hiding the black gauges in his lobes.

His lips fell on mine, hard enough to cause my stiff frame to stumble a pace. When he'd said the spell was invasive, I hadn't dreamt this. I fought to control my fists as my fingers curled into my palms. I had to get this creep off me. There was no way this had to do with magic!

My brain became numb, and the fight left my body as he pulled away. My mouth fell open, and I stood there dumbfounded as he watched—to be sure the spell worked.

A pit developed in my stomach. He hadn't cast a spell to find Rodney.

My vision clouded, same as my mind, then sharpened as rapidly. Like a switch, altering my brain. I blinked and rubbed the spot between my brows.

"How do you feel?" he asked.

Other than being cheated out of my first kiss, I felt fine. Albeit, different.

"Disappointed." I lifted my chin, refusing to let him believe he intimidated me.

A faint smirk threatened to cross his lips, then he cleared his throat. I couldn't perceive much more than that—at least my mind wouldn't let me.

I rubbed my face to encourage my foggy brain to focus.

Something wasn't right.

"Come with me." He pulled my wrist.

We progressed in the hall to a room holding training equipment for combat and strength. My interest piqued, recognizing my weapons on a table near the entrance.

"Go ahead." He gestured to them as he passed.

While he rifled through a closet, I donned my knives and gun. It was rather trusting of him to give me my weapons and expect me to not use them.

I still didn't believe he intended to return me to my Vampire with no strings attached.

Once I'd tucked the knives into my boots and the gun in my waistband, he reappeared with a wooden stake.

I frowned at the medieval weapon. He did have prior motivations.

"Take it,"

I did.

*Why did I do as he asked?* I had no intentions to kill any Vampires. I'd sooner plunge it through his heart.

Dammit, why couldn't I control myself? How did I stop from tucking the stake into my waistband alongside the gun?

*No!*

In his other arm, Ramone held a cloak—like his.

"Why are you giving me these?" I demanded, quivering with dread. Nothing good could come of him dressing me as his clone.

Ignoring my question, he sauntered behind to fasten the heavy fabric about my neck with an elaborate clip resembling a twisted ball of thorns. The center stone was a breathtaking depth of red.

Beneath the cloak, he buckled a harness for the stake and gun, looped around my waist and one thigh.

Then, I re-situated my weapons accordingly.

*Like a minion!*

What is wrong with me? What had I allowed to happen?

I knew better than to trust a Sorcerer!

"I'm taking you to your Vampire, but I caution you against feeding him. You have bathed in a blessed spring, designed to deter such creatures." He chuckled to himself. "Although it would be easier than what I have planned."

I gaped, realizing his talent at manipulation.

None of this had been about my tumble into the ravine. Everything had been a part of his scheme—letting me bathe, healing me. He'd cursed me at some point to give him information, something I would never do.

Every sharp object stored on my person should be thrust through his chest. Every bullet unloaded on his face.

My hands alone were trained weapons.

Yet I did *nothing*.

My muscles refused to strike, as if encompassed by concrete.

His teeth flashed identically to the treacherous gleam in his eyes. "You fight for me now, *Protector*."

*Please let them stop me.*

# CLOSER
## CHAPTER 10

Ramone's teleportation travel was much rougher than Preston's. I swayed as we materialized, my vision scrambled for an instant. Ramone stood behind me, hands on my hips to keep me close in front of him. Little did he know he also kept me from toppling over. We hid behind a mass of trees while Reggie and Preston slept on the dusty ground in front of a tent. Judging by the structure's worn fabric, it belonged to Reggie. I recognized it, usually attached to his backpack.

My hands trembled. I'd have to fight these men. I'd seen them in combat and had little faith my training would hold a candle to their experience.

Ramone's lips brushed my ear as he whispered how I would attack. Assuming I could focus on anything he said over the roar in my ears. The personification of not only the horror of what he expected from me, but his nearness.

My muscles merely tensed as his arm wound around my waist, his warm hand brushing against my bare stomach. Were I able, I would've righted my sweater, then pummeled him.

"What do you gain from their deaths?" I hissed soft enough only he could hear.

"Who said we were killing them all right now?" he plainly lied and his arm constricted around me like a vise.

I dipped my head, swallowing the threats collecting on the tip of my tongue. All his magic allowed me to do was wait to execute his plan.

*I can't do this!*

We'd worked too hard to get this far. I couldn't hand Rodney or the map to Ramone. I'd let Preston or Reggie kill me instead. They could finish the mission without me.

Reggie roused first, stretching, then staggering into the woods. Pressure constricted my chest, the urge to call for his help stunted. So long as the spell remained intact, I was helpless.

"This doesn't have to be forever," Ramone's voice warmed my ear. "Once you've fetched me the Vampire and map, I'll undo the spell." He thrust me out of the shadows, leaving him securely hidden within his lies.

I had no reason to trust him and also no way to fight him.

Under the magic's domination, I retrieved a dagger as I crept into their campsite. They'd carefully surrounded the tent with mature trees, leaving the only open approach over their resting bodies.

A leaf crunched beneath my boot; Preston's snores stopped, and so did I.

If he were to wake, I'd be forced to attack him. While it wouldn't feel good kidnapping my best friend, it would feel worse to fight the two people who'd volunteered to selflessly help us.

My feet moved on, ignoring my skipping heartbeat and the voice screaming in my head to stop.

Careful to avoid anything else that might make a sound, I crouched beside Rodney's sanctuary and undid the zipper. It only made a slight buzz that hopefully didn't wake the Vampire inside. Typically, their tendency to sleep hard overshadowed their enhanced hearing.

Rocking onto my knees, I pressed the blade against his throat, drums pounding in my ears. *Please let him fight me.*

His obsidian eyes flashed to mine. It felt like a stake to the chest. He wasn't supposed to ever look at me like that. *I'm his Protector.*

My hold on the dagger faltered for a split second before tightening. I couldn't fight the spell.

Slapping away the blade with incredible speed, Rodney reached for me. I dodged the touch, afraid of how much damage my poisoned skin could do.

I had to warn him.

Dropping his hand, he examined me same as we had the piles of Vampires outside Bathory. Disbelief and grief weakening the tight set of his jaw.

There had been many moments in our life Rodney could predict my thoughts, knew exactly how I felt. I begged for him to do that now. To see past the magic.

"You're alive," he murmured. His brows relaxed as the obsidian in his eyes softened, and his mouth popped open with more to say.

A gush of relief stole my breath.

Truly, I hadn't believed they didn't notice I'd fallen. My worry stemmed from a place I fought hard not to acknowledge—The fear I didn't matter to them like they did to me. That even though we were considered friends, I'd end up alone. Nothing but an orphan.

But it stung to think they'd given up so quickly. I'd fought so hard to get to Rodney—How long had they searched before declaring me dead?

I reached for the stake in my waistband.

*Let him stop me.*

He lunged for my arm, and I dodged him with ease. Unfortunately, my training assisted Ramone's spell.

*He couldn't stop me.*

"What are you doing?" Rodney demanded, his irises turning obsidian once more.

"I'm here to take you—"

His gaze flicked over my shoulder as I was ripped from the tent by my sweater.

Driving my elbow into the chest behind me, I whirled to level my dagger at his throat. My pounding heart shuddered as his wild, copper gaze locked with mine and his fingers curled around my wrist.

My suspicions twisted into a knot that sank low in my stomach. He protected my Vampire. *He hadn't been lying.*

I secured my hold on the dagger to slash at his face. Using the stake as a distraction ploy, I drove the point towards his chest. The dagger blade grazed his cheek, leaving a slight cut in its wake.

While avoiding my additional attempts to stab him, his gaze tracked from Rodney, trapped inside the tent until nightfall, and the shadows I'd slipped from prior.

"I'll fix this, Love."

He swatted my wrists out of the air so hard, my dagger fell to the ground, then jerked me into his chest. Cradling the back of my head, he pressed my lips to his, pinning my limbs with his free arm.

He did not mutter words I couldn't understand, nor make gestures with his hands. The curse slipped from my mind, as if Preston removed a sheet draped over my head.

*Wow.*

A very brief glimmer of resentment burned my throat that, yet again, I'd been robbed of a kiss. This wasn't how I'd wanted it to go—even if it hadn't been at the top of my priorities. It should've meant something and not been followed by the absolute lack of emotion that followed the curse withdrawing from my veins.

I felt like mush—the magic taking more from me than what Ramone had given.

"No!" I screamed as firm hands seized me from behind. Ripping me from Preston's hold so fast, he didn't have time to catch my hands as I grappled for a hold on him.

A wave of nausea crashed over me as we teleported in a blink. Materializing a safe distance from Preston so he could secure me as a shield.

"Why are you here?" he roared.

The look on Preston's face was lethal enough Ramone should have dropped dead. Suggesting he thought the same, he drew me closer. Hardly leaving an inch of him uncovered, aside from the parts of him past my shoulders.

"My ventures in the woods are not your concern. Why are you here?" His words were laced with acid and delivered less sarcastically than intended.

"You should be in hiding," Ramone bordered on hysteria.

*Hiding?*

Preston laughed flatly. "In fear of you?"

*So they knew one another.*

The familiar, hot tip of a dagger brushed against my waist, where he possessively held me. He cleared his throat. "I simply meant you typically hide from all of your faults. Didn't think this would be an exception."

Preston sidled casually in front of the tent to box Rodney in. "I wouldn't miss an opportunity to mock your pathetic leadership skills and elementary grade mind control spell."

He seemed primarily unbothered by Ramone, which led me to realize how flustered the Sorcerer had become.

I wriggled slightly, resulting in the dagger against my rib cage as a reminder. He didn't intend to allow Preston to keep him off track.

"Why haven't you blasted him yet?" Reggie entered the standoff, fists curled tight at his sides.

"I don't want to hit her," Preston grumbled over his shoulder.

Rodney stumbled from the tent, dagger clutched in his hand. He was careful to stand under the trees' protection from the receding daylight.

Which accentuated the shadows around his eyes—his tired and hungry eyes.

Ramone twisted us so we efficiently faced them all, straightened to his full height. "Your childish outbursts won't change the fact I have an army and you... You have a Leech and a dog."

Reggie's frame flickered with an iridescent glow and his gaze turned animalistic. *On the verge of changing.*

"Yet you have to enlist a novice Protector to do your bidding?" Preston jeered. He appeared light on his toes, ready to pounce.

*Novice Protector?*

"Arrogant prick," Ramone growled, shifting his weight so our bodies pressed together.

My flinch launched Rodney to the perimeter of the shadows, Reggie tight at his side.

"Stay back," I urged.

They did as asked, but their restraint was all too obvious. Which seemed to relax Ramone—at least his muscles softened.

I shifted the stake in my hand to reassure myself I still held onto it. While not much against Ramone's dagger, it was something.

"Let Josie go," Rodney snapped. "It's me you want, anyway. I have the map."

Ramone laughed, resting his chin on my head. His arms wound around my waist to squeeze me, and I grimaced. Too much of him touched me. "What's the matter, Vampire? Don't like that I have your snack?"

Rodney's eyes were nothing but pools of obsidian. "She's my best friend, asshole!"

"We can make this a lot easier. Shall we call him to feed?" Ramone's lips brushed against my cheek.

I gripped my weapon tighter. *How dare he use me as bait against my own Vampire.* Let alone touch me like his personal property. He made my skin crawl.

He withdrew the dagger from my ribs to touch the blade beneath my jawline. I stiffened.

"Stop!"

"What do you want?"

All three men shouted, hesitant to lunge in fear Ramone would harm me. His lips split into a smile against my skin, and the dagger pressed further into my neck.

Reggie let out a low growl as his wolf form fought to take control, rippling across his skin.

Rodney's nostrils flared as the dagger punctured my skin, warm blood trickling down my inflamed neck.

My whimper threatened to turn into a sob as Ramone retracted the blade. "You're sick," I squeaked. Frustrated immortality didn't mean pain no longer existed.

Ramone's focus remained on the feral Vampire he'd baited, holding tight to my hips as Rodney threw himself into an enraged hunt.

Reggie caught his torso and slammed the frail vampire into a tree, leaves raining down on them. Instinct had seized him—or maybe it was just his unbridled hunger from lack of feeding.

"Predictable creatures," Ramone chuckled, the sound radiating against my back. Like thousands of spiders charging across my flesh.

"This isn't right. They're not mindless monsters." The humor Preston boasted before was gone. He raised his hands to cast.

Ramone's hold slackened as he reeled to counter whatever approached him.

This was the perfect distraction. I twisted the stake to aim between my arm and torso, both hands locked on the hilt. With one forceful thrust, I drove the pointed end into Ramone's ribs.

He doubled over and backed away, swears spilling from his lips.

"If you incanted with that precision, you'd have better luck with efficiency." Preston laughed.

Blood soaked Ramone's shirt as he freed the stake from his side. The weapon fell to the forest floor with a thud. His haunting gaze fixed on Preston as he teleported.

I plunged to the ground to retrieve the stake then my dagger, wiping them clean with the end of my cloak.

"Love?" Preston dropped to his knees and pawed the blood tainted hair from my face. "Are you alright?"

Twisting my head to the side, his thumb swept across the slice in my neck. Sharp autumn air nipped at the exposed wound a second before he mended it. It tingled, only taking a moment to do so. Not even bothering to draw me into his healing world. Which I would've welcomed. Anything to stave off the barrage of emotions swooping down onto me.

With Ramone gone, I could feel again. At least, it felt like my mind fired once more.

"Not yet!" Reggie bellowed, adjusting his hold on Rodney.

He needed fed, but I couldn't do it. "He had me bathe in blessed spring water."

"You don't have to feed him." Preston dragged me to my feet. "We won't risk your life again."

"But he needs the blood,"

He slid his palm down my arm to lace our fingers. "He's had plenty of opportunities to do so. If he was starving, he'd tell you. We need to go. Ramone will return with reinforcements." Despite his prior less-than-intimidated state, his voice was tight with worry.

Was Ramone the reason he had wards over his apartment? Why was he allegedly in hiding?

"Who was that?" Reggie asked, releasing Rodney. His irises turned pink, and he slumped against the tree. "And what happened?"

"I fell down a ravine," I explained, ignoring the Archmage's impatient grunt. "Preston was right. I shouldn't have fed Rodney and should've taken better care of myself."

"We heard you scream," Rodney confessed.

"We searched for you for hours." Reggie added, dropping to his knees to disassemble the tent.

None of them could look at me.

It wasn't their fault.

"It happened so fast." My hand went to my throat. "There was an Ice Pixie waiting for me. They attacked me—"

"They froze your veins." Preston's fingers squeezed mine a little too tight.

"Yes." A lump of apprehension developed in my chest as I met his sad, haunted eyes.

"Froze her veins?" Rodney asked.

"Essentially, making her twenty-one forever."

I hefted a deep breath, still unused to the magnitude of that adjustment. "Ramone found me and took me somewhere to heal me. He cursed and questioned me, then...brought us here—"

"To kill us," Rodney finished the story for me.

"And to kidnap you and the map so he can eradicate all Vampires," I confirmed. Guilt turned my stomach sour. I'd held a dagger to my Vampire's throat.

Shouldering the tent bag, Reggie asked Preston, "Who is Ramone?"

"Didn't you hear? The leader of the Sorcerers who swarmed Bathory." Preston held his hands in the air dramatically. "Now, let's go, Love. He *will* return,"

"Are you afraid of him?" Reggie asked.

He received a scoff.

I held my arms out. "Surely, we aren't separating?"

Preston turned me, his exasperated face inches from mine. "Rodney would be safer if we do. If you hadn't yet gathered, Ramone has bigger plans for your Vampire's navigation capabilities."

Rodney scoffed. "He wants to get you alone so you can kiss."

I trembled with the need to punch Rodney. "When did you become an expert on magic and how it is applied?" Anyone could have seen the kiss was to help, not for enjoyment!

"There are plenty of ways—"

"You're not a Sorcerer, Rodney!" He'd detonate if he knew Ramone had kissed me first.

"We don't have time for this," Preston interjected.

"I can't just leave Rodney,"

"Reggie is capable—"

"He's my charge!"

"And for now, you are mine."

"What did you mean by Ramone has bigger plans?" I inquired between huffed breaths. We had put great distance between us and the others until the moon was high in the sky.

Preston lit a cigarette; precisely what his lungs needed. "Rodney poses little threat to his army's cause—"

"He said it was important for him to have the map—"

"You believe he'd reveal his tactics to *you*?"

He'd certainly had a lot to say. "I suppose not. He only said enough to get me to let my guard down so he could curse me."

Preston ran a hand through his sweaty hair. "He seeks to fulfill his father's ideal world—one without Vampires...where Sorcerers rule."

I grimaced. "Sorcerers rule?"

"They prefer to be the race in charge, as if they are some supreme bloodline and all the others are muddled wastes of flesh."

"You speak like you aren't one of them,"

He took a long drag. "I no longer share the same ignorance."

"Do most Spellcasters think like that?"

Preston held the cigarette between his lips. It bounced comically, and ash fell away as he spoke, "The numbers seem to be increasing."

"Why?"

"Persuasion, undoubtedly,"

"Why don't you follow him? I've seen the way you look when Rodney feeds."

Humor danced in Preston's eyes, and he smiled, pulling the cigarette from his lips to hold at his side. "I find drinking blood unappealing; in my old age I've realized that is no reason to kill—unless we're speaking of mosquitoes,"

I smiled at the poor joke. If Preston could empathize with the Vampires, then why did so many others choose to condemn them? I suppose I wasn't meant to understand.

"Is it because of a vendetta? Ramone said something about the Vampires using Mages to hide their city then killing them."

"That was an excuse for the Veiled Army to enact the next stages of the crusade. The Vampires were afraid of what would happen, so they hid their city. Their only choice was to use Mages and kill them once they were finished to protect the secrecy of the city's location." He chewed the inside of his cheek, then licked his lips. "So the Veiled Army far surpassed their claim to a vendetta. Especially now. It's become more than that, Love. They're after power and they believe the Vampires stand in the way."

"So, why does he want me? Can't he find another Protector and Vampire to manipulate?"

Preston heaved a sigh through his nose, smoke billowing out. "Besides the fact you two have one of very few maps to Carthage? Ramone thinks you'll...empower him."

This perplexed me. I was the best Protector in my graduating class—perhaps the entire school. What good did that do the Veiled Army? They didn't need a Protector trained for Vampires. Granted, some Sorcerers had Protectors. The more power they possessed, the more paranoid they became. We were overqualified bodyguards. While I could see the benefit a Protector would provide someone like Ramone, I failed to understand why it had to be me.

The fact a Pixie made me immortal, then the Veiled Army kidnapped me, to find out I'm somehow important suggested none of this was random.

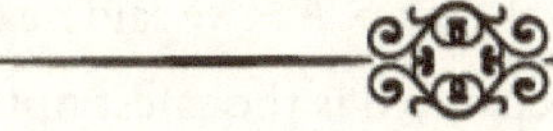

We paused to eat, the sun already up for hours. Preston handed over an apple, some trail mix, and a water bottle from the backpack he'd obtained at the bazaar.

Ravenous, I consumed the offering and slumped against a tree. "How long have you known Ramone?"

Preston's lips twisted. "Too long. We've never seen eye to eye. Ramone's always wanted what was mine. My friends, my family, my magic. He'd do nearly anything to get it. Which resulted in us getting cursed."

"*He* cursed *you*? Is that why you have wards over your apartment?"

Maybe my immortality was similar to a curse. Could it be undone?

Preston sighed and nodded. "He's always reacted negatively towards failure. Often, he blamed his struggles on me. Instead of bettering himself, he lashed out. Which ended poorly for us both. Now, we will forever suffer the same."

"How does that work?"

He shrugged. "I have yet to fully understand it. On occasion, I can hear the fool's thoughts and it pains me."

Simple, yet complex. *What were the curse's boundaries?*

"How come you haven't removed it?" I rubbed my tired face.

"We researched it for years; nothing ever came of it." He shrugged like he'd written off all concern decades ago. Were I not so exhausted, I'd bother to ask for him to explain in more depth. At his age, he should've found *something* by now.

"Can't we rest a little longer?" I gasped.

He swung the backpack over his shoulders, not even bothering to wait for me to get up. "The Vampire is in safe hands, Love. Reggie will take good care of him and the map. As I've said nearly a hundred times now, keeping you two separated is the safest option for now."

I shut my mouth with a sharp click.

*He's right.* We'd had this conversation over and over. To continue it once again was simply a waste of oxygen.

We walked for hours, basking in the autumn sun's heat. When I stumbled from lethargy, Preston scooped me into his arms. I clutched his dingy shirt front, focused on the tightness of the gesture to keep me awake.

His ability to continue baffled me. He suffered from fatigue, too. His eyes were bloodshot, yet he held them open wide; never wavering.

"Do all mind control spells work like the one Ramone used?" I chewed my bottom lip, anxious to hear his response. I needed to prove Preston hadn't done the same to me.

"The effects are the same, but the execution could go unnoticed depending on the Mage's qualifications." His eyes flashed.

"So, if you–"

"I would never do that to you. Had you made it known you wanted nothing to do with me, I would've left. You two appeared to need help, and I couldn't walk away."

Even if he hadn't meant to, Ramone had planted a seed of distrust in my mind. While I'd never suffered effects like I had yesterday, I still wondered if Preston had used any mind control on me. Perhaps when we first met him? When he healed me for the first time?

"This tactic is typical for Ramone. He's always had difficulties developing relationships, so he uses the cheat method. I understand why you asked, though."

Their strange interaction earlier made a little more sense now. They weren't friends, but they had history. History Preston chose to walk away from to be a better person. Something I should've recognized in him sooner. Had I not been convinced before Ramone kidnapped me, the way he'd jumped to Rodney's defense was enough proof he wasn't a Veiled Soldier any longer.

"I know I've asked this before, but why are you helping us?" I rested my head on his shoulder and subtly watched his expression harden. No matter how consistent he was with his replies so far, I refused to believe he just wanted to help us. Especially when Rodney made it so apparent he didn't want Preston around.

He glanced at me. "When I answer this time, will you believe me?"

I held the necklace charm in my hand, smoothing a finger over the decorative thorns. "Yes,"

"Since I was old enough to make my own decisions, I've done nothing honorable. I fought in a senseless crusade, fabricated enemies from distinguished people, and disappointed my mother time and time again. I promised myself I would change, and you were the cause I needed."

I struggled to believe he'd been as awful as he continuously insisted. We all made our mistakes, and it's admirable he made efforts to change.

"It's hard to imagine you care what your mother believes." I crooked a grin.

Preston's stony expression broke into a smile. "My mother is a wonderful and powerful woman. She had to be to put up with me,"

Preston's mother had to have his smile.

*Was she the woman who wrote the letters?*

"She would love you," he went on in reverie. "Especially because of how hardheaded you are—"

"You meant to say strong." I tugged his shirt.

He laughed. "I'll arrange for you to meet her one day,"

My heart skipped at the concept of keeping in touch with Preston once this ended. "Are you sure you could handle two powerful women together?"

His warm gaze fell on me, slowing the world's revolution. "It's everything I've ever wanted, Love."

Warmth flashed across my cheeks, and I tucked my head beneath his chin to avoid looking at him. He couldn't carry me and flatter me or else I'd believe he might *think* about me. I had enough on my plate with Rodney, I didn't have the capacity to deal with *feelings*.

I closed my lids and willed myself to sleep, listening to the rhythmic sound of his heartbeat and committing his bemused smile to memory.

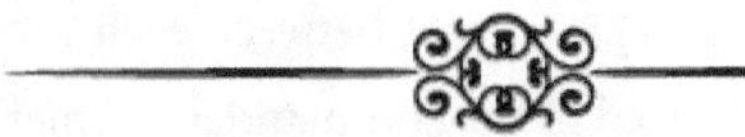

My nap lasted far longer than I intended. The moon and the stars had taken their place amongst the clouds.

I shifted my weight and realized we weren't moving. Preston sat on the forest floor, back against a smooth rock with moss grown over it. I rested in his lap, curled against his broad torso. My skin tingled with warmth, enjoying how comfortable it felt to be so close to him.

I studied his sleeping face, the way his closed lids were so peaceful, and his lips parted to breathe rhythmically. *I should give him space.* My added weight probably disturbed his already uncomfortable position.

Untangling myself from the cloak, I twisted to place my feet on the ground.

Feeling my weight shift away from him, Preston's eyes creaked open. He tightened his hold, and I froze. The cool night air as convincing as his big warm hands that I needed to stay nestled in his lap.

"Are we close to Carthage?" I didn't want to experience traveling by foot in the snow.

"I think so, but only Rodney can tell us that." Preston murmured, tucking the cloak around me like a blanket.

He gently cradled my head in the nape of his neck and I stiffened as his arm draped across my lap, hand cupping my thigh. His other hand perched on my outer hip.

"I wish I could burn that hideous thing," he confessed, nose wrinkled. "Probably would've already if it didn't serve a decent enough purpose for now."

"The cloak?"

"Mhm. Ramone has always dressed in that color. Every time I see it, I think of him,"

Tipping my head down, I upturned the pendant holding it in place. The polished metal shined, the contact between each thorn tarnished for depth. Had it not belonged to the commander-in-chief of the Mage army, I would've classified it as beautiful.

For now, it represented my failure to squelch an enemy determined to destroy the race I was born to defend. A reminder that I wasn't the badass Bathory made me believe I was. Not against Sorcerers.

A fiery rage heated my chest. Once more Bathory failed us. We should've been educated more on how to fight against magic. The Persecution hadn't been all that long ago.

"As soon as I get new clothes, you are free to do what you want with this cloak." I dug the wooden stake from my waistline. "Until then, you can burn this."

"Of course." He gladly took the stake.

I balled my fists in the center of my chest and curled up against him. His lap was a considerable improvement to the forest floor. One I could get used to. It's a much more intimate submission to his inviting scent than when I'd commandeered his bed.

More importantly, the way he held me provided a sense of comfort I wasn't used to. As a Protector, I did the shielding. Preston surrounded me with...*warmth*.

I never wanted this moment to end.

"I can't believe they still make these," he said. Stake held in his large palm, he stretched his arm out away from us. In a flash, it caught fire and dissipated into embers, blowing away in the wind.

"Thank you." It was a relief to see yet another reminder of what could've happened gone.

"I..." The center of his left cheek sank in and his glowing gaze swept over me. "You're welcome."

"Is the reason you know so much about the army that...destroyed Bathory, because it's the Veiled Army?" I asked tentatively, afraid it would sound like an accusation when he fought so hard to convince us he was our ally.

"Yes. Even though I'm not a part of their ranks anymore, I know things because I have unavoidable attachments to their army. Which is why I cannot stress enough that separating from Rodney was our best course of action. It protects him and you."

Confirming my suspicions only increased my worry for Rodney. This wasn't some army in its infancy, developing its numbers and campaigning its cause. The Veiled Army was historical and vast.

*And after us.*

Preston's stare was almost unsettling, a mixture of emotions spiraling within their depths. Thoughts I couldn't unravel—and wasn't sure I wanted to with Rodney being so far away.

Nuzzling against his neck, I stretched a palm out on his shoulder nearest my face. Mutely asking for permission, he hesitated to encircle his limbs around me. A sigh left his nose and tickled my hair as he relaxed, his body melding into mine.

I hadn't realized how rigid he'd been this whole time, which created a wave of awareness that swept through me, building a wall of stifling heat. I tilted my head to the glittering stars in the sky and he shifted to shamelessly watch me do so—*and Holy Mythos did that take my breath away.*

"What's it like having a mother?" I gingerly touched the ends of Preston's hair at his ear, knuckles brushing the developing beard encroaching on his hairline.

He laughed, a whimsical air whipping over his expression. "It's wonderful and horrible. She's always there when you need her and more so when you don't."

It baffled me someone as old as Preston still had a mother—*How old did that make her?*

I tracked the smile lines on his face and watched them disappear as I asked, "When is the last time you saw her?"

"Before the Blood Crusade." He turned his head and shrugged. "It wasn't until I'd taken many innocent lives, I realized the cause we led was...well." He succumbed, at a loss for the appropriate word to describe the carnage.

I suddenly felt odd in the lap of a Sorcerer who killed hundreds of Vampires. A killer I'd intended to ditch once he no longer served me.

Though he bore the tattoos as a permanent registrar of his savage past, he was no longer that man.

*I believed he wasn't that man.*

"I haven't spoken to her in decades, too ashamed of who I've become. Not since I fled the army..." The moonlight paled his complexion, and he fidgeted with my loose hair to avoid looking me in the eye. "I intended to write her with my whereabouts after I left the kind family in hiding who harbored me."

He swallowed hard, and the tendon in his neck flexed tight. The mention of this pivotal moment in his life still haunted him. The reason he strived so hard to help us.

"Had I not been with them, I don't think the Veiled Army would've ever found them." Pain flashed in his expression as if he relived every life he'd endangered or taken. I stilled his hands, squeezing them to assure him that part of his life was over. "Now I have to live with that burden for the rest of my very long life. That same shame is what kept me from reaching out to my mother. She'd see me for the monster I'd become—worse than the ones I set out to fight...Vampires feed on blood for survival. We spill it for pleasure and power."

# KALENTO
## CHAPTER 11

A FAMILIAR SNEEZE ECHOED ahead of Rodney as he stumbled from the thicket. A threat of violence crossed the Vampire's face as he freed himself from the vegetation, legs snapping from the tangled mess.

Nature was quickly becoming our nemesis.

Reggie passed through the same spot with ease, laden with the tent and his backpack. "Never thought I'd be glad to see your ugly mug, Spellcaster." He declared, dropping his load to the ground.

"Wish I could say the same," Preston mumbled so no one else heard but me. Still curled up against him to stave off the icy wind.

At least, that's the excuse I'd use if anyone asked why we were so close.

"I'm starved," Rodney bit out, and his tired eyes burned black with jealousy.

I hid my face against Preston's neck and sucked in a deep breath, until his sweet, tobacco laced scent soothed my tight chest. If I fed Rodney, I would poison him. Although, his forward behavior tempted me to let him. My duty was to protect, not wait around to feed him at a moment's notice.

The Vampire's fiery eyes scaled past us, and he exhausted a wavering breath. "Holy Mythos!"

"What is it?" Reggie asked.

Preston sat up and set me aside.

As I adjusted the cloak, I tracked Rodney drifting from the group. His eyes glimmered with fascination on the distant clearing ahead and he clutched the map between his hands.

"Rodney, what do you see?" I jumped up to follow, catching his jacket arm.

"It's the city," he breathed, a tentative smile twitching his lips.

I followed his line of sight and gasped. I could see it. The clearing below shimmered with lights and bustling bodies.

"Do you see something?" Reggie joined us.

"Carthage." I gestured for the others to follow.

They gathered our supplies and fell in step beside us. Their hesitant pace suggested they still couldn't see what we saw. The gabled structures and cobblestone streets. While the city was smaller than Little Hope, it was much larger than I'd ever imagined.

"You're sure we're going the right way?" Preston called, lingering behind to smoke his cigarette.

"We're almost there!" Able to see our destination, Rodney grew even more intolerant of any hindrances.

It was all I could do to keep up in the loose rock and patchy dirt.

"Oh, shit!" I gasped. My feet slid so abruptly, I clattered to the ground. The sound of my fall was as dramatic as the act, embarrassingly enough.

"Are you alright?"

"Are you hurt?"

"Jo, are you okay?"

I sucked in a sharp breath between my teeth and turned my hands over. The thin stone that seemed unfortunately abundant in this area had filleted my skin. "I'm...okay," I grumbled, gradually sitting up.

"You're bleeding," Rodney argued.

"I said I'm okay." My minor injury was significantly less interesting to me than the ice sheet that forged its way between the shale, creating the perfect trap. "How is that possible?"

I tapped the ground for emphasis. Had we grown accustom to the cooler air? It didn't seem cold enough to freeze.

"That's odd." Rodney helped me up while Reggie and Preston methodically swept the area. I was careful to not let him touch my bare skin by placing my arm in his outstretched palm.

"It's magic," Preston resolved, pointing to where the ice ended in a perfect, unnatural line. "To protect their borders."

The magic left behind by the Mages all those years ago.

The wind picked up, whipping hard against my ears. Dragging the cloak around my arms, I scurried to keep up with the others. Conscientious of where I put my feet and how much weight was pressed upon them. Which would be a lot easier if it were day time.

Reggie squinted, but otherwise appeared unphased by the wind. Preston kept his chin up, hair tousled to one side. I wouldn't blame them if they gave up now. We were close enough to Carthage; they had met the terms of their commitment.

The dry foliage latched onto our clothes as we trudged through. The brittle limbs cracked and clicked, the leaves threatening to spring free.

Reggie craned his neck to survey the path in our wake, even after we'd long passed it.

"What is it?" I asked, suspecting his enhanced hearing picked up something.

"I'm unsure," he replied, focus on the shrub in question.

We didn't stop, fear of the unknown our motivation. If Carthage went to great lengths to enchant the landscape, then we couldn't predict what else might happen.

"It's freezing," I complained, pulling the cloak tighter. Hopefully, we arrived before we froze to death. We'd trekked this far to deliver Rodney to his family, it would be a shame to fail now.

"I think it feels nice." Reggie countered, as if we were in a little too efficiently air-conditioned building.

Meanwhile, I shivered hard enough my teeth clattered and Preston zipped his jacket. What about Rodney? His core temperature was already cold, but what was the limit for him?

"At least it isn't snowing," Preston remained oddly positive.

"Really?" I shivered. "I can't feel anything anymore."

The Archmage eyed me, unappreciative of my melancholy sarcasm. It was difficult to appreciate the positives when my nose threatened to fall off.

A cluster of trees ahead startled to life; Something must be in there. The wind couldn't do such a thing. Pale blue light glittered like fireflies, glowing brightly, then disappearing. Flecks decorated the tree as it swayed, shining between the needles and branches.

"We must be cautious," Reggie's rigid whisper cut through the wind. "They're sprites."

We'd studied the tiny creatures in school, but I struggled to recall much about them. Other than they possessed wings and glowed different colors depending on their region of origin.

Preston grunted in agreement. "Territorial little shits."

"They can be friendly." Reggie's brows arched, and he cocked his head.

Preston's crow's feet deepened with doubt. "But they aren't,"

Deciding to heed the warning, I rushed to Rodney's side. How did one defend themselves against a sprite?

"So long as we leave them alone and preserve their peace, they won't bother us," Reggie insisted.

I wasn't sure which man to believe. Reggie had such a positive outlook on nature, while Preston had a more blunt one.

"I doubt they're regular sprites," the Archmage reminded us. "This area is enchanted—"

"They're still living creatures with a mind all their own,"

"If they're entrusted to protect the city, they'll do whatever they can," I decided. These creatures worked to do as I had trained. Conceivably, they'd recognize Rodney as someone they protected.

Rocks and dirt slid down the steep hill, scattered by our fatigued steps. The loose debris avalanched into our path. Unable to keep his balance, Rodney careened forward. I rushed to latch onto his flailing arms, wobbling dangerously myself. One unforgiving stone could send us both catapulting to the city's doorstep, a beaten and bloody package to discard.

Or worse, disturb the sprites.

Together, we lowered to our knees, the ground biting into our flesh. How much longer did we have to go? While we could see it, Carthage seemed to be an unobtainable summit.

"Don't move." Reggie crouched beside us. His eyes were wide, complexion pale.

"What is it?" I hissed, tightening my hold on Rodney.

His head whipped to find what perplexed the Werewolf and breathed, "An elk!"

It took me a second to spot it—even with my enhanced eyesight—first glimpsing its eyes reflecting the moonlight. The massive creature stopped, its ears flicking in our direction.

"Are they aggressive?" I asked, knowing little about them.

Reggie elicited an unsettling noise. "They despise Werewolves."

"Fantastic," Preston grumbled, coming closer.

As he did so, rocks scattered, loud as firecrackers. The elk stretched its muscular neck and chuffed.

*Shit.*

Preston froze beside Reggie, feet inches from my sore knees. A gust of breath formed in front of the elk's nose and it stomped a hoof. While I wasn't experienced in elk body language, I had a feeling our fate didn't look so good.

It charged. It's pounding hoof-falls rendered my spine solid. I balled a fist in Rodney's sweater. We had to run.

"Keep very still," Preston instructed, cupping his hands together. His eyes swirled brighter, a vibrant yellow hue with the influx of produced magic.

The surrounding space rippled like a mirage. He opened his arms, expanding the apparition to encompass us.

"What are you doing?" Reggie whispered.

"Camouflage," Preston spoke softer, breath forming in the air.

My heart drummed against my chest hard enough it hurt. We sat here like bait, waiting for the elk to trample us.

Its long legs handled the landscape nimbly, climbing nearer in a matter of seconds. Regardless if it could see us, its beady eyes were trained to our exact position.

*Could it scent us?*

I squeezed Rodney's forearm, doing my best not to crane my neck to see the elk. Instead, my red fingers caught my attention, tingling from the pressure I used.

The animal huffed and tossed its head in apparent offense as it skidded to a halt mere inches from us. It could smell us. A few more steps and we would be found out.

Reggie gathered a handful of rocks at the toe of his boot. With the subtlest movement, they sailed high into the nearest tree row.

Tossing its head with more vigor, the elk stomped a heavy hoof. Spit flecks sprayed us, expelled from its snout.

*Fuck, it's going to kill us.* I tensed, prepared for impact.

A hum of many working wings filled the air, spooking the elk to trample to safety. Darts of light chased after the retreating beast, targeting his thrashing antlers.

*We're so dead.*

We sprang to our feet, the trees alive with luminous sprites. Identical to hornets defending their hive, a swarm assembled.

"Shit!" Preston placed an insistent palm in the small of my back.

Doing the same to Rodney, we broke into an uncoordinated run. Rocks and debris scattered ahead, guiding our way down. We gained no ground; the sprites firing their natural magic upon us. Tiny icicles punctured my skin like arrows, stinging similar to paper cuts, and destroyed my clothes.

Blasts of sapphire magic brought the illusion icy flame burned my frostbitten skin.

Holding a spread palm over a shoulder, Preston conjured a wind gust to resist the sprites. The buzz of their wings ceased intermittently as they swiftly resumed pursuit.

The men in front easily scaled a fallen log, stepping over it without pause. Securing my waistline, I begged my short legs to not fail me. Maintaining momentum, I jumped over the log. On the other side, I slid on the rocks like a mini skateboard.

My leg muscles burned, but I couldn't stop.

Preston's pace slowed as he continued to push gusts at the sprites. He delivered in quick succession, so they struggled to keep to the air.

What could we do to get them to quit?

Tree limbs clawed our heads, bowing in the breeze that seemed to get worse the further we descended. It was easier for me to dodge them, while the others obtained scratches and bruised skulls.

No wonder Carthage stayed hidden so well.

Reggie batted the branches, launching a few sprites like he hit a home-run.

"Fuck!" Preston spat. "This weather makes casting a bitch!"

My fingers ached from exposure, I could only imagine how his felt.

"Don't give up now!" Reggie demanded.

"Didn't plan on it! I just wish I could conjure something more helpful."

Despite his complaints, we increased the space between us and the sprites with nature's assistance.

"They're going to leave us alone!" I cheered.

Tired from the gusts and trees, their flight travel slowed and their attacks ceased.

"I wouldn't celebrate yet," Reggie cautioned.

The sprites dispersed, their light disappearing into the trees. The hair on the nape of my neck stood straight and my numb fingertips tingled. They didn't retreat from us; they ran from something else.

A skeleton rattling groan echoed from the treetops, something enormous stirred nearby. Heads lifted to scan the horizon, we searched for the source. As if the horizon itself separated, a piece lumbered free.

Reggie gestured for Rodney and me to proceed, the city lights near enough to skew our visibility in the night.

Its tree-like antlers and great shoulders stood out against the night sky, stars hidden behind their mass. Either the ground quaked under its steps or my knees did with fear.

"What is it?" I whispered, moving hesitantly.

"Massive." His eyes widened.

It got bigger the nearer it grew—as tall as Preston's apartment complex. Its shoulders could vaguely be distinguished from its snow-matted mane, small, beady white eyes in the depths of its equine shaped head.

Every instinct I possessed instructed me to flee.

"It's a kalento," Preston supplied.

Something mythical, it must be rare. We'd never covered such a creature at the institute. Probably because no amount of training they provided could prepare us for combat against something of its magnitude. Even between the four of us, we wouldn't stand a chance.

"A product of dark magic," Rodney muttered so no one else heard.

Reggie thrust a finger at Carthage. "Help them get there. I'll keep it distracted."

Unable to turn our backs on the beast—with claws as long as my arm—Rodney and I fled while watching from our peripheral. A blue flash only briefly caught my attention as Reggie turned wolf.

Preston stopped to witness the Werewolf battle with the eerie creature.

Why had something so monstrous not stormed the city for food?

It lobbed stones at Reggie with enough force dirt and ice chipped into the air. Cutting from side to side, the wolf stayed light on his feet. While the distraction worked well, the boulders fell closer to Reggie with each pitch.

He'd throw his hindquarters into the air, whipping aside in anticipation. Fear shined bright in his eyes, but he kept his vow.

Preston pinched his lips, gesturing for us to continue. "He's going to get himself killed."

"It's too dangerous!" I exclaimed, stopping to watch him rush to Reggie's aid. "Preston!"

*They're both going to get killed.*

Hands lifted, he redirected some flying boulders to their pitcher. A guttural bellow echoed through the mountainside, shaking the trees and stirring the wildlife. Somehow, I doubted it hurt and instead upset the creature more.

Storming the pair, the kalento threw the stone hunks with more force. They hit the ground so hard they submerged in the dirt by several feet. It no longer lingered on the horizon, intent on crushing us.

"Jo, come on!" Rodney hadn't stopped. Several yards ahead, he neared the city limits.

My duty was to protect and deliver my Vampire to safety. But what about Preston and Reggie? Nearly strangers to us, they still threw themselves into danger without hesitation.

*For us.*

Reggie narrowly dodged the creature's swinging arms as a tree splintered under the mercy of its razor-sharp claws. They stood no chance, despite how slowly it moved.

I couldn't let them do this alone.

"Get to the city and find help!" I ordered, turning back.

Rushing to join Preston, I wracked my brain for an attack method. Any distraction tactic to give them time to get away. By then, hopefully, Rodney would find help.

"What are you doing?" Preston shouted.

"I can't let you do this—"

A boulder hit the ground nearest Preston, cascading enough debris to bury him.

"No!" I screamed. A few stones pelted my chest, feeling like daggers in the cold. Retracting my arms into my torso to not only soothe my pain, but catch my heart as it fell into the bottom of my stomach.

A bellow much louder and terrifying than mine shook the trees, and the creature's sights locked upon me.

*Shit.*

Swiveling to run, I shouted at Rodney who hadn't moved, "Go!"

The kalento's steps shook the ground, driving my trembling legs faster.

Reggie barked erratically, charging the creature's feet.

*We're goners.*

Preston's buried alive, Reggie was destined to be toe jam, and I would suffer a similar fate.

An uprooted tree sailed through the air, spinning like a baton. I threw my arms over my head and weaved in hopes to avoid an untimely death. The pointed end of the tree staked into the ground, scattering a wreckage tidal wave over me.

Closing my mouth on a scream, I shook my arms clean of bark chips.

A set of headlights flipped on, temporarily blinding us. Shielding our eyes, we slowed to a stop.

How long had they been watching us?

"Help!" Rodney cried, waving his arms in the air.

My heart leapt into my throat as the pickup truck rolled toward us. *Not fast enough.*

Reggie yelped, the kalento uninterested in the truck and instead concentrated on using him as a kickball. The wolf tumbled ahead of the creature's enormous feet, splayed out once he collided with a partially submerged boulder.

From here, it was difficult to see if the wolf's chest still expanded for air. Had the impact killed him? My nails dug into my palm as I fought the urge to run to him.

"Come on, Reggie!" I squeaked. I was mistaken. They weren't strangers. Quicker than I could've ever anticipated, they'd become friends to us.

We'd lost enough friends. I couldn't lose another.

He lifted his head to the kalento lumbering nearer.

"Get up." I pled.

With great work, he got his paws beneath him once more. Though his shoulders quaked and his head hung.

Rodney stiffened as the truck stopped and the passenger window lowered. A pair of officers sat on the inside, both clad in starchy black uniforms marked with reflective, silver-stitched badges.

"Hello," their greeting sounded silly after what we'd endured.

"Can you help us?" Rodney's inquiry delivered more like an order. "We seek sanctuary in Carthage."

The Vampire in the passenger seat squinted, stroking his thick brown mustache, while the driver watched Reggie race for survival.

*Seriously? Couldn't they hurry!*

"Where are you from?"

"Bathory,"

The passenger Vampire's eyes rounded, whipping in his seat to discuss with the driver. Both sprang from the vehicle, wielding staffs charged by magic. They emitted an electrical pulse, blue static bundled at one end. They waved the staffs in the air, calling out to the creature.

*Carthage has a terrifying guard dog.*

The kalento groaned and tossed its head similar to the elk. Eventually, it ceased its chase, and Reggie limped to join us, panting.

He slowed in his travels to dig at the mound where Preston disappeared.

I held my breath, waiting to see the shock of golden brown hair emerge, and stepped in their direction, fearful the dirt had suffocated him.

"You guys must've really upset it. Usually, it doesn't take that long to call off," one officer explained. I wasn't sure which, because I couldn't look away. Not until I saw Preston.

He'd fought too hard for all of us. He had to be okay. So he could see his mother again—

A dusty arm sprang free first, then the Archmage coughed. Relief wobbled my knees, and I pressed my icy fingers to my lips. We'd made it.

Using Reggie for support, he got to his feet. A plume of dust whipped around them, billowing in the wind. I'd never be able to repay them for everything they'd done.

Officers still shouting, the kalento's shoulders slumped, and it retreated into the landscape.

"Get in the truck," the mustached officer instructed.

He opened the back door for Rodney and me to get in. Now certain the pair would be okay, I did as instructed. Leaning around my Vampire, I held my fingers up to the air from the truck's vents. The sudden heat hurt as circulation returned to my digits.

"What did you mean by a 'product of dark magic'?" I asked, sinking into the stiff leather seat.

"When I was thirteen, I was really into reading about unique mythical creatures. A kalento is what happens when magic is used by many Sorcerers to do evil. It doesn't happen often because just the right amount of magic has to be used and, if my understanding is correct, they have to be trying to create a creature." Rodney craned his neck to see the officers. "I never read anything about them being able to be controlled. They're usually mindless monsters intent on laying waste to all that approach in the name of protecting the Mythos. Not people, but the land itself."

"Sounds like the perfect guardian for a hidden city," I confessed.

"Yeah. I'd just like to know how they managed to control it."

"I suppose anything is possible with magic."

Having to first locate his backpack and transition into his human form, Reggie fell behind. Preston stopped within the headlights' beam and swiped at his clothes to knock loose any residual dirt from his temporary grave.

My stomach clenched. *We could've lost them.*

The officers directed the battered duo to the truck bed, and I pivoted in my seat, fist lifted to pound on the window.

Rodney placed his hand over the glass where I intended to knock. "Don't,"

I jerked my hand away, fearful my tainted skin would harm him. "They shouldn't have to sit back there."

They'd continue to freeze!

"They'll be fine," Rodney assured.

I'm sure they would, but it was no way to treat them after what they'd done for us. We should sit back there and them in here to show our gratitude.

Their shoulders tightened abrasively as they climbed aboard.

Neither officer waited and joined us in the cab.

"You two are Bathory students?" the driver inquired, shifting the truck into gear.

"Yes, sir," Rodney answered.

"Who are your friends?" The officer peered in the rearview mirror at the men in the truck bed.

"They offered to help us," I replied. Even if it's their job, I didn't appreciate them prying.

"Per city ordinance, we'll have to escort you all to the station for questioning."

"Kinda figured," Rodney grumbled.

I watched out the window, the kalento melting into the distant horizon once more. To await its next unsuspecting prey as part of the tree line. I'd never forget its claws and the way the ground shuddered when it walked.

"What was that?"

"Carthage's guardian," the officer explained. "It kills or eats anyone, except Vampires, who dare to cross our borders."

"What about those who help the Vampires?"

"That's what the staffs are for. They're like magical cattle prods. Probably the only thing that can hurt the brute."

"Had you waited any longer, it would've killed us!"

"But we didn't," the officer remained blunt. "Our job is to protect the city. In today's world, you can't be too careful."

The air pressurized, and the temperature rose as the city revealed itself. Magic had been briefly touched in our education, including how some cities shielded themselves from the outside world. This one appeared to be programmed to unveil itself to Vampires and direct allies to their race, no one else.

Shops lined the curbs, Vampires and their Protectors bustling about the businesses. No one noticed us as we parked less than a hundred feet from them. The station was a small building nearly swallowed by the surrounding nature. Judging by its unkempt state, they rarely experienced visitors like us.

Upon exiting the vehicle, the officers wasted no time cuffing Preston. Reggie bled enough from his face and arm, they had him escorted to the emergency care unit of the building by a Vampire sitting at the front desk with her feet propped up.

"Are these necessary?" Preston held up his wrists, bound in plastic ties.

"Until you're cleared." The officer guided him to a cell.

A front desk divided the tiny sitting area from the singular cell and a 'secure interview room' as the door placard said.

"Lucky me." Preston hunched his shoulders and hung his head back. Blood spatters collected at the edge of his frown and jawline. Layers of dirt darkened his brows and added significant contrast to the dry grass in his wavy locks.

My stomach soured, remembering I'd planned to ditch him before now. Which would've robbed me of the opportunity to get to know such a selfless person.

Rodney and I were seated in the secure interview room across the table from the officer with a mustache. From here, we had the perfect view of the cell and Preston. The younger officer guided him to stand in front of the bars.

"Please stand with your arms and legs apart," he instructed, sliding his hands over Preston, working from one end of his body to the other.

He bit the inside of his cheek, fighting with an arrogant smile while the officer worked. "Watch out for my wand."

The officer's head whipped to first assess Preston, then his colleague in the office with us. "Spellcasters don't have wands...Do they?"

Groaning in answer, the officer with us got up to close the door on the chaos in the hall.

I watched Preston until I couldn't and he delivered an ornery wink just for me.

Struggling with a smile, I lowered my face to the table. The Archmage never ceased to amaze me with his many personality traits. His charm the deepest one.

"How were you able to find the city?" The officer retrieved a notepad from his pocket.

While he did so, Rodney set the map on the table and retracted his hands as if the parchment might combust. The officer collected the map, gaze lingering on us as he unrolled it. I bounced my knee, worried Beau would be angry we surrendered the item to someone other than him. Yet, it couldn't be the worst-case scenario, considering it was now in the city's possession.

"May I have your names?"

"Rodney—"

"Harper?" the officer guessed.

Rodney dipped his head.

"The mayor's kid." He turned to me. "And you are?"

Rodney's head whipped to me, and I stiffened. I'd never told him Preston had been right. I imagined he'd be delighted to know he was once again correct.

"Josephine Catherine. I don't know my full name."

"Pity." He recorded my information. "I'll direct you kids to the mayor from here. Once we clear your friends."

"They're good men," I insisted.

The officer's brows rose. "One's a Spellcaster, sweetie."

"Doesn't mean he's a bad guy! You can't condemn an entire race over what some have done."

Rodney's boot collided with mine, like a figurative hammer nailing my stupidity to the outside of my body. Like I hadn't done enough to shame myself. They were right to be concerned.

"You're sure neither one coerced you into leading them to Carthage?"

"I'd swear my life on it,"

The officer scribbled on his pad, then faced Rodney. "What about you? You're quiet."

Rodney's lavender irises turned gray. "They have proven to be faithful allies."

The officer expelled an amused breath. "Definitely the mayor's kid."

His chair screeched as he rose. "I'll grab some paperwork for you to fill out, then we'll shuttle you to the mayor. If he finds out you're in our custody long, he'll have our jobs."

I winced as the door closed; the sound solidifying our accomplishments.

We'd made it to Carthage and would soon be taken to Rodney's family. Who, from the sound of it, were well-known people eager to have their son back. I'd be a liar if I didn't say it hurt not to have a family of my own who would be elated I lived.

But that didn't matter. I had a job to do.

The paperwork wasn't much. They expected a recount of how we'd gotten to the city. On paper, it appeared a lot simpler. Especially when Preston's version had to be reiterated to the officers verbally across the hall. Every time they doubted him, my nails dug deeper into my palms.

They accused him of coercing us as well as lying to infiltrate the city. Just as we had, they found it hard to believe a Sorcerer existed who didn't have a motive to harm Vampires.

We were released from the station, meeting Preston and Reggie outside with a chaperone.

Rodney cast his faint grin on me. It had been some time since I'd seen him do so, and it triggered one from me as well.

"What?" I whispered, both to keep our conversation private and to not disturb Preston and Reggie's exchange about the many businesses ahead. It was odd to see the two getting along so well. Saving one another's lives must've made them push aside their animosity.

"You won't believe it." Rodney's lips parted into a smile. "While you were gone, I fought."

I tensed, stopping myself from giving him a proud hug in case my skin would still hurt him. "I do believe it!"

"It was amazing. I was against one Sorceress. Reggie guided me and told me what to do. I killed her all by myself. I felt so strong and fast—more than ever!"

I remembered my first real fight, it had been Rodney's first, too.

*An upperclassman cornered him in the hall and knocked his books from his hands. He'd held his head high, unafraid of the bully who wanted his homework done for him. When Rodney refused, the bully got angry. In self-defense, he raised his fists. The poor Vampire hadn't gotten to swing. The upperclassman clocked him good, dropping him to the ground.*

*Fury welled inside me, and I pushed my way through the crowd to attack the fellow Protector. I overpowered him, blacking his eye and busting his lip.*

*Having heard the commotion, a swarm of professors separated us, hauling the bully and me to the dean's office. Rodney was taken to the nurse—again.*

"I'm proud of you!" I squeezed his shoulder, suppressing the conflicted part of me. What if he got hurt? I wouldn't be there to provide him blood to heal and doubted the others would've done such a service for him. "I'm glad I gave you that knife."

I didn't sound glad.

I turned abruptly to watch an officer park their SUV along the curb to shuttle us. But stopped short, caught by the familiar faces staring at me. Their eyes still twinkled, unlike the last time we'd seen them—when they'd turned to stone.

My breath trembled, and I squeezed the necklace charm until it hurt. I'd done my job to ensure Rodney didn't end up on the billboard of missing Bathory students. A sob squeezed out of me. The weight of guilt that we'd survived and they hadn't, suddenly too heavy to bear.

How many families wouldn't get to be reunited with their children—but the *mayor* would.

"There's Zoon." Rodney pointed with his long, pale finger. He tore the poster of Zoon's class photo, demographics, and the police station's contact information from the billboard, tears distorting his cloudy gray irises.

"Tresillian?" I murmured. A dramatic last name, just like he'd always hoped for.

Time stopped.

Our best friend's enormous grin jumped from the stationary clutched in Rodney's trembling hand. I could still hear his laugh as we stood in line to have our pictures taken for our records. Never expecting they'd be used for this.

"Alright, kids. Let's go." The officer's serenely peppy voice sliced through the memory like a guillotine.

*He's gone and life goes on.*

Rodney and I climbed into the vehicle first, Preston and Reggie held back by the officer.

"My boss has asked me to remind you two, you're the Harper's guests. This means you will be watched under a no tolerance policy, due to the state of the situation. Under no conditions will the use of magic or shapeshifting be permitted. *Any* slip ups and it's jail for you both."

"Sounds pretty unjust to condemn us without first proving we're guilty," Preston remarked.

"Save it for someone who cares, Spellcaster,"

Reggie and Preston grimaced as they settled into the vehicle with us. I loathed how they were treated. We wouldn't be here without them. Wasn't that reason enough to trust them?

As we shifted onto the road, I leaned to gently touch Reggie's hand. Cleaned and sanitized at the station, the slight cuts and bruises on his face no longer hid behind a layer of dirt and blood.

"Are you alright?"

He cast a brilliant smile and lifted his arm encompassed in a sling. "A little banged up, but the big beastie wasn't so bad. Kinda reminded me of the silver wolves, mindless and lethal."

Preston snorted. "You're lucky to be alive."

"As are you!"

"Thank you." I spoke loud enough to stop them from arguing. "Rodney and I couldn't have made it without you." While confident in my abilities to fumble my way through it, they'd rendered the process much more bearable with laughs and infinite knowledge I could never match.

"Of course, Love."

"I'd do it again," Reggie insisted. His gaze dropped to his arm. "After a good long visit at home. I miss my village."

I was sure his village missed him. His incredible bravery and selflessness couldn't go unnoticed anywhere. What had I done to deserve such incredible friends from complete strangers?

# WELCOME
## CHAPTER 12

THE CAPITOL IN THE heart of the city had beautiful stone architecture that hid the moon from sight. Not an ounce of craftsmanship went wasted. The Vampires had a taste for the elite life. The buildings were an older style—not as old as Luxor. But the pitched roofs, turrets, and decorative trim were more common a hundred years ago.

Enamored, we climbed the stairs to pass through the gold plated doors. Rodney abruptly stopped, twirling to pin me with his wild eyes.

"What's wrong?" I asked, gripping his shoulders.

The shadow hadn't left his face since we'd seen Zoon's poster. Nor did the lingering tears in his eyes. "What if they hate me?"

They couldn't. They're his parents.

I rolled my eyes. "They've searched for you—"

"They don't know me—"

"They're your family, which is more than some people have." I reminded him. At least he had someone to call a family. While perhaps he shouldn't fall into their arms, wouldn't he be eager to at least know them? I'd give anything to meet my parents. "Come on."

I bypassed him to follow Preston and Reggie inside.

Head hung, he entered the building last.

A woman with blonde curly hair down her shoulders sat behind a marble desk. Her blue eyes pierced into us as we slowed to a halt in the lobby, smelling of polish. We didn't have to introduce ourselves. Upon sight of Rodney, faster than comprehensible, she streaked across the hall to tap on a glossy walnut door.

It swung open and a tall, sturdy Vampire with salt and pepper hair raced out. He approached us in a trance. Their genetic similarities made it impossible to suspect him to be anyone but Rodney's father.

"H-hello," I stuttered.

Rodney slid his hand into mine and squeezed tight. I had to admit. Meeting his family was a little more intimidating than I'd imagined.

Realization struck; his skin didn't boil off as I'd feared. My gaze flicked to him and my heart thrummed. Could he drink from me?

"Ashley, call my wife and tell her our son is home!" Mr. Harper instructed the woman behind the desk.

She did as she was told without objection, shuffling supplies on her desk.

Mr. Harper's eyes never left Rodney, his irises swirling with pink, lavender, and gray. He reached to shake his son's hand, the briefest indicator of tears in his eyes. "I can't believe it," his voice was gravelly and warm. "My son...I should've known you had it in you to be a survivor! You are a Harper,"

A smile wavered across Rodney's lips, and his gaze drifted to me. I accepted the lack of credit. This man was more interested in his son's survival, rather than the details of how it came to be.

Mr. Harper pulled Rodney in for an awkward hug. "My son, a hero."

I grimaced. We had done nothing heroic. We'd survived.

"I'd like you to meet Josie." Rodney stepped in reverse to pull me forward. "I wouldn't be here without her,"

Mr. Harper gathered my hand to kiss my knuckles. "I owe you a great debt, dear girl."

I gave him a small smile. "It was my duty, Mr. Harper,"

He waved a hand in the air. "Call me Burke,"

*I would call him Mr. Harper.*

Rodney introduced Preston and Reggie, gesturing to each one as he did so. Mr. Harper shook their hands, thanking them for their service. Though I did note the shift in his eyes as he reached for Preston. His irises turned coal black and his practiced smile degraded.

"I'll have a car brought to chauffeur you to our home. I'm sure you all need a good meal and rest. My wife will be elated to meet you all."

*Rodney's mother! He had a mother.*

I bit my bottom lip to keep it from quivering as another pang of jealousy accumulated. Wishing it were me in his place, even if it made me selfish to do so. I would never experience the sense of belonging to something bigger. The love of a family. Though I often pretended to be related to the larger, well known Protector family—the Deskovichs. Any member of their family was destined to be great, and I hoped to measure to their reputation.

Ushered out the door to a limo along the curb, the driver held a door for us to pile in. I sat by Rodney, clutching his hand—to keep reality set.

Reggie waited to get in last once he'd assessed how to fold enough to sit. His long legs stretched across the interior, shrinking the elongated vehicle.

The door clicked shut behind us and the limo set into motion. I gripped the seat beneath me in both hands to settle my stomach, still unused to car travel.

"It seems the Harper's are over the moon to have their little batling home." Preston crooked a brow and an ornery grin lit up his face.

"Batling?" Reggie raised a brow, too.

"The gallant *hero*," Preston continued.

"Shut up," Rodney bit out. Embarrassment turned his irises pink, and he directed his face to his lap.

It was a quiet ride across town, maybe fifteen minutes until we slowed at an elaborate wrought-iron fence encircling a mansion and its property.

"Wow," I breathed.

A teardrop drive led around a beautiful stone fountain and well-groomed shrubbery encompassed the intricate wrap-around porch. Sweeping up into the gabled roof and heavily curtained bay windows, towers on both sides of the mansion.

"Hm." Reggie motioned towards a plaque on the gate—'No Dogs Allowed.' "Suppose I'll have to stay in the car then."

I clapped a hand over my mouth, only for my laugh to come out in an unattractive snort.

Reggie seemed to grow as he basked in his comedic success.

"As if you have the choice to get out," Preston added, eyes twinkling with laughter. "It's a wonder you fit in the first place."

A man and a woman waited on the porch. The petite woman had fine lines etched in her face, suggesting she was quite old for a Vampire. Gray streaked her dark-colored hair, cropped short around her ears.

I was the first one out of the limo, relieved to put my feet on the ground. While cars were convenient, they would take some time to get used to.

"Next time, I think I'll walk." Reggie shared my disposition. The low vehicle made it quite a feat for him to get out, and his head thumped on the car's roof as he stood.

Preston's lips curled in a bemused smile he hid behind a hand, stroking his untamed beard.

He was much faster than I. My grin remained on full display for Reggie to scowl at.

Mrs. Harper shrieked and ran to sling her arms about Rodney's shoulders. He swayed under her weight, unprepared for the ambush.

"My baby boy," she sobbed, stepping back to view her son. She had to swipe her tears away with an embroidered handkerchief. "I'm so glad you made it."

Rodney smiled awkwardly through her affection. The attention foreign to him after years of stoic toleration by our educators.

She sniffled and dabbed at her lavender eyes. "I'm so sorry, I'm being rude. Introduce me to your friends."

He pulled me tight against his side and I did my best not to resist the gesture. "This is Josie. She has protected me nearly my whole life. She's the reason I'm still alive."

"Oh!" Mrs. Harper wailed. She pulled me into a vise-tight hug, then held me at arm's length. "The reward for returning my son to us will never be enough to thank you for what you've done."

*Reward?*

"This is Reggie and Preston. They helped us along our expedition." Rodney tossed a hand in their direction. As if they weren't the whole reason we'd made it here safely.

Mrs. Harper hugged both men and thanked them. Gushing over their chivalry.

I tuned out, more interested in the man on the porch.

His taupe-colored eyes already examined me from head to toe. He had black hair, cropped close to his head in a crew cut, which intensified his sharp jawline and serious expression. His built physique told me all I needed to know to declare him a *Protector*.

A glimmer of bemusement sparkled in his eyes as I squirmed. Knowing he was tearing me apart like Kade would during class.

"Oh." Mrs. Harper glided to stand on the porch steps. "This is Issak Deskovich, Lead Protector here. You'll see him lurking about." She laughed and waved a hand in the air. "Now, come on in. Let's get you cleaned up for supper. Josie, Issak can show you to the Protector's Annex."

This, potentially, was my boss—*a Deskovich*. He appeared fairly critical—*of course he is, he's a freaking Deskovich*. I'd have to be on my best game to prove myself worthy to protect Rodney—If I hadn't already done so by surviving a tragedy.

Rodney squeezed my hand one last time as we separated. I hoped he would get over his discomfort soon. This was his family. Yes, they were strangers, but he must possess some hereditary compassion towards them. At least, I'd always imagined it would be so when one possessed a family.

Mrs. Harper caught Rodney's arm and dragged him inside, babbling along the way.

Behind them, Reggie and Preston exchanged a hesitant glance, out of place in this strange debacle.

Nonchalantly, Preston's gaze slid past Reggie to me. The warmth in his copper eyes elicited a wave of awareness within me.

*We succeeded.* We'd brought Rodney home.

Issak glided down the steps to guide me behind the house to a smaller manor built with as much integrity as the rest of the estate.

He opened the door for me to enter after I finished ogling.

"This is where you'll sleep while you're here." Issak gestured to the small living room. Dust coated every surface, and the furniture showed no signs of obvious wear. Down a short hallway were the bedrooms, all with minimal decorations and possessions.

Like Bathory, the decor was simple and lacked character—a quality the Vampire community seemed to associate with Protectors. We truly didn't have time to live our own lives, especially when stationed over the mayor's family.

First providing black skinny jeans and a black crew neck sweatshirt, he left me to bathe.

I appreciated my tanned skin while dressing, having always been pale—thankfully a shade less translucent than the Vampires. Then folded my shredded clothes, the cloak last of all. I should let Preston destroy it, as promised. Once I acquired an additional layer to withstand the cold. While Carthage was warmer than the climate they'd created with magic, winter was here.

Issak waited in the living room, perched on a coffee table. He watched me with the same practiced intensity we'd learned at the institute. Searching for my weaknesses and any other condemning traits I may carry. Hoping he had no intent to question me, I pretended not to notice and passed him to hover near the door, impatient to rejoin my friends.

"You're well known in the Mythos." His stare bored into mine. "The whole world knows what you've done for the Vampire community."

I frowned. "It's what we're trained to do."

Issak snorted. "It's something your classmates couldn't achieve."

"You seem to know an awful lot about me,"

"I attended the same school." His shoulders broadened. "It isn't easy to forget how few Protectors took their occupations seriously."

The blood left my face, and I looked away from Issak. While his observation may be true—one I shared not so long ago—they hadn't deserved death. Many of them were kids, and none of us had any idea what the real world was like. Of course, they wouldn't take being a Protector seriously.

"Who was your mentor?" Issak stopped me from spiraling.

"Kade,"

A nostalgic gleam caught in his eye, and he folded his arms. "He was a young mentor, wasn't he?"

*He knew Kade.*

I nodded. "He was like a big brother to me,"

"He did a good job,"

"I couldn't have asked for a better teacher." No one could have prepared me for the way our lives changed. Kade equipped me as best he could for the challenging lifestyle of a terminally ill Vampire. He couldn't have known what the Veiled Army had planned.

"Are you and the Harper's son close?" Issak asked. "I could tell from the way he held onto you he cares for you."

I hardened my gaze on his. "He's my best friend,"

"Does he understand you're only friends?"

I swallowed the mud in my throat. Was this a test? Protectors and Vampires weren't supposed to have relationships, especially if they were already engaged in a career contract.

The first time I'd ever seen Rodney look at me like the world spun in my palms, he'd fallen off the swing at recess, knocking the wind out of him. I'd rushed to hold his hand until he recovered his breath and helped him to his feet.

His lavender eyes met mine with confusion at first. He wasn't used to his peers' help. Usually, no one except staff members cared. I'd noticed long before we were paired up. It didn't set well with me and I'd decided not to watch him suffer alone anymore.

Once understanding set in, Rodney's expression became one of wonder and a slow smile creased his lips.

I awkwardly returned the gesture and invited him to play on the seesaw.

*Best friends ever since.*

Until we made room for Zoon, who Rodney befriended whilst in the dean's office. I often suspected Zoon saw Rodney as an opportunity to assist in his endeavors to avoid detention. Whether via pity for having an invalid in his company or he assumed Rodney had inside knowledge on how to dodge getting caught.

Regardless, we became an inseparable trio.

"I've done all I can to protect him since the third grade," I explained, deciding it was a test. "I suppose when you've been the lightning rod for someone for so long, feelings are bound to surface."

"So, it's complicated?" Issak crooked a grin.

"I suppose you could define it that way." I pinched my lips together and squeezed the necklace charm. Rodney had feelings and I did not. That's all.

This Protector was good. I could learn a lot from him. He reminded me of Kade, which tore open a wound in my soul that would likely never heal.

"Tell me more about the Vampire,"

I swiped my thumb over the thorns along the dagger charm. "He is sick, as I'm sure you know?"

Issak nodded. "Enough so they held him back a year so he could build his strength,"

Maybe all of his information wasn't from attending Bathory. Did every Vampire family have the same access to their children at the institute? And why weren't they more concerned about his health?

"Doesn't mean he isn't strong minded." I smiled, my chest squeezing. Our school days felt like such a long time ago. "He'd be a great lawyer."

Issak rolled his eyes. "Articulate mandibles run in this family. They're all politicians."

I genuinely laughed, and my posture eased. It had been some time since I let my guard down. We were finally in a place we could do so, where a Sorcerer didn't wait around every corner.

"He spent a lot of time in the nurse's office, as well as the administrator's," I explained. "While I often found myself disciplined there, Rodney discovered new ways to avoid such punishments,"

"Diplomatic,"

I nodded, and the smile vanished. We'd spent twenty-one years in the institute and had little to show for it. Graduation stolen from us, as well as any friendships we'd taken time to build.

I brushed the tears that snuck free with the back of my hand.

Kade taught me how to fight once I could walk. But he was more to me than a teacher. He didn't treat me with the same indifference the others did. He cared.

He made it known when I experienced difficult emotions and obstacles, I could seek him out. He could always be found at his desk in his office reviewing sparring rosters—Something I often begged him to let me help with. Of course, he denied and tucked them away to give me his full attention.

I had eagerly awaited the day I'd get to shake his hand and leave the campus doors a certified Protector. Now...now I'd never get to.

Issak squeezed my shoulder. "We better get inside; we'll be late to dinner."

The dining room wasn't far from the entry hall, through a set of French doors reflecting the house entrance. It was large enough to hold a massive table beneath a crystal chandelier, a buffet table adorning a tea set, and an entrance to the kitchen.

Everyone already seated, the three Vampires sipped from black crystal chalices. Issak left me at the doorway, and I sat at Rodney's side. He was rigid as a plank, his fists rested in his lap.

Across the table, Preston and Reggie squirmed in their seats, uncomfortable in the semiformal setting. Especially out of place in their ratty clothes, despite how much primping they'd attempted beforehand. Only so much hand soap could wash away the blood and dirt embedded in their clothes.

"Josie?" Mrs. Harper called to me from the head of the table. "Rodney told us some of the cutest stories about you two and your friend. Zoon? Was it?"

Rodney's arm snapped out to lace his fingers with mine, as if I were the last lifeline to bring him ashore. Slate stalactites encroached on his sad, lavender irises and the tendons in his jaw flexed restlessly.

I squeezed his hand until his cool palm no longer felt so cold and he blinked. Realizing the entire room stared at him, waiting for him to acknowledge Mrs. Harper.

"Yeah. Zoon." His lips wavered as he stretched them into a painful smile, one that seemed to get stuck at his fangs. No matter how much time passed, it would never become easier to talk about Zoon.

The tension shifted as a server entered from the kitchen to deliver food for those of us who ate. My stomach growled at the glazed salmon, garlic roasted potatoes, and steamed mixed vegetables.

"It's a pity you weren't able to graduate this year," Mr. Harper said, his chalice raised. "We'll have to see about getting you a certificate, under the circumstances."

I sipped water to wash down the swell of emotion in my throat. Graduation was something I'd looked forward to for a long time. The day we'd finally get our certifications and enter the job market. No more training on lifeless dummies, no more lectures from a grouchy Space Pixie—just living.

Rodney placed a roll from the basket in the center of the table on my plate. Leaning so he could harshly whisper in my ear. "How was your visit with Issak?"

*Holy Mythos.*

He's going to start a fight here? In front of his parents?

"Refreshing." I lifted my fork to my mouth. "He seems well qualified."

*Of course, he's qualified.* Why else would he be the Lead Protector for the mayor?

Rodney glowered into his blood chalice. "He seemed rather interested in your qualifications."

*As he should be!*

Reggie pounded on his chest, having inhaled a piece of food.

Issak *should* want to know if I was qualified to protect Rodney. Whatever the tyrannical Vampire was trying to insinuate was *wrong*.

Mrs. Harper cleared her throat, voice stern, "Issak graduated top of his class fourteen years ago. I'm surprised you didn't know him."

The air in the room shifted, dense thanks to Rodney establishing his jealousy as a public affair. The household held Issak in high regard and their son—who slouched in his seat to pout—tattered the man's image after knowing him a short time.

I smiled politely. "The school's rather big, it's hard to know everyone. Especially when you're just a kid."

"Right you are," Mrs. Harper agreed, lowering her quaint hands to the tabletop. "Well, I've arranged for fresh clothes to be delivered tomorrow for you gentlemen. I apologize for not having something suitable on hand. I'm sure you are more than ready to retire your travel clothes."

Reggie creased his eyes in a gesture of thanks for the hospitality as he shoveled food into his mouth. Covered in filth didn't strike me as uncommon for a Werewolf. Though it probably irked Mrs. Harper's tendency toward polished cleanliness.

Preston didn't appear to hear her, his head bowed over his plate while he ate. A bat fluttered in my stomach, stirring a cloud of worry.

Mrs. Harper continued, "You are welcome to stay here in our home. There are beds prepared upstairs for the gentlemen and, Josie, I had Issak select a Protector's suite for you."

The bat in my stomach dropped, smothering my appetite.

*Protector's suite?*

I hadn't slept alone in *weeks*. In fact, I wasn't too sure I could anymore. How would I know Rodney was safe?

Or Preston?

Or Reggie?

Rodney tensed beside me.

"What's gotten into you?" I whispered, bouncing my leg off his.

"Issak gives me the creeps, I don't want you alone with him." His harsh whisper teetered on the edge of full volume.

Thankful Reggie recounted our journey to Mrs. Harper, I turned to hiss at him, "He's the household Protector. He wanted intel on you—"

"He wanted to know more about you, it has nothing to do with me,"

"I forgot you were there to hear our conversation," I bit out. Issak had done nothing suspicious. "Quit acting jealous!"

Rodney touched his tongue to a fang and slouched. His dark glare cast from Issak to Preston, who finally looked up from his plate to return the favor. Promptly, the Vampire dropped his head into his lap.

Mr. Harper licked his lips clear of blood. "Tell me, what is it you two gents do? Anything interesting?"

"Not sure I'd call it interesting." Preston poked the food on his plate. "I retired from the military some twenty years ago or so."

He'd never answered my question about the wards over his apartment. I suppose war trauma was a valid reason to have them.

Mr. Harper's black brows pulled together. "Retirement?"

"Yessir." Preston sipped from his water. "After two centuries of traveling the world, I landed in a mundane city called Little Hope."

The Archmage's history didn't appear to sit well with Mr. Harper, the gears whirling in his kaleidoscope irises.

Reggie pushed his plate away and leaned over the table to obtain Mr. Harper's attention. "I'm a second generation board member in my village's government."

Mr. Harper perked up in his seat. "Which village?"

"Welch. It isn't far from here."

"Oh, damn." Mr. Harper lifted his buzzing phone from his coat pocket. "I hate to eat and run, everyone, but I've got some business to finish at the capitol before the sun is up."

We rose from the table so Mr. and Mrs. Harper could exchange their goodbyes. Judging by her lack of enthusiasm, he was gone often. Or perhaps his schedule changed after the Bathory attack.

Issak slipped to my side. "I thought I'd let you know we have other Protectors scheduled to watch the house while we rest. They were all handpicked by me."

"Thank you," I murmured. Not that it reassured me one bit. No one knew Rodney like me; therefore, no one could protect him like me. "Can I meet them sometime?"

Did they sleep during the night so Issak could during the day? There had been no sign of them in the Protector's annex.

"Of course." He took my arm to lead me. "Let me show you to your room."

Mrs. Harper herded the other three upstairs to their bedrooms like children late for their bedtime. She never stopped talking, covering from the cold weather to when breakfast would be served.

Rodney ignored her, preoccupied with the copious effort he put into glaring at me.

It took every ounce of energy I had left in me not to roll my eyes. "How many Protectors are employed here?"

"Three. We work in shifts, so we can watch over the Harper's while they sleep and when they are awake,"

I nodded; *Knew it.*

The bustling town had gone silent, the sky growing lighter as the sun returned. Heavy curtains shrouded every window, and each door was sealed tight. Creating a sense of security I'd once trusted myself—*before.*

"Your Vampire appeared upset," Issak observed, walking sideways along the stone path to the Protector's annex.

My nails dug into my palms. Had anyone else asked, my eyes may have finally rolled. Not only had Rodney made a spectacle at dinner, he'd planted a seed of suspicion in my future boss's mind.

"I recognize jealousy when I see it." Issak laughed. "He seems to have a vendetta against the Sorcerer in your company."

I gave a nod and exasperated sigh; Would he ever get used to Preston? "Rodney has a vendetta against any male who gives me attention,"

Issak inclined his head and slid a hand over his face to hide a facetious grin. "Tell me about the Sorcerer and the Werewolf. Mr. Harper said to watch them closely until their visit is over and report anything unusual to the city patrol officers."

Now I knew how Preston felt having to defend himself repeatedly.

Inhaling a long breath, I recounted our expedition, careful to establish Preston's loyalties. Issak had asked about both men, but I could read between the lines. He wanted to know the same as the officers—Had we been coerced?

I skipped the Ramone encounter, embarrassed by my naivety. A practiced Protector should have known better than to trust a stranger.

Issak would've known better.

# COMFORT
## CHAPTER 13

THE BED WAS SMALL like the one in Bathory, only with silky soft sheets. With the blackout curtains drawn, the room was dark. Too dark. Thankfully, there was a lamp on the bedside table, but not even it could drive away the crushing terror of isolation. It was worse than listening to birds chirping while trying to sleep. More horrific than sleeping on the forest floor.

Because I was alone.

Alone with my mind. It wasn't the same mind from Bathory. The one used to sleeping in my dorm room and dredging up sweet scenarios to fall asleep.

No. This one conjured the sounds of footsteps in the hall. Ominous shadows that swirled like Ramone's eyes.

I drew the blanket over my head, certain I could smell the scent of charred flesh.

"It's not real. You're safe here." I whispered to myself.

Rodney's safe. *I'm safe.*

*Rodney.*

He'd humiliated me at dinner. Accusing the Lead Protector of inappropriate behavior within hours of meeting him. In front of his parents. Not only was it embarrassing, it was a direct hit at my capabilities as a Protector.

They'd think he only wanted me because of his misguided feelings. Not because I was qualified.

He was about to find out how qualified I was.

*Oh, Mythos.*

He'd always been possessive. But nothing like this. He'd kept his feelings under wraps since Zoon was rather forward with his.

Only he never made me feel this way. Trapped. Degraded. Incompetent.

*"You're right, Jojo. This is totally worth skipping lunch."* Zoon called, *standing along the gym wall.*

*He'd teased me for skipping meals to practice high kicks, so I'd invited him to come watch. Because I knew he'd show up and I knew he'd say something stupid.*

*"Your ass is far more fulfilling than a blood pouch."*

*The lanky Vampire went rigid as Kade seemed to materialize from nowhere. "With a mouth like that, I sure hope you have the physical capability to back it."*

*His sea-blue eyes widened, as did my grin.*

*There, in front of a full gym of our peers, I practiced my kicks, using him as the target.*

*No one else dared to hit on me after that. Not even Zoon had the gall to be genuine about it. At least not crudely.*

I missed him. Missed Kade.

My fingers wrenched tight in the blanket—the scent of charred flesh seeping through the threads.

Whirling the blanket over my shoulders, I shot from the bed and into my boots. I couldn't sleep here and I desperately wanted the rest. Needed it.

The cool morning air licked at my bare legs, easily passing through the thin blanket, then the cloth shorts and crop-top. Its icy claws tightened around my chest as I darted through the yard. It's broad daylight in a nocturnal city. The streets were quiet, the yards still. Although every house had its curtains drawn, it felt like I was watched.

I questioned the so-called Protectors who were supposed to guard the house when I opened the *unlocked* front door. Anyone could've waltzed right in!

The house was dark, the blackout curtains drawn, and the lights shut off. My heart skittered in anticipation of complete darkness.

The staircase light remained on. *Thank the Mythos.*

Tucking the corners of the blanket to my chest, I darted across the entry room to climb the stairs—and nearly toppled down, colliding into a firm chest at the top.

Issak steadied me by my arms and potentially saved my pathetic life.

If Rodney's behavior at dinner hadn't convinced him I wasn't qualified to be a Protector, bumping into him like this would certainly do it.

I stepped out of his reach and cinched the blanket tighter. I'd never impress him if he found out I needed a life-sized teddy bear to sleep with.

He turned and bowed his head, too, as we awkwardly progressed along the hallway shoulder to shoulder.

"I won't ask where you're going if you don't?" he bargained softly. I couldn't see his expression in the poor light.

"Deal." I gave a curt nod.

He swooped into the last door on the left without another word or even a glance back. Like he was late for something.

*Or someone.*

Mrs. Harper was the only person living in this house who was home right now. *Were they having an affair?*

My cheeks heated, and I suppressed a giggle.

Maybe Rodney's spectacle wasn't a big deal after all.

Not that I forgave him for it.

I hadn't a clue which rooms held my friends, let alone *who* would put up with me. I pressed my ear against the first door on the right, recognizing the familiar animalistic snore which kept me up while traveling—Reggie. Even if he was comfortable with me as a bedmate, I was not.

The next door held a softer snore. I turned the handle.

Had Rodney's room arrived beforehand, there was little to no chance I'd join him. We had some boundaries to set and, frankly, I was too tired to do that right now.

My heart pounded in my ears, threatening to burst from my eardrums. I could still be wrong about the door. What if one of these unseen additional Protectors slept here? Maybe that's what Issak was up to and why the annex was so barren?

I trudged on, knowing damn well I couldn't sleep on my own.

The sunlight through the open curtains traced a golden outline of the bewildered Sorcerer, arms raised defensively. His hostile grunt drove me back a step, and I threw my hands up in surrender. The blanket fluttering around my ankles.

"It's me," I hissed in a whisper.

Combing a hand through his tousled hair, Preston blinked until his sleepy eyes focused. "What a surprise, Love."

I kicked aside the blanket and my boots, shutting the door behind me. "I...uh." I hovered near the foot of the bed. "Couldn't sleep,"

Preston fell into the mattress, rolling onto his side to pin me with a sleepy smile that made my heart do stupid things. "Issak didn't provide you enough comfort?"

"Shut up!" I punched him in the arm, causing him to swear. "Rodney's jealousy is annoying enough. I can't have you sulking, too."

He motioned for me to join him. "I was kidding, Love."

I groaned, lowering onto the edge of the bed. The moment I felt the mattress beneath me, any energy I had left after what we'd been through drained out of me.

I was exhausted.

My thoughts couldn't get to me in here. Not when…Not when he was dressed like *that*.

His pajama bottoms hugged his hips, drawing attention to the defined lines gliding from his waistband. Then the rhythmic rise and fall of his tight chest. Faint scars decorated his bronze skin, highlighted by the sunlight.

His warm gaze awaited mine, stopping the breath in my lungs.

*Holy Mythos.*

I dropped my eyes to my lap.

"What's on your mind, Love?" His fingers tangled with mine.

*He expected an answer?* I couldn't tell him I'd been envisioning what it would be like to tuck my head under his chin when he was dressed like *that*. How his arms would feel wound around me—dressed like *that*.

How his skin would feel beneath my fingertips.

His lids flickered while he waited, a sleepy sigh expelled from his nose.

"I guess Rodney is." It wasn't a complete lie. "I sacrificed to get him here…to his family, something I'll never have…and he's worried about made up scenarios in his head about the Protector giving me too much attention."

Preston's tired eyes went soft and the residual, spicy scent of body wash cascaded over me. "Are you mad at him for being jealous?"

A swarm of bats vortexed in my stomach and I put my back against the pillows, bending my knees. He couldn't believe I shared Rodney's feelings. *Right?*

"I'm used to that." *Unfortunately.* I drew my knees to my chest. "He's acting out because he's scared. What he doesn't realize is there's a lot of people who won't get the opportunity he has. He's taking his parents for granted."

Tears dampened my cheeks, more welling in my chest. "I'll never know mine." I whispered. "Not even their names."

Preston sat up beside me, the same shadow casting over his face that surfaced when he talked about his past.

"Even if he doesn't *like* his parents, he gets the opportunity to know them. I'd give anything to have a dad to spar, a mom to fret over my every mistake," my voice wavered until I ceased.

Preston's hands slid into mine. "In time, they'll become your family, too," his words were slow and careful.

I blinked away my tears and squeezed his hands. "Don't get me wrong, I'm excited for this new chapter in my life. The Harpers. Fulfilling my dream as Rodney's Protector. Getting to know my new friend."

The shadow lifted. "You like Reggie that well?"

"I mean you!" I thrust his hands into his chest and scowled.

His smile didn't quite meet his eyes, and the warmth in them was softer. "You're free to visit me anytime, Love."

*Visit?*

It had yet to occur to me Preston wouldn't stay here. That his temporary access to the city would expire and he'd return to his life in Little Hope.

*When had I decided he was a permanent fixture in my life?*

The pit that developed in my stomach dragged me beneath the covers and onto my side.

Rodney's role as mayor's son would soon consume my time. I wouldn't have any to spare for friends. Or anything but my duty as a Protector.

Isn't that what I'd always wanted?

After breakfast, I perused the browning floral garden in the yard's corner. Tierney prided herself on presentation, and it showed in her home's details. As promised, fresh clothes were delivered and I'd changed into the same black sweater and jeans as we'd been assigned at Bathory. Pretty sure it was as scratchy, too.

How long would it take to fit in here? With Rodney working against me every step of the way. He didn't even give me a chance to show them the skills I'd obsessively trained for alongside Kade.

The skills I failed to adequately utilize until it was too late.

Breath rattling in my chest, I wiped away the tears. Things changed so frequently, it left me feeling empty. We'd only just got to know Reggie and Preston. I wasn't ready for them to go just yet.

Lowering onto the stone bench in the garden's center, I stared into the carefully pruned shrubbery. It hadn't been a surprise, so it shouldn't hurt this bad. Just because Preston had to return to his own life didn't mean mine would fall apart. After all, I am exactly where I should be.

A Vampire Protector, not a Sorcerer's—

I yelped. Reggie's towering figure rose from behind the sphere-shaped bush in front of me, nearly ejecting my skeleton from my skin.

"You needed the fresh air as badly as I did," his voice was soft and his unbuttoned flannel billowed in the slight breeze. Retying his wild hair into a ponytail, he joined me on the stone bench.

I gripped the stone's edge on either side of me, afraid it couldn't support his massive frame. So much to say came to mind. The ideas crowded my throat until I was struck silent.

"This place is...something else." His massive shoulders sagged, and he let out a content sigh. "You must be relieved we finally made it."

"I am," I confessed. "We couldn't have done it without you or Preston."

He chuckled, and it was a sound I wished never to forget. "Ah, you would have. Granted, it may have taken a little longer and a few more scars. But you are capable, my dear."

I struggled to suppress the bubbling insecurities climbing past the clog in my throat. "I hope his parents see it so."

"It sounds like they intend to get you certified," he reassured me.

Lifting one shoulder, I bowed my head to my lap. Where had this hopelessness come from? This is what I'd fought so hard to accomplish. Being here. The version of me just a short time ago would've been honored to work for the mayor.

So what's making me hesitant to embrace the position?

Clearing his throat, Reggie sat straighter. "I'm afraid I'll miss the big day. My village is near the Pixie village invaded yesterday. As part of the board, I must help prepare, in case the chaos reaches my people."

I whipped to face him. "What can I do to help?"

He held up a meaty paw, flaunting his freshly healed arm. "Your responsibilities lie here. I appreciate the offer, though."

His soft smile warmed me from the inside out, driving me to rest my head against him. I owed so much to this man for protecting Rodney in my absence. As well as all the help he'd provided along our journey.

He patted my knee. "I hate to leave you on your own with those two nitwits."

I grinned. "They aren't so bad."

"The Vampire you can handle," Reggie agreed. "But *Lover Boy* seems to believe he holds some special place in your life."

Swallowing the lump in my throat, I scrambled for an excuse to defend Preston. "He's a good guy."

Reggie wiggled his brows. "So, he *is* special to you?"

Shoulders hunched to stare at my toes, I rocked forward in my seat. "Friends are few and far between in today's world—"

"Right you are." He slapped his hands on his knees and stood. "I best gather my things."

Household alerted of his departure, we gathered on the front lawn to give Reggie a proper sendoff. He had his pack on his shoulder and a shaky smile pasted on his face.

I squeezed the wolf tight, sad to see him go.

"I don't live far from here." He held me at arm's length, compassion in his tight face. "Don't hesitate to visit."

I hugged him once more. "I will, I promise."

"Not far!" Preston scoffed and extended a hand to Reggie. "It's far for people with two legs."

Reggie laughed, pulling the Archmage in by his arm to clap him on the back in a hug. Preston winced under the force of the man's heavy palms, shouldering away to gather his composure.

Reggie proceeded to shake the other's hands, holding onto Rodney's for an extended period. He crouched low to give advice that made Rodney laugh and throw a glance in Preston's direction.

With one last theatrical wave, he climbed into the limo Mrs. Harper insisted he take to the city's edge. From there, he was on his own. It would shorten his walk by twenty minutes. She ensured he left with a bag full of food and plenty of water.

I remained in the lawn, sitting on the fountain's edge, unable to go inside. Afraid, somehow, it would solidify my future—that I belonged here now. The finality insinuating I'd never see our new friends again.

Cigarette smoke drifted in the air, reminding me Preston was still here. I watched the burnt ash's reflection on the water's surface. It melded amongst the glittering stars.

"I'm going to miss that flea-bitten mutt,"

I splashed Preston. "Would it kill you to say we lucked out, stumbling on him?"

"It might." He brushed the cold water from his shirt. "I suppose he was helpful against the kalento."

He'd been helpful for more than that—the silver wolves, food, and I'm certain he stepped up while I was gone. Rodney wouldn't have accepted Preston's help.

I opened my mouth to inform him of such when a blast of icy water landed in my lap. "Asshole!"

I jumped to my feet, any remorse for letting Reggie go set aside. Making room for the determination to…I wasn't really sure what I could do to an Archmage that would stick.

He skirted around the fountain, staying just out of reach. In one scrambled sweep, he tossed away his half-smoked cigarette and twisted to catch me against his chest. I leaned away to strike, but he grappled my wrists, firm against his torso.

"Just remember, you started it!" he claimed.

I laughed, writhing helplessly.

His golden eyes darkened, and one side of his lips curled. I froze. Not only did he look menacing, he took my breath away.

"Shit." *He's hot.*

Again, he caught me distracted. Dipping to lift me over his shoulder, his arm locked across the bend of my knees to keep me in place.

"No!" I cried. "No, no, no!"

He dumped me into the frigid water. Maybe a foot deep, it crashed around me, soaking my clothes and freezing me to the bone.

"Holy M-Mythos," I chattered. *So cold.*

"Fascinating," Preston said, backing away slowly and his lips curled devilishly. "You look even better wet."

*He did not just say that!*

"When are you leaving again?" I rose menacingly into the bitter, wintry air. At least, I hoped to be menacing. The way the water dripped from my clothes and hair, I undoubtedly resembled a drowned rat.

"Hey!" Issak's call distracted us and brought to light we were the last two outdoors. He stood on the porch, hand on the front door. "It's time for lunch."

"You're ready for me to leave?" Preston teased as I wrung out my clothes as best I could.

"Let's go eat. I'm starving." I insisted, hustling up the stairs. His inflated ego didn't need anymore help, so my preferences about when he left would remain as my little secret.

In the entryway, Rodney finished a conversation with Mrs. Harper about his future in politics. Deciding they would discuss his position in office at a later date, he faced me. His glower lingered on Preston as he climbed the stairs to freshen up.

"Please, stop," I snapped. The boundaries had to be set now. I couldn't continue to live like this.

"I don't understand what you see in that creep." Rodney gestured in his direction. "He's a Sorcerer. I don't actually believe for a second he's on our side."

I rolled my eyes. "You don't know anything about him—"

"We've known him a few weeks; of course, I know nothing about him! *You* don't know him!"

I folded my arms. "I trust him. He's considered an enemy to our enemy, which knights him an ally in my book."

"He could as easily be our enemy as theirs!"

"You want him to be an enemy because you're jealous. Which is highly unnecessary. We've got enough going on without you instigating a pissing match. There will never be anything between you and me."

His fangs poked into his bottom lip. "We've been through so much. Why can't you give me a chance?"

"I'm your Protector. It would be inappropriate." His confession wrenched the icy fixture in my chest. I expected it, yet it still struck hard.

"Under the circumstances, the world could forgive us,"

I sighed. "It's more than that. I don't have the same feelings as you do."

"What does Preston have that I don't?" His eyes flashed. "We hardly talk anymore! You're always with *him*."

"Come on, you two, lunch is ready!" Mrs. Harper swept through the room, Issak hot on her heels.

"And why are you wet?" His voice rang out.

I strode away. He wasn't listening to me and likely wouldn't until Preston was gone.

My chest squeezed.

The tightness in my lungs didn't go away through lunch. He fumed the entire meal, glaring between Preston and me while Mrs. Harper, or Tierney, as she preferred, went on and on about how hard her husband worked.

While she talked, I ran my fingers through my hair. I grimaced. A wet grass clod had navigated its way there from the fountain and it reeked. The Vampires likely resented the way I smelled.

Across the table, Preston stifled a snicker by sipping from a water glass. Of course, he choked and cleared his throat.

*Asshole.*

I pressed my lips together and bowed my head to hide my grin. He shouldn't look that appealing after the trouble he'd gotten me into. But my stomach fluttered anyway, making it difficult to eat.

*It's the grass clod. Not him.*

A determined boot brushed against my leg, wrinkling my soaked pant leg. A chill shot through my entire body and my grasp constricted on my fork. Looking from beneath my lashes, Preston's gaze met mine.

My breath hitched in my throat, convulsing with laughter once again, and I bit down hard on my lip to hopelessly keep the sound in.

A smirk tugged his lips, eyes darting to Rodney. The Vampire already glared, heat radiating from his onyx eyes. Unphased by his anger, Preston offered an ornery wink.

*Oh no.*

Rodney went rigid in his chair, nails biting into the wooden arms. "What's so funny?" His glare shifted from Preston to me. "*You* are acting *so* immature."

*Me?* What about him?

Sufficiently scolded, I bowed my head to my plate. He'd relentlessly keep this up so long as the Archmage was here. It didn't matter who was at the table, nor if it embarrassed me. Let alone, this was the most fun I had since Bathory. Since it didn't involve *him*, it wasn't okay.

The silence stretching across the table led me to check Preston from my peripheral. He sat pin-straight in his chair, unwavering stony glare on Rodney.

Exactly what we didn't need. *A pissing contest.*

Bangs elevated on the arch of her lifted brows, Tierney cleared her throat and rose from the table. "Alright, well, did everyone get their fill?"

"Thank you for the meal, ma'am." Preston seemed to have been waiting for the dismissal. His chair screeched back, and he rushed straight outside.

"Yes, thank you," I murmured, discreetly preparing to escape next.

Except Rodney beat me to it. Table manners forgotten, I chased him upstairs. Seizing his upper arm, I dragged him to a halt in the hallway at the top.

"When will you stop acting like this?" I demanded. When would he stop treating me like I belonged to him? Not just when Preston's around. He'd been like this long before and would treat Issak the same.

His onyx eyes widened, and he ripped his arm from my hold. Looming over me, his fangs poked into his lower lip. "When you treat me like your friend again. You know, the one you've known since the *third grade!* I don't get how you so easily replaced me with some *Sorcerer,*" he growled.

"Just because *you* don't know him, doesn't mean I don't!" my cheeks warmed and my voice wavered. The longer this argument went on the more stupid I felt. It wouldn't be such a big deal to me if he was as willing to fight about Reggie.

Shadows crept across his face, as if I'd slapped him. "You do like him!"

"I..." I stammered, unsure how to admit my speculations aloud, "I'm unsure."

He stepped back. "He's over two hundred years old."

Age didn't matter. Not anymore.

"I'm immortal now. Soon, two hundred years will feel like a couple months." The bats in my stomach were fighting one another—at least it felt that way. "I've never *liked* anyone before. Preston...h-he makes me feel..."

I couldn't say it. Because my best friend didn't want to hear it and I knew he wouldn't approve. Which shouldn't matter to me, I suppose, but it did.

"Jo?" He too was at a loss for words and his lips curled over his fangs.

"I don't understand it either, okay?" I bit out, arms over my chest. Feelings weren't part of my training, therefore they weren't supposed to be a part of my life.

Protecting. That's what I was supposed to do.

Shaking his head, my best friend slammed his bedroom door. Thrusting the realization in my face he wasn't my best friend. At some point, he'd become something different. Someone jealous and possessive.

My lungs ached, fighting the sob creeping up my chest.

I fled the house to the rear patio, so frustrated it was easy to ignore the crisp late night air. Paver bricks imprinted the ground in an ornate design that complemented the architecture well. Carefully planted flowers and shrubs decorated the perimeter. Near the house sat a bench beneath an overhang adorned with ivy.

I lowered myself onto the bench, hands held in my lap, and shoulders sagged. I loved my best friend, but he behaved as if I belonged to him, like property. Sure, he was technically my future employer, but I'd always thought we were friends first.

A tear slipped free, and I swiped it away. He meant the world to me, being the only family I'll ever have. The only person in the Mythos whose opinion truly mattered to me.

A chilled hand rested on my shoulder. I hadn't heard Tierney come outside. Hadn't seen her approach to stand over me. Her eyes were a pale lavender and the lines around her lips made her frown that much more empathetic. She'd come here to console me instead of her son?

Sinking onto the bench beside me, she placed a hand on my thigh, and I fought the urge to recoil.

"Your patience with my son doesn't go unnoticed," she murmured, picking apart every imperfection of the house she could see from here.

I gave a tight-lipped smile. How could anything between us go unnoticed? Rodney involved the entire house any time we fought.

"He seems to have his father's temper." Her lavender irises turned gray. "They mean well. They simply don't understand how to express their emotions in a well-received way."

I nodded. Rodney always had a temper; fortunately, it hadn't ever aimed at me.

"I've considered your situation." She pivoted in her seat, placing both hands on my knee. "He doesn't know how to tell you he's afraid to lose you, after so much loss already. It's pretty obvious you are most precious to him, more than his Protector."

I squeezed the necklace charm in my palm until the smooth edges pressed into my palm painfully. "He won't lose me." Albeit, I tired of fighting over trivial things.

She smiled, but it didn't reach the lines around her eyes. "It's important to understand feelings are inevitable, no matter what the world believes."

The muscles holding my mouth shut about gave up the ghost. Did she—? She just gave me permission to date her son?

# BREAK
## CHAPTER 14

There wasn't much of a gathered meal the next day. Tierney had a light lunch prepared for those who had time since Burke was at the capitol again. If he stayed away this often all the time, it made sense how easy it was for Tierney and Issak to have an affair. Especially since I had yet to see another Protector shadow her while she tended to the house's mechanics. Nor had I seen one at all.

Rodney sat at the dining table, staring into a cup. He swirled the contents, careful not to spill it. I'd never seen him so patient to consume blood. Even at campus he was ravenous.

I found myself hovering. Something was on his mind, the emotions whirling in his irises. I wanted to approach, but wasn't sure he'd want me to.

"It tastes so bland," he spoke to the glass then watched me shuffle in the doorway. "I don't feel as...strong when I drink this."

What did he mean by 'strong'? I'd never known Rodney to be physically remarkable.

I brushed my hair from my face and came further into the room. "What do you mean?"

He set the glass aside and gave his full attention. His lavender irises glittered. "Your blood is—um, better, somehow."

I shifted, the slow way he spoke peculiar. Was this how Vampires flirted with their food?

His optimism faded. "I'm sorry. I..."

I held up a hand to deny his apology. His mother gave me enough to mull over. While I resented his behavior, I was willing to work past it.

His lips pinched together. "I understand about you and Preston...I...I'm different."

"You're the closest thing I have to family," I provided, reaching for his hand.

He clasped my fist inside his long fingers. "I know...and I don't want to lose you."

"Josie," Mrs. Harper's voice drew my attention to the entry hall. "Would you meet me in Mr. Harper's home office?"

I followed her, Issak in line behind me, to Mr. Harper's office tucked behind the grand staircase. Embarrassment hung heavy on my sagging shoulders, afraid to be scolded further for inappropriate behavior—or worse, for disturbing their fountain.

She gestured for me to sit beside her on the love seat against the wall. While Issak closed the office door, she poured a cup of tea to offer me. I held the small teacup of herbal bliss in both hands while studying the room. A wooden desk sat along the opposite wall. Two small armchairs faced the desk and a huge painted portrait of a Vampire I didn't recognize. Judging by his hair color and angled face, he shared Rodney's lineage.

Tierney clasped her frail hands in her lap, exhibiting the most awkward smile. It brought out her crow's feet and aged her. Perhaps the shallow depth set it apart from her typical smile.

*Something's shifted.*

Issak stood behind the woman, his arms at his back. His gaze ever so briefly crossed mine, triggering a guilt driven shoulder drop.

*I knew his little secret.*

"We wanted to thank you, once again, for all you've done for Rodney. He's a special boy and I don't believe there's another person in the world who would've cared for him as you have."

I blushed. *They knew I fed him.* "He would've done the same for me."

She reached out to pat my knee. "Of course, dear. Now, money doesn't mean much when you've saved a life; however, it's the best we can do."

Issak produced a thick envelope of money.

I hesitantly accepted the payment, studying the suspicious pair. "Thank you. Although, I don't understand, it's my job to protect Rodney. We don't get paid unless we're certified and I certainly don't deserve the reward money."

The smile on Tierney's face condensed further. "Josie, dear, you've done so much for him and again, we truly appreciate the lengths you went to, but your services end here."

I stood, full teacup discarded. "Does he know about this?"

"He will later." Tierney reached for my hand. "I need you to understand our decision, dear."

"I cannot. I've trained since the third grade to be his Protector—"

"And I admire your dedication, dear. We simply don't need you. We already have a full staff here and Issak is more than qualified to protect Rodney—"

"Qualified?" I laughed. "He doesn't know a thing about Rodney! Does he know how long his energy lasts between feedings? Does he know his sleep cycle? Or his ability to heal?"

I was hysterical.

"I know enough, thanks to you." Issak bypassed Tierney to clutch my hand. "You're a superb Protector. You won't have trouble finding another Vampire to care for."

I swatted his hand away. "I don't *want* another Vampire! Rodney's my best *friend.* What happened to you understanding he doesn't want to lose me? Now you're taking me from him!"

The Vampiress quaked with a sense of fury I'd seen my instructors possess once I provoked their authority. At school, they would've sent me to detention—she could have me arrested. The fierceness in her stare told me she not only could, but would.

"Josie..." She didn't want me here. She'd consoled me after our fight in hopes I would leave quietly. That much was as plain as the fangs poking into her lower lip.

I stormed from the office, tears loose and embarrassment heating my face. With little consideration, I went to Preston's room upstairs. My abrupt entrance startled him and he narrowly avoided the door as I threw it open.

Slamming it behind me, I launched the crisp cash into his chest.

He caught it, perplexed brow line locked on my driven strides. "What happened, Love?"

"They no longer want me to protect Rodney!" I paced the room, throwing my hands in the air.

"What?" Preston said, his eyes round.

"They're over-staffed and don't need me," I fumed. "Like any halfwit here stands a chance at protecting Rodney from a ray of sunlight!" I wanted nothing more than to wring Issak's neck. He couldn't do a better job caring for Rodney than I could. It would interfere with his agenda to fawn after Tierney.

"What are you going to do?"

I whirled to scrutinize him, nose to nose. "You need a Protector!"

"What?" He smiled. "I don't—"

"You do," I decided. "As the Veiled Army's enemy, you need protection."

"That was a long time ago, Love, they've forgotten all about me. Rodney *needs* you,"

*If only his mother saw it so.*

"I'm done babysitting Vampires; they don't appreciate it anyway." I feigned.

"Love," his frail attempt to scold me was near inaudible.

I laughed, tossing my hands dramatically. "I've got to get outta here. Is there a hotel nearby? We can rent a room until we figure out what we'll do."

"We're going now?" he asked, baffled. He stepped back to watch me tentatively.

"I can't be in this house one more minute,"

"Don't you want to say goodbye to the batling?"

*I couldn't bear to say goodbye.*

"Pack your bags, Preston, we're leaving,"

I left to gather my clothes gifted by the Harpers. Although I didn't wish to leave him, I couldn't help but wonder if the distance might give Rodney the chance to come to terms with the fact we were nothing more than friends. He'd initiated the first step by apologizing to me.

Though I would worry every second we were apart.

*But that's his mother's fault.*

I charged, scouring every building we passed for hospitality from the cold. The time it took to find a place to stay helped alleviate my temper, willing me into a silent depression.

Preston trailed along, opinions kept to himself, if he had any. A cigarette clung to his lips, smoke whisking over his shoulder. In all his infinite wisdom, I figured he would have something to say about my reaction to this situation. Instead, he pandered to whatever I decided.

There was a bed-and-breakfast three blocks away from the Harper residence. Recognizing my face from the news, the inn keeper waived the fee for our room. I must admit, it was rather honorable to be commended for all the effort I'd put in—to end up *fired!*

Once in the antiquated bedroom, I threw myself onto the creased bed. The firm mattress cradled the weight on my weak shoulders.

I lifted my head to observe the complimentary gift basket Preston discarded onto the dresser near the door. He curled his fingers above the cork in a bottle of red wine. With a pop, magic removed the stopper so he could pour a glass. I accepted the bottle, leaving him with the contents of the glass, and downed a mouthful of the bittersweet liquid.

"Are you sure this is what you want to do, Love?" He sat on the edge of the bed beside me, wine glass set aside. His expression primarily indomitable, a hint of concern traced his tone.

"They made up their minds. There's nothing I can do." I sat up to rest against the headboard, knees bent to cradle the wine bottle in my lap.

Preston sighed. "You didn't give Rodney a chance to fight for you."

I stared; he knew as well as I did there would be no talking Mr. and Mrs. Harper out of anything. They were politicians—*and assholes.*

"Are we going to sit here and wait for them to change their mind?"

*We'd be here for all eternity, since I'd be alive forever now!*

"No, we'll sit here until you and I make up *our* minds. Where do we go from here?"

Preston rolled his eyes. "This is out of character for you, Love."

He tucked a loose hair strand behind my ear and tipped my chin. I dodged the gesture, frustrated he would never understand. Protectors do not get to choose their Vampires. In the political world, Rodney doesn't get to choose either.

"I'll be back, Love." Preston left for a cigarette break, obviously unprepared to bask in my rage.

It felt nice to have a moment alone to process.

Knocking back more wine, I explored the attached bathroom. As hoped, it held a jetted tub, the perfect place to enjoy my wine and wallow in misery.

Living in a school my entire life, I'd never been drunk. I tried rum Zoon stole from the teacher's lounge once. A few sips convinced me liquor wasn't it. I didn't prefer the burn or the fuzzy brain it gave me.

This time, I found wine easy to choke down. My current emotional state as well as the bubble crested tub aided the effort.

Using the wall to stabilize myself, I left my sanctuary to towel off. The water went cold, and I grew bored with solitude. My clothes did not pass the vibe check, so I tried out one of the provided fluffy white robes. The fabric caressed my bronzed skin, an excellent replacement for the water. However, the body coverage aspect prevented me from exiting into the bedroom.

*What did it matter, anyway? Preston wouldn't notice I'd bothered to bathe.*

I gulped some more wine for liquid courage, then opened the door. He sat on the edge of the bed, fidgeting with some archaic technology I'd seen in movies.

"Those still exist?" I exclaimed, sauntering to stand at his side.

A crooked grin pulled on one side of his face, and he looked up from the tiny tube TV. Quick as magic, his expression changed, his brows at his hairline. While I'd imagined his bold scrutiny would drive me to cower in the bathroom, it felt empowering now. Chin lifted, I chewed my bottom lip and searched his glowing eyes for a train of thought.

He didn't speak and returned to the TV, the muscles in his jaw flexing. My confidence flickered, disappointed in his interest redirection.

He pressed the power button, and the clunky device hummed to life. An old black and white western performed on the curved glass screen, the poor sound quality vibrating from the speakers.

His eyes twinkled. "I love this movie. It's an absolute classic."

Jittery, he kicked off his shoes and twisted the TV on the bedside table to face the queen-sized bed. Scooting into the pillows, he laced his fingers in his lap.

I observed him long enough his gaze flicked toward me.

"What, Love?"

"How old *are* you?" I quirked a grin, resisting the urge to laugh.

Preston pulled his attention from the escalating saloon scene to scoff. "You don't have to be old to appreciate a good story line."

I snorted. "It's in black and white—"

He hurled a lace fringed pillow from the bed. The stiff cushion barreled into the side of my head, and I stumbled to catch it.

First setting aside the wine bottle, I pelted Preston with the pillow. He held his arms up to protect his face, catching the lace to rip from my grasp. He then deposited the pillow behind him and scowled.

"Give it a try, Love." He patted the space of bed beside him.

I pulled the robe tighter, uncomfortable and sobered. His expressive brows exposed his prior deliberations. While then, I'd convinced myself it didn't matter—it *terrified* me. Standing beside the bed in lackluster coverage was one thing. Curled up in the bed with him a next tier confidence level. One unachievable without a lot more wine.

I retreated to the bathroom to change into the pajamas the Harper's gave me. Once finished, the wine bottle and I joined Preston. Sipping, I scooted close to see the tiny screen.

He looked at me, honey-colored eyes softening at my closeness. His gaze stopped the world and my breath echoed in my ears.

Returning to the TV, he draped an arm across my shoulders. His casualness muddled my perception. He was so comfortable around me, meanwhile I couldn't form a coherent thought.

I glanced at his fixated expression, then rested my cheek on his shoulder, wine clutched to my chest. *What did he think of me?*

My lids lulled, bored with the simple plot; I preferred thrillers. Preston's occasional giggle at the old-fashioned humor provided the real entertainment.

At a particularly pathetic joke, I twisted and he turned to return my diligence.

"You are *such* an old man," I teased.

His ornery smile hid within his beard, and his nostrils flared. To shield his reaction, he stole the wine to finish its contents, deposing the empty bottle to the floor beside the bed.

I chewed my bottom lip and twirled a finger in the chain around my neck, mind on Rodney. I regretted not saying goodbye. If I was right and the Harper's never changed their minds, when would I see him again?

I sighed and rolled to lie flat. At what lengths would they go to in order to keep me away? In a short time frame, I'd lost two best friends—first Zoon and now Rodney. Reggie had gone home, and I doubted Preston would put up with me much longer.

How was I expected to keep myself together? My entire life had shaken apart.

As if he could sense the landslide of my emotions, Preston left to shower.

Shifting to his side of the bed, I shut off the whistling western ballad credit scene. I wasn't in the mood to watch TV, it would distract from my pity indulgence.

*What led them to fire me?*

They could've replaced one employed Protector or afforded a fourth.

*Was it my inexperience?*

I recalled the awkward encounter between Issak and me. If my assumptions were true, then perhaps this was to protect their secret adultery.

I thrust myself from the bed to paw through the wicker basket on the dresser. Rose petals covered the bottom to cradle the contents. There was no longer any use for the second flute included, so I cast it aside to inspect the remaining items.

A package of gourmet chocolate-dipped strawberries found their way to my lips. I returned to the bed to munch on them as Preston departed the bathroom.

Much as his had, my brows rose. His damp hair clung to his head, teasing his cheeks. His exposed torso glistened with stray water droplets. A globule trailed to the waistline of his thin pajama pants.

*Holy Mythos.*

Swallowing a much too big bite of strawberry, I lowered my head to the sweets in my lap. I cleared my throat to prevent choking to death and flushed in humiliation. He'd seen my *stupid* expression and if there was a *minute* chance he hadn't, my choke certainly revealed it.

I jumped, the bed bouncing as Preston placed a balled fist on the quilt at either side of me. He leaned forward, his lips parted. My hands trembled and I became sober in an instant.

For a split second, I thought he wanted a kiss, then rationalized he wanted a bite.

Cheeks red, I placed the chocolate-glazed fruit to his waiting lips. My stomach fluttered as he took a bite, his unwavering stare on the fruit in my hands.

I looked away—Unfortunately, able to inspect his flexed arm muscles.

*Was he—? No, surely, he wasn't flirting. No.*

Frenzied, I set aside the sweets to push past him and make a show of picking through the gift basket. He stepped out of the room and, of course, I spiraled.

*Had I scared him off?*

*I was so awkward. Why was I so awkward?*

My actions felt severed from my brain. In a daze, I padded to lean against the intricately small, square-paned bay window and peered outside. It shifted. First pushing open the thick velvet curtains, I discovered the window to be a set of double doors.

I opened them to step outside, where I could see the entire block. All the other houses were silent, everyone in town running errands and living their lives. The lights presented themselves as the entrance to a promising future when we discovered the city in the forest. Here, in the midst of them, the city was as defeating as the rest of the world. Beautiful, in its own nighttime aura, even if I no longer held the same excitement for it.

I chewed my lips, mind drifting to Preston's berry-stained ones. Hands trembling, I curled my fingers around the balcony railing. Did I make it all up? Was he interested? *How did one know?*

The bedroom door startled my thoughts of Preston's decadent lips away as he arrived with a fresh wine bottle. Without eye contact, I confiscated the bottle to sip, thankful for the distraction in hopes it would quiet my newfound nerves.

I heard the familiar snap of him lighting a cigarette and braced myself for the smoke cloud. It never came. He took a long drag from the cigarette, his head hung and shoulders slumped. The smoke trailed over his shoulder, against the wind.

I pinched my lips, fidgeting with the necklace. What had I done? I must've done something to make things so uncomfortable. Was it the strawberry situation? Had I been too obvious?

*Oh Mythos.*

He leaned against the wrought iron around the balcony and my stomach did a flip as his hand darted to still my fingers. The touch lasted a second before our eyes met and he shied away.

I definitely screwed up.

He held the cigarette at his side, a light cloud pouring from his nostrils. As it whisked across his arm, the stacking of V's and scars distracted me from the roiling sensation in my stomach. Many years of life left behind a roadmap of memories.

He must've tracked my line of sight, because he ran a hand through his damp hair, leaving it unruly and yet, still complimentary.

I swiveled to look at the stars, unable to look at him. Not when my thoughts should be more concerned with my Vampire. Like when I'd see him again. Or if I'd have anyone left after today. Preston could go home at any time and I'd be...*alone.*

Would Ramone be able to find me?

"Are you sure they couldn't be persuaded to hire you?" Preston spoke, his voice unexpected. "It seems like this decision was made hastily, or perhaps even before they met you. I doubt they even consulted Rodney."

I braced against the chilled air and dared to turn around. His exposed skin responded to the cold, urging me to guide him inside. Then again, he is a grown man who could have easily put a shirt on and I am not his Protector.

"Mrs. Harper was confident they didn't need me and that Issak would be sufficient." While I didn't care for the idea, she was right. He could do my job easily. Over twenty years of training and we'd both nearly died multiple times since leaving Bathory. I didn't deserve any certifications. "There's nothing we can do. It doesn't matter anymore; I'll focus on you."

Preston lifted his chin. "I have no need for a Protector, like Rodney does."

*Dammit, he's right.*

"Well, technically, I have no degree or certification, so we would complete a perfect set."

His cheek wrinkled with disbelief. "It doesn't mean you aren't qualified. There is still time to figure this out."

Except I wanted to live in petty ignorance. "I refuse to beg for my job! If they don't believe I'm the best to care for their son, then I'm not. There's plenty of Spellcasters to fight, anyway."

He placed the cigarette between his lips and the cherry burned brighter. "You don't need to search for trouble. *You* are the one who needs protected now, Love. Staying here in Carthage is your best option."

He seemed all too relaxed to be delivering prophecies like that. "I can't read a map, let alone lead them here. So what use am I to them?"

His lips contorted as he exhaled smoke and flicked the cigarette off the balcony.

I paced closer to him; afraid he'd walk away from my question. How did he expect me to survive not knowing what I'm hiding from?

Licking his lips, he lifted his gaze to mine, and I held my breath, waiting for him to speak.

"The Harper's should be glad to have you." He cupped my chin and the intensity of his copper eyes weakened my knees, drawing me nearer. "You are destined to be an excellent Protector and shouldn't waste those talents on someone like me. But I'll be damned if I let someone like Ramone get their hands on you instead."

Darkness crept over his features, and the weight he carried on his shoulders multiplied. If only he would tell me what it is so I could help him with it. Protector or not, I considered him a friend.

I looped him in my embrace, his warm skin melting it all away. For a moment, we could both pretend we were good enough. That crippling burden we both housed had to wait.

One arm snaked around my waist, and he rested his chin on my head. It felt right, being here with him. Even if it meant my life would change drastically from what I'd envisioned.

I pressed into him, hoping to still the thoughts swirling in his sad eyes. Finally, he lifted his other arm to cradle my shoulders.

The bats in my chest fluttered so hard, I'm sure it echoed into him. This embrace was different, we both needed it. Needed to feel one another, the connection. It wasn't a nod to attraction, rather our promise to one another to protect the other. Nothing like my obligation to Rodney.

We stayed locked in each other's arms until the cold became too much to bear.

Uncurling my arms, I stepped back to study his solemn face once more. He lifted his head to stare past me. While I'd hoped to comfort him, whatever regrets plagued him stole the light from his eyes. He needed time.

Leading the way inside, I fell into the bed, noting the strawberries were gone. Preston flipped off the lights with a twitch of his fingers as he climbed in beside me.

He cuddled close, smoothing my hair. Breathless, I ogled him, able to see vague features. Day time approached and soon light would fill the room.

His hand stilled, fingers dragging across my cheek. The air filled with electricity, stopping my heart. I wanted to kiss him so damn bad.

*But did he want to kiss me?*

# FLOURISH
## CHAPTER 15

PRESTON INVITED ME TO breakfast in the quaint dining area. The few tables were positioned so the other guests weren't so obvious. As if the arrangements of greenery weren't enough, the walls were coated in pale blue floral wallpaper.

My vision should have disintegrated the vase of delicate flowers. Preston watched me over his coffee mug's rim, a bacon slice in his free hand. I couldn't look at him yet. Every time I did, his strawberry-stained lips resurfaced in my memory.

Stabbing a forkful of scrambled eggs, I delivered them to my mouth. *Fuck, why are feelings so difficult?* Even avoiding him didn't help—I'd tried hiding in the bathroom until he'd insisted I come to breakfast.

"Do you know how to relax?" He rocked back in his seat.

I lowered my fork. "Yes. I just haven't been allowed to lately."

He smiled at my defensive tone. "Fair enough."

I placed my palms on the tabletop, overflowing with frustration. *I need answers.* "Why didn't you leave like Reggie?"

"Love," Preston frowned. "You know my concerns about Ramone."

Was that really the reason he stayed? "If you don't want to be here, you can go. I can take care of myself. I'm not a child."

He returned the bacon to his plate and exhausted a laugh. "I know, Love. Believe me."

My cheeks dared to declare how flattered I felt. Before they won out, I hid behind my coffee mug. Once again, he'd rendered me speechless. At this rate, I'd never know if he wanted to kiss me as badly as I wanted to him.

Finished, he dismissed himself for a cigarette. Finally, I could compartmentalize the circus inside my brain while exploring the bed-and-breakfast.

Across from the dining room, a roaring fire kept the nighttime chill out of the beautiful library, beckoning any bookworm to curl up in one of the wingback chairs positioned in front of the bay window.

I glided a hand along the many wooden shelves on the wall, tracing the frayed spines of each piece of literature. Rodney would kill to be here. He'd spread out on the floor and surround himself with stacks of books. I'd spent many hours complaining, bored to tears, watching him read.

My eyes burned, and I turned away from the memory.

I bypassed a roll-top desk to stop at what appeared to be a buffet along the opposite side of the room.

Once closer, I could distinguish the top lifted to rest against the wall behind it. Inside was what resembled a plate. I touched the engraved lines on the disc's surface.

A hand met mine and I whirled around. Preston smirked, close enough to tower over me.

*Fuck.* Oxygen grew thin again and bat wings pounded against my chest.

"It's a record player," he explained, golden eyes glimmering.

I smiled, knees weak. "Another old man thing?"

He leaned to adjust the record player, and a static pop emitted. The disc spun and smooth jazz filled the room. The sound of the instruments deposited sparks in the depths of his glimmering eyes. Much like the western had, this piece of the past brought Preston to life.

I became hyperaware of his closeness, able to hear him hum along to the music.

*Of course, he knew it.*

The tease on my lips softened as I listened. Never had a man hummed music to me. However, this one in particular could hum just about anything and I'd turn to jelly.

He laced our fingers together, and the other squeezed my hip.

My cheeks burned; I couldn't dance. Social events at the institute were mandatory, yet I'd purposely avoided them all. While Kade pressed the importance of building relationships with my peers, I failed to see how dancing with any of those dopes could help me in the future. Only training would.

He shifted us to and fro as we migrated closer to the fireplace; the heat caressing my skin. The flames' reflection flickered in his eyes, blended with their natural glow.

He released my hands to loop his arms around and pull me close. One of those bats finally escaped my chest to clog my throat. Being this close only made the desire to kiss him undeniable.

Arms loosely around him, I dared a glance. His gaze waited to meet mine, still humming.

*Shit, think of something else.*

I recalled how ominous he'd appeared when he'd taken down the band of Spellcasters easily, like it was second nature to him. Now he hummed jazz and held me.

*Stop, that isn't helping!*

The concept stirred fancies of what other talents this beautiful soul held.

He squeezed us nearer, head bowed so his lips were at my ear, his stubble scraping against my jawline. Once again, my heart raced with the same energy as the flames in the hearth danced. I closed my eyes and focused on the vibration of his hum.

He stopped and straightened, still holding on to me. I opened my lids, immediately caught by his steadfast copper eyes.

*Oh, fuck.*

My breath hitched in my dry throat and my legs weakened. He filled my vision; the world shrinking away with each heartbeat.

His hand caressed my cheek, fingertips striking magic into my veins. There's no other explanation; *he absolutely wants to kiss me.*

His lips parted, and the space between us felt so tight my ears rang.

"Oh, shoot,"

The music player crackled, the smooth jazz gone as quickly as my breath. Preston hurried to shut it off and panic swelled inside my empty lungs.

I fled.

*Ugh, I am an idiot.* An absolute coward. I'd rather be thrown into a pack of silver wolves than have to sit through that again. I wanted to kiss him so bad, but the absolute terror that coupled it was so draining.

I darted upstairs, glancing over my shoulder to ensure no one followed.

It would be easier as a Protector if I never became romantically involved, I recited the code. If there were any issue in a romantic relationship, it would impact the way my job was done.

I shut the door carefully so it made no sound, then slumped against it.

*Preston didn't want me as his Protector, anyway.* I'd have to find another Vampire to care for, which meant my silly infatuations would only endanger them.

My chest heaved for air as tears flooded my eyes.

*Could I do this?*

Could I walk away from the only family I'd ever known? Walk away from whatever stirred within me for Preston?

Or would I finally become the one thing I feared most? Nothing but an orphan.

"Love, this is pathetic, you need to get up." Preston threw away the stale covers. "It's been two days and you've spent it wallowing."

"Go away." The ceiling light burned my retinas, shunning the pale moonlight's reflection on the double doors. The night had merely begun.

"You can't pout forever, Rodney's life is going on without you and you have to accept it,"

"I expected to be with him forever! Forgive me if it takes more than two days to move on!"

"Move on?" He raised his brows. "Are you sure you don't have suppressed feelings for Rodney?"

A lump developed in my throat and tears spilled out. I *didn't* have feelings for Rodney. I'd recently realized I had *any* feelings! My training as a Protector led me to believe feelings were optional. While all my peers fell in love and fraternized, I focused on my career. It was imperative in my profession to put the Vampire first. Whatever or whoever would disrupt their welfare must be eliminated. Which included unnecessary life events—like dating.

"Love," Preston got close enough to send my fury through the roof, "if I gave up over something so trivial, I wouldn't be here in this room."

I dug my fingers into the bed; Mister Know-It-All really wanted to meet the pointy end of my dagger. "I'm grieving, not giving up! A career change this dramatic isn't trivial—"

"You lose friends and jobs in life—"

"I never imagined losing this one was an option." It was difficult to control my voice's volume and refrain from adding '*he's my family*'.

Preston intensified his scowl. "A juvenile mistake."

*Juvenile?* I'm far from an inexperienced child! I've taken lives, journeyed into the unknown, and narrowly escaped death. Losing my sense of purpose for experiencing all of those things was just the icing on the cake.

The fight left me; he was right. I hadn't come this far to quit now. Kade would tell me the same thing.

"We could go to my apartment." He pried my hands from the mattress and squeezed them. "In a few days, you'll decide I'm boring and be ready to find a job." He placed a hand on his chest while etching as many age lines in his face as physically possible.

I opened my mouth to speak, merely to be interrupted by an urgent knock. We stayed here all this time without a disturbance from housekeeping.

Exchanging a hesitant glance, Preston answered the door.

Issak stood on the other side, peering around Preston at me. It embarrassed me for him to see my current state. I hadn't bathed since the first night here and resembled a wreckage victim.

"Josie is needed at the estate," he muttered to keep the conversation private.

I smirked, wishing to rub in his face he hadn't been able to adequately care for Rodney in the two days I was gone.

"Rodney refused to drink any blood provided since you left—"

I sprang to my feet, pulling my hair into a bun as I sought my boots and cloak. If he hadn't fed in two days, then he was beyond starving. If he waited any longer...

My chest tightened in reminder of the last time he'd waited this long—he'd been tempted to drain me.

*It doesn't matter. He needs me.*

"Can we teleport?" I laced my fingers with Preston's. "We have to hurry."

"The Sorcerer isn't permitted to use magic—"

"For fuck's sake," I muttered, barreling out the door and hauling Preston to the car outside.

How far gone would Rodney be? Two days danced dangerously on the edge of death for him due to his illness.

Mr. Harper's bellow rattled the entire house. He was upstairs in the hall, verbally tearing his son apart. Mrs. Harper endured her husband's tirade, arms crossed to hold herself together.

As we stepped from the stairs, relief loosened her shoulders, and she clung to my arm. "I appreciate you coming—"

I held a hand up, unwilling to hear a word she said. I was here for Rodney, not to help her.

Preston shouldered past the Harper's to block the doorway behind me.

Unlike the school, Rodney's room held no coffin, entrusting his safety to blackout curtains. He laid in the king-sized bed, hair matted with sweat, barely breathing.

Mrs. Harper sobbed from the hallway, and I suppressed the urge to silence her. Had she actually cared for her son, she wouldn't have sent me away.

Preston peered at me over his shoulder and my heart skittered. It wasn't disgust twisting his features this time. He worried for my safety. His time fighting in the Persecution made him no stranger to the dangers of feeding a starving Vampire.

"This is pathetic! Refusing to eat to get his way?" Mr. Harper fumed. "What a brat!"

Issak had misled me to believe they could care for my Vampire—That they understood his illness. This rampaging bigot solidified they knew nothing of Rodney's disease.

Fists clenched, I spun to glare at the cluster in the doorway. Insults loaded behind my pinched lips, threatening to spill.

"I think it's best if you two wait out here." Preston stepped into the room and closed the door behind him. Anything they said too muffled by the heavy wooden door.

"Thank you," I murmured, then faced Rodney. While his methods were illogical, I feared his theory about my blood being 'better' was true.

For his current wellbeing, we'd hope so.

I sat on the bed and held my wrist above his lips to coax him to feed. His lethargic face twisted in recognition of my scent and for a second, I worried he wouldn't eat.

He seized my forearm and sank his fangs into my skin. It was sloppy, nowhere near as gentle as he'd tried to be before.

I flinched. The endorphins couldn't kick in soon enough.

From my peripheral, Preston turned away. While it could be a multitude of reasons, I couldn't shame him for his reaction; the act had once disgusted me and I, too, feared for my safety.

Rodney's free hand clasped my upper arm, and he drew my blood in ravenous gulps.

My arm burned from the force, and the room spun.

"You've had enough," I stammered.

*Did the endorphins kick in?*

He tempered his hold like a child who refused to have a toy taken away.

"Please, it hurts," my words slurred. I pulled weakly on my arm, afraid to pull too hard.

"Can I help, Love?" Preston came to my side, all the color gone in his face. He swayed with me, fighting his instinct to grab me.

"Stay back," I breathed. A Vampire wasn't predictable when they were like this. We couldn't chance interfering.

The longer Rodney drank, the louder my heartbeat grew and the stronger the waves of nausea hit. Ramone had said, immortal or not, I could still die.

Tears trickled down my face as a pang struck through me like a bolt, casting a white streak across my vision. Preston swiped the tearstains from my cheeks, his emotional battle plain in his butterscotch-eyes.

By now he'd had enough. I could feel it. I felt cold and sweat permeated my sweater. "You're hurting me."

Tierney had listened through the door and swooped in, Issak close behind. Her stark, charcoal eyes latched onto mine and her lips pressed into a tight line. "Honey?" She brushed a hand over Rodney's head, and spoke in a soothing voice. "You've had enough. If you drink anymore, you'll kill Josie."

If I hadn't panicked already, I did now. Wondering if I'd die was far less terrifying than hearing someone else say it.

Rodney groaned, as if to acknowledge he could hear us.

A scream ripped through my lungs as my forearm cracked from his possessive grip. The spike of white temporarily blinded me.

"Rodney!" Mrs. Harper called.

The Vampire released.

I cradled my arm against my chest and fell away from the bed into Preston's arms. My vision swam as it came back to me, and I swallowed bile.

"He broke it," I gasped, drenched in sweat.

*Being immortal and still getting hurt was a sick joke.*

"This shouldn't have happened!" Mr. Harper charged into the room as Rodney's hazy eyes creaked open. "I will not tolerate—"

"Jo?" Rodney attempted to stand, but Issak pushed him down. His skin was flushed and his eyes were pink.

*He's okay.*

"It's going to take a minute for the affects of her blood to kick in," Issak explained.

"Is she alright?" Mrs. Harper asked. "I can fetch her something to eat—"

"I have to heal her," Preston explained, cradling me to his chest. The pressure of his hard torso was the only thing confirming to me I was still conscious, still breathing. Because I felt myself slipping.

"Get her out!"

"Burke!" Mrs. Harper cried. "She's helped our son and you're sending her away?"

"I'm thankful for her help. Regardless, he must realize this is unacceptable behavior. He manipulated this situation to get his way and I won't allow it!"

I reached to touch one swaying display of Preston's indignant face—his skin balmy against my chilled hand. His warm butterscotch eyes were the only clear thing in the room as it seemed to dismantle. Falling into pieces of blackness and swallowing us up.

I should be scared. But he wouldn't allow anything to happen to me.

Preston's apartment door materialized, and he set me down to gather his keys from a coat pocket. The room hadn't been falling away, we'd teleported. *He'd used magic within Carthage city limits.*

Three men rounded the east side of the complex, two taking hold of Preston, while one smacked him over the head with a gun, knocking him unconscious.

The all too familiar maroon cloak billowed as Ramone slipped between to grasp my broken arm. Black starbursts littered my vision and my fingers tingled.

"Let go!" *Oh Mythos.* My arms hurts—My *head* hurts. "Let us go!"

He pulled me against him to teleport us once more, something I wasn't too sure I'd survive. Not when it hurt this much to stand.

My stomach developed a sour taste in my mouth, threatening to spill over as we arrived in a walnut laden lobby. The tall ceilings limited the light provided by the antique brass fixtures.

"Where are we?" I gasped, knees wobbling hard enough I slumped into him.

His fingers cinched tight, and I whimpered, stumbling along as we marched into a cell hall. The other Sorcerers struggled with Preston's limp body, dropping him into the nearest cell.

One kicked him in the abdomen while the other held him by the arms from behind. With a groan, he appeared to stir from unconsciousness, his lids pinched shut. The henchman delivered another kick to crunch Preston's nose.

"Stop!" I screamed, tearing from Ramone's hold.

They easily seized each of my arms, wrenching on the broken one to manipulate me into the hall. Ramone locked the cell door behind us, Preston left to bleed on the concrete floor.

*I failed him.* We were supposed to protect one another.

"Obtain her weapons and tie her up," Ramone instructed, waving a hand in the air.

My stomach churned as their grubby hands slid over my clothes in search of my knives and gun. The creep smirked, dark gaze filled with pleasure at the sight of my discomfort.

"What do you want from us?" I rasped, stumbling as the smaller Sorcerer tied my hands in front of me tight enough it burned like a brand. My blurred sight distorted my view of the other henchman as he delivered my weapons to a table in the glass walled office nearby.

No one answered me, or if they did, I couldn't hear them. Not over the pounding in my head.

Ramone gave them further instructions as he wheeled me into the walnut lobby, the heavy door slamming shut behind us. I stumbled and staggered, my head throbbing like a vice crushed it.

Plaques beside the doorways listed the room's function—at least, I assumed. My vision was so blurry, I only barely made out 'Luxor Capitol'.

*Luxor.* This wasn't just the army's headquarters, this was the central location for the politics of all Sorcerers.

*Preston's right, they are after world domination.*

We crossed the lobby in front of a massive desk and a few staff members who ignored our existence. Like hostages were a normal occurrence in their field.

"Careful!" The resistance of the tile floor acted as a magnet, folding my wobbly legs beneath me. Without Ramone's support, I would've fallen.

*As if he cared.*

Adjacent to the desk, we entered a door labeled 'Mayoral Wing', 'Authorized Personnel Only'. This led to a hallway of doors—the same one from last time Ramone abducted me.

He escorted me to the room I'd slept in last time. Where he sank me down in the hard wooden chair.

"Careful!" I sobbed when he touched my arm to remove the rope, doing my best to mock him.

"You've let him drink from you again?" Ramone's lips curled in disgust at my mangled wrist. I was right; Rodney tore my skin. "I thought that was forbidden."

"What does it matter to you?" I snapped.

"Did he break it, too?" He crouched to cradle my arm, gently smoothing his fingertips across the wounds. "Disgusting creatures."

"Funny. I could say the same thing about you and your army," I growled.

He squeezed my wrist, shooting pain up my arm. White spiked my vision and my stomach lurched.

"Bastard!" I hissed.

"Oh, does that hurt?" His soulless eyes lifted to mine, and I clenched my jaw. "I'm sure it doesn't hurt any worse than a stake in the ribs."

"You deserved it—" A scream cut me off as he twisted my arm until more blood spurted from the wound. I dug my nails into the chair's arm as his vindictive eyes swallowed me whole.

The weight of the darkness pressed into me until I felt the crippling paralysis in my subconscious and the pain slipped away. Eventually, the darkness pushed aside for a vivid image and, in place of the pain, heat lapped at my legs.

I lay in a heap on the fur rug in front of the warm fireplace in the cabin of his healing world. Tangling my fingers into the rug, I watched the flames dance. The vibrant orange color reminded me of the charred carnage throughout the institute, the ashen scent unforgettable.

"Would you fancy some warm tea?"

I shot into a sitting position, fear stricken. He sat on his knees at the opposite end of the rug, two steaming mugs in hand.

I backpedaled into the fireplace utensil rack. Luckily, my arm was healed, so I grabbed the fire poker before the rest clattered to the stone hearth.

Ramone quirked a pierced brow, waiting patiently to offer me a mug.

I raised the cast iron over my shoulder and gestured with my chin for him to discard the tea. Healing world or not, he's still the enemy. With magic, his options to harm me were limitless, and I had to stay alive—for Preston and Rodney.

"Can't we save the fighting for another time?" He sighed, setting one cup down, then sipping from the other.

"So you can get the upper hand?" I swung home.

He ducked the attack, tea cast aside so he could roll away.

He caught the fire poker as he somersaulted and jerked it from my hold. While he stood, I collected the shovel from the floor.

"What do you want from me?" I demanded, shovel drawn over my shoulder.

Ramone smirked, eyes dancing. "We can discuss my plans for you later."

Swinging for his head once more, our weapons met with a *clang*. I stumbled towards the fireplace, flailing to stop my fall. Ramone tossed away the fire poker to catch my arm and pull me with more force than expected into his chest.

We tumbled to the wood floor, but I refused to allow him the upper hand. As we landed, I held the bar across his throat with both hands. Leaning forward on my knees, I put weight on it.

He raised his hands in surrender, a slow grin stretching his mouth so the hoop in his lip pressed against his teeth.

My heart skittered. *What is this weirdo's problem?*

I primed my hold on the shovel and bared my teeth. "I should have killed you,"

He laughed. "Yes, you should have."

Taking my shoulders and lifting his leg, he launched me over his head and onto the sectional behind him. Afraid to hurt myself, I let the shovel clatter to the floor and held my hands in front of my face as I landed.

"Ow. Fuck." My neck kinked, the words came out in a grunt.

Ramone sprang to his feet, chest heaving. "Why didn't you kill me?"

I rolled to sit, mouth uttering uselessly. I could've killed him if I had the chance.

He smirked and disappeared from the room, like vapor.

A chill ran down my spine. *Why hadn't I killed him?*

The side effects of his spell shouldn't have been enough to stop me. Not when Rodney's safety was on the line. I'd let him escape.

*Why?*

Curtains drawn on his show, his healing world shut off. Abruptly, I was bound to the chair in the Mayoral Wing by my arms and ankles. I assessed my forearm as best I could, appreciative he'd taken the time to heal me, although I was his prisoner.

The pale moonlight through the window illuminated him on the twin bed, arm thrown over his face. His cloak hung in the closet and he'd changed into a set of silk pajamas. The bottoms clung to his hips, and the fallen open button-up top exposed his chest and hipbones. The bold purple galaxy tattoo infringing on his torso, a complimentary addition to everything I could see.

Hearing me shift under my ties, Ramone lifted his arm from his face. He watched me long enough I worried he'd seen me ogling his tattoo.

My heart pounded faster as he climbed to his feet.

"I'm thankful for you, Josie." His lips twisted as he approached, and I dug my nails into my palms. He brushed my hair from my face, fallen from the poor bun I'd tied it into. "You naively believed you got away that night in the woods."

I clamped down on my jaw to avoid snapping at his fingers like a dog.

"You led me right to the Leeches' lagoon."

I lunged against my restraints. "You can't get in."

He laughed. "Wrong again. With your help, I can smuggle my army right in."

Nails sunk into the wooden chair, I snarled through my teeth, "I won't help you."

"Oh, you will." He squeezed my knees. "Because I have Preston."

I tensed, igniting a solar flare within his eyes. This sick fuck enjoyed watching me writhe.

"If you do not help me, I will kill him."

I refused to lose him; he meant as much to me as Rodney now. If I had to help Ramone to keep him alive, I would—until given the chance for us both to escape.

Ramone patted my knees, then rose to close the curtains over the window and shut off the light. A chill lingered along my thigh after his touch.

*Invasive creep.*

My anger shifted into fear, the weight of the darkness crushing. Ironically, while I lived primarily during the night, I'd never gotten over my fear of the dark.

*Get it together, Jo!*

I could *hear* myself breathing—panting in distress.

*There's nothing in the dark more dangerous than what's there in the light.*

I swallowed and leveled my breaths—it didn't help. The dark far scarier than anything he could do to me.

"Um, R-Ramone," my voice quavered. "Are you still awake?"

"What is it?" he grumbled.

"This, uh," I cleared my throat, "this chair is uncomfortable."

*Should I stoop low enough to beg?*

He scoffed. "Comfort wasn't on my mind when I selected it for you,"

I inhaled a deep breath and shut my lids.

*It's not dark in here, your eyes are just closed.*

I *could* envision I was somewhere else, anywhere else. Like at campus, prior to the attack, or safely in Preston's apartment after all. Instead, I begrudged my stupid fear, wishing I could sit here and be a normal prisoner. Rather than throwing my dignity away, begging to be freed from my ties via any means necessary—such as wearing on Ramone's patience.

"How do you expect me to sleep?"

He sighed. "I didn't care to consider it."

Several moments passed while I sweat through my shirt. My dry throat desiccated by my incessant pants. I couldn't stand the sound of my heart any longer; I had to get out of this chair. "R-Ramone,"

"What?"

"Any chance you enjoy cuddling?" I cringed at my own words, ashamed to sound so pathetic.

He laughed. "You're that desperate not to sleep in the chair?"

"You can keep my hands tied, if you prefer."

The light came on and relief washed over me. He ran a hand through his hair, gray circles encompassing his droopy eyes as he filtered through the closet for something specific.

"No!" I protested.

He forced the bandana into my mouth and secured it behind my head. The fabric tasted dusty, triggering my gag reflex.

"You can't do this!" I complained, not that anyone could understand me, and pulled against my restraints.

The light disappeared as he returned to bed and, if possible, the darkness felt *worse*.

I pinched my lids closed, wet lashes against my cheeks. The room was so quiet, my muffled sobs pierced the silence.

There wasn't a single thing I could do about any of it.

He left me in the chair most of the next day. My muscles ached to move, my lips raw from the bandana.

*I'd kill for that hot tea from the dream right about now.*

When would he return? Would he let me out of the chair when he did?

To pass the time, I did my best to nap. I wouldn't sleep a wink during the night and sitting here worrying about Preston was just as draining.

Trapped here, I had no idea what torture he endured. Was he even still alive?

Dark came before Ramone's return. I sobbed until my throat burned, tears soaking the fabric twisted in my mouth. This irrational fear frustrated me more than how I allowed myself to arrive in this predicament. It crept through my skin like mist that turned into sand. Pulling me into the Mythos, weighing me down, and stealing my air.

The light flicked on, searing into my eyes and through my pounding head, all while putting my puffy face in the spotlight. As if I weren't humiliated enough.

"I suppose you've earned some time out of that chair." His boots clicked along the floor as he settled behind me to remove the bandana from my mouth.

I exercised my jaw and sighed hoarsely. A punch to the face hurt less than this.

My scant breath caught in my windpipe as he jerked the bandana tight into my throat. Unable to free my arms from their restraints, I did my best to stretch my neck out in resistance.

His breath tickled my ear. "Let this be your reminder. I have Preston and many years of resentment towards him. Do not test me."

I struggled to swallow. To prevent Preston's fate, I *wouldn't* kill Ramone in his sleep. Though at present, I'd do just about anything to crush his windpipe with my fist.

His amused breath brushed my ear as he removed the bandana. Then he untied me, tired fingers fumbling the knots.

"It's been a long day." He gestured towards the bed.

I kicked my boots off and plodded into the comfort of the blankets against the wall, pressed away from where he would lie.

He locked the door and muttered a spell under his breath prior to shutting off the light.

I spoke to distract myself from the darkness, "What did you do to the door?"

"It cannot be unlocked unless I do it." The bed shifted under his weight as he joined me.

I dragged the covers to my chest and pushed out a hand, feeling for him.

To make sure he stayed over there—*definitely not because I'm pathetic and terrified.*

He allowed me to clutch onto his shirt front, releasing the pungent aroma of his citrus-based cologne.

"A Vampire Protector who fears the dark?" He stifled a laugh.

I scrunched my nose, annoyed by his insensitivity. It wasn't the dark, more-so the helplessness and defenselessness when I couldn't see my own hand in front of my face.

"Have you considered maybe this is all a ploy so I can slit your throat while you sleep?"

I winced, his hand at my throat, squeezing until I struggled to swallow. Gripping his wrist in both hands, I scolded myself for not heeding his warning.

He had all the cards.

"I cast a weak spell on you on purpose. I intended to follow you and your Vampire to Carthage." His tone lowered, like he's speaking to himself, "I didn't know Preston was going to be there."

His grip on my throat relaxed, and I pulled his hand away from me. He tucked my hair behind my ear and I flinched, his fingers trailing my cheek.

"He never fails to complicate my plans," Ramone complained.

I noticed a pattern here. Both men believed the other was out to get him. Guess that kind of made sense, since one of them is the *bad guy*.

"I have a favor to ask you." Ramone's weight shifted, and his hand left my face.

I groped for him, the darkness doing just as I feared—making me defenseless. He could do anything and I wouldn't know until it was too late.

His open shirt front brushed my fingertips, and I realized he'd propped himself on an elbow. "A favor? Do I really get an option?"

"I suppose that depends on your behavior." As if he could see perfectly fine, he gently clasped my searching hand. "I can either hold you against your will here. Or you can agree to be my partner?"

I considered the question, and the unspoken words. "As in your partner in arms?"

He came nearer.

I bit my bottom lip hard enough it stung to keep from telling him to shove his proposal up his ass. If I wanted to free Preston from his cell and save the Vampire race, I had to think strategically.

"As in the key to my success. Wherever I go, I will flourish with you at my side."

I didn't like the sound of 'flourish', but at his side meant not being in this room. Which is exactly what I needed.

But could I *flourish* alongside the warlord who stole my future and locked Preston in a cell? Who'd instructed his henchmen to beat him as I lay here—or worse.

"Josie?"

The longer I remained locked away here, the longer Preston was, too. The longer Rodney had to go without me—without my blood.

I squeezed Ramone's hand. "Okay."

He combed his fingers through my hair and I fought the immediate reaction to break his nose—something I'd have to get used to as I played this role. "I knew you'd see it my way."

# MISMATCH
## CHAPTER 16

RAMONE LET ME BATHE first in the morning, allowing me some privacy this time. While he showered, I pilfered through his closet for something suitable to wear, wrapped in a fluffy towel. I decided on one of his V-neck shirts and a pair of boxers. If I must suffer in his presence, it could be done in comfortable clothes and I suppose it didn't hurt to appear...*relaxed*. Just enough to convince him I intended to play along as his 'partner'.

At least as comfortable as his limited options would allow. Judging by his wardrobe, the guy never took a second off the clock. *No wonder he had such a bad attitude.*

I sat cross-legged on the bed and waited.

When he returned, he wore gray sweatpants and worked to thread in his lip ring.

*Or did he hide the comfy clothes?*

I traced the edges of the dagger necklace charm as he ran his fingers through his damp hair to create its wild style. When dry, it appeared satisfying to touch. Especially when it clung to the freshly groomed stubble on his cheek.

*Shit, what is wrong with me? Once again, this is the guy responsible for the war.*

Noticing my warm cheeks, Ramone grinned.

*Oh, gross.*

He thought—He thought exactly right and I should be ashamed of myself. Because I couldn't even pass it off as committing to the bit.

He crossed the room to adjust the bed covers habitually. His torso took most of my line of sight, therefore his tattooed V's caught my attention. His kill count was much smaller than Preston's, covering the topmost part of his upper arm. Beneath it was a solid bar and an intermingled galaxy mural.

Three bars meant general. What did one bar mean?

"How did you become mayor of Luxor?" I couldn't imagine him out polling and giving political speeches. Especially not with piercings and tattoos. "Aren't old guys without piercings and tattoos usually in charge?"

"Usually. The previous mayor offered to step down. He hated his job." Smoothing the pillows one last time, he straightened. His eyes flashed and his lips twitched. "To be sure he didn't return, I had him killed."

Briefly, a flicker of surprise sparked to think he let the man live, only for it to snuff out when he finished. I shouldn't be surprised. *He's the bad guy.*

"Did everyone...I mean, your citizens, support the change?"

Ramone shrugged. "My family is well known here, so few people questioned the change. They trust that, like my father, I have their best interest in mind."

*His father?* "Preston said you plan to carry out your father's legacy—"

"Preston is a know-it-all. It doesn't surprise me he thinks he knows everything going on with *my* army." he put emphasis on the last part, as if it were a competition between them.

"Then what do you plan to do with me once you've...gotten into Carthage?"

The shadow of a smile passed over his lips. "That's why I offered to let you stand with me as my partner. You're too useful to throw away."

I narrowed my gaze. "Useful?"

He paced. "You're skilled and dangerous. I'd be an idiot to have you against me, rather than at my side."

His schmoozing had to be a distraction tactic. He knew I wouldn't cast away my beliefs to join the Veiled Army, that's why he had Preston. To ensure I act as his partner—even when I changed my mind. Because it was a ruse. I unfolded my legs to let them fall over the bedside. There must be more than using me as a key to Carthage. Preston had said as much, that I was important.

Ramone stopped to look at me, and his admiration made my heart kick. The orange sunlight haloing his head, intensifying the effect it had over me. Were he not a power-hungry monster, I may have allowed it to flatter me.

Kade wasn't generous with compliments, which partially drove my determination to work so hard. I wanted one more than anything. The last person I expected to hear it from was the enemy.

"You managed to survive an attack no one should have and kept your Leech alive. Against all odds, you've slipped through and fallen into my hands. I'm not dull enough to let an opportunity like that pass by." His eyes whirred like a mechanism and my stomach dipped. "You're special."

I tussled my hair, as if the movement would sever his intense line of sight. The longer he looked at me, the greater the conflict of emotions inside me became. His opinion didn't matter. At least, not in the way a compliment should. My capabilities should threaten him, not *impress* him.

"We'll achieve great things."

*We? Mythos, he's delusional.* This was an arrangement by *him*. Whatever plan he had was his and should be operable without me. "I'm sure you'll make sure of that."

His fingers balled into fists, and his whimsical veil darkened. A sense of self-loathing that often overcame Rodney. While I couldn't care less how this dictator perceived himself, I'd agreed to be his partner in arms. Therefore, I had to feign emotional investment in his welfare.

I caught his hand, pulling his attention from the angry place it ventured. Smoothing my thumb over his knuckles, I did the same as I'd done many times for Rodney. I held his stare, searching his eyes for the piece of him threatening to fall away in the darkness. The cloud drifted slowly, his pinched brows softening.

"Excuse me." He jerked his hand away and backpedaled. "I have to tend to...something."

He whirled out of the Mayoral Wing, leaving me behind in what would swiftly become my prison. Although more elaborate than Preston's, that's exactly what it was.

"So much for partners," I muttered, fruitlessly rattling the locked doorknob to the lobby. What could he have to do? He didn't strike me as the type to surface in the world underdressed. We were supposed to be *partners*. Partners didn't leave the other behind like a prisoner. For that matter, they didn't freak out when they should feel consoled.

Raking my teeth together, I sauntered into the sitting area.

He could touch me, but I wasn't allowed to touch him? How did he expect this to work? Was it some perverted kink of his to believe I'd work with him? It had to be. Why else would he flip around and act so strange when I tried to connect with him? If he didn't have to act empathetically, then I didn't either!

Our partnership was a business deal and nothing more. I had to respect his wishes, as he had to respect mine.

The built-in shelves smelled of polish, just like the lobby. Every book, statuette, and piece of artwork clear of dust. I ran a finger along the edge, skimming the spines for something interesting to read. A thick, black folder stopped my finger in its track. The surname Crosstone inscribed into the leather with gold ink glittered in the sunlight from the bay window. Why did Ramone have something belonging to Preston's lineage?

I retrieved the portfolio and unlooped the string holding the folded leather closed. It was filled with ledgers, legal files with vibrant red stamps to declare them official.

Soft footsteps alerted me I was no longer alone, his quick 'errand' already completed. The shift that had jerked him from the room remained stamped in his expression. He stopped in the doorway, the white flecks gone from his eyes. From this distance, they were two bottomless black cavities waiting to swallow me.

"What was so pressing you had to go out dressed like that?" I asked, gesturing to his current outfit. It was more of an accusation than an inquiry.

"Nothing that concerns you," he grated. He'd plummeted from the depths of self-loathing to the next stage—brooding.

"If I'm your partner, it should concern me. Shouldn't it? Secrets don't make good allies." I brandished the portfolio. "Like, why do you have this? It doesn't belong to you."

"I possess many things which belong to others," he replied dryly.

Shaking the documents hard enough they threatened to spill out the open top, I dared a step towards him. "These belong to Preston—"

"That's not how this partnership is going to work." Shoulders drooping under a dramatic sigh, Ramone lifted his brows and shook his head. "Put it back."

"Then what exactly does this partnership entail? Because I was under the impression it included—"

"*Put. It. Back.*" his voice boomed in the cramped room.

My gull diminished, I clutched the portfolio to my chest in both hands. I may not argue further, but it wasn't going back on the shelf. If he was going to continue to treat me like a prisoner, then I was going to act like one. At least until he changed his tune.

"Whatever it is, isn't relevant." He gestured to the built-in shelving. "I should've thrown it away ages ago."

If he'd had it a long time, then Preston must have searched for it. Which only made me want to fight him on the matter more. *I had to return it.* "Then it shouldn't hurt if I keep it. It'll give me something to do while I'm locked away in here."

"If it's been here long enough I've forgotten about it, do you really think Preston cares about it?"

"I think you're the last person to listen to about what Preston wants."

He swept across the room to box me in. Recoiling against the shelves, I turned my head away and dug my fingertips into the leather binder. "Is this really a battle you want to fight? Over something trivial? I expect some push back, but this isn't something I would've expected to fight over."

"I think you're just upset you underestimated me."

His pointed nose mere inches from my face, the puffs of his enraged breath tickled the skin at the base of my neck. He grasped the top of the portfolio with one heavy hand.

I braced myself.

"Give it to me," he growled, tugging at it.

"Not until you tell me where you went. *Partner.*"

He yanked the folder from my arms, scattering documents across the room. "This is such a waste of time!" he growled, throwing the empty portfolio onto the floor.

I fell to my knees to gather the paperwork and yelped as it all combusted at once. "You could've just let me have it if it was so unimportant!"

He cocked his head to the side. "You're wasting time crying about it."

"I'm not crying!" I snapped, climbing to my feet. "It obviously wasn't a waste of time if you'd rather burn them than let me read them! How am I supposed to learn anything about being your partner if you hide everything from me?"

"I'm not hiding anything." He extended a hand to me.

"Liar!" He ran from me right after asking me to be his partner and now he wouldn't share information with me. Wholly, I expected it. What I didn't expect was to still be treated like a prisoner. To still be kept in this hall. "Tell me what the extents of our partnership are! Tell me the truth!"

"That is up to me to decide as I please. I never said we would be equals and if you were so naïve that you convinced yourself of that, then I may reconsider my proposal." The hand he offered to me swung to point to the doorway. "Return to the bedroom until further notice. It appears you need to cool off."

"You can't keep me locked in here forever!"

"Actually, I can." The darkness stretched from his eyes to overshadow his face and tempered his voice. "Hostage or partner, I am the leader of the Veiled Army. You answer to me or Preston pays the price."

The day swept by while I rotted in solitary confinement. Tortured by loneliness until the sun came up. I must've fallen asleep at some point, otherwise I'd have seen him drop off the warm, cream cheese muffin with a pad of butter, a knife to spread it with, and a bottle of green tea.

*Fuckin' weirdo.*

Sends me to the room after threatening me, then leaves me a weapon on the bedside table?

Muffin consumed and clothing adorned, I tucked the butter knife into my sleeve for safe keeping. The hall was empty, so he must've left for 'mayoral affairs', as he liked to call it. Which meant he could be gone all day—just like when he'd left me in the chair.

I had to do *something*. Sitting in that room by myself, day or night, was among some of the most unbearable things I'd been forced to do.

Thankfully, he'd left the door unlocked for me to roam the Mayoral Wing. Not that there was much to explore. I stopped at the closed door a few paces from the bedroom and tried the handle, ear against the cool surface.

Nothing stirred inside.

It easily could've been a maintenance closet, though I had a feeling it was something more. *'I possess many things which belong to others.'*

It would have to wait. I didn't have the means to unlock the door and was unwilling to waste the butter knife on curiosity. So I went to the sitting room to read the newspaper—something I never expected to do.

The Veiled Army had advanced into the rest of the Onatah Territory, forcing the Pixie villages into an alliance.

The only reason Sorcerers would be interested in such a primal race would be for formidable soldiers. They'd be easy to enlist, whether against their will or not.

I crumpled the paper, as if it would dismantle the war swiftly building across the Mythos. One I, single-handedly, could've ended had I stabbed Ramone a little higher.

My chest ached, envisioning Preston in his cell. He would've stabbed Ramone higher and he damn sure wouldn't be reading the newspaper. The Archmage had done his best to protect not only me, but my Vampire.

*It's my turn.*

The lobby should be empty by now, everyone already at their desks for the day. A Sorceress likely manned the front desk, but I could handle just one—*I hope.*

Sliding the butter knife from its hiding place, I pried at the lobby door. Pushing my weight behind the silver, it slipped from the lock and staked between the door and its frame.

*This isn't going to work.*

Footsteps pounded in my head like a drum as they came closer. A voice murmured on the other side.

"Shit!"

The door jerked open.

Hiding the butter knife behind my back, I shied away from the Sorcerer in the entryway. I hadn't seen this one before. The deep circles around his eyes and the shadows under his skin were unforgettable. He seemed to loom over me, stealing all the space in the building and sending a chill across my scalp. It wasn't his size, in fact, he was comparable to Rodney in physique—it was something else entirely.

Something foreboding.

"Really?" He stepped forward to swipe the knife and laughed. The silver turned red hot in a flash of heat that started at the ends of his fist. The metal trembled, then pooled in his open palm.

*Oh Mythos.* My lips stirred without purpose. There wasn't anything that could be said to get me out of trouble. No reason for me to have a butter knife near the door.

"I should report you to Mayor Salvatore." *Ramone Salvatore.* We hadn't learned that name in school. How long had he been mayor?

"Do it then." I folded my arms.

"Oh, I will." He pointed the disc of silver at me. "In the meantime, I suggest you return to your holding place."

I set my jaw stubbornly, tempted to stay right here.

He lunged, and I scattered, much like my heart within my chest. Perhaps I'd underestimated Ramone. He'd told the truth. Partner or not, I was still his hostage with the threat of a reward for good behavior—and consequences, if not.

*Then what was the point?*

I found myself in the private gym's closet, the one Ramone had entered before when he gave me the stake. Stocked to the ceiling with weapons, one entire wall was daggers and swords. His collection's beautiful. One I envied and hoped to one day replicate.

"Not very smart to leave these out," I murmured, pulling one old knife from its hooks. The wear on the sharp side intrigued me—not wear, but inscriptions were carved into the metal. The design's familiar. Several of the texts in the astronomy room bore the same runes on their covers.

I traced my fingertip over the grooves, racking my brain.

*Onataian.* This was a Space Pixie design. A blade he'd collected from a victim, no doubt.

I jumped, warm breath on my neck and hands beneath my rib cage. "I see you found my collection," Ramone's soft voice echoed against my skin.

*Shit.* He'd incinerated those documents to keep them from me. What would he do to keep me from his weapons?

"They're, um." My throat went dry and my fingers coiled tight around the dagger's hilt. "They're gorgeous."

I put the dagger in its place on the wall before the temptation to stab him won out. If he knew I'd tried to escape, he wouldn't be so tolerant of an assassination attempt.

"A lot better than a butter knife, aren't they?"

I twisted in anticipation to defend myself—only to be met with smiling maroon eyes. The white flecks glimmered, like stars in a miniature galaxy.

*He isn't mad?*

My adrenaline crashed so abruptly, my knees wobbled. "I wouldn't have guessed you to be a collector." I attempted to redirect and deflect.

"Magic isn't my preferred method of defense. Since I'm less talented with it, my father had me trained to use more conventional tactics." He shrugged.

I gawked. "You know how to combat?" So far, he'd sent others to do his dirty work, even using me as a makeshift soldier. I'd assumed politics were more his thing.

"Of course I do. We don't use magic for everything." Ramone crooked a grin. "I especially wouldn't waste it on a measly Protector."

*Measly!*

"I thought I was impressive to you?" I narrowed my gaze. "You don't know anything about hand-to-hand combat, do you?"

He laughed, it was low and genuine. Not a taunt. Which I wasn't sure how to feel about. "You don't have to believe it."

That's where he was wrong. I *had* to know.

"Prove it." I inched closer.

"Why?"

I shoved him. "Are you scared?"

He stumbled a step, grin still in place. "Scared?"

Once more, I pushed him. Again, he faltered and smiled.

*Damn him.* I had to know. Had to know if our fight in his healing world was an accurate depiction of his abilities.

I grappled his arm, pulled him over my shoulder, then stooped low and flipped him onto the padded floor. He landed flat on his posterior, the smile on his face still there, just smaller.

"You know what I think? I think you're a coward—"

*Ouch.*

Ramone dragged me to his level by the leg, then slammed me into the ground with one arm angled across my chest. Determination darkened his features, the smile gone.

"Man, you're sensitive." I groaned, writhing on my sore back.

He rolled to his feet, a graceful whirlwind with impressive speed.

I heaved myself up to partake in the chase, unsatisfied. Just like when Kade sparred with me, it was never enough.

Ramone faced me, and I swung out only for my hands to be evaded every time. He ducked, dodged, and twirled out of the way with practiced skill. It was like watching a dancer perform ballet.

He grinned, waiting for me to attempt again. I hefted for breath and my muscles ached. His tactics were maddening. Worse than when Kade sparred with me.

I clenched my fists in front of me—*So impressive*. The longer I fought him, the more I learned about him—about how to escape him.

It's going to be a lot more difficult than anticipated.

Sucking in a deep breath to still my mind, I kicked—Deflected. He swiveled me around by the arm to slam my back into the brick wall, then pinned my arms to my chest. Like a bow on a wrapped present, he had me set in place.

*Damn.* My chest heaved while he wasn't even breathless!

"Had enough?" He rested his cheek against mine, and his voice tickled my ear. "Because I can keep going."

I bit my tongue to keep from saying anything hateful. I'd trained to fight in excess and I couldn't beat *Ramone*. Preston had been wrong to classify this man as weak. He may be mediocre at magic, but in hand-to-hand combat, he excelled.

*Fucking impressive.*

Taking my silence as defeat, Ramone chuckled. "Don't be too hard on yourself, I've got nearly two hundred years of experience on you." He released my arms and stepped away.

*Two hundred.* No wonder he was kicking my ass.

Being a sore loser, I took him to the ground from behind. He wound one arm around my waist as we fell, whipping me against his chest. After the initial impact, I pushed myself up to straddle him and brushed my wild hair from my face.

A light lavender blush formed across the bridge of his nose and cheeks.

*Lavender?*

I brushed his black hair from his face and bent to analyze him from an uncomfortably short distance. Checking the depth of the color and how it dipped across his skin, leaving room for faint white freckles. "You're part Space Pixie!"

"How could you tell?" He rubbed his neck and wriggled to get free. But I wasn't done.

I sat back and squeezed my thighs so he couldn't escape. "It's pretty obvious. Your eyes, the purple blush…" The knife in his collection…

"My mother's a Space Pixie," he explained, stilling against the floor. "It's part of the reason my magic leaves much to be desired."

Were he not the enemy, I might've felt bad for him. Halflings were common, albeit less appreciated in the political world. Each community wanted to be represented by someone who would understand their race. Someone who wouldn't find themselves obligated to another community.

Absolute idiocy, if my opinion mattered at all.

"You're pretty bold to run for mayor of a city who wouldn't accept you,"

"Which is why it's imperative they don't know." The purple blush faded as his expression turned steely. "Many would jump to prey on my weak genetics."

"Seems we can make an agreement." I tilted my head and put my hands on my hips. "You know my secret, and now I know yours."

"I'd hardly call being afraid of the dark secret worthy,"

"Do you want people to know you're a Pixie?"

"Fair enough."

Not only did I have valuable information against Ramone, now I had leverage.

"If you were so bad at magic, why did you bother involving yourself in their community, going to school for it? Why not a Pixie school?"

"I'm not *Onataian* enough to fit into their community, too capable with magic and not enough like them to be trusted with their culture." I forgot Pixies preferred to be known by their territory, a term forgotten as the Mythos expanded. Pixie much easier for others to remember.

"Capable enough you have everyone else fight your battles?" Being a Halfling meant just that. They were only half, which meant his magic could only be half as good as a full-blood Sorcerer.

Ramone flipped me by the arms onto my back, reversing our roles. "You asked why people choose to follow me." His face was close to mine, and I twisted away to stare at the ceiling. "I'm decent enough at illusion magic."

Same as he'd brainwashed me into his bidding, he'd indoctrinated an entire city into his scheme. Twisting, I wrapped my legs around his waist and flipped him. When he attempted to sit up, I thrust him down hard enough my arms nearly buckled from the force.

The necklace swung from my chest to dangle in his face. Fixated on the jewelry, he snatched the charm to hold it still. His lips curled, and he cast a thumb across the small dagger.

"This is one of my first pieces,"

I wanted to argue there was no way he created the necklace; it belonged to Preston. He'd never own anything associated with his nemesis. But two-hundred years was a long time.

"You make jewelry?"

He tucked the necklace into my shirt and gathered himself to sit up. This time I let him, distracted by my own curiosity.

His eyes danced, the white flecks shifting like nighttime snowflakes in the wind. "Do you want to see?"

I did.

Small tools and stones littered a desk in the far corner of the gym. At the center of the work area, various pieces of jewelry were displayed in a case.

Ramone held each item individually and explained their purpose, chattering listlessly. I did my best to absorb everything he said, but most of it went over my head.

He spotted the confusion drawing my brows together and ceased to speak. His shoulders slouched, and he studied a polished stone held between his hands, turning it over.

The defeat in his posture spoke more than words could. It must be lonely when you're the guy giving instruction and manifesting terror.

Toying with the stone, he avoided eye contact. Without a family to aspire for, I often sought validation from my educators. Kade saved me from becoming like Ramone. A single wing flutter in my chest considered empathy for him.

"Did you make the brooch for my cloak?" I fidgeted with Preston's necklace, tracing the thorns along the blade.

His head lifted, enthusiasm building in him once again. "You noticed it?"

"It's lovely." I released the necklace and considered reaching for him. He's strange—yet my soul ached for him. It's hard to believe a war lord could be simple enough to enjoy hobbies such as this one.

The care free light in his eyes suggested him to be a different man entirely. One who could be manipulated and distracted.

*Note taken.*

He cleared his throat, the lavender blush donning his features, and set aside the polished stone. "How about lunch?"

# GUILT
## CHAPTER 17

RAMONE SHOOK ME AWAKE, the white flecks in his eyes glowing like the bit of sun creeping through the curtain. "Get dressed," he demanded. "I have something to show you."

Had he given me a chance to wake up, I may have thought to argue with him. Then again, it had been three days since I'd stepped foot outside the hall. We exited the lobby through the front, rounding the rear of the building. He stopped us at the tree row, starting the nearby forest. The sun lowered in the sky, casting long shadows in its wake.

I began to ask what we were doing when he grasped the pendant holding his cloak in place. His focus fixated on the woods' depths, and he whistled low.

Foliage rustled and parted.

My breath caught in my throat as a silver wolf emerged. The others had been scuffed and dull, something I hadn't noticed until now. This one gleamed and glistened. Its fur almost could've been mistaken as soft.

Tentatively, the creature paced towards us, as if it were as nervous as me and allowing me a moment to appreciate its beauty—and the fact it wasn't trying to kill me.

"Can I pet it?" I asked, already crouched to do so.

One side of Ramone's lips curled. "I suppose."

Timidly, the wolf's nose touched my outstretched hand. I waited for it to acknowledge I meant no harm before petting its head.

The wolves *were* linked to their Spellcaster. I dropped to my knees to observe the canine's magical, almost mechanical, design. A magnificent red underglow cast between its flexible chest panels. At the center rested a crest identical to the one on Ramone's cloak-pin.

I cupped the wolf's snout in my hands, the wire brush fur uncomfortable to pet. Craning my neck, I asked, "How does it work?"

His subtle grin stretched into an arrogant one. "Magic."

I rolled my eyes and stood to maintain his gaze. "You called her?"

He nodded. "Each wolf's created with a specific symbol and matching trinket for its owner." His hand went to his pendant. "This is mine."

The same fire opal crystal from the pendant glittered in the wolf's sockets.

"Does it have a name?"

He shrugged one shoulder, a few white flecks fading from his eyes. "It doesn't need one. They aren't pets."

I narrowed my gaze, failing to understand how he could resist naming a loyal animal. My career path left me as a solo operation; a companion such as this would be beyond appreciated.

"How long have you had it?"

He made a face. "Well over a hundred years."

They technically weren't alive, since they're machines. *Fascinating*.

The wolf's ears flattened against its head, and its lips curled into a vicious snarl. I stepped back to watch it turn to survey the forest edge.

Ramone saw the threat first, spreading his arms out wide to put himself in front of me.

Curious, I leaned to see the massive grizzly bear, focus locked with the wolf. This being the first bear I ever saw, its thick defense coat and lumbering physique impressed me. But was it enough against a silver wolf? My bones ached, recalling how it felt for their razor-sharp teeth to carve away flesh.

Straightened, so I remained behind, I studied Ramone for an answer. He held onto his pendant, mumbling.

As the wolf darted to attack, the bear charged and met its adversary halfway, snarling in return.

I gripped his cloak, poised on my toes as if I could help. While he claimed the creature wasn't a pet, it already seized my compassion. But not a glimmer of emotion displayed in his dark eyes as he watched.

While the massive creatures continued to quarrel, he twirled to pull me into a run. I matched his pace—out of fear and worry for the wolf.

We scaled the capitol's steps, stopping outside the doors. We'd abandoned his companion, like cowards.

He drew me against his heaving chest and I stretched to search the way we came for the wolf.

"Don't worry." He smoothed my hair, and a chill prickled along my cheeks and down my neck.

I sighed. Despite his confidence, I worried.

*Why?*

If the wolf survived, it would go on to murder innocent Vampires—like Rodney. But I couldn't help myself. Even if it were a mindless creature, it acted on Ramone's command, not its own. It didn't deserve to be destroyed by a bear just because its owner was too cowardly to defend it.

"You have magic, you could stop that bear from..." A lump crowded my throat, and I choked.

"I'm not worried about the bear winning. The wolf will take care of it."

"How can you be sure?"

"I've watched them kill, like I said, for over a hundred years. I know their capabilities and even in the event something *did* happen, I'd just rebuild the wolf. It's not like they feel pain."

The while flecks were gone and the absence of empathy for the wolf in his expression sparked to life the reminder of who held me against his chest and combed my hair from my face. The warlord whose touch should repulse me.

This stupid arrangement with Ramone stood between me and my life. Rodney and Preston. I had to get out of here. No more waiting around, playing prisoner.

"Am I able to visit Preston?" I asked.

"Not today,"

"Why not? I'm tired of rotting in that bed!" I folded my arms. "You said we'd be partners. Did you just need a playmate, so you forced me to be your *friend*?"

His jaw hardened. "This won't get you what you want."

"You can't dazzle me to do what you want," the words sounded snottier than I intended. "I'm not some dumb bimbo easily impressed by your materialistic bullshit!"

Any trace of the person I'd begun to see in Ramone disappeared behind the thick walls of the dictator he's supposed to be. "My mistake," his words dripped with venom.

His fingers bit into my arms as he hauled me to the area of the building I loathed and the force with which he thrust me into the floor of the hall told me he was done playing.

*Good.*

Light shined through the gap between the curtains, an excellent back light to harrow Ramone's features as he observed me reading in the sitting room bay window. It took great strength not to swing, his proximity taking me by surprise.

He waited for me to tuck away the book, eyes twinkling like glossy ink.

"Since you believe it awful to be my *friend,*" he tipped my chin, "I'll show you how it feels to be my enemy."

What did the lunatic mean? I *had* experienced what it was like to be his enemy. "What do you want?"

He squeezed my chin between his thumb and curled index finger. "First off, I'd like to report that I was right. The bear wasn't successful and the silver wolf is fine."

I chewed on a response for a moment. His thumb glided gently across my chin, inching too close to my bottom lip. "The wolf's capabilities weren't my concern. It was the fact you could've diffused the situation but chose to walk away."

"I *chose* to get you away from what was going to happen." His fingers curled around my jaw.

"You expect me to believe that? To fawn at your feet and thank you?" I swatted his hand away. "I'm beginning to think your army lets you believe you're in charge when, in reality, you have no idea what you're doing."

A chilling smile twisted his lips, and the pits of his eyes sank into bottomless caverns. "I have a request."

The air suddenly felt too dense to swallow. Too heavy to bear, I leaned into the window.

"I want Preston to teach me dark magic,"

*He's alive.*

While Ramone hadn't let me go a single day without reminding me Preston was locked away in a cell, I'd begun to lose faith he was still alive. Every time I'd asked to see him, Ramone turned me down. It had been yet another way to keep me trapped in the Mayoral Wing—secluded from his plans and the world outside.

"What do you mean, dark magic?" Saying it aloud made the hair on my head stand up.

Smoke coiled in his laughter. "Have some imagination, Josephine. It's powerful magic. Something only Archmages can wield because the universe itself fears it."

"Because it's unpredictable and dangerous?" I thought of the kalento and how the Veiled Army had already wrecked hundreds of lives in one night and continued to do so.

He didn't need anymore power.

"Aren't all things worth having a little dangerous?" He turned away to straighten the books on the wall.

I crawled from the window seat to stand toe to toe with him. My patience thin. "What are you going to do with it?"

His smile didn't reach his dark, soulless eyes as he gathered my face in his hands. "Don't worry. I don't plan to use it on Preston. It would be a waste."

I didn't believe him. "What about the Vampires?"

His smile faltered. "After what that Leech did to you, you'll continue to defend those vermin?"

Rodney mutilated my wrist and nearly drained my life, but it wasn't as he saw it. It had been an unconscious act of survival. One I know he'd beat himself up for forever.

"It was an accident,"

"That's foolish to say." He swept to stand in the archway. "People who think like you do are the perfect prey for them. You humanize them too much just because they've fooled you into believing they need you. Protectors are nothing but a sense of security for them in the event they're hungry."

"That's not true. You don't know—"

"I've known them longer than you have. I've seen what they do when they're comfortable. They're an invasive species and if left untended, they'll swarm the Mythos."

"They've evolved. They're not like...like that." Briefly, it had been mentioned in our history books that Vampires were more feral before the Persecution.

"Get your boots."

I bypassed him a little faster than I probably should have. Eager to see Preston. To be sure it wasn't a trick, and he was okay.

Ramone followed me. "If you're to be my partner, you'll have to see them for what they truly are."

I bit my tongue hard to keep from pointing out he was the one who didn't see them accurately. Because proving him wrong wasn't as important as getting to see Preston or getting a chance at escape.

*Play the part.*

Boots laced, Ramone led me by the arm to the cell hall. I upturned my head to explore the drab concrete walls and ceiling. The rest of the capitol was drenched in intricate wood accents and decor, a great testament to the treatment of their prisoners.

"How can he not teleport out?"

Ramone released my arm to draw me against his side like some eager to learn prodigy. "The hall is warded to neutralize and absorb any magic, so it cannot be used within its walls. The concrete's infused with an alchemical property that preserves the ward magic so it doesn't have to be maintained daily like most."

*Logical*; Otherwise, the cells would be pointless. "Who maintains it?"

"A crew of hired professionals who both watch and regenerate the wards as needed,"

I pictured a band of security guards behind a computer screen, watching closely. It likely had nothing to do with such technical devices and instead measured the magical charges from the wards. *What level of the capitol were they on?*

I bowed my head as we approached Preston's cell, embarrassed to be tucked against the enemy's side.

He still laid on the floor, dried blood on his face and chest.

"If we weren't *partners*," Ramone's whisper caressed my skin and warmed my ear, "you'd be in a cell next to him. Left to rot. And being a plaything for my men is far worse than being *mine*."

A chill shot down my spine and I felt the blood in my face drain. *Shit.* His minions didn't scare me nearly as bad as hearing him refer to me in that way did.

He squeezed my shoulder before leaving to converse with his men in the glass room. As if he'd planted a seed of *knowing* within me. Like he didn't have to worry about what I'd do without him in earshot.

Rubbing my arms to ward off the chill, I crouched outside the cell and reached through the bars, calling Preston's name.

I needed to hear his voice, to feel him, to assure myself I hadn't accidentally slipped into Ramone's proposal without realizing it. That I hadn't lost myself—or Preston and Rodney.

"Preston, *please* wake up," I murmured, afraid Ramone could hear me beg. Afraid to show him I was scared. "*Preston.*"

Lying face down on the cold concrete floor, he twisted his stiff neck towards me. His bloodshot eyes gradually focused, drawing tears to my eyes as potent relief broke through the pained twist in his features.

"Love?" he croaked.

"Are you okay?" I gasped.

He slid across the floor, wincing as he stretched to squeeze my fingers. "I am now,"

My heart ricocheted around inside my chest. The world felt lighter just to see him. Even if he looked on the verge of death, at least he's alive. "I'm s-sorry," I stammered, a sob climbing past my lips. "I'm sorry it took me so long to come see you. I-I tried. He wouldn't let me. He keeps me locked away in the Mayoral Wing—"

His fingers tightened around mine and his golden eyes caught mine as if he'd reached out and touched my face. "Has he hurt you?"

"No." He hadn't. Not since the day he tied me to the chair. "I'm playing along with his terrible plan to sneak his army into Carthage. He's going to use me to do it."

"You can't let him do that,"

"He said he'd kill you if I don't cooperate." My voice broke, and I swallowed the lump of emotion that wouldn't stay tucked away. I couldn't let him worry about me, not when he struggled just to stay alive.

"Let him."

I shook my head and my lips quivered, tears sliding down my cheeks. "I won't. I'll find a way to save you. All of you."

Preston coughed and laced his fingers with mine. I felt the strength weaken in his grasp.

*Mythos. He's dying.*

"Love, if it comes down to it, I matter so much less than an entire race."

"That's untrue," I squeaked. I wiped my face, turning a bold glower at him. It may be selfish to, but he mattered as much as saving the Vampires. My entire being ached to imagine a world without him in it.

His lids drooped as he fought to produce a wavering smile. One that split his scabbed lips and a cut along his brow. I cupped his hand in both of mine, wishing I could squeeze hard enough to put him back together.

"He wants you to teach him some dark magic."

Preston gargled, then spit blood. "Over my dead body."

The reality of how near he was to that rattled me. "Don't say that."

"Don't worry about me." The failed smile slipped from his lips and he shut his eyes for a moment, drawing a deep breath.

One that shuddered.

"I don't care how dangerous it is. You've got to show him. We can stop him once we're out of here—" I stiffened, the office door swinging open.

Ramone stepped out, a new cloak for me in his hands.

I leaned to press a kiss to Preston's busted knuckles, a few stray tears falling from my lashes and washing away the bloodstains on the back of his palms. "Stay alive. *Please.*"

A muscle in his jaw flexed as his steely gaze swung past me to Ramone. For a fleeting moment, his strength returned in his fist as he drew it from my grasp. I didn't want to let go—didn't want to take my eyes off him for a second. Afraid if I did, the life in his eyes would flicker out like a burnt out bulb.

"I hope you're enjoying your stay here, Preston. Unless you're ready to discuss that spell with me, you'll be spending a lot of time in that cell." Ramone sneered, offering me a hand up.

It physically hurt to take it, because I could feel Preston's eye cut through me from behind.

"I'll be sure to give it a generous one star review." Preston growled, inducing another chest caving cough. He trembled and spat more blood.

"I assume that means your efforts weren't successful?" Ramone tucked me within the cloak, pinning it carefully with a brooch just like the one before.

"He'll come around," I insisted. "It would probably help if you'd give him a chance at healing—"

"I'm fine, Love. Don't barter with him on my behalf."

Ramone's lips peeled back as his gaze shifted to the broken mage on the cell floor. "Yes. You look as healthy as ever. In fact, I prefer your new look."

"Still better looking than you."

"Where are we going?" I cut them off, unable to listen to their childish bantering any longer. Preston was *dying* and they had the audacity to hurl insults at one another.

A pretentious sheen pressed Ramone's lips together as he slipped a hand into mine, towing me along. The muscle in Preston's jaw flexed tight as he watched me go. Ramone's back turned to him, the feigned strength melted from his features and he sagged on the floor.

*Please don't die.*

"We're going to get you some real clothes." Ramone led me outside and down the stairs. The cool late afternoon air nipped at my cheeks.

"*Real* clothes?" What was his definition of 'real' clothes?

His smile tugged higher on one side of his mouth. "You're my date and I can't have you looking…"

"A date?" I ignored his decision to trail off. I couldn't be seen in public with him. Not as his *date.* "This isn't what I agreed to."

"Need I remind you again so soon that the discrepancies of our partnership are primarily up to me?" He tilted his head. "Besides, I think you'll be pleasantly surprised with what I have in mind."

My heart turned to stone and dropped to the bottom of my rib cage, cracking open the place where I stored my composure. My insecurities feasted on the crumpling morsel. Not only did I have little experience shopping for a *date*, the concept of where something like that could lead utterly horrified me.

Had this been what he meant by partner? Behind closed doors, I was his hostage, in public I was to pretend to be his *girlfriend?*

His fingers tangled with mine, the soft pad of his thumb gliding along my wrist. Ice bolted up my arm and I trembled. The gesture was so casual, I almost couldn't tell if he realized he did it.

The distance between us shrank as we walked further into the city. The streets were crawling with pedestrians, leaving no room for vehicles of any kind. I found myself gripping his hand as many of them stopped to stare at us. People with big bright eyes and hair, some with wrinkles and no hair, even children. All ages and walks of life.

The families pointed and waved. Men gave a courteous nod.

The women were the worst. They sneered and whispered horrible things—about *me.*

They loved him. Even though he killed Vampire children and their Protectors. As if we were a true threat to the Mythos.

I hated all the attention. Protectors were to be inconspicuous—the most efficient way to perform our jobs. Which could be defined as a useless argument at present, since I didn't protect Ramone. In fact, it bothered me he could roam anywhere with little threat when Vampires had to look over their shoulders—because of *him*.

His thumb skated along my wrist faster the closer the crowd got. Because even he couldn't ignore the jealous remarks said loud enough anyone could hear.

I drew a sharp breath and blocked them out. Pushing my sights past the too close bodies to absorb the architecture. Tall, beautiful buildings with columns, pointed arches, and colorful, detailed stone moldings loomed over the civilians. The roads well-worn brick, curbed with modern sidewalks.

I committed the path we took to memory, logging the abundance of columns to hide behind in the event Preston and I escaped successfully. He wouldn't be able to teleport, so I'd have to navigate our way to freedom.

Ramone turned us into what I wouldn't have guessed to be a mall until we entered. He led me to a woman in fishnets with lime green hair. She smiled politely, head tilted to the side. Her vest declared her a design expert, while her floral perfume suffocated the suggestion.

"I've already made an appointment. Pick out whatever you want." Ramone pushed me towards the woman.

What I wanted, he kept in a cell, under a crippling amount of pain.

All sense of being vanished the second the clothes rack sea came into view. Without my combat boots to weigh me down, there may have been a chance I'd float away. Who could pick out anything with this amount of selection?

Mystery, her name tag said, guided me by the arm, thankfully. While she intimidated me, her knowledge would come in handy. This was her profession, not mine. I had no clue where to even begin.

Mystery shoved me into an open salon chair on the other side of the clothing sea. The most time I'd ever spent in a salon chair was one provided by the institute. We weren't allowed much personalization to our hairstyles, only general trims.

My hair was cut, my face pasted with makeup, all while beautifying my nails and toes. The woman was like a makeover pit crew.

Turning the chair, she held a mirror so I could see my transformation. *Shit!* I loved it and hated it simultaneously. She'd shortened it maybe one or two inches and layered it to frame my face and enlarge my eyes.

Tossing the mirror aside, Mystery called for assistance.

I gaped in terror. *What would they do to me now?*

She mumbled to the assistant as they hustled into the clothes racks.

"Come on,"

I regarded her hand like it was venomous, afraid to go with this cosmetology-psycho.

*Weird.* My hands and feet were soft and dainty. I possessed little doubt I would break if thrown into battle.

Tired of waiting, she pried me from the seat to drag. "So, you're with Mayor Salvatore. How is it?"

"Strange," I mumbled so she couldn't hear, then cleared my throat to speak louder. "Oh, you know…"

"No, I don't." She wiggled her brows. "Is he a good kisser?"

I avoided eye contact, my cheeks warm as the image of Ramone fresh out of the shower intruded into my thoughts, same as then.

*He's the enemy!* I thrust the image from my mind and defied a shiver.

"Yeah." *Ramone so owed me.*

Mystery squealed, excited to get dirty details. "He is talk of the town," she expressed. "Everyone wants to know what he's like."

*So much for being well known by his people.*

"There's not much to tell, yet." *With Ramone?* Hearing myself say it sounded traitorous. What was I doing? If I told her the truth, there's nothing he could do—nothing Mystery could do. One negative comment from me wouldn't change his entire followings perception.

"He's so gorgeous!" she crooned.

My hand shot to the necklace as Preston's rattly cough echoed in my thoughts. Dragging forth a crippling weight of guilt. If he could hear the lies I uttered to play along—or the thoughts that invaded my mind against my will...

"Would you like a piece to better match your outfit?" She craned her neck to catch a peek at the charm clutched in my fingers.

"No." I whipped to the side. But I couldn't escape the guilt. The realization that even pretending to be Ramone's partner was traitorous. Because when did I draw the line? When would I be able to save Preston?

Mystery held her hands up. "I understand."

But she didn't.

*Oh, no, no, no, no-o.*

The assistant met us at the dressing rooms with gifts worse than what she'd already given me—clothes unfit for physical combat.

Cloak returned to my shoulders, and my old clothes in a bag, she led me to Ramone. *I missed them already.* Especially when Ramone's eyes widened to better linger at the edges of the frightfully short and formfitting dress.

My gut wrenched, wishing it were Preston looking at me like that and I flushed, knowing well how mortified I'd be either way. I ran a hand through my hair, trying to distract myself. The attention from him made my heart jump the longer it trailed on. I'd never felt pretty, not really. The dresses at Bathory were more like bed sheets.

*What am I thinking?*

I'd agreed to this arrangement to rescue Preston. Ramone's nothing but a manipulative creep. Nothing he could do or say would make me feel pretty.

He caught his bottom lip in his teeth, drawing attention to his lip piercings.

"Is this stylish enough?" Mystery's voice had grown heavy and she flipped her hair, as if it would sweep me out of the way.

It didn't work. Ramone nodded like a bobble head incapable of speech, and his eyes never left me.

*Fuck, why wouldn't he look away?*

Smiling, Mystery left for another customer to satisfy. *Or torture.*

I sighed, then *click-click-clicked* towards the exit, Ramone left behind in his stupor. My ears rang, solidifying the hatred I had for heavy footsteps. Stealth was difficult to achieve when one trotted like a horse through town.

Breaking out of the stun, Ramone rushed to catch my free hand. This time, he took it with such possession it staked me clean through. He held onto me because he wanted to be seen with me, not because he feared I'd escape.

And, *Mythos*, did that hurt. Worse than if he had sliced my chest open with a dagger. Because it should be Preston at my side—not *him*.

"Josephine?" He lifted our joined hands and drew us to a stop just outside the mall. The sun rested low in the sky, its warmth blanketing my skin like an embrace. Chasing away the chill from his unwavering stare. "You're beautiful."

Against my will, my gaze darted to his. The heeled boots put me closer to his height, which made it easier to tumble into the depths of the universe within his eyes. The lavender blush became more saturated along his cheekbones the longer I stared, the more I forgot to look away.

"I thought we'd go out to dinner." He tucked me against his side and abruptly set us into motion.

"Where?" I tried to hide the waver in my voice. Perhaps hard to get was the vibe I sought here.

His entire persona glowed as he flipped on the charm. "My colleagues rave about a restaurant in Carthage."

"You can't teleport in," I stated. Despite the kalento's ability to wipe out Ramone, I wasn't willing to risk my life against the great creature *again*. Once was enough for me. "Their guardian will—"

"The creature won't bother us." My warning didn't penetrate his stone wall of confidence. Head tilted back, his gaze challenged my own. "I'm an educated man. I studied the kalento, and the stored knowledge of Carthage's wards."

It couldn't be so easy, not for him.

# NETWORKING
## CHAPTER 18

He teleported us to the forest at the city's edge. The wind whipped my bare legs, biting the skin within seconds. I pulled the cloak around me, clenching my teeth so they didn't chatter.

I deserved to freeze to death, leading him here into the heart of the world I'd sworn to protect.

The kalento emerged from the distant tree row. My hair raised when the ground shook under each of its steps. I clutched Ramone's arm to keep from falling, off balance thanks to these *stupid heels.*

"How is it possible you can teleport this close? It took Preston until we got to the city to be able to see." I demanded, nails digging into Ramone's sleeve. "It's enchanted."

The cloudy skies camouflaged the creature, its heavy footfalls the best way to keep track.

"All you need to get this close is an ally. When you entered last time, you were accepted as such by the magic protecting its borders."

"But you—"

"I'm riding on your visa's coattails,"

I shook my head as we neared the city limits. As if we hit a wall, our feet stuck to the ground, rooted to the spot. The officer with the elaborate mustache came into view like a curtain lifted.

Ramone clutched me against his side; a poof of his breath formed in the air. His uncertainty reflected my own; fingers dug into my hip. His ruse would end here once we were denied entry.

The officer's gaze swept over him once before me. "Back again?"

I sucked in a sharp breath, unable to dredge up any sort of response. If I told him the truth, Preston would be trapped in Luxor until I found a way to get back to him. If I stayed silent, I betrayed Carthage—and Vampires as a whole.

"Still with that Sorcerer, eh?" He adjusted a strap across his shoulder—a sheath for the staff they used to control the kalento.

My mouth fell open. He thought Ramone was Preston!

It couldn't be this easy! They were so thorough last time!

"We were told you'd probably be back. Same rules apply as last time, buddy. We're really cracking down on things since other cities are experiencing raids." He hooked his thumb in his belt, gaze darting to the kalento as it drew nearer. "I've even heard rumor we might increase the wards, which hasn't been done in...Well, since the Blood Persecution."

Unlike Preston, Ramone kept silent and dipped his head in obedience, face hidden by the clouds shielding the moonlight. Not that the officer looked at him anyway, too distracted by the creature bounding only a hundred feet away.

"Anyway, enjoy your visit." The officer sighed. "I've got to deal with this brute before he gets any closer and scares the civilians." He grumbled to himself as he bypassed to confront the city's guardian.

Ramone thrust us into stride, pushing me faster to put space between us and the others. I couldn't help but wonder if he feared the officer or the kalento more.

The wind disappeared, elevating the temperature to a bearable autumn night, and the city revealed itself to us.

I'm useless and the system is useless. The officer should have interviewed us no matter if he recognized me!

"Nothing like the Vampires' lack of consideration for their people," Ramone celebrated. "This will be so easy."

His reaction to the city was similar to Rodney's. His mouth fell open, and he pulled me close against his side. I could've fought back—probably should have. But I couldn't. It was too late now. He could get into the city, the magic establishing him as an ally—as he said.

Now I just had to stick by his side and ensure he didn't harm anyone, until he took me to Preston again.

The warm buttery smell of pastries filled the air, luring us along the strip mall. Hunger alone kept my feet shuffling, my attention harnessed on him from my peripheral. He commended the shop fronts and architecture, noting each detail.

"Josephine," he murmured, spinning us and catching me by the shoulders. His whirling gaze delved into mine and my stomach did a cartwheel, seizing any air I might've possessed. "Magnificent. You're magnificent," he breathed.

The cartwheel rose into my chest, and I gripped the edges of his cloak to keep from crumbling. Behind bars is where traitors belonged. Not on a romantic stroll under the starry sky. "Don't thank me—"

"I couldn't have done it without you." He cradled my face in his hands. "But it's not over. Our night here has just begun and you look as if you've seen a ghost. Play along for me and this doesn't have to be ugly."

The density of the weight I carried multiplied as he unshelled his warning. Now, not only did I have to bear the burden of treason to save Preston and in the future, Vampires, I had to make sure I played it right so no one died *today*. "Okay," I murmured.

We held hands through the cobblestone streets, pointing at different shop fronts and landmarks. His eyes' movement without a pupil became more apparent to me. The way they narrowed to take in every detail, he plotted instead of enjoying the sights. My wallow grew into paranoia. *What if someone recognized him? Or me!*

Strapped to his side, I hardly saw an older woman as she approached from the opposite side of the street. Her solid build defined her as a Protector, Vampires leaner. As well as her short, gray streaked hair gave away her shorter life span.

"Excuse me," she called, briefly assessing me in advance of Ramone.

He drew us to a stop alongside her, and my hands grew damp. This was it. She recognized him and if she had an ounce of sense, she'd kill us both.

"Aren't you the mayor of Luxor?" She placed her hands on her hips.

This woman should be defending the border! Not that mustache with a badge.

"Yes, ma'am." His voice was smooth and inviting, like the breathtaking smile he unearthed next.

She fell for it, unable to hold back her own flattered grin and pink donned her cheeks. "What brings you to Carthage?"

I hoped it was compulsion magic misleading her and that she'd feel it. In case, I scanned for her weapons. She must've kept them concealed beneath her layered clothes, because I saw no daggers or guns.

"Other than its fantastic ambiance," Ramone purred, securing his hold on me as I writhed for some separation, "I'm here to network."

Let her see through it. *Please.*

"May I offer any guidance?" The crow's feet around her eyes deepened, and she combed a hand through her hair.

*She believed him?*

"Could you recommend a restaurant? My Protector and I could use a good meal."

"Oh, yes." She bounced in place, as if no one had ever asked for her opinion before. "There's a great one at the end of this strip mall, on the corner. Best one in town."

"Thank you for the recommendation." His hand coiled around my waist, fingers gliding along my hipbone and pressing in, because he knew what he said next would set me off. "And thank you for protecting this beautiful city and its inhabitants. I'm sure you bring great comfort to them after what happened at the boarding institute. Such a tragedy."

*Ah, yes, flattery and pandering to her emotions.*

She pressed a palm to her chest and her lips mashed into a fine line. "We're doing the best we can."

Ramone curled his arm, so he smashed my face against his shoulder. "Someone will answer for what happened. Justice will be served."

It's a good thing he'd thought ahead, because I couldn't look at her when he lied to her. Couldn't bear to think she believed him—trusted that he was here just as he said, to network, and assumed he worked to help solve the mystery of the Veiled Army's rise from the shadows.

I curled my fist in his shirt front and clenched my jaw as they bid one another well-wishes. Furious she didn't question every word that left his lips.

He's a Sorcerer, for Mythos' sake. I hadn't trusted one since Rodney and I stepped foot outside Bathory—until I did.

Ramone stroked my hair and brushed his cheek along mine to speak softly so no passersby could hear. "You've got to check your expressions. Anyone could see you were ready to explode just then and while you may think it would help your case, it wouldn't. You're here with a Sorcerer and I just established you as my Protector. You'll be held in contempt, too."

Were Preston not held prisoner, it would've been a risk I was willing to take.

He tucked a lock of hair behind my ear and tipped my chin, forcing me to look at him. "Now smile and remember we're here on a date. We're having a good time and eager to see the city."

My abdominal muscles tightened as I did what he asked. Fighting to appear believable and keep my composure.

We traveled the entire business district before backtracking to the restaurant. It was bustling with patrons, dressed as sharply as we were and the smell of oregano hung heavy in the air.

My cheeks tingled, the cold leaching from my body as we waited to be seated. I grew more impatient with Ramone and, in turn, myself. Maybe Preston was right. Maybe Carthage mattered more and I should out Ramone right now, no matter what would happen to me.

But an ember of doubt weaseled into my mind. If he could so easily look anyone in the eyes in this city and *smile*, not a bit of guilt weighing on his shoulders, then he had a plan in mind. One that would secure his safety in the event I tripped up.

He may have a strange way of thinking, but the Sorcerer wasn't stupid.

"Welcome. Just two today?" The hostess's pleasant voice matched her polished customer service regard.

Ramone reflected the gesture. "Yes, please. We heard this is the best place in town." He winked and pulled me close to his side.

"Oh, are you just in town visiting?" She filtered through the menu stack.

My mouth went dry, afraid he'd finally slipped up.

"My Protector's from here. She used to care for a Vampire. We thought we'd stop in and see if there was anything we could do for the community after the tragedy at the boarding institute."

"You're so thoughtful." She clutched the menus to her chest and led us to our seats. "Not many outsiders thought to reach out once the news got to the media. Most we've seen show up are reporters."

The lies just kept coming and everyone we met ate them up. No one thought to challenge the Sorcerer who seemed too comfortable visiting a city that should've turned him away.

I fidgeted with my skimpy neckline as heat climbed up my throat. This was too easy—like he said. If they wouldn't make this excursion challenging or in the least daunting, I had to.

But I had to be careful.

The hostess left us at a booth in the corner, taking our cloaks to hang up. Shouldn't those be a glaring signal to *someone* that we shouldn't be trusted?

Not a soul bat an eye.

I slid into the booth and pressed against the cool stone wall, dress rolling up my thighs. He swiftly filled the other end, trapping me.

"I hate this dress," I muttered, jerking it into place. *Among other things.*

"You look lovely in it," he countered, skimming the menu. Completely at ease, despite the fact we earned glances from other patrons.

As if I *cared* what he thought of me in this dress!

"Everyone's staring," I growled, holding up my menu like it would help. Protectors were allowed to go out on their own. But they all knew the man at my side wasn't a Vampire and while they should trust the police to keep a dangerous Sorcerer from entering the city limits, I hoped they didn't.

"Because they think you look *delicious*?" He *finally* looked at me, a devious curl raising his lips.

My throat closed on what I wanted to say, which fell short of the role I was supposed to play. His cedarwood, citrus cologne smacking me in the face far more potently than any of the stares. "Are you sure this is a good idea?" I whispered, leaning behind the barrier of his menu. "We could've eaten when we got back to Luxor."

"Coming here to eat was the entire point. Remember?" He flipped the menu for the drink options. "I'm not afraid of them."

"Then why are you so worried about exterminating them?" I spoke through gritted teeth, hoping no one could hear.

He set aside the menu and draped an arm across the back of the seat casually. While he fought to remain unbothered, the tension around his eyes and lips told me his patience with me was breaking. He leaned to speak in my ear, his breath and low tone striking a bolt through me. "They're just the first step in what's to come. My father campaigned to solve the Mythos' problem decades ago, and I intend to finish his efforts."

"What problem?" My grip tightened on the menu as his hand slid off the back of the booth and he brushed his fingers along my cheek.

"The imbalance of power. It's in the communities and governments. Stretching far past the borders. Something has to force the Council to reform, and it seems brute force does the trick."

"Why the Vampires? Why Carthage?"

His fingers lowered, first to my shoulder, then traced a figure-eight along my upper arm. With each pass, the motion grew slower and more intentional. A strange sensation climbed into my veins like the endorphins from a bite. Lulling me into a false sense of delirium as his repetitive track synchronized with the puffs of his breath, caressing my skin. "Because of what they have done to survive."

I jerked back to reality and his fingers suddenly felt like claws skating across my flesh and his breath like the icy chill of death.

The server appeared at our candle-lit table, a female Vampire, likely a few years older than Issak, with layers of dark circles around her eyes. Her toothy smile was as strained as her voice. "What can I start you two off with?"

A glimmer of hope crossed my mind that she could be the one who saw through Ramone's facade. Until I realized she just hated her job.

"We'll take the best wine you have." He cast her off with a flick of his wrist. One she was eager to oblige.

I placed my menu with his and twisted so our knees touched. "Why is it so important to you to carry on your father's legacy? I assume he's dead, so what do you get out of it? Besides the shift of power."

He studied the dining room, turning a deaf ear to me. Lacing his fingers, he rested his chin on them, elbows propped on the table. Unexpectedly, a smirk surfaced, and he leaned towards me.

"Isn't that your Vampire over there?" He lifted a finger subtly to point to a table across the room.

Rodney sat with his parents and the blonde woman from the capitol... *What was her name? Ashley!*

I slumped in the seat to hide behind Ramone. Rodney would shamelessly remove any hope I had of getting Preston out of Luxor before enacting a plan to stop Ramone.

"I assume that's his father with him." He sat straighter in his seat for a better view. "He's sharply dressed."

The server blocked his line of sight as she delivered the wine and Ramone leaned to peer around her. "Tell me, who is the man over there? The one in the suit."

She glanced over her shoulder. "Oh, he's the mayor." A dense cloud encroached across her features, intensifying the circles. "That's his son there beside him. Must be nice to have money. He doesn't have to morn like the rest of us."

"Hm." Ramone behaved uninterested. "Send them all wine on my tab."

She grunted and left us alone. Realizing her jab at the mayor fell on deaf ears. Ramone didn't care about her lost loved ones. Didn't seem bothered she thought Mr. Harper knew about the Bathory attack before it happened.

"Why did you do that?" I hissed, leaning over him to watch the server deliver the Harper's drinks.

*Shit, shit, shit!*

I hunkered deep within the booth and gulped from the stemless wine glass. The sweet nectar burned my throat and warmed my belly.

*Think, Jo, think!*

My nerves seized as Ramone smiled and waved at Mr. Harper, sweeping to his feet to approach the family.

It felt like the wine bubbled in my stomach, boiling into my chest and up my throat. Threatening to blow like a steam engine and announce me to the entire restaurant as a traitor. A spineless coward who put her own feelings before her duty.

I shot out of the booth to retreat to the restroom, fighting with my dress every step of the way. Weaving between the many tables, I ignored the glowers and judgment twisting the guest's features.

*Did any of them see me?*

No matter how hard I tried to break through the hiss in my ears, I couldn't form a cognitive thought. Consumed by blind panic, I allowed my instincts to locate the nonchalant sign hung along a wall to indicate where the bathroom hall was.

Ducking my head, as if it would slow the steam rising inside my skull, I barreled past a few stragglers, and only slowed once in the vacant bathroom.

The door swung closed a second after I locked myself in a stall.

I'm a *traitor*.

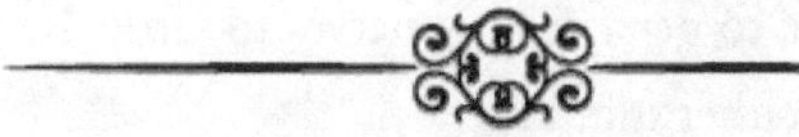

I leaned against the cool stall door and pinched my eyes shut. Didn't Ramone know Rodney would recognize him? Even if he hadn't gotten a good look at him during his hunger craze, he'd still recognize the name.

Ramone had to know that and must've had a plan or he wouldn't have approached them. Or would he? He had access to the city, he didn't have a use for me anymore and he said he wasn't afraid of the Vampires, so maybe he didn't think they could catch him to arrest him?

No matter what, my luck's fucked.

I'd end up someone's prisoner.

But I couldn't just give up. It's not who I am. Preston had been right. Walking away from the Harpers when they fired me wasn't okay. I should've given Rodney the opportunity to have the final say. Being fired by people who didn't have the authority to do so wasn't something I should let rule me.

Neither was being Ramone's prisoner.

I'd make my plan to distract Ramone work. *My skeleton of a plan.*

Some composure gathered, I left the stall to gawp at my foreign reflection in the sink mirror. The woman staring at me was unrecognizable. What happened to the determined Protector Kade trained? Had my ego kept me afloat in school this whole time?

I patted cold water on my neck to soften my nerves and smoothed my dress before stepping into the hall.

Thus far, Ramone had access to the city and a decent enough layout of the business district. I had to get him out of Carthage before he could map out the entire place—or whatever else he intended to accomplish.

Ramone waited for me to assume my seat, watching me slink across the building in hopes the Harpers didn't notice me. One glimpse of Rodney and everything would crumble.

I gulped more wine to persuade my nerves to settle. Ramone didn't appear panicked, so neither should I.

He stretched along the booth, eyeing me closely. "Burke is a pleasant Leech," he resolved, pushing a glass of ice water to me. "Who is the woman with him?"

"His wife or his assistant?" I leaned to peer around him, hand on the condensated glass.

Mrs. Harper spoke to those at her table with great flamboyance while no one listened.

Ashley's leg stroked Mr. Harper's from beneath the table.

My forehead wrinkled with the arch of my brows. *Gross.*

Ramone's lips curled. "I take it you see what I saw?"

"They're having an affair, too." I gasped.

"Too?" he inquired.

I cast aside the water glass to continue drinking the wine. "While I *briefly* stayed at their estate, I...I saw Mrs. Harper's favorite Protector sneaking into her room."

"Is that so?" He drummed his knuckles on the table, shifting his invasive stare in their general direction.

How long had she and Burke been out of love? Were they aware of one another's infidelity? Perhaps they were in a stalemate, waiting for the other to end the marriage.

I gulped the rest of my wine as the server arrived with our meal. I hadn't placed an order, so I assumed Ramone did so for me. The pasta sauce smelled delectable—surprising since the restaurant appeared primarily operated by Vampires who didn't eat.

"Didn't your mother ever teach you it's impolite to assume what a lady wants to eat?" I grumbled, casting him a displeased glare beneath my lashes.

Either he didn't hear me, or he ignored me.

"More wine, please." Ramone gesticulated towards my empty glass.

Blatantly inconvenienced by the inquiry, she raced away at inhuman speed to retrieve a wine bottle. I watched her pour the blood red liquid, happy to consume more. I was going to need it to get through the rest of this night.

Ramone stacked ziti noodles onto his fork. "What is your opinion of Mayor Harper?"

I nearly choked on the wine. He was asking me? "He...He reminds me a bit of R—my Vampire. They both have tempers that tend to get ahead of their logic."

"I get the feeling a lot of people don't care for his temperament."

"The server?"

"And others."

Who else?

Ramone sipped his glass of wine, then pushed my plate closer to me. "After this, I'd like to mill about the town some more. Get the feel of exactly what his constituents think of him."

I didn't like the sound of that. "Why? What do you have planned?"

"I've already told you," he sighed. His expression became clouded. "The imbalance in power is felt all across the Mythos. I suspect, even with the city closed off, Carthage feels the imbalance, too. It all roots to the governments. My father knew it and tried to change it. It was the only thing he truly cared for."

"That can't be true," I said, scooting so I could study the side of his head because he wouldn't look at me. "He must've left some impression if you're carrying out his legacy."

The wine undoubtedly caught up to him, or he'd ventured to the same dark place I'd lost him to the day he'd asked me to be his partner. "The only impression he left was one of remorse. That I'd never be good enough."

A stake plummeted through the center of my being to hear him talk like that. To see the glistening in his soulless stare. I plucked a cloth napkin from the table and clutched it in my lap.

"He used me when I convenienced him. That's all." His voice grew tight, like it pained him to relive the memories.

I knew the anguish of holding yourself to an unreachable expectation. Trying to make someone proud who wasn't even here anymore. Someone I never really knew.

Without instruction, my hand darted out to grasp his forearm. A ripple of tension coasted up his arm and settled in his shoulders. A muscle in his jaw flexed, and he squirmed to the edge of the booth, drawing his hand from mine.

I lowered my head to the napkin clutched in my other hand, recalling how he'd run away the last time I'd tried to console him. Then couldn't help but wonder if he had ever been shown an ounce of compassion? If he had, maybe he wouldn't be so intent on destroying the Mythos.

By dinner's end, I was pickled. So much so, we staggered along the road—Ramone trying his best to keep me upright. Clutching my unsettled stomach, I swayed toward the decorative shrubs along the walkway. Ramone tightened his hold on my hips, putting me center with gravity.

"Either you can't hold your liquor," he complained, "or you have a drinking problem."

"I had a bit of wine," I stammered, my stomach swimming. The physical benefit of the alcohol was the warmth it provided, even if it all resided in my face.

The second he released my waist, I did a swan dive at the cobblestone road.

"Dammit," he grumbled, catching my arm a second before I hit the ground.

I curled my fingers into his shirt to stabilize myself as he dragged me upright. The world spun, my feet were giant, and oxygen definitely was not my friend.

"Can you try to walk?" He braced me in front of him. "At this rate, we'll be deterring the citizens."

Taking tentative steps, we moved a few paces further.

"Ramone..."

I expelled my stomach onto my shoes.

# DRIP
## CHAPTER 19

FOOTSTEPS FOLLOWED THE ECHO of the lobby door as it slammed shut, each sharp click a direct jab into my skull. No matter how much I'd tried to nap in the sitting area, even forcing myself to read a book about precious metals, my hangover persevered. In spite of my eight hours of rest and a revitalizing breakfast.

Ramone jerked me to my feet by an arm. My head pounded from the swift transfer and my stomach soured.

"I need you to help me."

"With what?" I struggled to keep up as he hauled us to the lobby. Especially with my head pounding like a drum.

"*He* refuses to cooperate," he spat. "I believed he would oblige to protect you, but he's stubborn and thinks he has grounds to defy me!"

"Can't imagine how that didn't work for you," I grumbled.

Some of the weight plaguing my skull lifted. Preston sat on his cot, arms rested on the knees of his blood spattered jeans, and a lit cigarette between his scabbed lips.

My stomach did a weird flip. Relieved to see he was more himself than he had been in five days.

"This is a government building!" Ramone fumed, his fingers curling tight into my arm. The restrictions on magic likely the only reason a spell didn't jet from his fingers. "You can't smoke in here!"

I hid a smile behind my hand. *Damn, it felt good to see him vertical.*

Preston raised his brows, pulling the cigarette from his lips to hold his hands out. "I don't see a sign anywhere."

"There doesn't have to be, it's just common knowledge." Ramone fanned the air, coughing. "How did you even light that?"

Preston lifted his destroyed reading glasses to perch on his nose. The glass broken out of them and the frames tweaked.

*And yet he's still breathtaking.*

"Should've taken those." Ramone huffed, pushing me closer to the cell and finally letting go.

I slipped my arm through the bars, tangling my fingers with Preston's. He leaned against the bars so I could press his fist to my chest, resting my forehead against the cool metal between us. Somehow, beneath the stench of dried blood, he still smelled warm and welcoming. Like he hadn't been close to death while waiting for me to save him.

"Are you alright, Love?" He squeezed my hand and placed the cigarette between his lips. "If he's laid a hand on you—"

"You'll what?" Ramone sneered, folding his arms across his chest and leaning against the opposing wall. "You can't get out of there."

Preston's gaze narrowed, but he said nothing, his lips pressing together when I placed my hand to his cheek.

"I'm fine. He's..." My mouth went dry, unable to dredge up what I'd been about to say. He could've been much worse as a captor. In fact, I'd expected him to be. But I couldn't bring myself to say any of that to Preston.

"A gentleman?" Ramone provided, chin lifted spitefully.

Preston raised a brow in contest. "Who told you that, your mother?"

He pushed from the wall to toss his arms in the air. "Josie has agreed to be my partner. I'm sure some of her cooperation can be attested to the fact I have *morals*."

A line chiseled into Preston's cheeks, and his expression turned steely. They'd known one another a long time, which meant they knew far more about one another's pasts than I'd ever know. It didn't surprise me to hear Preston had been with other women.

I smoothed my thumbs across his knuckles, begging him to ignore Ramone. He was obviously trying to get a rise out of Preston. I didn't care about his past. He'd shown me compassion when I thought no one could. Stood at my side when my best friend was taken from me.

He's a good man.

"It's easy to appear as if you have *morals* when you aren't noticed." Preston fired back, some of the warmth returning in his eyes.

Catching my bottom lip between my teeth, I begged my cheeks to remain colorless. Ramone was furthest from repulsive; the women in this city flocked to him. Although I failed to see how any of this was relevant right now. Not when Ramone wanted access to dark magic and had Preston trapped in a cell to ensure he got it.

Ramone jerked me aside by my arm, once again eliciting a sharp pang in my head. He plucked the cigarette from Preston's lips and crumbled it in his hand. Tobacco and ash fluttering to the ground, the paper falling after it.

"I'm not going to play your childish games anymore," he declared. His fingers bit into my arm and I clenched my teeth.

Preston's eyes flared, shifting from me to lock on Ramone. His hands coiled around the cell bars, cinching tight until his busted knuckles broke open and blood seeped through the cracks. "If you're going to waste time, I figured I might as well make it fun."

"You're the one wasting time!" Ramone argued. "I'll keep you locked in here forever—"

"You're both wasting time!" I countered, ripping my arm from his hold. Pushing him aside, I angled myself between the two. "Neither one of you is going to get what you want, acting like that."

It became starkly obvious to me they'd always been like this. Arguing constantly.

"I asked him to teach me a simple spell—"

"You *know* it isn't simple," Preston snapped, head whipping in his direction. This magic, he referenced, was one spell in particular rather than a genre. How horrible could it be if Preston would rather die to avoid Ramone using it?

The Veiled Army had decimated an entire generation in one night. I couldn't even imagine what they'd do with dark magic.

My gaze stayed on Ramone a long time. What choice did Preston have? Lying? If he were to send the Veiled Army on a wild goose chase, it could buy us some time to work out an escape.

The bottomless depth in his black eyes persuaded me to speak, "Ramone, why don't you go cool off while I speak to Preston?"

He pushed away from the cell. "Fine. My men will be in the office, so don't try anything stupid or it'll cost you *her* life." His glare lingered on Preston before he proceeded down the hall, the door slamming behind him.

*My life.*

If we couldn't escape while they were hopelessly chasing our lead…I didn't allow myself to finish that thought.

I drew his ruined glasses from his face. "You have to give him something to work with," I whispered, in case the Sorcerers in the office could hear. "Even if it's a lie."

"He'll know if I'm lying." He caught my hand to pluck his glasses from my grasp and tucked them in his pocket. "I won't risk your life—or the Vampires'—for his stupid plan."

"I need time to find a way to get us out of here. What is the spell he wants you to teach him, anyway?"

"Impossible." Preston shrugged.

"Is this a power trip for you or something?"

"Of course not! This is dark magic, unpredictable chaos. In Ramone's inexperienced hands, it's a death sentence for the entire Mythos."

My stomach sank. Intentions aside, Ramone would destroy us all.

"Besides, the talentless prick cannot slay me nor will he harm you. So, I refuse to help him and there isn't anything he can do about it, Love. End of conversation."

I caught his jaw in one hand to force him to maintain my gaze. "Stop being so selfish! You have to pretend. For me. I really don't want to spend all of my immortal life stuck here, playing Ramone's partner, and before you say something stupid, *no*, I will not just leave you behind."

He rolled his eyes, cheeks squished together. I assumed his reaction as compliance and let go.

"I'm willing to rot here if it means keeping the Mythos from suffering at his hands. While you're, strangely, alright with risking the Vampires' lives for what? Me? I've lived a long life and if you think for one second he's going to be easy to trick, I've done an incredible job convincing you he's incompetent. Ramone is magically weak, he's not unintelligent."

Fire ignited in my chest and my palms ached for my blades—to prove I was still the driven Protector who'd survived the Bathory massacre. "I never said he's unintelligent. I just think he's...easily manipulated."

A muscle in his brows twitched and his cheek sunk in on one side. "You're falling right into his plan by staying here. You should leave and protect Rodney."

I'd chosen *him* to protect. He would not rot here in this cell, not when he'd made me have *feelings*. "That's not going to happen. If you won't step up and help me, then I'll continue to screw up Ramone's plans until I can get you out of here. I'm not betraying the Vampires by being here, either. I'm protecting them too, by monitoring him."

His shoulders tightened, like something hit him. "Monitoring him? Do you hear how naïve that sounds, Love? He holds all the power here. You're not his partner. You're his puppet. So long as you stay here, you're endangering the Vampires. Stop trying to be my hero. I don't deserve it."

*Naïve.*

"Just because you're two-hundred years old doesn't mean you know everything! Ramone believes I'm a very capable Protector and I'm going to prove him right! You're going to leave here with *me*."

I rushed for the exit to hide the tears welling in my eyes. His lack of faith in my capabilities stung. Worse than him asking to be left behind.

He'd given me feelings only so he could *crush* them.

Over the next three days, I learned Ramone's routines. Gone all day, he'd return in the evening to prepare dinner. We would eat, then retire to the sitting room for chamomile tea and a book. I, however, wasn't a reader. Typically, I sat beside him while he read, pretending my escape to be as simple as crawling through the window and racing through the streets.

Tonight, I glared holes into the opposite wall. Preston had so easily disclosed his lack of faith in me. Even if I broke him free, he'd given up hope on our overall mission. He'd said Ramone was weak. Then why did he believe the war was already won?

Without realizing it, I twirled my fingers in my hair. The strands got so bound up, it's a wonder they didn't knot.

Ramone stilled my hand, restricting it between us. His gentleness surprised me. He held his book in the other hand, vision never leaving the pages.

My cheeks burned as I whispered an apology. At the sound of my voice, he lowered the book to face me.

"Don't apologize," his voice was soft, and he released my hand. "I'm sure you have a lot on your mind."

I did. As if he controlled what went on in there, my thoughts quickly shifted to the many times he'd complimented me.

*'Magnificent,' he'd said.*

"You should try drinking some tea. It would help calm you down," he insisted for the hundredth time tonight. This time, it was less scolding and more attentive. Like he genuinely cared if I relaxed.

His unwavering stare reeled me into the caress of his citrus scent. The tension melted from my shoulders and settled in my veins, whipping through me like warm summer wind.

His camomile laced breath tickled my lips—

The walls shuddered, and a thunderous boom rolled through the Mayoral Wing.

"What was that?"

Ramone snapped his book closed and tossed it to the bedside table. "I'll return. Stay here."

He rushed from the room, leaving me to climb from the debris of my conscious that shattered under the sound. Back to reality.

*Had I...tried to...*

I shook my head to rid myself of the notion. *No.*

Preston had gotten into my head. Making me believe I was that *naïve*. I'd never fall for something like that.

The bedroom door burst open, ripping me from my slumber. I'd given up on waiting hours ago and went to bed.

Ramone's eyes were unnatural; pits of bottomless darkness. He locked the door and flipped off the lights. Before we were thrust into darkness, I'd noticed his entire face flushed purple, as if he'd yelled.

A darker shade than when he'd argued with Preston about the dark magic spell.

He slid into bed, heat radiating from him like steam from the spring.

"Is everything alright?" I whispered, reaching towards him in the darkness.

He shifted so his breath tickled my face as he sighed. "Yes, it was...the maid."

I wanted to question his response, considering his disgruntled state. Why would he be so angry about a maid slamming a door?

Lying came so naturally to him that even if he told the truth, I wouldn't believe him.

Because Preston had been right about one thing. Ramone isn't stupid, and I had likely misjudged him. Everything he did had motive. Whatever had made that noise was something important. I'd have to figure it out on my own, but I'd have to do so carefully.

I found his hand near his face. It wasn't something I was proud of. But it was the only way I could sleep at night. The only way I could stave off the nightmares that Sorcerers were crawling through my dorm room window and the haunting faces of my deceased classmates.

He squeezed my hand—as if it hadn't been him who had stolen our lives. Who threatened to do the same to many more.

*Him* who I'd delusionally—*naively*—tried to kiss moments ago.

A fluorescent pink sticky note fluttered on the mystery room door. Migrating down the hallway and rubbing my sleepy face, I leaned close to read the message scrawled there.

After several tries, it occurred to me my eyes weren't tired, the words were in Onataian, the old language used by Pixies—written similar to ancient hieroglyphics. Since Ramone possessed Pixie lineage, I assumed either the note had been left by him or for him. It also suggested the message contained some protected information, unless I'm the only one here who couldn't read it.

Did it say what's inside?

I reached to turn the handle but didn't have to. The ajar door swung open at my gentle touch. I glanced over my shoulders to be sure neither Ramone nor the fabled *maid* watched. There were no signs of life within the hall, nor the cluttered and disheveled room.

I entered.

Stacks of files and paperwork littered the floor and desk against the cobweb ridden walls. I touched an expansive piece of parchment on top of the desk. Tracing the outline of a barrier around a rudimentary drawing of a castle. Bold, black ink circled the exits and entrances, with detailed notes written in the empty spaces along the margins. All of them written in Onataian, too.

*These were the plans used to attack Bathory.*

Swallowing my tears, I pushed the map away. Like ants, they'd filtered into our school. They had every upper hand, magic, stealth, and inside knowledge.

*We didn't stand a chance.*

A folder labeled 'Administrative Documents' caught my attention. I pushed its contents across the desk's surface. Each paper stamped with the school's insignia and a signature from the dean. *Why were these here?* No one except a campus staff member would have access to these.

A pit filled my stomach, and I filtered through the documents in search of a name. Whether it be a staff member or a student. These had to be sent to someone. I plucked a roster from the stack, beginning with the dean, it went on to list the board of directors, then the professors and mentors.

*Kade.*

His name was at the top of the list because he was the best. He cared about his students' education. It wasn't just a job to him—we weren't just his students. We were *family*.

His lifeless corpse swung from the chandelier burned inside my pinched lids and a wave of nausea swept over me. A sob clogged my throat.

*I can't do this.*

Sniffling, I pushed everything back into the folder and shoved it away. Exposing the leather portfolio Ramone had burned.

*Magic's an interesting thing.*

Quick, as if expecting company, I retrieved the senseless documents inside. If they weren't ledgers, they were ramblings scribbled by the author about some power enhancer for Sorcerers.

Maybe he hadn't lied about their uselessness after all. No one could've deciphered anything from these. The words were arranged like a puzzle. Obviously related to the same subject, but erratic and written with poor penmanship.

I scanned the area for more clues. A twin bed, similar to the one in the other room, sat in the corner. I hadn't noticed it due to the clutter. The rumpled sheets suggested the bed had recently housed an occupant.

Inching closer, I used the toe of my boot to shift the clothes pile on the floor. Ramone brought almost the exact pair to me on my first visit here.

I straightened. *Is this the maid's room?*

The echoing sound of entry drove me out. I pulled the door closed, hoping Ramone wouldn't suspect I'd trespassed. A lump in my throat, I scanned the hallway for a sign of who came into the hall.

*Maybe he'd already entered another room?*

After confirming he wasn't in any known area to me, I chanced a try at the handle to the lobby door.

*Oh, shit! It's unlocked!*

Chest heaving, I only opened the door an inch to peer into the empty lobby. It was oddly quiet.

Inhaling a deep breath, I stepped into plain sight. The lights were dimmed, not a soul around.

*Strange.*

Light on my feet to not make a sound, I crossed to the cell hall. If Ramone wasn't nearby, I could speak to Preston—*or retrieve my weapons.*

The door clicked shut, and I froze.

Preston's cell stood open, Ramone and his two henchmen inside. Thick, crimson liquid smeared across the floor, a slow, steady stream trickling into the metal drain in the corner.

The large henchman laughed as he stomped on Preston's face. A fleshy thud, as blood cascaded over his ear and soaked his hair.

"What are you doing?" I screamed, rushing into the cell.

Ramone whirled to face me, his maroon eyes wild and a dagger in hand. His expression flickered like an old projector, disappointment seeping through the cracks. He hadn't meant for me to see this.

He hesitated to snap out, "I'm tired of playing nice! I don't have forever to wait on him to get past his moral compass."

A gristly, wet sound rattled from Preston. The longer it persisted, it became a tormented laugh. "I won't waste the energy; you're too stupid to learn it!"

He pinched his lids shut tight and fell into a coughing fit, blood strung from his lips like molasses. My stomach wrenched, sickened by the thickness and magnitude. How did the snake expect him to do anything in this condition? His face was bruised beyond recognition, the swelling giving his boney skeleton the illusion of health.

Much more and he'd die!

I trembled, fingers itching to take the dagger from Ramone and plunge it into his heart. *This isn't what I'd agreed to.*

Roaring, Ramone kicked him in the stomach hard enough to lift him from his hands and knees. Preston cradled himself as he choked on the liquid in his throat.

Unable to watch any longer, I lunged for the dagger. Swift as the wind, he held it out of reach, thrusting me to the floor with one hand.

Slipping in the sticky, crimson liquid coating the floor, I did my best to forget where it came from. Climbing to my knees beside Preston, my eyes burned with hot tears. Weaponless and outnumbered, my services as a Protector were void. But I could comfort him.

*Where would it hurt least to touch?*

"You'll teach me, even if it costs her life." Ramone shoved him with the toe of his boot. His footsteps echoed as he left, and the door to the lobby banged shut behind him.

"Not if I kill you first," I muttered. My arms shook so hard I couldn't have wielded a dagger, anyway. But I'd damn sure try.

The henchmen sauntered to stand in the hall. They whispered to one another but didn't tell me to go.

I took Preston's face into my hands. His brows pinched together and his lips quivered.

"I'm so sorry," my voice broke. I hoisted his torso into my lap so I may better cradle his head to listen for his wheezing breaths.

His fingers tightened into a fist, and I gathered it into mine. The unswollen eye creaked open and his mouth split for blood to spill out. He cleared his lips with a flick of his tongue, grinning.

"How do I look?" his voice was strained and rough.

Tears loose, I laughed. "Shitty."

His free arm clutched to his chest as he coughed some more. If there were a way, I'd take all of his pain.

For now, I'd settle this with Ramone.

Preston's lids pinched closed, and he relaxed in my lap, as if asking for oblivion.

I bent to kiss his head, smoothing his copper colored hair from his bloody face. Careful, I lowered his defeated bulk onto the floor, a hand to his in promise I'd return. Ramone's game would come to an end.

I rose to my feet and stormed to the office holding my weapons. The door handle didn't budge.

I shouted and kicked the door hard enough to leave a small dent in its metal surface.

*Fine, I didn't need my weapons! I'd kill him with my bare hands.*

One henchman clattered to lock the cell while the other trailed after me.

"You're to return to the Mayoral Wing,"

I thrust open the lobby door, the hunk of wood slamming against the outer wall. The employee behind the desk appeared startled by my abrupt entrance. I ignored her and the coward tailing me; glare on Ramone's back. He shuffled some paperwork on a nearby table; odd behavior for someone who *mutilated* a man.

No care for stealth; I crashed into him like a bull. We slammed into the small table, shattering its frail fabrication on the tile floor.

*I'd break him like he'd broken Preston.*

Ramone's cranium hinged on the wall as we fell to the floor, so he landed on his posterior. I punched him in the face repeatedly, knees in his chest.

"You said you wouldn't hurt him!" I screamed.

He shielded his face from my blows, attempting to catch my wrists in his hands. Frustrated, I got up to put my boot on his throat. I gritted my teeth as I pushed hard. His eyes bulged and his face bloated under the pressure.

The two henchmen seized me from behind.

Relief washed over Ramone's gasping purple face as they hauled me away, struggling to keep my limbs pinned.

"This isn't what we agreed to!" I yelled. "I just needed more time!"

He rose to his feet, smoothing his clothes and licking the blood from his lips. "There weren't any finite obligations to our agreement," he croaked.

"I'm done being your puppet! You're a liar and a coward!"

"Lock her up." Ramone crooked a grin.

"Locking me away won't stop me! You'll pay for what you've done to him and to Bathory!"

# Isolated

## Chapter 20

My first day incarcerated, I seethed around the cell's perimeter. I wanted to rip Ramone limb from limb. He'd promised not to hurt Preston and made a fool of me. I'd almost—almost...I hefted a sigh, which morphed into a sob.

The rage passed, and I shook from my cries on the pathetic excuse for a bed in the corner. I failed my mission. I didn't even know what time it was anymore. How could I do anything locked in here?

I silenced, to listen to the faint voice from the stall next door. "Love,"

I spotted a grate in the wall, low to the ground, nearly touching the floor where Preston still lay. I dropped from the cot to put my face near the slatted metal sheet.

"Love, are you there?"

I sniffed, placing my fingers on the rough, rusted grate. After all he'd endured, he still could talk.

"Yes, I'm here," my voice was raw and defeated. It hurt to admit I was jailed, too.

*We'd failed.*

"Are you okay?" I asked, well aware he wasn't. If quiet enough, his rattled breath filtered through the grate.

We both needed comfort, and I couldn't hold him. He'd healed me many times; while I couldn't offer the same service, I hoped my voice would suffice.

"Oozing with perfection," his shattered speech turned to a cough.

I got angry all over again, my nerves piqued due to the low light conditions. "I should have killed him," I hissed, banging my hand on the wall.

Preston cleared his throat. "I'm much better now that I have a neighbor,"

I smiled and wiped the tears from my face. "Shut up,"

"That's not neighborly,"

I rolled my eyes and listened to him cough. I hated myself.

"Preston," I whispered, tears welling, "I'm sorry, I failed you. I failed Rodney and all the Vampires, too. Mrs. Harper was right to fire me."

"I don't blame you." He hocked loose whatever coated his throat. "I'm sorry for what I said. You're not naïve. You're just not used to someone like Ramone."

But he was wrong. I bowed my head. I was naïve.

"I've had the unfortunate displeasure of knowing him for nearly two hundred years." He huffed several times to catch his breath. "It's acceptable for someone so experienced to have tricked you."

*Tricked me.*

I'd fallen into his hands without slowing a minute to truly assess the situation. Had forgotten he wasn't just a person like I was used to. He's the leader of the Veiled Army.

Murderer of innocents.

Trickster of hearts.

All things I should've expected because I was trained to.

The click of boot heels ceased as Ramone stopped outside my cell. His cloak enhanced his image to fill the entryway. The lack of light increased the intensity of his perusal, which made my skin crawl.

His smile glowed in the darkness. "You look well rested."

All night, I'd strained to ensure Preston hadn't stopped breathing. Even holding my own breath at times when his grew too faint.

"What do you want?" I grumbled. Struggling with my sore muscles, I got to my feet to stand in front of him. My fingers curled into fists, the knuckles eager to come into contact with his face. To remind him I hadn't been bluffing when his henchmen hauled me away.

His arrogance diminished as he inched closer, gripping the bars. A flash of guilt crossed his face, the subtle change reigniting the fire that had consumed me last night. The uncontainable desire to hurt him as he'd hurt Preston.

As he'd hurt Kade.

"Why do you look so guilty? You did this!" I bit out, voice still hoarse. "Isn't this what you wanted?" my voice cracked, but I straightened to my full height.

His mouth opened as if he would speak, instead he lowered his gaze and turned his head to view the hall.

I crossed my arms, suspecting he bore some remorse that his plan had derailed from its original path.

*Or he pretended to.*

"I didn't want..." He faced me. "I didn't mean for it to go so far."

I scoffed. "You threatened to kill him and nearly did after you promised not to! You'll lie about anything, Ramone." *He'd pretended to possess a decent bone in his body.* "You're two-faced! I saw it in Carthage. How you shift into whatever you think most suits your situation."

He shook the bars until they rattled. Through gritted teeth, he growled, "You don't understand."

"You're right! I don't understand! You treated my wounds when you didn't have to and made sure I ate, even after we fought. You were so *nice* to that Vampire Protector." He was a snake, and I an idiot for believing him; *simple.* "Do you even know who you are?" I challenged, taking a step from him. Tears burned my eyes, threatening to expose their existence in my voice.

His expression softened, and he slid a fist through the bars as if he expected me to hold it. I grimaced, holding in a shout, and sat at the grate.

A faint clink hit the ground when he left, and I shifted to find a bracelet on the floor.

For some time, I stared at it.

*Was it a peace offering or a trick?* Just another gust in his whirlwind of actions.

Curiosity won out, and I crawled to retrieve it. I twirled the stone beads over, pinching the smooth and lightweight texture between my thumb and index finger. They were the same aquamarine color as my irises, but bore no obvious evidence of enchantment—Not that I'm an expert.

*Thanks, Bathory, Institute of Wasted Time.*

For now, I slid it on my wrist as a reminder to never trust him. A mockery of whatever semblance of a partnership we'd shared.

Hours passed. Preston's occasional rattly breath the only thing keeping my mind off my ravenous stomach and the pressing weight of the darkness. Straining to listen, rather than succumbing to sleep, no matter how heavy my lids became.

I raked a hand through my hair and froze. A soft blue light ringed my wrist, the aquamarine beads glowing.

I squeezed the bracelet in my other hand. It wasn't a trick. It was bribery.

Bribery to keep quiet about his little secret, because he knew mine. All of them.

Footsteps echoed throughout the hall, driving me to the cell bars. An air of satisfaction cast over Ramone at the sight of Preston as he sauntered to stand before me.

"Enjoying the amenities?" He gloated.

*What amenities?*

"You spend a lot of time here for someone who's supposed to be leading a war," I stated.

He stood straighter, hands clasped behind his back, and a playful smirk on his lips. His eyes danced with laughter at my disheveled state.

*There's the miserable dictator I'd forgotten he was.*

I pounded a fist against the bars. "What do you want?"

"A date to dine with the Mayor of Carthage,"

"I won't help you,"

"I'm not asking." The laughter in his voice sickened me. All this a game to him. "And since threatening your precious *Anteomancer's* life doesn't seem to cover all my bases," he took one big step closer to the cell, "I'll place a compliance spell on you."

*Anteomancer.* That's what Rodney said he thought Preston was. A Sorcerer who could wield many magics in strength.

"Eat shit." I couldn't bear through another one of his compliance spells. Especially if the application's the same as last time.

His white teeth flashed. "Again, I'm not asking."

On the doorstep of the Harper estate, the icy wind whipped the cloaks on our shoulders. I'd bathed and outfitted myself in the dress from the last dinner date. This time, makeup was an absolute necessity to cover up the evidence of all the tears shed over the last few days.

Including the fresh ones that still stung in my eyes from seeing Preston on the way out. Judging by the path of blood, he'd crawled to put his back to the wall nearest my cell. He'd been that close and I could hardly hear him breathe. It didn't seem right I couldn't tell how faint his heart beat. How withered he'd become.

How many more beatings could he withstand?

Tierney opened the door, her perfect hostess greeting crumbling on her face. Her brows pooched as if they might become one and her lips fought with a frown.

"J-Josie?" Her gaze flicked between us and she put her weight on the door like she considered closing it. "I wasn't aware you knew Mayor Salvatore."

He chuckled and wrapped an arm around my shoulders. "I've recently employed her as my Protector."

*I'd rather die.*

The vacant countenance on the Vampiress's face reflected my own.

*Please refuse to allow me in.*

Like the flip of a switch, the grand hostess, Tierney, laughed emptily, waving a hand in the air. "Come in, come in!"

I rooted my feet to the wooden porch, clenching my jaw tight enough my teeth squeaked. His spell would have to make me do it. Someone had to make an effort to protect Carthage since their leaders were failing to do so.

Ramone put a firm hand on my back and thrust me into the house. Set into motion, his spell kept my feet going. I bowed my head to avoid eye contact, my shame scrawled across my face like graffiti.

*Traitor.*

I led the wolf into the flock. None of them were aware, but it was all my fault. Every single life taken in this city by the Veiled Army would be because of me.

Tierney rattled on about dinner as she led us to the dining room. Rodney and Burke already sat at the table, Issak near the buffet. I didn't have to look to know they all stared at me.

Ramone and I sat side by side, across from Rodney. Tierney and Burke sat at either end of the table, Ramone the closest to Mr. Harper. They began small talk instantly, something I couldn't bear to listen to. Because the Vampire should be able to sense this wasn't right.

Why didn't they question how he'd made it into the city in the first place?

Beneath the table, Rodney brushed his foot against mine. I refused to lift my gaze.

"I'm glad to see you found employment so quickly, Josie," Mr. Harper congratulated me, holding his glass up for cheers.

I lifted my chin enough to give a polite, tight-lipped smile.

Ramone patted my leg. "I couldn't let such a gifted Protector go unemployed."

He regarded me proudly, making my stomach twist. Too many red flags should've alerted them to this sham. Ramone never should've made it into the city in the first place, their officers should've stopped him and I couldn't take on a new charge because I never received any certifications.

I'm still considered a Student Protector.

My muscles went taut. The truth backed up in my throat, crowding behind my lips to escape. They needed to know.

"Have you heard any news about the rogues who attacked the school?" Mr. Harper's gaze fixed on Ramone. "You mentioned at the restaurant you were tracking someone."

He straightened in his seat, a hand possessively in my lap. "Nothing new yet, but I can assure you we are making every effort to figure this out. We won't let it pass without justice."

My abdominals contracted as if he'd gut punched me. It was all lies and I couldn't stand it.

I chanced a look at Rodney, unable to believe he hadn't said anything. From beneath my lashes, I could see his rigid shoulders and jawline. His fangs dug into his lip and his slate-colored eyes smoldered on Ramone.

"We'd like to form an alliance with you, publicly. Assisting in the effort to find these treacherous rogue Sorcerers would bring hope to our city."

I clicked my teeth together hard, biting my tongue. *Alliance?* This fool invited the enemy into the last safe haven Vampires had left!

As the spell ensured, I could do nothing about it.

"So many lost beloved children, they need something to lift their spirits," Tierney added to her husband's testament.

A low rumble tickled the base of my throat, the magic stopping it from becoming much more than a garbled sound.

"I'd be honored." Ramone squeezed my leg tight.

I stiffened to keep from doubling over from the pressure he applied. His devious message was loud and clear.

Rodney rose to storm from the room. Knowing his emotional instability well, he couldn't keep his mouth shut any longer. Magic couldn't be the reason, but somebody had persuaded him to stay silent. I knew him too well to believe he'd go along with this otherwise.

The kitchen staff brought food to the table for Ramone and me. A vibrant collection of vegetables accompanied with seared chicken. The taste of blood in my mouth would have to do; I couldn't stomach a bite.

"Please excuse our son." Tierney smiled awkwardly. "It's still hard for him to recall what happened."

My jaw ached. Had Rodney told them, and they didn't believe him? If the spell didn't stop me, would they believe me?

"I understand." Ramone waved off the apology, brow line wrinkled with feigned sympathy. "Such a tragedy."

Both of us pushed the food around our plates, Ramone undoubtedly too disgusted by the Vampires' meal to eat. I was afraid if I opened my mouth for a second, the truth would spill out with the blood from my tongue—Regardless if the spell ensured it impossible. The surface of my water rippled with the faintest shade of red and I watched it spread to the edges of the glass.

Burke brought his hands down on the table, startling me. "Shall we retire to my office to discuss details?"

The Mage radiated happiness. "I thought you'd never ask!"

While Burke adjusted his place at the table, Ramone leaned into me. His breath was harsh against my ear, "Don't forget about your Anteomancer."

My heart faltered, Preston's battered figure fresh in my mind. He couldn't risk another beating. Not so soon after the last one.

Rising from his spot, Ramone offered a polite smile to the others as Burke stood to lead the way.

Massaging my irritated leg, I pondered his warning. My focus drifting to the bracelet. He'd admitted his magic wasn't as strong because of his Halfling status. Was there a chance his spell wouldn't hold up? Could it be broken?

A smile twisted Tierney's lips but never met her eyes. She didn't want me here. Afraid her son would have the confidence to stray from whatever they'd done to force him to stay quiet while Ramone was here.

"Issak," she turned to the statue of a man, "will you escort Josie to the Protector's Annex while Mr. Salvatore and Burke are...busy?"

He gave a nod and rounded the table.

Was this a way to ensure I couldn't interfere with their meeting? I cast a glance at Tierney, hoping she could somehow see through the spell that they were in danger. The entire city was in danger.

Without a word, I followed Issak. Ramone wouldn't have said anything if there wasn't a chance the spell could be faulty. Nor would I have been able to make that sound. At least I hoped.

My palms grew sweaty. Would Issak ask the right questions? Could I find a workaround?

He held the annex door open for me; Inside, Rodney faced us. His arms folded across his chest, fit to burst.

I bowed my head and stopped so Issak could step in. Even if this increased my chances of telling *someone* the truth, I hated for it to be Rodney. This would put him in harm's path, no matter which way the outcome swung.

Despite my efforts to appear unapproachable, Rodney pulled me into an embrace so tight I crumbled in his arms. I wished once he let me go, the world would be put together, and I'd wake in my bed at campus. I'm so tired of trying to save the Mythos when I'd only been trained to protect a Vampire. *One.* Not all of them.

He let me cry into his chest until I quieted, then cradled my face in his hands. His icy fingers wiped my tears, then tipped my chin. His irises were rain cloud gray as they studied me, worry dropping his brows together.

"Tell me what's going on," he instructed.

I stepped back to wipe my face, trying to build composure as I imagined all the horrible things magic could do to me or Preston for going against Ramone's wishes.

"Is there something I should know?" Issak ambled to Rodney's side. His dark eyes were on me, sympathy shadowing his intense features.

Rodney gestured to the main house. "That asshole in there isn't who he says he is. He's responsible for what happened to our school."

"Rodney," I hissed. *What if Ramone found out? What if Issak said something?*

"How do you know?" Issak looked between us, eyes round, to consume us both.

"Because he's kidnapped Josie before. He plans to attack the city and my dad is helping him do it; he just isn't aware yet." Rodney's voice grew louder, and I nodded, like the useless bobblehead the spell made me.

Issak's brows hunkered low, and he rubbed his neck, shoulders hunched forward. We watched him go back and forth for some time before he spoke. "Mr. Salvatore said Preston was the enemy, and he'd brainwashed you into believing he was innocent."

"I don't care for Preston, but he's not the enemy." Rodney roared. "Why would any of you believe Ramone over me?"

Issak's hands dropped in conquest. "What can we do?"

I maintained eye contact with Issak, struggling to keep my emotions in check. My voice wavered, "I don't know."

Rodney bent to retrieve his dagger from his boot, concealed by his pant leg. "Would this help?"

I wrapped my fingers around the hilt, the familiar stitches instilling some comfort. *I had a weapon.* While not much against magic, it might be enough. It certainly beat waiting for something else to present itself.

Careful to tuck the knife away from us, I hugged him tight again.

"Thank you." I stepped back.

His lips pinched. Same as me, he wasn't sure how much help the blade would be.

"We must speak to Mr. Harper about this," Issak decided, gears turning in his eyes.

Rodney scoffed. "I've tried. He doesn't want to hear it. He believes he's performing some heroic act by entertaining Ramone."

Issak scowled, brows quirked as if he wasn't surprised. I recalled what Mr. Harper had said when we'd first made it to the city. Declaring his son a hero for surviving. Everything had to be a show to the public for him, and the realization pained me. Because it only enforced the rumors circulating around the city about him paying for Rodney to survive the Bathory massacre.

A half hour passed before Ramone was ready to leave, a future, formal meeting arranged with Burke—*in one week*. I was careful to tuck the dagger into my spandex, pulling my cloak tight to conceal it.

Our entire world had changed. There were bigger threats than we'd ever realized as children. History had only been ancient stories that couldn't happen again. Yet, here we were reliving the past. We had to rely on one another if we intended to survive.

The Harpers summoned a car to deliver us to the city's edge so we may teleport to Luxor capitol.

I possessed a weapon, but no plan. Which was something I'd grown to resent. Waiting. Always waiting for the opportune moment. How much had gone wrong while I *waited*?

Grip tight on my arm, Ramone dragged us to a stop in front of my cell. The practiced, attentive guest veil was gone from his face. Now he was a soulless, stony warlord who almost seemed *tired*.

Lightning went up my spine, tightening my shoulders as he closed the space between us. Impatience ticked in his jaw as his warm hands slid over my body, tracing every curve with invasive detail. Slowly, he inched along my thighs and my fingers coiled tight into a fist.

*He'd find the knife.*

If I wanted any chance of escape, now was the time.

Fumbling to retrieve the blade from my spandex, I thrust an elbow into Ramone's chest. He stumbled a single pace, rebounding quickly from my attack.

I sliced at him.

He blocked my wrist, his free arm across my throat. In one step, he pinned me against my cell, then grappled the knife from my fingers. Leveling the blade's tip between my eyes, his fingers cinched so my breath whistled.

"Did you really think that was going to work?" he asked, a dim light illuminating his eyes. "That I wouldn't expect you to pull something like this?"

"Just kill me then," I rasped, gripping his wrist with both hands. Nothing he could say would make me feel worse than I already did. Once again, I'd screwed up.

"Kill you?" Unhinged laughter shook his voice. Lowering the knife, he guided me into the cell by my throat and thrust me to the concrete floor.

I choked on a gush of air, drawing my fists to my chest as it convulsed.

"Killing you would be too easy."

The jarring racket of my cell door shattered the daunting silence, ripping me from the edge of slumber. Ramone appeared both exhausted and irritated by the bloodshot and groggy film in his eyes, telling me he, too, hadn't gotten a chance to sleep.

He motioned for me to get up, rubbing his face with his other hand. "We have to return to Carthage," he yawned, stumbling in place.

I sat up to slip on my boots, which were deposited in my cell sometime while we were gone, along with my sweater and leggings. I'd changed shortly after our return, eager to escape the restrictive dress.

Stretching my arms, I got to my feet. "Why?" Surely, he didn't plan to attack now?

"Tierney called, Burke and your Leech got into a dispute." He paced from the cell entrance so I may exit. "He's hurt and requires your blood." His face twisted in disgust.

My pulse thrummed through my veins, concern for Rodney and excitement for the endorphins grappling for traction. "Did they say how bad he's hurt? When he last fed?"

"It's late," he grumbled, jerking me by the arm into the lobby. "You can ask them when we get there."

The city's magic prevented us from teleporting straight to the Harper's doorstep. We had to start at the border and no matter how fast we walked, it wasn't fast enough.

Not for me.

"I hate this obligation. Hate pretending to care about them. Is this a trick? Why do they need your blood?" he growled. He'd grown more awake as we walked in the early sunlight and, as a result, grouchier. "Can't he drink what they have?"

"Yes, he can." I snapped, ignoring the blatant revulsion in his tone. It seemed unlikely Rodney would refuse to drink what they offered, considering he's aware of my predicament. Had he attempted to talk to Burke about our discussion in the Protector's Annex?

"So, why do we have to be here?"

"Do you want your alliance to go as planned or not?" He didn't need to hear our suspicions about my blood and that it might work differently for Rodney. He had enough leverage over the Harpers.

The estate was a wreck. Undoubtedly, the 'dispute' between Rodney and Burke escalated into a full-on brawl. Furniture laid on its side, vases broken, and Burke bore a swollen lip and blackened eye.

Rodney had gloated about defending himself when I'd been kidnapped before. Hopefully, that small experience had been useful against his father.

My nails bit into my palms. He shouldn't have to defend himself against his *father*. I should've been here.

Is this why they'd gotten rid of me?

Was Issak okay with this?

Silently, her head hung in embarrassment, Tierney led us upstairs to Rodney's room. Her eyes were vacant, a smoky shade of gray. The same shade I'd seen in Rodney's when he thought of Zoon.

*Please let him be okay.*

Issak stood at Rodney's bedside, blood leaking from his slightly agape mouth.

"We've given him plenty of blood, but he won't heal," Tierney explained, her voice weak. "We didn't know what else to do, so I called for you."

I dipped my head and pinched my lips before accusations flew from my mouth. They'd acted so happy when we'd made it to Carthage. So proud to have their son home.

Any belief either of these Vampires cared for Rodney's wellbeing—or anyone's, for that matter—had dissolved to ash on the walk here.

The ash turned to stone as my muscles constricted. His bleeding face was so swollen with bruises, I hardly recognized him. Had his chest not pumped with shallow breaths, I would've assumed the worst and come completely undone.

Everyone would answer for what they'd done to him.

"Should we call a doctor?" Ramone feigned concern, but his face contorted in undeniable abhorrence.

I stopped at Issak's side and held my arm out, palm up. "Can you cut my wrist a bit?"

"He won't drink," Issak said. "We've had to pour it down his throat."

I nodded. "Cut my wrist."

Ramone whipped in my direction, eyes swirling like a galactic war model. The muscles in his neck strained to keep from ordering me to abandon all efforts. He was stuck between his moral beliefs and his fake persona for the Harpers.

"This is risky," Issak insisted, retrieving his dagger from the sheath on his hip. With a quick swipe, he did as asked.

I winced. Blood spilled from the split skin as I hurried to place my wrist to Rodney's lips, lids pinched closed as I waited for his fangs to sink in.

"Why are you letting her do this?" Ramone asked, purple climbing up his neck. "Isn't there a facility for this? A hospital?"

A whimper stung the back of my throat as I met Ramone's gaze. Rodney latched onto my arm, dragging me closer. "This is the only way for Rodney."

Ramone jerked, like my words hurled into his chest, and his fists tightened. He couldn't stand to see a Vampire feed.

I gasped, Rodney's fangs digging deeper and tearing the slit open further.

*Please don't drain me.*

Ramone raked a hand through his hair, and his complexion turned pale, glistening with a layer of sweat. "How much does he need?" his voice was loud and uneven.

*Fuck, where is the endorphin high?* I held my breath as my vision narrowed.

"He's healing!" Tierney celebrated as his split brow mended at an accelerated rate.

His gulps should've slowed. He should've backed off. Should've showed some signs of consciousness.

He didn't.

He squeezed my arm tighter, trying to wring out every last drop, and sucking on my skin like a straw.

My knees wobbled as the room grew narrow, and their voices became muffled.

Ramone's was the loudest, "...*too much*!"

# Alive
## Chapter 21

I wasn't sure how much time passed; the sun shone through the window onto the familiar small bed. No one bothered to change me from my bloodied clothes. The salt and copper concoction on my skin reeked. Judging by my healed wrist, I'd been left here for rehabilitation. Which would explain why I dreamed of Ramone's cabin in the woods. Fortunately, *he* hadn't been there to ruin the bliss of unconsciousness.

Moving slowly due to the dull headache behind my eyes, I dropped to the floor to search for Ramone. To ask him if Rodney made it.

Most of the doors shut and locked, it didn't take long to declare he wasn't in the Mayoral Wing.

I sucked in a deep breath as my head pounded in time with my footfalls. The last time he'd left me here alone, he'd gone to Preston's cell and beat him.

That couldn't happen again.

I hesitated to twist the lobby door handle. What if a henchman stood guard?

*What would it matter if the door's still locked?*

"Yes," I breathed.

He must've been too exhausted to remember to lock it!

A Sorcerer strolled from the elevators near the front desk. He pushed faster, chewing a bite of the candy bar clutched in his fist—it was the one who kicked Preston. "Why are you out here?" he demanded.

My confidence plummeted along with my lead stomach. I couldn't go back to that cell.

"Where's Ramone?" I asked, retrieving a vase from the console table beside me. Launching it through the air, I swept the area for another weapon.

The Sorcerer dodged the heavy ceramic and discarded his candy bar. "I'll pretend you didn't just do that if you'll give up."

A blast of magic thrust me into the wooden chair on the other side of the door to the Mayoral Wing. The wood bit into my tailbone and I clutched the arms, swallowing the groan that followed.

"It's been a long night for everyone," he said. "We were up all night pumping you full of blood and Mayor Salvatore healed what that Leech did to you."

Nails dug into the chair, I sucked in a deep breath. "Rodney is not a leech."

Throwing myself into a run, I lifted the chair over my shoulder. The Sorcerer drew his hands up to cast another gust. The chair splintered on the tile floor in long, ugly splines.

My chest heaved, relieved the pieces hadn't been me.

"You're really starting to piss me off!" He pushed me down with magic.

"Ow. Shit." I caught myself on my hands and knees. The frayed edges threaded into my skin as my fingers curled around the fragmented wood scraps. Baring through the pain, I secured a piece the length of my forearm and narrow at one end, then climbed to my feet once more, careful to hide it behind my back.

The Sorcerer held out his hand. "Let's get you to your cell before I have to do something regrettable."

I nodded and took a step forward.

Realizing I wouldn't give him my hand, the Sorcerer lunged to take it, just as I expected. Weight thrown into it, I plunged the wood scrap into his jugular.

Whirling to kick the back of his knees, I thrust him to the floor, and the wood pressed deeper into his neck. He gurgled, blood pooling around him, the same as it had around Preston when they'd had their fun.

Satisfaction supplemented the disgust I should harbor for what I'd done. But it was difficult to feel empathy for someone who had shown none.

I darted into the cell hall. Expecting to be met with some resistance, I was surprised to find the Sorcerer in the glass-walled office kicked back in a wooden chair, arms folded behind his head while he napped. An absolute miracle, considering the commotion in the lobby could've wakened the undead.

*Now to get the keys and my weapons.*

Biting my bottom lip, I twisted the knob to the office slowly. Letting out a breath, I entered, careful to control the speed at which the door closed behind me.

It shut without a sound.

While the Sorcerer snored, unaware of my presence, I adorned my weapons, every step taken with vigilant judgment.

I gripped one dagger tight in my hand as I stood over him. It went against my morals to kill him as he slept. But, I had no choice.

As I leveled the blade across the Sorcerer's throat, his lids flashed open. He gripped the seat to stand, swearing loud enough my ears rang.

Once on his feet, he lifted his hands to cast.

I gripped my knife tight, braced for the spell.

"Shit," he swore. We'd both forgotten magic was blocked in this area.

Relief washed over me, while he fell into panic. He scrambled across the room to a red button on the wall. *'In Emergency Only'.*

A shrill alarm shrieked throughout the building, raising the hair on my neck.

*Now or never.*

Backed against the wall, I cornered the Sorcerer.

"Just do it!" he snapped, jabbing a finger at the hallway. "I'm so fucking tired. I've been here for forty-eight fucking hours because of *him*."

"Why didn't you just leave?" I asked, caught off guard.

"You think I'm gonna tell you? Blood whore!"

With practiced skill, I plunged the blade into his chest, right between the ribs and into the heart. He choked on the blood in his lungs, gritting his teeth through the pain to die courageously. It hurt worse to kill someone while looking them in the eye—someone who bore through it instead of fighting back. Despite what he called me.

Arms trembling, I watched as his heavy corpse fell to the floor with a thud.

*Blood whore.*

I fed Rodney because he needed it, not because I craved the high and certainly not over sex.

Pinching my lips together and holding my breath, I turned away. My breath rattled as I let it out.

The alarm broke through my remorse, reminding me capitol security would be here in minutes. Stealing the keys from the vacated chair, I fled. My heart pounding in my head, I leveled my breath. Any second, someone would find I'd escaped the Mayoral Wing. They'd see what I'd done to the guards and our escape would be over.

"Love, what happened? They said you were unconscious?" Preston sat erect in his bed as I fumbled to unlock his cell, struggling with the heavy keys. As I flew through the entrance, he tried and failed to stand.

"Don't worry about that right now." I bent to help support him, a shoulder under his arm.

"How did you escape?" his voice was a hoarse squeak.

My blood boiled and suddenly the henchmen's deaths were not enough. Ramone had put him on the cusp of death. And for what?

*A death sentence for him I'd be glad to execute.*

"We'll talk about it later," I said. He flinched in pain as I pushed us into motion. "For now we have to get out of here."

A clamor echoed on the other side of the lobby, several voices shouting over one another.

*We'd never make it through.*

"There's a door this way." Preston gestured opposite of the lobby. "It leads outside. From there, we can teleport."

I questioned if he possessed the strength to do so, but hadn't the heart to argue. Nor did we have any other options. Together, we stumbled toward the steel door at the end of the hall.

"Jo?" a familiar voice called. "JoJo, is that you?"

I stopped dead in my tracks and spun to observe the towering Vampire in the cell nearest our exit. He leaned against the wall, just out of reach of the sunlight shining on the floor through the thin rectangular window just below the ceiling.

"Zoon?" I gasped, pulling Preston with me. I kept him propped up, spreading my stance wide to do so, as I opened the cell faster this time, the alarm shrilly reminding me to hurry.

"I thought you were dead!" Zoon walked along the wall, sticking tight to the shadows.

The same confession froze on my lips as the hall door burst open, three security guards squeezing through at the same time. They had weapons lifted, sweeping the office first.

"Come on. Hurry!"

Without question, Zoon rushed to lift Preston into his arms. He was thin as a rail, but unnaturally strong as Vampires should be—*healthy* Vampires.

"A friend of yours?" the Archmage wheezed, then coughed. The sound was barely audible beneath the floundering guards in the office.

"We can trust him." I looked between the two. With a tight nod, I intended to assure Zoon more so than Preston.

The Vampire didn't give any sign he questioned me.

"Get them, you idiots!" Ramone's instruction barked over the chaos, piercing my nerves with fear.

"Go!" I rushed to hold the steel door open for Zoon.

His ocean blue-green eyes sparked in determination as we marched into the sun. His porcelain skin burned crimson and that acrid smell from the Bathory massacre singed my lungs.

*He's alive.* I reminded myself, clasping tight to his arm as the whirling separation of air and existence tugged at my center.

Zoon crumpled on the doorstep of a small cabin, like one in the western at the bed-and-breakfast. The rickety porch roof shielded his scorched skin from the sun, the pale tissue an angry shade of red.

"Fuck, that hurts," he groaned.

I moaned and clasped my queasy stomach. The teleportation quick and more rough than I'd ever experienced. Which made me wonder exactly how dangerous teleportation was when a Mage didn't have the strength for it.

Preston rolled from Zoon's lap, attempting to get up. He fell.

So weak and defeated, so unlike the man I'd grown to admire.

"Where are we?" I peered at the dirt road behind me, wracking my brain.

Almost in answer, the thin screen door opened, and Reggie stepped outside. His eyes were wide, and he didn't hesitate to help Preston up. Had he not stepped out to greet us, he had amazing timing.

"Damn, ugly, you look worse than usual," he teased, but his pinched brows said he worried.

Balanced with a trembling arm on the door frame, Preston cradled his agonized torso with the other. A fragile smile tugged at his cracked lips.

Hooking a hand under his shoulder, I leaned to support him. I'd kill every last soldier in the Veiled Army if he didn't survive.

Reggie's gaze swept over me, then stopped on the gangly addition to our crew. "What are you?"

"A well-done Vampire." Zoon pulled the tied bandana from his head to dab his blistered skin. "Also known as Zoon." He lifted his gaze to meet Reggie's and extended a hand to shake the Werewolf's. They were matched in height, opposite in build.

Reggie sniffed Zoon. "More like medium rare. I'm Reginald Rayham. You can call me Reggie." He winked, then turned to face Preston. "What got ahold of you?"

Sweat beaded across the Archmage's forehead as he fought to keep on his feet. His breath shook, but he trialed a smile, anyway. "What do you mean? This is the newest style,"

Reggie snorted and rolled his eyes. "Agh, you stubborn jackass. Let's get you off your feet."

He scooped an arm under Preston's and hauled him into the house. *He'd be fine. He just has to heal himself.*

Zoon and I followed into the narrow living room. The furniture was dated and smelled dusty. Maybe this *was* a shack from an old western.

Preston stretched across the low-to-the-ground, olive-green couch. He pinched his eyes shut and groaned, clutching a fist in his shirt.

"What do you need?" Reggie hovered over him.

"Food." I dropped to my knees at the Anteomancer's head. "And water."

Reggie crossed the tiny house in just a few strides and dishes clinked as he prepared a meal in the next room. The top of the doorway was worn in a concave shape. In fact, all the entryways bore similar wear.

I grinned; *Many years of head collisions?*

While we waited, I smoothed Preston's hair from his face; He paced his breath and the fist in his shirt loosened.

This was unbearable. *Why isn't he healing himself by now?*

"Not to be insensitive..." Zoon lowered into the rocking chair across from us, dwarfing it, and ridiculously so. "How did you acquire a Sorcerer, Jo?" His thick brows knit together as he tied the bandana around his forehead, clamping his medium length, dirty blonde hair to his head. His skin already lightened to pink, only dried blisters left behind.

*He's actually alive.*

I twisted to view Preston, placing a hand in the center of his chest. "After...what happened at Bathory, he found us in the forest and offered us shelter and food." I could've explained more, like how he'd grown to be so much more to me since then, but it hurt to say.

Especially when his lids opened and he quirked a tentative grin. "And saved your life."

"How humble," Reggie provoked, coming into the room with two plates laden with stew. The way he ducked through the doorway confirmed my theory.

"Thank you," I gratefully accepted the oddly plated offering, a reassuring hand on Preston as he scooted into a sitting position for his share of food.

Zoon was quiet while we ate, rocking in the chair and staring at the floor. I couldn't help but stare at *him*. We'd watched them throw his corpse into the pile. He had been dead.

Yet here he sat.

As Reggie took our empty plates to the kitchen, he lifted his oceanic eyes to mine. "You said 'we'; did Rodney make it?"

My breath hitched. He had to be okay. I'd know if he hadn't come out of unconsciousness. *Wouldn't I?*

"Yeah. He's with his parents." I omitted Mr. Harper had nearly killed him—*While throwing a tantrum.*

"I worried with his condition..." he trailed off, ashamed to mention Rodney's illness.

"He's a survivor," I reminded him with a soft smile. He'd healed with my blood and now, undoubtedly, did his best to make his father miserable until he could get out of their house. Until I could get to him.

Because his parents didn't get to decide if I was his Protector or not. He did. I didn't care about the money. We'd make it work. Staying with them wasn't an option for either of us.

Zoon's shoulders relaxed, and he tilted his head back to rest on the chair. "He is."

"Last time I saw you two, you were safe in the mayor's estate. What happened?" Reggie pressed for more information. He leaned against the wall at the foot of the couch. The space of wood paneling he occupied was a lighter shade, implying he often stood in this position.

I squeezed Preston's hand, afraid to let go. Afraid he'd disappear. That this was all a dream, and we were still trapped in our cells. "After you left, they told me I had to leave. That I couldn't be Rodney's Protector—"

"Who did?" Zoon's head snapped up. "What kind of idiot would—"

"Sh!" Reggie held a silencing hand.

I dragged my knees to my chest with one arm, sweeping my thumb across Preston's scabbed knuckles. "So, we went to Preston's apartment to discuss what my options were. Ramone and his men ambushed us the second we got there."

Reggie grunted. "Bastards. How did you escape?"

I explained the previous night and today's events.

As I finished, what I couldn't absorb in the moment sank in. How the Sorcerers had supposedly stayed up all night to give me blood. That Ramone had healed me. All of them so tired that they'd made silly mistakes—leaving the door unlocked, not noticing the woodshard behind my back, begging for his death.

"We have to meet with the Harpers." Reggie's creature flickered across his skin. "I'll make them listen."

I shrugged one shoulder. "I'm not sure they want to believe us."

Preston's grunt derailed the conversation. He *finally* healed himself, which appeared to be less enjoyable than when he healed others. His face twisted as he held his palms out above his abdominal region.

I rocked toward him, hands lifted to assist in some way.

"Son of a bitch," he gasped. His wounds were gone, but the color still hadn't returned to his skin. The glow in his eyes dim.

I dropped my hands into my lap, wringing my fingers until they ached.

"I heard everything," Zoon said, poised on his toes, still seated in the rocking chair. "He took one helluva beating."

"I can heal from a beating," Preston bit out. "I need to rest...I'm exhausted."

The way his words cut through Zoon's set me on edge.

"Anything I can do?" Reggie pushed away from the wall.

Preston shook his head, sliding into the couch cushions to rest his head in my lap. I leaned to clasp his hands, searching his golden eyes for reassurance he would be alright. For a moment, they fell on mine, and he gave my fingers a squeeze as his lids fluttered closed.

*Damn.* I'd missed him.

I brushed the hair from his clammy face. The temptation to touch his lips, hidden in his wild facial hair, surfaced and I dismissed it immediately. He needed rest.

"Seems he did more than save your life, lass." Reggie chuckled as he slipped into the kitchen.

The house suddenly felt too hot. *Was it really that obvious?*

"I still can't believe you're alive." I scrambled for a distraction. This wasn't the place to hash out exactly how I felt about the Archmage. Why it mattered so much that he stayed alive.

"Me neither." Zoon tossed his hands to rest on his knees.

"How did you...? We—" I heaved a breath that made my lungs sting. "We saw you in the piles."

His stare became far away. "A Sorceress dragged me out and brought me to the cell where you found me." Pain deepened the angles of his finely boned facial structure. His vast lips converted into a frown. "Once I was healed, they beat me for fun, then fed me and interrogated me."

To imagine Zoon lying on the floor of his cell, just as Preston had, nearly sent me marching back to Luxor. To think I'd believed Ramone capable of...anything besides what horrible things he'd done. Believed he could treat anyone with compassion.

"What information were they after?" I asked, filtering my fingers through Preston's matted hair.

"They saw you and Rodney escape, so they asked about you. Where you might go. Who you were. For days, I pretended not to know either of you." His shoulders slumped and he wouldn't look at me. "Eventually, they got me to talk. I didn't tell them much before Salvatore found you on his own."

"I'm sorry I wasn't there," my voice wavered. I should've gotten there sooner, to protect them both.

He buried his face in his hands, his broad shoulders appearing small. Weighed down with everything he'd survived. Everything *Ramone* had done to him.

I closed a hand around the bracelet on my wrist, and rage whipped through my veins. He'd pay for what he did to us.

*I knew his secret.*

"You shouldn't be out here smoking. You're still recovering."

Preston sat on the splintered step to Reggie's back porch, face inclined to the lavender sky, the sun below the horizon. His shuffling footsteps had alerted me to his whereabouts as he slipped through the screen door.

"It helps make the misery bearable." He rolled his eyes and rested his forearms on his knees, cigarette in hand as smoke billowed from his nostrils.

I leaned against the post parallel to him, the darkness of worry consuming me. Before, I believed I could do anything on my own. That the only person I needed was Rodney.

Now, I couldn't imagine going another day without Preston at my side. Not because I couldn't survive without him, but because I didn't *want to.*

He coughed, running his free hand through his bangs, so they parted on top of his head and framed his face.

"Just because your life is long doesn't mean you shouldn't take care of yourself," I scolded, stooping to sit beside him.

"I've lived several lives." He placed the cigarette between his lips, the cherry red hot. Blowing the toxin from the corner of his mouth like a steam engine, he said, "I'm done prolonging the inevitable."

*Not this again!*

Ripping the cigarette from his hold, I threw it into the yard. "As long as I'm around, which could be a long time, you have to live!"

Licking the nicotine from his lips, his brows arched. "It would save you a lot of trouble to give up on me now."

Scooting so our thighs touched, I touched his forearm. "I won't. I can't."

A gust left his nose as he stared into the yard shaded heavily by trees. "I'm unwell, Love," he stated. "My magic's weaker."

"What do you mean?" My heart pounded, recalling his groan as he'd struggled to heal himself.

"Ramone has been syphoning my magic since we escaped. He had to have a plan in place."

"Syphoning it?" What could he do with Preston's magic? A chill ran down my spine at the thought of Ramone having that kind of strength. "Like, taking it for himself?"

Preston shook his head. "It doesn't work like that—"

"Is it because you're an Anteomancer?" Rodney had tried to explain the term to me, but I still didn't fully understand it.

"Anteomancer is just the sect of magic I can wield. It means I can use all types of magic at impressive strength. Which is why he can only take it from me and it releases into the Mythos. This way, I'm not as much of a threat to him."

"How do we stop him?"

"Don't worry, since I've got you so weak in the knees, I'll figure it out." His ornery smile, the one that did exactly as he suggested, slowly curled one side of his mouth. Stretching the faint scar on that side. "My mother's an extraordinary alchemist."

He fretted inside his jacket for another cigarette and I stilled his arm, meeting his gaze boldly. "Preston," I squeaked, studying his stony expression.

His golden eyes lost their sheen, now stale and tired. My hand operated on its own, gliding over his stubbled jaw to his cheek. Each digit could have been a chisel, the way his face broke. His lids slid shut and a heavy breath escaped through his nose. His chest sunk in as if he held the sigh for some time.

My abdominal muscles convulsed as my brain calculated how close we were. Close enough, I felt the urge to run rise again, just like at the bed-and-breakfast.

He squeezed my upper arm and his eyes opened, a hint of luminescence in their depths. They didn't hold my attention long, the faint scar on his lips more distracting.

The world froze.

His cigarette laced lips collided with mine, quick and possessive like he knew I'd run and he had to hurry. All hesitations melted as I leaned into him, entangling a hand in his soft hair.

His spicy scent chased away the hint of nicotine on his tongue. His warmth pooling across my skin as his hands slid up my arms. Gentle, yet firm, so he could trace every inch.

*Why had I waited so long to do this?*

Waited to acknowledge my feelings wouldn't go away even if things hadn't gone awry with the Harpers. He's all I thought about.

Reggie and Zoon's voices boomed from the kitchen behind us, and I sprang to my feet. The withdrawal from him was like letting go of a piece of my soul. But I had to go. Before I had to explain *this* to Zoon, when I wasn't even sure how to explain it to myself.

I sucked on my bottom lip, still able to taste him and unable to look away from his golden glowing eyes.

*Damn.*

Reggie proved to be a much better nurse than his bedside manner led one to believe. By the time night fell, we were all pretty content. Preston had gained some energy, more than he'd had yesterday, but still didn't behave quite like himself.

Something that couldn't happen until the spell was removed. Which haunted me every time his lips stretched into a grimace.

An alert tone cut through the living room TV to announce the breaking news. The channel wasn't great—Welch Village had terrible connection issues.

Reggie, Preston, and I sat shoulder to shoulder on the couch, Zoon in the rocking chair. We swore under our breaths as the news anchor disclosed the alliance between Luxor and Carthage. A clip of Burke Harper played, stating the rally would be held in three days in front of the capitol. The Vampire public was invited to attend, and it would be televised for the rest of the Mythos.

"A great way to honor the Bathory massacre, nearly a month later." I read the banner at the bottom of the screen.

*A month.*

"Someone has to assassinate that worm," Reggie growled.

"I'd be happy to set a magnifying glass on him in the sun," Zoon sounded bleak, rocking forward in his seat.

"It took him a month to get into Carthage. One month." I said, voice wavering uncontrollably. The most well-hidden city in the Mythos would fall victim to his plans. "How long before all Vampires are gone? Before the Mythos is his?"

"That won't happen," Preston insisted. "If we can't get Burke to listen to us, his people will."

"And how are we going to do that?"

"We're going to the rally."

# About the Author

## Jessie Kreidler

Born and raised in Kansas, she has been writing since the age of nine. Since age sixteen, it has been her dream to become a published author. In her spare time, she writes as often as possible. Although most of it is taken up by her beloved family and four sassy dogs. She enjoys reading, hiking, and garage time with her husband and son, helping work on their list of projects that is nearly as long as her never-ending list of books to write.

https://jessiekreidlerauthor.com/
https://www.facebook.com/jessiekreidler.writer
Don't forget to leave a review!

Book Cover and Art by @TheMythicStorm